SWEET FORBIDDEN FRUIT

A Novel By

KEN. N. ROBINSON

Survivor Publishing

Acknowledgments

First of all I would like to thank God for all of the blessings and gifts that have been and continue to be bestowed upon me. Thanks to my ex-wife Gwendolyn and my son Myles for allowing me the time, space and opportunity to see this thing through. It has truly been a process. Thanks to my wonderful parents who I am so lucky and blessed to still have with me and always a mere phone call away. And thanks to my entire family for being so fantastic. To every sibling, cousin, aunt, uncle and so on who are certainly too numerous to mention individually. Not every family is fortunate enough to share the bond that ours does. A special mention goes to those friends who always encouraged me to write when not many people even knew that it was something that I did at all. Thanks to Lisa Vignola, Lynn Ensley and Dana Parker. To the late Mr. Alan Lowenstein; I will never forget you telling me that writing is something that I should pursue. R.I.P. Sir. To Roberta 'Bobbi' Tyler for not only giving me your insights but also that final push I needed to get to the finish line. To friends Lynn Smith and Charisse Taylor; your feedback on my manuscript was invaluable. Thanks to the many writers who have inspired me with their work and shown me that there is indeed a market for this type of story and the content it includes. To Michael Baisden, Zane, Mary B. Morrison, Gloria Mallette, Carl Weber, Eric Jerome Dickey and so many others. Much respect to you all. And last, but certainly not least, I want to truly thank all who have or may support me by purchasing a copy of this book. That could not be appreciated more.

K.N.R.

Special thanks to Tatiana Vila for creating an excellent cover and for the editing assistance.

This book is dedicated to all those individuals who like me, sat on a dream for quite some time before finally deciding one day to get up and make it happen.

PROLOGUE

"Hurry up, let's go," Sherri shouted to her two oldest children Abby and Tyler. Seconds later they hustled down the stairs and reached out to grab the jackets their mother held for them.

"Mom are you sure I have to go," a forlorn sounding Abby pleaded. "I just don't feel up to it."

Sherri cut her eyes sharply at her daughter. "Yes you have to go. Now get outside. Wait on the porch, I'll be right out."

"Uggh, I hate Mondays," Abby replied as she walked out the door.

"You're ten; that's too young to hate Mondays," Sherri countered.

With that she turned her attention to her youngest, the just recently turned four years old Zach. She buttoned up his shirt after guiding his arms into the sleeves. Eight year old Tyler then brushed his hands through Zach's hair on the way past him, drawing a predictable response.

"Hey cut it out," he said in his soft voice. "Mommy tell Tywer to stop it."

"Tyler please leave your brother alone. Let's not get him started okay."

"Okay I'll leave the baby alone. And my name's Tyler not Tywer."

"I'm not a baby, you're a baby," Zach fired back, before his Mom cut off the exchange.

"Tyler, outside!" she snapped. "Let's go. I have an appointment this morning so I have to hurry back."

She pulled up at the kids' day camp at 8:55, just 5 minutes before the 9 am start to the daily activities.

"Okay you two, hustle on in," Sherri said before giving both Abby and Tyler a quick kiss on the cheek. "I'll see you guys later; have a good day."

"Okay Mom bye," Tyler said as he hurried out of the car.

"Bye Mom," said Abby. "Bye squirt," she said to Zach, after kissing his forehead lightly

Tyler on the other hand, wasn't quite as endearing in saying good-bye to his little brother.

"Bye little baby," he quipped.

"Mommy," Zach complained in a whiny tone.

"Don't worry about it honey," Sherri said in a comforting voice before turning back to the front.

"Go," she commanded Tyler. Just as the doors closed, her cell phone beeped twice, signaling that she had received a text message. Pulling the phone out of her jacket pocket, she began to read the brief message on the phone's screen.

"What are you doing?"

"Good morning to you too," she quickly typed in response.

"Oh my bad; good morning. Now, what are you doing?"

"I just finished dropping two of the kids off at camp. Why?"

"You feel like swinging on by and doing that little thing for me this morning before I start my day?"

Sherri knew that in his own indirect way, he was requesting an early morning blowjob. She shook her head from side to side before typing her reply.

"I'm sorry but I can't. In case you forgot I have that Doctor's appointment this morning so I need to get back home."

"You can't? You can't or you won't?"

"I mean I can't Gee."

"And why not?"

"I told you I have an appointment. Don't you remember me telling you about it while I was on vacation? Once again I'm sorry."

"What time is your appointment?"

"10:45. And I have to get dressed because I just threw something on to drop the kids off. So I have to get home, get showered, and then get dressed. And of course drop my youngest off at his sitter and then drive there."

At that point Sherri had decided that she needed to call rather than continue with the texting.

"Hello."

"Hey listen, I can try to come by tomorrow rather than not seeing you until Thursday. If I can work out a sitter for my youngest I'll do that. Does that sound okay?"

"Nah forget all that; I need you to set this Monday off right. Whatever you're going to the Doctor for can wait for another day I'm sure."

"No it can't wait. It's a pretty important office visit actually."

"So in other words hell with me huh?"

"Listen it's not like that; you know I would if I could but I just can't this morning, sorry."

"Yeah you keep saying you're sorry and you know what, you've got that shit right. You're getting to be about one sorry ass bitch if you ask me. But you go ahead; I've just about had enough of you anyway." His words cut Sherri like a knife but she said nothing.

"That's right. There are a lot more hoes out there that can fill your shoes. And probably better too."

"Please don't say that. Give me a break. I'll make it up to you; I promise."

"Oh bullshit, whatever; take your ass on home then."

"Don't be mad okay, I…"

Sherri held the phone to her ear for several seconds while saying hello before she'd accepted what had happened. That he had hung up on her. A bit shaken, she placed the phone back in her pocket, put the car in drive and pulled away from the curb. About 5 minutes or so later she made the turn onto Ridge Valley Drive, the street on which her home was located. Moving along slowly, she pulled her phone back out of her pocket. She stared at it briefly before tossing it onto the seat beside her. Once within 50 yards of her driveway she suddenly slammed on the brakes, paused and then turned into one of her neighbor's driveway.   Reaching over to the passenger seat, she snatched up her phone and started dialing numbers.

"Hello."

"Great, I'm glad you answered. Don't go anywhere. I'm on my way, bye."

She then took a brief moment to look at Zach who was quietly staring out the window from his car seat, and then quickly executed a K-turn and headed back in the opposite direction. Her new destination—Route 287 South.

CHAPTER ONE

"Come on sweetie, blow out the candles.   You can do it; come on baby. Blow real hard for Mommy."

And with that little Zach puffed up his cheeks and with a mighty exhale extinguished the little flame on all three of the candles on his birthday cake. As he did so all of the children present, along with their parents, began to clap in unison.

"See there, that a boy. I knew you could do it," proud Mother Sherri Connolly King said to her youngest child Zach who beamed in delight.

"I did it, I did it Mommy."

"Yes you did little guy," Sherri said as she wrapped an arm around his shoulders and pulled him close. "And now you get the special first piece sweetie."

"Really Mommy? Wow."

"Yeppers, now come on, why don't you help me cut it for you."

Sherri loved to see the joy on her kid's faces as they celebrated another birthday.   She only wished Zach's father could have been there for the occasion.   But she understood. Such was life when you're married to a partner at a prestigious law firm. Sherilyn Connolly or Sherri for short, had married Clayton King thirteen years ago, when she was a junior associate at a Manhattan law firm and Clayton or Clay as he is called, was on the fast track to partnership at the large and very prestigious Bridgewater, NJ firm of Bergen, Schott, Pilsner and Wise. They had met 3 years earlier when she did a stint as a summer associate at BSPW. He was attracted to her immediately and it wasn't hard to see why with her long, chestnut-brown hair and beautiful face, highlighted by sparkling green eyes. And even at the age of 39 and with three children under the age of 10 she still carried but a petite 120 pounds on her 5 foot 3 inch frame. For her part, it had admittedly taken Sherri a bit longer to take to Clay. She found him attractive enough with his faired-haired, blue eyed looks but, she initially felt he might be somewhat too cocky and arrogant for her taste. She still remembered her first day that summer when the stocky, 5 foot 11 inch fellow first popped his head in her office.

"Hey there, I'm just checking in with this year's summer crop. Going door to door introducing myself and offering up my vast expertise if you choose to accept it. I'm Clay King. Please make a mental note of the name."

He then stated that he was joking, but Sherri wasn't so sure at the time. But he did eventually win her over with his charm, his confidence and yes his wit. At the end of her summer at the firm, he had asked if he could contact her sometime. Initially hesitant, she soon relented and he called her a couple of weeks later. She was in her second year of law school at NYU at the time and thus very busy with her studies. They talked occasionally over the course of the next few months before he decided to finally ask her out. School was in its first semester break, so it seemed a good time for it he figured. On their first date he took her ice skating at the famous Wollman Rink in Central Park. She had a great time and readily agreed to see him again. And so it began; a courtship that would continue on for the next 14 months or so until one day out of the blue, he dropped to a knee and proposed to her in full public view at the very place where they had gone on their first date; Wollman Rink. They were wed a year and half later in a traditional Catholic ceremony. She was 26 at the time and working at the New York offices of the international firm of Jarman, Klein and Bruer and he 29 and comfortably situated at BSPW. Yet due to his highly ambitious nature; three years later he began a stint as an assistant county prosecutor, which would last 4 years in duration. Following that he would return to his position as a criminal litigator at BSPW, which this time came with full firm membership. With his experience and through his working at the very politically connected firm, Clay had recently began to have his name floated as being on a short list of possible candidates to be named lead Somerset County Prosecutor; if the upcoming election led to the election of the Republican candidate for Governor as the polls were indicating may well happen. He certainly had the desired background for it. Ivy-league educated, and staunchly conservative, he has also been very active in local Republican circles, something that has certainly not gone unnoticed by the state GOP.

As for herself, Sherri had given up the life revolving around brief filings, dockets and court injunctions for one filled with diapers, feedings, naptimes and Doctor's appointments. She and Clay made an agreement after the birth of their first child that she would stay at home with the children once the family expanded beyond that. And she was perfectly okay with that. But that is not to say that she didn't have her occasional misgivings. She loves her children dearly as well as the amount of time that she got to spend with them. But on the other hand it was only natural to sometimes think about the countless hours she'd put in to become an attorney, only to walk away from it after only 6 years. Who knows, maybe she might get back into one day when the kids were older she figured; especially the youngest Zach. But for the time being it was life as the typical PTA/Soccer Mom.

It seemed to her that her biggest challenge during the course of the school year was occupying her mind and her time while her 2 oldest children, nine year old Abby and seven year old Tyler were in school. Sure Zach could be a handful by himself at times; but he was also at an age where the junior Nickelodeon channel was his biggest interest for a large portion of the day. Indeed it made for the ideal babysitter whenever she just wanted to unwind for a while.

"Mmmmm this is yummy Mommy, I like the strawberries in the middle," little Zach said after he tasted the cake for the first time.

"I knew you would honey, that's why I got it. I know strawberry filling is your favorite."

"Mm hmmm," Zach beamed, the whipped cream frosting already covering the entire area around his mouth.

Her friend Lily from across the street approached and offered her assistance to Sherri in handing out slices of cake to the ten or so children present.

"Sure that'd be great, thanks Lil. I'll go get the ice cream and bring it out."

Once inside the kitchen, Sherri retrieved the ice cream from the freezer and placed it on the counter while she went over to get the ice cream scooper.   As soon as she picked up the ice cream and was headed back out the phone rang.

"Hello."

"Hey how's the party?" Clay asked.

"Oh it's almost over. We're doing cake now. He got a lot of nice presents and the piñata was a big hit naturally."

"Sounds good; I wish I could have been there, I really do."

"Yeah it would have been nice. He did ask about you once or twice and I just tried to explain to him that Daddy wanted to be here but he really had to work today. Of course he doesn't really understand that, but I think he's okay."

"And you; you're okay with me not being able to be there today right?"

"Yeah sure," Sherri answered dryly.

"It's just that this is such a big high profile case and with us having to prepare for our summation---I mean certainly you understand honey."

"Of course, you don't think I've forgotten what it's like to be an attorney do you?"

"No I don't, but I just wanted to make sure. Anyway don't forget we're all going to Chuck E Cheese later on this evening okay."

"All right; we'll see you later then."

"Okay bye."

"Bye, I……..'Sherri started

Click

"I love you," she continued though she was now only speaking to a dial tone. She twisted her face a bit before hanging up and heading outside with the ice cream. The party broke up about 4:00 and then the cleanup began. Lily stuck around to lend a hand and that enabled it to get done rather quickly considering the number of young children that had been running roughshod through the backyard for a few hours.   Once that was completed Sherri and the children went inside; she to relax for a few minutes, while the children returned to doing what it is that young children do. While Abby and Tyler retreated to their rooms to entertain themselves with their video games, Sherri decided to lay Zach down for a nap. Once he was asleep she popped her head into Abby's room.

"Sweetie, why don't you start getting your things together for your sleepover? I'll drop you off once Zach is awake from his nap okay."

"Okay Mom."

Taking a seat in the family room, Sherri comfortably seated herself on the leather sectional, reclined it back and flipped on the TV. I could easily sit here and fall into a deep sleep myself, she thought as her body sank into the softness of the leather. Rather than take a chance at doing so she decided that it was better for her to get up after a few minutes. Glancing at her watch she noted the time was 4:55 as she headed into the home office where she powered on the computer. She logged onto Facebook and checked out some of the updates posted by some of her 75 friends. She commented on a couple of them before adding a status update of her own.

"Birthday party today for Zach; can't believe my baby is 3 already. Next up is Chuck E Cheese tonight. Pictures from the party coming soon."

She always found checking in on Facebook to be an easy way to pass an hour or so of idle time. And that was something she had plenty of on occasion. She didn't notice it immediately but she had received a new friend request. Upon clicking on the link she discovered it was from someone named Miguel; Miguel Larios to be exact. "Hmm Miguel; I don't think I know anyone named Miguel," she said to herself. "I don't know maybe it's someone I used to work with or went to high school or college with. I've met and known a lot of people over the years. And with him not having a picture on his profile..." She clicked on accept without thinking too much about it before logging off the computer.

Sherri pulled out of the driveway at about 6:00. It wasn't a long drive to Abby's friend Courtney's house. About 10 minutes each way, and that was a good thing because it didn't take long for Tyler to start antagonizing his younger brother in the back seat. She had also left a note for Clay in case he arrived home while they were gone, which he in fact did.

"Daddy," Zach said excitedly just as he entered the house upon their return before rushing over to greet Clay with a big embrace.

"Hey sport, how you doing buddy?"

"I had a party Daddy. I got presents and we had candy and cake and ice cream."

"I know. Daddy's sorry he couldn't be here but I had to work today. Next time okay buddy?"

"Okay daddy."

"But we're going to your favorite place tonight to have some fun."

"Yeah, Chuck E Cheese. I like Chuck E Cheese."

"I know you do; now why don't you go to your room for a little bit so I can talk to Mommy okay?"

"Okay bye-bye," Zach said before running off.

"Hey Dad," Tyler said once Zach had raced to his room.

"Hey what do ya say there Tyler," Clay replied before giving him a high five. He then looked in Sherri's direction.

"Hey you're home," she said as Tyler walked away.

"Yeah I got in around six," Clay said before planting a brief kiss on her lips.

"Oh I guess we just missed you because we left about that time."

"It's been a long day; I had no idea we'd be putting in that many hours. Again I apologize."

"Don't worry about it. I understand."

While she occasionally wished it wasn't the case, Sherri didn't often complain about the hours Clay put into his work. Especially considering that it was Clay's success that allowed them to live as comfortably as they did in a 4,000 plus square foot home in the tony suburb of Basking Ridge, New Jersey on his salary alone. Yet there were those moments when it did get to her.

"I figure we can leave about 7 or so for Chuck E Cheese," Sherri suggested. "Get there and order some pizza so the boys can eat and then have a good amount of time to play; three hours or so."

"Where's Abby?"

"I guess you must have forgotten that she was going to Courtney's for a sleepover. That's where we were, dropping her off."

"Yeah I guess I did forget. You said about 7:00; hmmm let's see. Listen, honey I'm dead tired," he continued after a pause. "I was thinking about lying down for a while. Would it be okay if you guys were to go ahead and then I came and met you a little bit later?"

"No problem, I guess that would be fine."

As it turned out Clay didn't make it to Chuck E Cheese until about 10:30. And that might have only been because he finally answered the home phone the 3rd time that Sherri had called in an attempt to find out what was keeping him. It turned out that after she and the boys had left he'd gotten up and done some more case-related research before eventually falling into a deep sleep. So by the time he walked in Zach was tired, irritable and clearly ready for some sleep. But this time Clay offered no apologies.

"Hey everybody, are you guys ready to have some fun?"

"Clay it's 10:30, Zach is exhausted. I think he's had about all the fun he's gonna have for the day."

"Oh no way, don't be silly. Let's go sport you ready?"

Zach slowly walked over and extended his arms out to him in a gesture indicating that he wanted Clay to pick him up. As soon as he was in his Dad arms his head slumped onto his shoulder and he fell fast asleep.

"Come on, let's go home," Sherri said softly.

By 11:30 and with the boys long asleep in their rooms, Sherri sat up in bed reading while Clay was in the office; having just watched the nightly news while seated at the computer.

A few minutes later he popped his head into the master bedroom.

"Come here for a second I want you to read something," he said before heading back into the office.

Sherri sighed and rolled her eyes before getting up and making her way off the bed to follow him.

His eyes were glued to the monitor as she entered the room, yet he still knew just when she had arrived.

"I want you to check this out before I post it. See, this is why I love the anonymous nature of the internet. You can just speak your mind, you don't have to worry about all that politically correct crap, and nobody knows a thing."

He was logged into a forum devoted to local and statewide issues, where he often made his opinions known. Having been called on to read some of his postings before, Sherri could kind of sense what sort of comments they were that he had typed, but she still went over and stood behind him. Focusing in on the screen, she began to read.

"The reasons why our property taxes in much of New Jersey have gone through the roof are obvious to many of us. I mean after all its only fair that the rest of us subsidize the immoral, indecent lifestyles of the lowlifes that reside in places like Newark, Paterson, and Camden etc. And why is this? Well that's just as obvious. These social programs shoved down our throats by the liberals are like prescription drugs these minorities rely on to survive. I mean what else would they do? Work? God forbid. Why would they when the rest of us work for them."

Fed Up Taxpayer.

"Well what do you think," he asked once Sherri had finished reading.

"What do I think? Well to be honest with you it sounds pretty racist to me."

"Oh please, since when is telling the truth being racist? Besides you know me better than that."

"Yeah I think I do, but that doesn't mean that I don't wonder sometimes. Anyway I'm going to bed. Good night."

"Well you don't have to wonder. That's not me; I just have my views like everybody else. And anyway, my Black friends at work would laugh at even the suggestion of it."

"Your Black friends huh? Well how come you've never had any of those Black friends over like so many of your other friends?"

"Well it's just that they fall more into the category of strictly work friends that's all."

Once again rolling her eyes, Sherri was thinking that's it's not like these Black friends Clay spoke of have any idea of some of the views he harbors inside, because if they did she doubts they'd consider him any friend to them at all. After Sherri left the room, Clay immediately turned his attention back to the computer. Leaning in he studied the monitor briefly before clicking on the post message box on the screen in front of him.

While she was a registered Independent who sometimes voted Republican herself, Sherri was far more moderate in her views than was Clay. After all she had grown up in a family of Massachusetts Democrats. But she was careful to never make politics a divisive issue in her marriage.

CHAPTER TWO

Sherri awakened the next morning at her normal hour of 7 am. She got up and looked in on Tyler and Zach and upon discovering that both of them were still sound asleep, headed to the bedroom before passing straight though to the adjacent bathroom. She brushed her teeth and then walked back out to the bedroom suite's sitting area, where using the natural light from the morning sun, she sat down and began to read the book she was currently at work on. Clay woke up about thirty minutes later and immediately went into the bathroom. He emerged a few minutes later and made his way over to where Sherri was seated.

"Good morning," he said as she sat there, focused on her reading.

"Are the boys still sleeping?"

"Yep, soundly."

"Well do you wanna come back to bed with me?" he asked while touching her hair.

Sherri lowered the book to her lap and looked him in the eyes for several seconds before answering. "Okay sure."

This was a far too infrequent opportunity for some lovemaking and there was no way that she was going to pass it up. She stood and followed him over to the bed and they both took a seat on the side of it. He kissed her briefly as his hands began to run over her upper body. He then gently pushed her onto her back and reached under her nightgown and started to remove her panties. After standing up, he quickly removed his clothes and then laid down beside her and started to climb on top of her.

"Why are you rushing?" she whispered. I don't think the boys are going to be waking up anytime soon. They're exhausted.

"Yeah but I just want to do a little work this morning."

"Okay that's fine but,"

"Shhhhh," he interrupted her. "Why are you still talking?"

She felt like she was barely wet when he worked his way inside of her. With her eyes wide open and focused on the ceiling

Clay began to pump in and out of her rapidly. As he moaned and groaned she just laid there silently.

"Ooh yeah baby, is it good," he grunted between deep breaths.

"Oh yes, yeah it's so good; that's it yessssss," Sherri feigned in a bravado performance.

"Oh, oh ohhhh," he bellowed as his release built.

"Mmmmm, mmmmm, mmmmm," she cried as she expertly faked her own simultaneous orgasm.

Having deposited his fluid inside of her, he rolled off of her and onto his back with his chest heaving as he caught his breath.

"Oh my, that was amazing," she lied.

"Thank you baby," he countered before he kissed her on her forehead and quickly headed into the bathroom to shower.

Sherri stared at the bathroom door for a few seconds as she got dressed before climbing to her feet. Shaking her head, her eyes narrowed into slits and she let out a deep sigh as she stepped away from the bed. She then headed right back to where she had laid her book and after picking it up, resumed reading.

∞∞∞∞∞∞∞∞

A few nights later Sherri was back on Facebook uploading the pictures from Zach's party to her profile. She had just about finished up when a chat window suddenly appeared in the bottom right corner of the screen.

"Hey, Sherri, what's going on? It's been a long time."

"Hello"

"How have you been?"

"Um I've been okay, but I'm not sure we know each other."

"Huh; you're Sherri Connolly right?"

"Yeah but I doubt very seriously that I'm the only one with that name. And actually my name is Sherri Connolly King now."

"Oh okay, so you got married?"

"Yep, long time ago. If you know me wouldn't you have known that though?"

"Come on Sherri, not if I haven't heard from you in years. But I thought about you and somebody told me that you had moved out to Jersey so I figured I would try to locate you on Facebook."

"Yeah that's true but I've been married for 13 years. Anyway I'm sorry; your name is Miguel right? I don't think I know any Miguel's."

"You don't remember me; Miguel Larios from URI?"

"URI?"

"Yeah URI, University of Rhode Island. Come on Sherri stop playing with me. Wait a minute, hold up; you are from Rhodie right?"

"No; actually I've never even been to Rhode Island which is odd being from Massachusetts."

Realizing then what had happened, Miguel paused before responding.

"Oops, I guess I definitely have the wrong person. Sorry about that."

"That's okay, but couldn't you tell from my picture that I wasn't the Sherri Connolly that you thought I was?"

"Actually you really kind of look like the Sherri I went to college with and who knows how much she might have changed in 12 years."

"True, but no I'm not that Sherri. I must say though you had me going when you said that about having moved to Jersey, because I did move here from out of state. But like I said I'm from Massachusetts. And then with you having no picture on your profile I had no idea what you look like so I couldn't be sure. But like I said I don't recall ever knowing anybody named Miguel."

"Yeah I guess I need to get around to putting a picture up."

"It certainly helps when you might be searching for people."

"Well I'm still new on here. It's only been a few weeks so I just haven't gotten to it yet, but I will, as soon as I pick out the right one. Anyway, I'm sorry for the mistake and to have bothered you Sherri Connolly King."

"Well again its okay; don't worry about it Miguel. And besides I don't mind making new acquaintances."

"Hmm, well okay then, you take care and since you put it like that feel free to say hi anytime you see me online."

"Hey I might just do that one day since we're on each other's friend's lists now. You take care also. Bye-bye"

"Bye."

Sherri then finished loading the pictures and with the clock approaching midnight prepared to call it a night. After all another day of errands, chores and motherhood awaited her; so she soon joined Clay who was already fast asleep, in bed.

The new school year was fast approaching and with it a change in the routine; but at that time Sherri's days pretty much kept the same script. She would see Clay off to the office; relax for a while longer until the kids were awake and then chauffeur Abby and Tyler around to either day camp or soccer practices. Abby had also decided to get into cheerleading so that added a little extra diversion as well. But other than that it was just her and Zach sharing quality time in between his naps and his occasional moments of independence where he just wanted to hang out in his room alone. That presented a challenge for Sherri because even with three young children there was only so much laundry to be done, so many bedrooms to be tidied up or errands to be run. And it isn't like she was able to entertain herself a great deal with the typical daytime television fare. It just didn't interest her all that much, with her finding both the soaps and courtroom reality shows boring and redundant and the talk shows only as interesting as whomever that day's guests might be.

Therefore she often had a bit more free time on her hands than she knew what to do with. Both day and night actually, because once the kids were in bed and asleep Clay was soon to follow on most nights including the weekends. He considered every day a workday and believed that an early start gave him that little edge he always had over his opposing counsel in big cases. But what it also equated to was precious little quiet, alone time together for the two of them. And having very sporadic lovemaking sessions with her husband was but one of her concerns. While Clay may never have been any big john stud, he at least used to not approach sex with her like a parking meter was running short on time with no more change to refill it. Foreplay had become like a premium event apparently reserved for holidays or other special occasions, and her satisfaction was not something that seemed to fit in his agenda either. Presumably because it would take up too much time and wasn't billable. And worse; all of her occasional voicing of her feelings seemed to have fallen on deaf ears. Sherri loved Clay dearly and she had no doubt that he felt the same.   She just wished that he'd put more effort into showing it. After all kind words are great and gifts are usually sent from the heart; but sometimes a woman wants and needs to feel that real heat, that searing passion and that powerful desire from the man in her life. She wondered if he had forgotten that.

∞∞∞∞∞∞∞∞

In an attempt to simply switch things up a bit Sherri had began to take Zach out in his stroller at times. They would go to the Bridgewater Commons mall, to the park, or even just around the neighborhood. And although Zach walked very well, she found it much better to make use of the stroller because otherwise it would not be very long before fatigue would overtake him and she would end up needing to carry him.   Besides, she liked pushing him along in the stroller due to the fact that it provided the added benefit of exercise along with just the enjoyment of being outdoors. Basking Ridge is awash with stay-at-home moms so wherever she chose to go on a given day it was a safe bet that she would run into familiar faces, particularly when she stayed local. And they'd often stop and talk about various neighborhood, or school-related topics, or most frequently their children.   Just the usual idle chit-chat that she quite frankly felt often went on a bit too long, was a bit too boring and let her know that there were many others in her shoes. That is to say, they had too much time on their hands and too little to fill it with.

About two weeks after her previous brief conversation with Miguel via Facebook, she happened across him again on a Saturday morning.   Only this time it was she that initiated the chat.

"Hello, how are you?"

"I'm good, how are you doing", he replied.

"Hanging in there; not a real lot to complain about I guess. I mean I always could but I won't."

"Oh okay. Glad everything is pretty well."

"How's life been treating you? And did you ever locate your friend Sherri that you mistook me for?"

"Everything is just fine, but no, no luck with Sherri. I don't know; it could be that she's also married now and has a different name. And that would make it very hard to locate her. That's assuming she's even on here at all."

"Yeah that's true."

"So anyway we'll see I guess."

"Hey Miguel do you mind if I tell you something?"

"Sure, go ahead."

"Don't take offense but I must say when I first saw the friend request from you I pretty much just assumed that you were just some guy trying to meet random girls on Facebook."

"You did? Why?"

"Yeah I kind of did. I mean I know people do that because some of my friends say they've gotten those types of friend requests. And then if they happen to accept and hear back from the person they admit that they don't know them but just liked what they saw and wanted to try to get acquainted."

"Damn; people trying to hook up on Facebook?" Well it hasn't happened to me yet but like I said I'm pretty new here." Only thing it makes me wonder is why they would accept the friend request from a stranger?

"I don't know maybe they liked what they saw too and said what the hell. I didn't want to ask but that's a good question."

"But no that's wasn't my intent in any way, shape or form."

"Okay well I'll take your word on that. I was just wondering though. No biggie."

"I don't know I just don't view Facebook that way. I mean I guess I could see it happening in some instances. I'm talking about people hooking up, but not me. Now I do know of some major hookup websites out there that could serve that purpose much better."

"Oh really; such as?"

"Are you sure you wanna know?"

"Yeah why not, I'm just curious."

"Uh huh, sure."

"For real; I might just check it out to see what its like."

"Well I can tell you this, they're not tame, so be warned in advance."

"Hey that's okay, I'm a grown up woman."

"Yeah okay, but I'm telling you they play hard at these places. So don't expect it to be like match.com or eharmony. These sites are just raw and direct and so are a lot of the members."

"Sounds like you might be on there."

"No comment," Miguel typed back as he smiled.

"No need to comment at this point."

"But seriously though, yes I used to be on both of them but I've changed my ways."

"Uh huh I bet."

"Really I did."

"All right, I have no place to question you anyway. I don't even know you really."

"That's right, good point Sherri."

"But anyway, are you going to tell me the names of the sites?"

"Okay, well if you insist."

"Yes I pretty much do at this point."

"Uh oh; another married woman is about to be corrupted."

"Oh please, I just wanna look at them."

"Yeah that's what a lot of them say at first I bet."

"Miguel!"

"Okay, okay, forgive me Lord. One of them is called redhot2trot.com—now that one is geared towards people who are married or involved with somebody. I know--go figure. And the other one is asudesire.com."

Sherri quickly jotted the names of both sites down on a large sized post-it note and stuck it on her arm until she would have time to put in a secure place. After doing that she typed another reply to Miguel.

"Okay I've got em, thanks. That 1st one even sounds kind of direct. Actually they both do I guess, but especially what is it hot to trot.com?"

"Redhot2trot.com. Come on now, you've got to have it right if you intend to get in on it."

"Who said anything about getting in on something? I'm just the inquisitive type by nature that's all."

"Okay well we'll see. Anyway Sherri I have to get ready to go but if/when you do check them out let me know what you think."

"I will definitely do that. In the meantime you take care and I hope you locate the other Sherri."

"All right thanks and you take care also. Bye."

"Bye-bye."

Sherri immediately got up and took the post-it containing the name of the websites into the bedroom, where she placed it in the bottom drawer of the nightstand on the side of the bed on which she always slept. A little later that day she rounded up all the kids and off they went to the mall. She wanted to get in some final school shopping and figured with Abby and Tyler along to help tend to Zach she might just be able to pick up a few things for herself as well.

That night about 11:00 she entered the bedroom where Clay was seated on the bed with the TV on, but his attention was focused squarely on the notebook computer resting on his lap. He had been focusing a ton of time on the defense of former South Jersey Congressman Max Faulkner against extortion and tax evasion charges. Sherri actually stood in the doorway for several seconds without either him not sensing or if he did, not even acknowledging her presence. Noticing this, she called out to him as she slowly walked towards the bed, holding something in front of her.

"Hey honey."

"Yes, he replied without veering his eyes away from the laptop at all.

"Look I bought this at Victoria's Secret today; want me to model it for you?"

"I'm sorry sweetie, not right now, maybe tomorrow or something."

"But you didn't even look at it Clay," she noted with a bit of exasperation in her voice.

Sighing as if he was frustrated by the interruption, he looked in her direction.

"I like it, that's real nice. but please Sherri; I'm sorry I have a lot to go over in preparation for the Congressman Faulkner trial. It's scheduled to start next week. I think I might have mentioned that," he added with a hint of sarcasm.

Upon hearing that, Sherri quickly turned and headed out of the room; pausing to place the baby-blue, one-piece teddy in one of the dresser drawers before slamming the drawer closed. "Sorry to bother you," she huffed.

About an hour later she returned, this time only to climb into bed beside him with her back turned. Not a word was exchanged in the process. Unable to fall asleep she lied still, staring at the wall before her. Eventually she turned to Clay who was still busying himself with work.

"Can I just ask you one question?"

"Sure," he replied while squinting in an attempt to focus in on the screen in front of him.

"Am I less attractive to you than I was in the past?"

"Of course not, don't be silly Sherri."

"Oh I'm being silly, well just what is it then Clay."

Clay lifted the laptop, sat it beside him to his left and then turned towards her.

"Listen, honey; this is a really big case coming up, and a very high-profile one at that. It's just the type of case that could be the final step towards propelling me into that Chief Prosecutor position. Now I guess you may be feeling like I haven't been as attentive as I should be or could be, but I'm just really focused right now. And you know how I get when that's the case. I just get that tunnel vision going; I can't help it. But its part of what's put me where I am, I thought you understood and accepted that."

"I have and I do but; would it be so hard, so detrimental to what you have going on to turn that focus to me for an hour, a half-hour, fifteen minutes even. I mean once in a while rather than once in a blue moon as it seems to be now."

"Sherri I am sorry, I really am, but please support me on this; please."

"Okay Clay fine. Have a good night," Sherri said flatly before turning back onto her side.

Gently placing a hand on Sherri's shoulder, Clay then said something he thought might pacify her.

"Hey listen; when this trial is over maybe we can go someplace nice for a few days; just the two of us. We can ask my brother or sister if they would take care of the kids and just fly away. How does that sound?"

"Oh that sounds great but I'm afraid it would wind up just like when we went to Aruba over the holidays last year. Remember that? When you seemed to spend most of the time making calls or sending emails from your Blackberry? It was almost like I was there by myself I spent so much time just lying by the pool or on the beach reading. At least I knew to take a couple of good books along."

"Hey, you know in this profession work never stops."

"Yes I do, but I also know that being a husband is not supposed to either. See you in the morning."

CHAPTER THREE

Not a lot changed over the course of the next couple of months. Yes a new school year commenced just after Labor Day, and of course the weather cooled considerably once it was mid-October. But what didn't change was the level of intimacy between Sherri and Clay. Clay and his team of Associates had gained acquittals on all charges in the Faulkner case so life was good for him in terms of his career. The trial had garnered him a great deal of publicity, not only locally but on the national stage as well. He had also began to put in less time on work but that was largely due to the fact that his increased profile allowed him to spend more time hobnobbing with the who's who of the state GOP. The campaign for Governor was in its stretch run and that meant fundraisers, personal appearances and get out the vote efforts galore. At that point he'd gone from a speculative candidate to an outright shoo-in for the job of Chief Prosecutor of Somerset County if Senator Christian indeed became the state's next Governor. Sherri and the kids were even invited along to some of the social gatherings that dotted Clay's early fall calendar. He realized that with the GOP being very image conscious it was a good idea to roll out your pretty wife and adorable children for all to see. However, what that pretty picture failed to portray was the continued lack of romance and passion inside the bedroom at the King house and it leading to a rising feeling of frustration on Sherri's part.

She and Clay had made love only a few times since she had clearly let her dissatisfaction be known back in August. And even on those occasions it followed the same familiar script; with Clay moving things along in a way that made it seem for the entire world that she and her needs were merely an afterthought. Yet through it all she had continued to play the role of the good wife on the rare occasions they did get intimate. That is she continued to portray him as the possessor of earth-shattering skills in bed. Even with her frustrations, she saw nothing to gain by bruising his ego. So instead she just went with the flow, accepting things as they were, while feeling powerless to change anything about her circumstances. That was until the day she made an impulsive decision; one that would alter the course of her life from that day forward.

∞∞∞∞∞∞∞∞∞∞

It was just a typical midweek day, with Clay at work, Abby and Tyler at school, and Zach having begun his nap. Sherri was taking a few minutes to relax on top of the bed herself when she reached into the nightstand and pulled out the paper with the names of the websites Miguel had provided her a couple of months previously. Them being asudesire.com and redhot2trot.com. She studied the names of the 2 sites briefly, trying to decide which one she wanted to take a look at first. Once decided, she went in to the office, logged onto the internet and quickly typed www.asudesire.com in the address bar. The first thing that appeared on the screen were images of beautiful, nude or scantily clad women. This came as no surprise to her because she figured that any website of this type had to be driven by male members if to succeed. There were areas from which you sign in for existing users or to sign up as a new member. Also drop down menus in order to select your criteria to search members from. It was all a bit overwhelming to her initially, so the first thing she opted to do was to view some of the existing profiles. She got a kick out of the usernames selected by some of the site's members. Pussy Galore, Sweet to Eat, and Nutty Fuckbuddy were just a few handles used by women which she found amusing and Tongue Fu Panda, Tricky Dick and George Bushwhacker were usernames of some males that bought a smile to her face. As well as a mental note to herself to keep the name of the member Tongue Fu Panda in mind.

Most of the profiles included only facial pictures if any at all, yet many others had sometimes eye-openingly graphic photos staring out at anyone who viewed them. As she perused some of the numerous member pages for about thirty minutes, Sherri was struck by the wide geographical reach of the site. Members hailed from all 50 states as well as dozens of foreign countries.

That night in bed Sherri mulled her impressions of the site over in her head as she lied there beside her sleeping husband. Before long she had made a decision; she was going to become a member of asudesire.com. Now, what attention grabbing screen name could she come up with? What witty double entendres could she throw in to liven up her profile? This was the time to think it all through; because in the morning she was going to jump in feet first.

Sherri heard the rumble of the thunder and saw the flashes of lightning well before daybreak. It was not expected to let up all day, but there was no chance it would dampen her enthusiasm on this morning. She was excited about the task at hand and anxious to get started. Abby and Tyler were to be driven to school as was always the case on days in which the elements were not very favorable to kids waiting on a school bus. Luckily, Lily had called and informed Sherri that she would handle the driving that morning. So there was nothing left for her to do other than to get Zach's morning going once her two oldest were out of the house. Once Zach was fed and dressed for the day, she occupied him in his room with his favorite children's movie. And with that done she was ready to begin.

Staring outside into a miserable, gray haze, Sherri's mind was moving quickly yet getting her nowhere. As much as she was sure of some of the content she wanted to include in her member profile, there was still one big roadblock to steer past. She couldn't settle on a uniquely fresh screen name. She wanted something that would be all of descriptive, catchy and captivating. Something that would speak the words that her mind often spins; while reciting the tale that her longing heart told as it spoke to her restless flesh. In the end it was what she saw outside her window that wound up as her motivation as much as anything.

STORMY

Anybody else like to play in the rain? There's a quiet storm building inside of me.

Sweet and slightly shy, petite Princess is on the lookout for a bad boy who can make me act like a bad girl. I would love to engage in some fun and naughty conversation with someone capable of drawing me out of my shell. Can you help this bored lady re-discover the "other" side of me? Come on; let's get just a little bit wet. Total discretion is a must.

She hoped that the masses would see it as she did. Simply stated yet clear in its intention. The way she saw it she didn't really need all the flash or the shock value; after all her stated goal was merely to encounter someone interesting to chat with; nothing more than that. She read over her profile several times before deciding that she was content with it; now on to the next step.

The next thing for her to do was to specify her criteria; age range, physical appearance, ethnicity, geographic location etc. She left the location open to all 50 states figuring that since she was not looking for any face to face meetings it didn't much matter. As for herself, she did list her age, state of residence and a slightly more detailed physical description in the allotted drop down menus. She even listed her astrological sign of Aries. Though she didn't have much use for that sort of thing she knows many others do. She uploaded a simple picture of herself that had been taken in the backyard that previous summer yet opted to limit its accessibility to be viewed to only those of her choosing. Discretion was foremost in her mind. With that taken care of there was but one thing left for her to take care of.

Married
Single
In a relationship
Divorced/Separated
We'll talk

Those were the choices in the drop down menu she saved for last. She was unclear on what she would select. She didn't want to mislead or misrepresent herself yet at the same time she didn't want to minimize her appeal to those who might bypass her for being married. After taking all of that into consideration she clicked on the final choice on the list.-We'll talk.

With her new member profile all completed, Sherri continued on with her day. She couldn't wait until she got her first whiff of attention from some of the men out there, but she decided that she would do best to let some hours go by before checking back in. Besides the accounts had the option of being set to notify member via email when they received anything like a message or a wave. A wave being something that members can send out to anyone on the site who they wanted to show some interest in communicating with. In fact before signing out after setting up her account, Sherri sent out a wave to the person who used the screen name of Tongue Fu Panda. She was intrigued by just the clever choice of name alone and thought he might be someone fun to talk to.

In between taking care of Zach and preparing dinner for that evening, Sherri snuck in an hour-long workout downstairs in their home gym while her son napped. While she didn't have the time to do it as often as liked to, she enjoyed getting in some good exercise whenever she could. She also certainly liked the benefits from it. Especially that which she got from using the tread climber by Bowflex, a hybrid machine which is basically a cross between a treadmill and a Stairmaster. She credits this piece of equipment more than anything else with trimming her waistline after Zach was born. But more than that she loved the fact that it gave her what she refers to as her nice patootie booty. She enjoys looking at herself in the mirror wearing those nice snug fit jeans or on occasion nice body-hugging skirts or dresses. She was blessed with a nice-sized pair of boobs even before the rest of her anatomy started to fill out as she matured and had children. But now that she had added a little roundness to her ass she really felt good. If she must say so herself she kind of had it going on for a mother of three who was going on 40. Even if her own husband never said so.

With the kids due in from school in about ninety minutes, Sherri decided to check her Blackberry for any emails. She was super excited when she saw that she had already received six message notifications from asudesire. She quickly logged onto the site and saw that she had received 4 messages along with 2 waves. The first message was merely from the site's administrator's welcoming her to the site and further informing her of some of the rules and guidelines. The next two messages were frankly a bit off-putting to her. One read—"So, you like to get a little wet I see. Well come over this way if you want to get a little golden showers action going on."

The second one was certainly even more disturbing in her eyes. "I hope you're not a tease, get down on your knees; I want to fuck you till you bleed." Yikes, she thought to herself; that's enough of the messages for now. She then decided to look and see who had waved at her. The first was from some guy from Southern California. As for the other one, she was pleased to see that it was a returned wave from Tongue Fu Panda. She took a little bit of time to look at his profile more closely. She hadn't even noticed before that he listed his hometown as Boonton, New Jersey which is straight up 287 North in Morris County. Hesitantly, she then went back to check the last message she had received. But unlike the previous two this one brought a little smile to her face. "Hey, how are you? This is Craig aka Tongue Fu Panda. Got your wave and couldn't send one back to you fast enough. Why don't you send me a message back and then we can see what there is to talk about. I have some ideas. Until then, take care."

Sherri decided to do a little housecleaning on the site before trying to reach out to Mr. Tongue Fu Panda again.

She erased the two crude messages from the sick pervert and the wannabe poet with the twisted sense of humor, and blocked them both from contacting her again or even being able to view her profile at all going forward. She then turned her attention back to the Tongue Fu Panda. She figured that any site like this was sure to draw in some creeps and she wasn't going to let a couple stop her from seeking out some fun. As she clicked in the place to reply to Craig's message she got an onscreen notification that the ability to send messages was restricted to premium members. She had signed up for a basic membership which while free of charge carried far more restrictions than the paid monthly membership. Knowing that she really wanted to get back with Craig, she charged a month's worth of premium membership to a credit card, figuring that if she didn't encounter anyone of interest in that amount of time she would just cut her losses and move on. With that bit of business handled she then proceeded to send her reply to Craig.

"Hey yourself Craig; I must say I love the name Tongue Fu Panda. I wonder if you're an expert in the ancient Chinese art of Tongue Fu. Anyway, I look forward to hearing back from you again. Bye-bye for now; Stormy."

Sherri spent the rest of the late afternoon and evening in the usual way; tending to the children as well as the household while awaiting Clay's arrival home. By 11pm everyone was sound asleep, so it was her time to spring back into action. She quietly slid out of bed and made her way to the computer where she immediately logged into asudesire. She was quite anxious to see if the mystery man with the catchy username had responded to her most recent message. Indeed he had, but while she was pleased at that, she was also a bit disappointed that they seemed to just be sending each other messages while the other was logged out of the site. She thought for a moment, trying to figure out the best way to overcome this obstacle. After a short time pondering it she had thought of something and prepared to send her suggestion out to Mr. Tongue Fu.

"Hey it's me again. I see that you left me another little note. I appreciate all the attempts that you've made to establish some contact. However, given that we seem to be doing nothing but playing a little game of email tag here on this site why don't we try something else. You can email me at my yahoo account and perhaps if we hit it off from there, we can then instant message each other going forward. I'm a night owl relatively speaking, so if you have some time after 11, hopefully we can begin to engage in some conversation and get to know each other a little bit. What do you think? Anyway, my email address is sherri_ck@yahoo.com.   I hope you don't see this as me being too forward, but I've just decided to go with the nothing ventured nothing gained attitude. Besides I'm really eager to speak to you. Bye again, and I hope to hear from you soon."

It took only a few minutes after sending that email out that she received a reply.   She was on CNN's website checking out some of the headlines when the little box popped up in the lower right corner of the screen notifying her of a new email from a bmalecky@yahoo.com.   In the subject line was: Let's get acquainted.

"Tag, you're it. But seriously, in case you're not certain who this is, yes it's Craig. But that's tongue fu panda to you. Anyway I'm wondering when we're going to have the chance to connect. You sure we can't just IM chat?   I enjoy the quick back and forth of that so much more than emailing. I'll be up for a while; let me know. Bye."

After taking a walk into the kitchen to grab a glass of water Sherri sat back down at the PC and typed out a response.

"Okay Craig, I see your point and I must agree with you.   I mean if we've exchanged email addresses anyway, it makes more sense to just IM each other.   Give me a minute to add you to my contacts and you go ahead and do the same okay. Talk to you soon."

After logging into her IM account she added his contact info and then sat back and waited to see just how anxious he was to make her acquaintance.   And she didn't have to wait long to find out.

"Hey, is it still stormy where you are?"

"Oh yeah, there always seems to be some upper level disturbance all around me."

"Upper level disturbance? What are you a weather girl in your spare time?"

"No, but I did stay at a Holiday Inn express last night.   Oh Lord that was so corny.   Forgive my lame attempt at humor."

"Yeah I was thinking maybe somebody has been watching a little too much TV."

"Maybe so, I guess that's part of the reason I'm on here right now. Looking for a more interesting form of entertainment. Can you help out with that?"

"Oh I think I can; certainly will do my best. Anyway, how are you?"

"I'm fine Craig, how are you?"

"Craig? Who's Craig my name is Jeff. You mean to tell me you don't know who I am? This is Dina right?"

"Ha ha very funny Craig; anyway, you can call me Sherri."

"Okay will do, Sherri baby.

"Oh I know that song. I wasn't born when it came out but still had people singing it to me all through my teens and beyond as a joke. After about the thousandth time it got to be just a bit annoying."

"Okay well I'll make a mental note to refrain from any further references to it."

"No it's okay. It's a nice song. I can pretend it's my song for a little while."

"Okay yeah, let's go with that; a song dedicated to you."

"Why thank you. So having said that, how else are you going to make me smile tonight Craig?"

"I don't know. Don't have any ideas on what softens you up and makes you smile and relax, so I'll just have to feel you out first."

"Oh I'm relaxed, now as far as the smiling part, well you can start by telling me why you chose the username Tongue Fu Panda."

"Well I thought you'd never ask. Well unlike in the movie where the focus was on the ancient Chinese art of Kung Fu, I instead set out to master the just as ancient, erotic art of Tongue Fu."

"And have you."

"If I can be the opposite of modest for a second I most certainly would say I have."

"MMMMMM, so what color belt have you obtained?"

"Oh a black belt of course; but I can't yet tell you what I like to use it for."

"Ooh naughty, naughty. I can only imagine what you use that black belt for."

"And you'd probably be correct in whatever you're thinking."

"So tell me Craig, what would you say is the key to becoming a tongue fu master?"

"Well—let's see, I think the real secret is much focus, concentration and setting goals Daniel son," Craig answered.

"Okay Mr. Miyagi; care to expand on that a bit."

"Certainly; well first one must focus and concentrate my dear. So I focus on the clit and concentrate on my goal of bringing about an orgasm.

"Well that certainly sounds like a worthy goal to me."

"Yes a most worthy one and one very achievable with patience."

"Oh yeah, have to take your time and do it right."

"And I certainly pride myself on that."

"So I imagine it must take years of practice to become a master of such an art form."

"Oh yes but I have studied for many years, until I was able to pass all tests along the way. And once that is achieved it is just a matter of staying in condition and keeping your skills sharpened."

"And how have you been doing with that?"

"Well there's never as much practice as I would like."

"Ideally, how often would you like to practice your craft?"

"Oh that's easy, daily."

"Oh my, that's quite an appetite you have there."

"Yes it is; I am always starving."

And so it went until a quarter past midnight, at which time Sherri reluctantly decided that she should turn in for the night. After all she did have the task of getting the kids off to school and taking care of Zach in the morning. She and Craig did decide that they would chat again real soon however.

All of that spicy back and forth with Craig seemed to have a bit of an effect on Sherri after she snuggled up in bed. She was quite restless and sleep was not coming easily at all. After much tossing and turning, she slid over close to Clay in an attempt to possibly entice him. She started to softly run a couple of fingers up and down his back in a subtle attempt at rousing him awake. Failing with that, she tried toying with his ear closest to her. After first shaking it off while still sleeping, he eventually awakened somewhat and started to shrug her hand away.

"Just what is it you're doing Sherri? Can't I just sleep in peace without you playing this little game you've decided to amuse yourself with?" He grunted once his eyes opened slightly.

"Sweetie, come on; it's not a game. I was just trying to get your attention."

"Well you've certainly got my attention now, so can you just back off so I can continue to get some sleep please. For crying out loud it's the middle of the night!" he snapped.

Hurt by his reaction, Sherri slowly backed away from him before turning her back.

"Thank You—geez," he then said coldly.

Her mind racing, Sherri stared off into the darkness of the room; tears welling up in her eyes. It took some time but she did eventually manage to drift off to sleep.

She was usually up and at em by 7:00, but she couldn't crawl out of bed before about 7:45 the next morning. She slowly walked into the kitchen while trying to rub the sleep out of her eyes. Looking straight ahead, she saw Clay standing at the stove.

"Good morning, she whispered while stifling a yawn.

Turning to face her he shot her an icy glance. "Oh yeah it's a great morning. My sleep is disturbed in the middle of the night and then I come in here and see that I have to make my own damn coffee."

"Oh sorry Mr. Sunshine, I hope that doesn't overextend you too much." she responded back.

"You know Sherri, sarcasm is the last thing I want to hear from you right now. Especially after that little stunt you pulled at God knows what time of the morning. And then this," he added as he banged a coffee mug down on the counter.

Sherri turned and stormed out of the room only to return a short time later.

Walking over to Clay she too slammed something on the counter beside him. "Here's five dollars, next time you can go to Starbucks," she snapped before leaving the room again.

"I don't know what you're so pissed off about," he yelled out as she was walking away. "I'm the one who first of all was awakened in the middle of the night. And, even though you're here doing whatever all day long, it's apparently too much for me to expect to have some coffee prepared when I get up for the day to actually go to work."

"Here all day doing whatever?" Sherri fired back after returning to the kitchen. "You know something Clay you, you, oh never mind I won't even go there." She instead threw her hands up over her head in frustration and headed back out of the room.

"Come on Sherri, go ahead and get whatever you have to say off your chest."

Like I need this shit first thing in the morning, she thought as she returned to the bedroom. It's like I'm nothing more than one part maid, one part chef and the rest live-in nanny. And it's not like I'm getting much in return. Sure there's this great house and all the creature comforts, but where is the caring and the respect? And somebody tell me, where in the hell is the love and affection, not to mention any sort of physical fulfillment? I'm apparently just here for his convenience and to be his occasional showpiece outside the home.

Later that day as Zach was well into his daily nap, Sherri logged onto the internet in search of a brief diversion. She first logged onto Facebook as was her norm. I wonder how Miguel is, she thought to herself. I haven't heard from him in several weeks. She decided to send him a message, after which she navigated over to Yahoo to check her own email. Almost as soon as she entered in her user name and password, a popup appeared indicating that she had received an instant message.

"Hi Sherri; just wanted to say again how much I enjoyed chatting with you last night. It was a blast. You are one interesting lady and I look forward to catching up with you again sometime in the near future. Like as soon as you have time for me. I have a pretty big job I'll be working on until the early evening so I won't be available until tonight. So if you are also, maybe we can sort of pick up where we left off last night. Have a good day."

Craig had told her the previous evening that he was a self employed contractor/handyman type who provides services in every area from painting and siding installation to carpet laying and minor plumbing. She smiled broadly after reading the message and immediately started to type out a reply to him. "Hey you, rumor has it that you're a jack of all trades and master of tongue. Now if that's so, why don't you look for me the same time tonight; about 11:00 or so. Hope to talk to you then."

The interaction between Sherri and Clay that evening was pretty much limited to discussing issues surrounding the kids, and even that was short-lived, direct and very much impersonal in nature. By 9:30 she was thinking that she couldn't wait until he went to bed so that she could comfortably spend some time getting more acquainted with Craig. So she was not at all upset when Clay approached her in the living room about 10:30.

"I'm gonna call it a night; see you in the morning," he said before touching her lips lightly with his.

"Okay, good night," she replied before glancing at her watch as he turned and departed. She was wishing she could go and seek out Craig online right then and there. But no, she would wait until at least 11 as she had said to him in the earlier message. Instead she continued to flip through the pages of the boring magazine she was attempting to pass time with. When the time finally reached 11:00 Sherri jumped to her feet and tossed the magazine aside. After taking a peek at Clay who was by then sound asleep, she went straight to the computer and logged into Yahoo chat. Craig wasn't logged on so she decided to just sit back and relax while she waited for him to sign in to join her. As it turned out it was only about five minutes later that she saw the popup indicating that he had indeed signed his way on.

"Hello Craig."

"Well hello to you to Sherri."

"Let me just get this out there, before I say anything else. Assuming that you logged on with the idea of chatting with me that is?"

"I indeed did."

"Okay good. Well I know you probably have been wondering what I look like, so I just want to tell you that I gave you access to my pictures at asudesire.

"All right great; I guess you could say I have been naturally curious. Mind if I go take a look right now? It'll only take a minute."

"Sure, go right ahead; that's why I opened them up to you. There are only two of them. Hope I don't scare you away."

"Now I wouldn't worry about that happening."

"How do you know?"

"Just what my gut tells me; but let me go check them out real quick and I'll be right back."

"Okay, I'll be here."

True to his word, Craig took only a minute or so before resuming the chat.

"See, my gut was right again. They're nice, real nice; you're downright hot to tell you the truth. Has anyone ever told you that you look similar to Cindy Crawford minus the mole?"

"Really; you think so? I mean thanks. Wow, that's some compliment because I think she's beautiful. My husband never even speaks of me in such glowing terms anymore,"

"What? You mean to tell me you're married?"

"I'm sorry I didn't mention that in our chat last night but I was definitely going to put it out there this time around. Maybe not in the way I did, but more in a direct oh by the way I'm married sort of way. But anyway, is that a problem for you Craig?"

"No, not if it isn't for you or for your husband," he kidded. "I mean you might have even listed that in your profile for all I know. To tell you the truth I didn't and usually don't pay much attention to that because, I figure that if someone is on that site regardless of whether they're married, single or whatever there's a reason for it."

"Good point, and very true I guess."

"Yes, every one of us is looking for something."

"You're right again."

"So Sherri, having said that, why is someone like you on a site like that?"

"Well I don't want to go into any specifics on my marriage right now. Besides, like you said, just the fact that I'm there says something right?"

"That's true, but that's not exactly what I meant by a site like that."

"Huh?

"I meant a site like asudesire; you know with how out there it can be sometimes. How graphic in nature it is I guess I'm trying to say. Let's face it this is not the kind of site on which you'll find people discussing current events or exchanging casserole recipes."

"I'm there for pretty much the same reason as everybody else I guess. Why do you ask?"

No offense, but in addition to being so hot you also strike me as sort of the Sweet Polly Purebred type."

What? Sherri thought to herself before typing her next message.

"Really, you say that based on what? I mean you don't even really know me."

"Like I said no offense Sherri, but you just have the appearance of the sweet, innocent type."

Somewhat taken aback, Sherri paused before replying back once again. As she ran her response through her mind, she also began to clearly recognize what Craig was doing as a ploy. A clever way of steering the conversation in another direction. But what the hell; she was game to play along. She figured that it was a good time to show Mr. Tongue Fu that she could be very blunt and quite comfortable in initiating some very pointed dialogue too.

"Well Craig," she began. "The truth is I haven't been innocent for quite some years now. But yes I do admit to being sweet. In fact you'd be searching quite a while to find a pussy any sweeter than mine."

"Hmmm; really, you don't say?"

"I certainly do say. You'd best believe it."

"I do like the sound of that."

"And you'd like the taste of it even more."

"So I guess I'll just have to take your word on that huh?"

"Maybe, maybe not; that depends on you."

"Well in your ad profile it said that you were looking for just some fun, spicy conversation. I did take note of that part."

"Yes it does say that. However I've learned to never say never. But yes, right now that's as far as I'm thinking. Just some hot and heavy chatting. Just trying to throttle up my life a little bit. Yet at the same time I'm not really trying to get myself in a situation."

"Anything I can do to help, just let me know. Without getting you into a situation (as you put it) of course."

"Okay, well just be who you are. That seems to be just fine so far."

By the time it was 12:30a.m, Sherri was left wondering where the time had gone.

"Well you know what they say right," Craig pointed out.

"What about time flying?"

"Yep it sure does when you're having fun."

"And this time flew by like the space shuttle."

"Can I take that as a compliment Sherri?"

"You most certainly can Craig."

"Okay; well thanks. And you're pretty damn interesting yourself. By the way where is your husband while you're here being dirty and flirty with me?"

"Oh he's in bed. Sound asleep; has been since about ten-thirty or so. But I guess I should go and join him now though."

"Well thanks for all the time Sherri. And I'll have to dig up a picture to show you now that I've seen one of you. I'll take care of that soon; maybe by tomorrow. And once again, hopefully we can do this again sometime soon."

"I hope so too Craig."

"So I guess I did okay tonight then?"

"Let me put it this way; my panties are still a little moist I think."

"Oh my, well on that note---Good Night Stormy."

"Good night Tongue Fu Panda."

CHAPTER FOUR

When Election Day arrived Clay was in an upbeat, optimistic mood. Everyone from pollsters, media pundits and Republican insiders were comfortable in saying that Senator Christian would soon be elected as the next Governor of New Jersey. Privately, even many Democrats admitted that the outcome was not too much in doubt. Nevertheless, the GOP didn't want to become too overconfident and assured of victory, so they were still maintaining their get out the vote strategies. And Clay was right in the middle of that effort, having put together a local team to mail out reminders and make phone calls. For that day he was working out of a little office that had been set up in Bridgewater. Sherri knew she wasn't likely to see him all day once he left early that morning. His plan after leaving the location in Bridgewater after his days work was over was to head right up to Bergen County. He had scored an invitation to what he expected to be a celebration of the highest order at the Hilton in Woodcliff Lake. It was the Christian team's election night headquarters and he was very excited about the prospect of being front and center as Mr. Christian gave his victory speech. For not only was he one of the 600 people invited to the festivities, but Clay had been personally told by Senator Christian that his was one of the faces he wanted surrounding the podium as he spoke. This was something that meant a lot to Clay because it meant prolonged face time not only on every local TV outlet, but also the strong possibility of being seen in living rooms across the nation on CNN, Fox News etc.

As for Sherri, she had declined a plea by Clay to attempt to find a sitter for the night so that she too might attend. While she was a Christian supporter she wasn't as caught up in the euphoria as her husband was. In fact with the kids all home due to the schools being closed, her plan was too spend the day with them. First, they were to go hang out at Chuck E Cheese, having lunch and enjoying themselves with games and amusements, and then watch a movie and munch on popcorn after dinner. She had already voted early that morning, so with that out of the way it was strictly fun for the rest of the day; albeit tiresome fun for her.

The word came down from all of the networks as soon as the polls closed that Senator Paul Christian had indeed become the Governor-elect. When Clay called the house about 8:30 to share some of his excitement with Sherri he seemed disappointed to find out that she was watching an animated film with the kids rather than election results.

"Well are you at least going to watch the Senator's speech later on. I'm gonna be up there on the stage with him if you recall."

"I don't know we'll see, depends on the kids and then some stuff I have to do after they go to bed."

"Well get the kids off to bed early, get to the other stuff now and then that won't be an issue."

"Like I said, we'll see. They're enjoying a movie right now and it'll be on for another half-hour. And I'm also pretty tired, so I may just want to finish up my chores and relax."

"Okay, well I can see you're really stoked about the possibility of seeing me on TV."

"Clay I've seen you on TV before remember, during the Dellasandro trial?"

"Yeah but that was a while ago; besides this is different. Anyway never mind; it's no big deal right?"

"Well it is to somebody, that's obvious."

"So can you at least TiVo it? That way not only can you watch it some other time, but so can I."

"Okay, no problem I can do that; sure."

"Thank You."

"You're welcome. Anyway let me get back to the kids and I'll see you whenever you get in."

"Okay well word is that the speech should begin about 10:00 if you happen to change your mind about watching."

"I'll keep that in mind. Bye, see you later."

"Bye."

Sherri didn't want to say it to Clay, but she knew she had no intention of watching the soon-to-be Governor's speech. So as soon as she hung up the phone she went to set the TV in the master bedroom to record it before getting back to the kids. Zach fell asleep about 8:45, while Abby and Tyler prepared to go to bed as soon as the movie ended at 9. Sherri then tidied up a bit before killing some more time by calling her Mom. They talked about twice a week on average, which sometimes made it a challenge maintaining a conversation if there wasn't much new to talk about. And with this being one of those instances, Sherri found herself watching the clock early on in the conversation. She basically just wanted to pass time until 11:00. She and Craig had by then pretty much made it a nightly occurrence of chatting at or around that time, so she was already looking forward to that.

She ended the call with her Mom around 10:45 in order to give herself some time to prep for bed before seeking out her new online friend. Due to her being a bit tired, she decided that rather than sitting up at the computer, she would chat with him using her handheld. That way she could engage Craig from the comfort of her bed. As it turned out, that was a bit too comfortable and she fell fast asleep at some point during their chat. She realized that when Clay awakened her upon arriving home about 12:45. The last thing she could remember was that as usually was the case, things started to get a little steamy between she and Craig. So much so that she had placed a hand under her nightgown and started to masturbate. As she got her bearings a bit, she began to recall that she had fallen asleep in mid-chat. From the lingering wetness she felt between her legs, she had little doubt that the session had also included a happy ending for her. Sherri also noticed that her Blackberry was right beside her, so she snatched it up quickly and looked at the screen. She immediately started to hope that Clay hadn't taken a look at it, because she hadn't logged out of the chat session and some of the erotic exchange between she and Craig was still visible for any probing eyes to see.

When Clay made no mention of anything, she started to relax, comfortable that he hadn't seen anything. She knew that it would have been out of character for him, but certainly not out of the question. As he made his way to the bathroom, she quickly erased the conversation, logged off and placed the device in her nightstand.

Clay soon emerged from the bathroom and immediately climbed into bed beside Sherri, placing his body snuggly against hers. Without hesitation he began to slowly rub his hands all over her backside and around her thighs and up to her breasts. Sherri's initial reaction was to pretend to be sleeping.

"Babe, wake up, come on babe. How about a quickie? Sherri come on, how about it, whaddya say?" he added when she didn't respond.

She finally turned until she was facing him. She hated his approach at that moment and decided to let him know about it.

"Well aren't you Mr. Charm," she said softly. He also reeked of cigar smoke and alcohol and she hated that even more. I guess taking a quick shower and brushing his teeth before trying to make moves on her would have been expecting too much.

"I'm sorry honey; okay can I have a quick piece please? That's better right?"

"Not really but I guess it's about as good as I'm gonna get out of you."

They looked at each other for several seconds before he broke into a smile.

"Okay, come on," she said. She realized that she wasn't in the best bargaining position. She was still a bit horny from her chat with Craig and knew that although she wouldn't get what she wanted, it would be a case of biting off her nose to spite her face if she declined. After all 50% of something beats 100% of nothing anytime.

As usual Clay had little time for foreplay, not that she wanted much from him right then. This was an instance when she didn't even want him to kiss her, and any oral was out of the question unless it was gonna be him giving it. But she would have appreciated it if he could have at least made time to suck on her tits for more than 10 seconds or so before climbing on top of her. As he thrust his way in and out of her, Sherri allowed her mind to wander. Mostly to thoughts of Craig and what it might be like if he were the one making love to her right then. Who knows maybe it would have been satisfying to me also, she guessed once Clay came inside of her before rolling onto his back.

"Good night," he whispered before kissing her lightly on the forehead. "And thanks."

"Good night," she replied softly.

As he rolled onto his side and quickly fell asleep, Sherri folded her arms across her chest. She wondered if there was any chance that Craig was still up. Quickly pushing those thoughts from her mind, she too decided to focus on sleep.

∞∞∞∞∞

Before you knew it Thanksgiving was quickly approaching and that meant hectic times for Sherri as it was her family's turn to host dinner. It was rotated between theirs and the homes of Clay's brother and sister. There was a lot of shopping to be done in order to feed so many people. There was her family as well as Clay's siblings Kevin and Colette, their spouses and five combined children, three of whom were perpetually hungry teenage boys. This was one of those times when it was really advantageous to be able to shop during the weekdays when many people were at work. Three days before the big day was when she decided to pick up the bulk of the things she would need. As she was strolling up and down the aisles at King's Supermarket thoughts of Craig crept into her mind. She hadn't heard from him in several days and just wondered if everything was okay. Pausing in the middle of one of the aisles, she started to type an email message to him.

"Just wanted to say hi, been thinking about you and miss chatting with you these last few days. Hope all is well with you and of course with us. Message me back when you can. Take care."

She then continued on but stopped just about 25 feet ahead and pulled out her Blackberry once again.

"Sorry, it's me again. I've been thinking, and if it would be easier for you why don't you text me? The number is 908-448-7813. Talk to you soon, bye."

Craig's appeal to her had only grown after she had received the picture of himself he emailed to her a few weeks earlier. In his profile he had listed himself as 5'11" and about 175 pounds with brown hair and blue eyes. And once she saw the picture she was more than pleased that he had described himself with pinpoint accuracy. In the photo, which was obviously taken while he was working, he was wearing a wife-beater tee shirt, jeans and black work boots. She still recalls getting a lump in her throat as she gazed at his muscular arms and shoulders. A bushy yet well-trimmed mustache adorned his upper lip and topped off his rugged looks perfectly in her eyes. He was quite the contrast to her husband's bookish appearance. And of late she'd had more and more thoughts of him.

Sherri made very good time at the supermarket; the aisles were not terribly bottled up with shopping carts as it tends to be on weekends. It was populated largely with other fellow housewives, retirees and the scattered person just picking up a few things while on their lunch break. And to make things even easier, Zach was reasonably well-behaved while seated in the cart's upper basket. At times he can really impede her by being overly restless, but on this occasion he wasn't bad at all. The produce aisle was the last one she had to navigate before heading to checkout. She was picking out some fresh squash when her phone sounded off, informing her that she had received a new text message.

"Hey sexy, not to worry; all is well. Just been a busy few days that's all; you doing okay?"

"All is well; especially now that I know it's not that you've tired of me."

"Don't be crazy. Nothing of the sort, trust me."

Sherri held fast right in that spot in order to continue the conversation. A couple of other shoppers excused themselves in order to try to get around her to reach the stacks of produce near her.

"That's so good to hear Craig."

"So what are you doing with yourself today?"

"I'm just doing the shopping for Turkey Day. Cooking and hosting are on my agenda this year."

"Sounds good; am I invited."

"Yeah sure come by around 6; you'll miss dinner but I'll certainly be serving up desert."

"Okay no problem. Oh and by the way good call on the texting. I love the quick back and forth as much as using instant messaging."

"Yeah that's what I was thinking."

Sherri by then had moved on down the aisle. She narrowly averted running into a couple of other shoppers with her cart as her attention was drawn to texting with Craig.

"So what will you be doing for the holiday Craig?"

"Still up in the air; I may head up to my parents, and if so I'll make it an early night."

"Why?"

"I just don't get so much into all of the post dinner stuff. I tend to eat and run. I find that more favorable than spending extended time around my insufferable sister-in-law. Besides I want to get some work in on Friday."

"I see, and I understand because I have one of those type of sister in-laws myself. Where do your folks live by the way?"

"Up in Rockaway Township."

The texting continued through her check out process and up until she reached the parking lot.

"Okay well I'm done at the market and headed home so let me go on. If I don't hear from you before Thursday have a great Thanksgiving."

"Thanks and you too sexy. And try not to eat too much so you can stay that way."

"I'll do my best. And you don't eat too much of whatever it is you'll be eating—wink wink."

"Well that's healthy eating, as long as it's not the wrong one. But unfortunately I don't think that pussy will be a part of the menu this time around."

"Ohhhh that's too bad, I wish I could bring you some; served up all warm and delicious."

"Mmmm that would be the best part of the feast. That's one plate that would be completely cleaned."

"You are so very naughty do you know that?" a blushing Sherri replied.

I do, but would you have me any other way?"

"Oh no, I like you just like that."

"Wanna know how I want you? Naked and spread-eagled."

"Come on stop it Craig. I think I feel a little wetness between my legs."

"Cool; now let me take care of that for you."

"Now don't tease unless you plan to please."

"Sherri you know you actually look a bit tired; why don't you have a seat. And on my face looks like the perfect place."

"What am I going to do with you?"

"I have a few ideas."

"Bye Craig."

"Bye, Sherri, talk to you soon."

∞∞∞∞∞∞∞∞

Sherri got up bright and early on Thanksgiving morning to get started on that day's cooking. She is actually quite the cook when she puts her mind to it and Thanksgiving was definitely one of those occasions where she enjoyed showing off her skills in the kitchen. The menu included the traditional fare of turkey, stuffing, mashed potatoes, gravy and corn, but Sherri also enjoyed experimenting with different dishes for the day as well. To that end she also prepared prime rib au jus, squash soufflé, a green bean casserole, cranberry-orange relish, glazed carrots and sourdough yeast rolls. Needless to say it was a busy morning in the kitchen, but at the same time she didn't mind the work. Colette and Kevin's wife Nina were bringing the desserts so that would certainly help also.

Dinner was at 4:00 and the major issue of concern was keeping the kids occupied and out of Sherri's way. She and Clay had discussed the possibility of his taking them into Manhattan for the annual Macy's Thanksgiving Day parade but that would have necessitated an extremely early start to the day. Something that they couldn't really see the kids getting on board with. Not to mention that it was a 31 degree morning with the high temperature expected to be no more than 40 degrees. Plan B was that they would all go to Extreme Kidz play emporium along with two of their young cousins. Unfortunately that plan also fell apart over concerns that the children's three father's would not be up to par as chaperones. Sherri for one felt pretty certain that Clay would be more concerned with watching football than paying close enough attention to their 3 children, and Zach in particular.

As a result Abby, Tyler and Zach were left to their own devices to keep themselves entertained. That wasn't much of an issue with Abby and Tyler as they each had plenty of games they loved to play on their individual Wii entertainment systems. It was little Zach who presented the biggest challenge. His two older siblings weren't generally enthused about him intruding on their play time, and at times there could be a question of whether anything else could hold his interest long enough to keep him from latching himself on to his mother's apron. As luck would have it, on that day he was fine on his own. He was perfectly content watching cartoons up until the time they started watching him once he fell fast asleep.

With all of that handled the cooking went very smoothly. Sherri was able to complete everything by 3:00 and at that time get showered and dressed in advance of their company. She decided to dress very casually, in jeans and a light blue tunic worn over a tee shirt. The kids had gotten dressed hours earlier with Abby lending her a great hand by assisting with Zach. In the meantime Clay had been parked in front of the TV for hours watching football while occasionally glancing over case documents. Colette and her husband Frank were the first guests to arrive, doing so at 3:30 on the button. Sherri greeted them both with a hug as they entered and gave big hugs and kisses to their children; 15 year old Vincent, 13 year old Anthony and Jenna 10. Colette King Ricciardi was at 45 the oldest of the three King children. She stands 5'7" and has the same fair-haired, light-featured looks as her brother Clay. She had recently cut her hair to a short, easily manageable length. She also has long had a penchant for overdressing for this sort of gathering and that day was no exception as she was outfitted in a slitted, floor length Salvatore Ferragamo skirt, sexy knee length leather boots by Prada, and a sharp Christian Dior sweater. Her large chest stood out from the moment she removed her coat. In contrast Frank was dressed simply in a pair of black Dockers and beige mock turtleneck.

"Okay, you said to bring whatever kind of deserts I wanted so I went with an Italian cheesecake and a carrot cake," announced Colette.

"Oh that's fine," Sherri said as she led Vincent and Anthony into the kitchen so they could place the items down. Naturally they were store bought. Colette wasn't known for being very domestic at all. In fact Frank prepared many of the meals for the family; particularly the Italian dishes he is most fond of. Vincent and Anthony were the spitting image of their father; both tall, strapping young men who may be well on their way to equaling or even surpassing Frank's 6 feet 4 inch height. They also have the same olive-skinned appearance with dark hair and eyes topped by full, thick eyebrows.

"Frank, Clay is downstairs watching football I believe if you and the boys want to join him," said Sherri.

"Okay, but I think they're in between games now. We were actually watching one game before we left the house. I guess we'll try to catch some of the Dallas-Miami game after dinner."

Jenna had already gone off in search of Abby. No sooner than had they greeted each other than the two of them were playing Just Dance on Abby's Wii game system. Tyler on the other hand broke away from his game of Punch Out as soon as he heard his older cousin's voices. He had a level of admiration for Vincent and Anthony that almost bordered on idolization. He spoke often of how he couldn't wait to be a big football star just like them. Vincent had just completed a very successful season with the high School freshman team while Anthony was the quarterback for his middle school team.

The doorbell rang again at ten minutes to four, signaling the arrival of Kevin and Nina along with their two children Scott-14 and 12 year old Katie. Sherri excused herself from her chat with Colette in the kitchen in order to go answer the door.

"Hi, I didn't know if you guys were going to make it on time," said Sherri as she opened the door to greet them. "Oh my God Katie," you're getting so big," she noted as she hugged her shoulders. "You're a young lady now aren't you?" she added.

"Yes I am," Katie beamed proudly as she looked over at her Mom.

"Oh yes, there's no doubt about that; at least not if you ask Katie. Now that she's turned 12 you would think she's ready for her own car, her own place, everything," Nina chuckled.

"Oh Mom please," Katie protested before turning to Sherri. "Where's Abby?"

"She's in her room," Sherri replied prompting Katie to head in that direction. "Jenna's back there with her too."

"Okay cool."

"Katie don't forget we're going to be eating soon," Nina called out to her as she looked to Sherri for confirmation on that.

"Yes, four o'clock sharp," Sherri then stated.

"4:00 that's only like ten minutes from now so don't get too comfortable."

Sherri took everyone's coats and hung them in the closet in the foyer.

"I'm sorry we got here so late, blame it on Nina," Kevin said with a grin.

"Okay, okay I admit it was my fault. I was trying to finish up the pies. I got a later start than I wanted to," Nina confessed.

"Oh that's fine I understand. Let me take those in the kitchen," said Sherri before she started to pick them up from the table where Kevin and Scott had placed them while they removed their coats.

The ladies split the load with each of them carrying 2 of the homemade coconut custard pies into the kitchen. "Clay, Frank and all the boys are in the downstairs family room I believe if you guys want to join them," Sherri offered to Kevin and Scott as they departed. Clay and Frank were seated in front of the 50 inch television talking while Vincent and Anthony were engaged in a game of pool while Tyler looked on, when Kevin and Scott entered.

"Okay let me guess, you guys are talking politics," said Kevin as he approached them with his right hand outstretched.

"Yes we are but I guess we'd better stop now that the family's resident Democrat is here," Clay said in jest.

"Well no need to stop on my account. And to tell you the truth, I admit that I'm not all that upset with Christian winning. Governor Corcoran has been a disappointment even to us Democrats so maybe a change is good right now. What's best for the state is what's most important."

"So Kevin, can we take it that you cast your vote for Christian then?" asked Frank.

"No you can't. I actually sat this one out. As much as I tried I just couldn't bring myself to pull the lever for a Republican," he quipped.

In the meantime Scott lurked in the background. He's the quiet, unassuming type and was not wholly comfortable in this type of setting. Even when it involved being around family. After some prodding he eventually made his way over to his 3 male cousins and watched them as they continued their game of billiards. Scott has the same red-headed, freckled appearance as his mother Nina and has just recently matched her 5'6" height. Unlike Vincent, Anthony or even Tyler he has never demonstrated much of an affinity for any sort of sports and has interests that run more along the lines of nature and science. Sadly, that in itself is enough to have one quickly labeled a nerd, a fate that had certainly befallen the bespectacled Scott.

Over dinner; the conversation first centered on Clay's likely appointment as the next Somerset County Prosecutor. Kevin, who is a mirror image of Clay except 2 years younger, was effusive in his praise of his brother, pointing out that such a position may well be the stepping stone to becoming state attorney general or possibly even a federally appointed judge one day. "But of course that would more than likely require a Republican in the White House so while I love you brother I can't say that I'm rooting for that to happen anytime soon," he admitted.

"Nor would I expect you to little brother, Clay replied. But it's gonna happen anyway; it's inevitable. The American people will come back around to our way of seeing things soon enough."

"Yeah, yeah, sure they will," Nina chimed in. "You keep waiting for that day and we'll keep the White House thank you."

Not wanting to see this go the way that it was likely headed at that point, Sherri decided to jump in and change the subject of conversation. She deftly steered it over to Vin and Anthony's prowess on the football field. She didn't have a lot of interest in the sport personally, but she loved and supported her nephews. And besides, she had no interest in seeing Thanksgiving dinner deteriorate into petty bickering over politics. The discussion of football got Tyler revved up quickly. So much so that he took the opportunity to ask his parents if they would allow him to sign up for midget football next year rather than soccer.

"We'll see Tyler," is as far as Sherri would go, drawing a frown from Tyler.

"Dad!" he protested.

"Like your Mom said, we'll have to see," said Clay as Tyler folded his arms across his chest in frustration.

"Oh let the boy play if he really wants to, "Colette interjected. I was the same way with Vinnie back when he first wanted to start out playing. And look at him now. His coach seems pretty certain that he'll start for the varsity as a sophomore next season and should start getting some attention from colleges by the year after if not before. I sure hope so. A football scholarship would be a great help financially. So I'm just saying you never know"...

"Well that's all well and good Colette," Sherri snapped, cutting her off mid-sentence. But Tyler is our son and like Clay and I said we'll see. Let's just leave at that shall we?"

"Hmmph, well I guess we shall," Colette said in a huff as several of the adults at the table shifted uncomfortably in their seats. Sherri and Colette have never gotten along terribly well. In fact their relationship could best be described as them just tolerating each other. Sensing the need for it, Clay decided at that point to jump in and lighten the mood a bit. Truth is, he either had no idea or didn't at all care that it was he who was the reason for much of the tension Sherri was feeling. He hadn't made love to her in a few weeks, and even when he last did, the only orgasm that resulted from it was his own. Furthermore, her period was due any day and she had no reason to feel like she would receive the kind of release she was longing for before its arrival. Nor at its conclusion for that matter, so Sherri was just a bit uptight and had very little patience for Colette putting herself in something that was strictly a family decision that would be made when the time came to do so.

"Hey Nina did you remember to bring your Taboo game?" Clay asked.

"Sure did, its right over there on the cocktail table."

"Great, let's get a game going later."

"Okay, but I know you guys will probably want to watch some football after dinner. While you're doing that I guess us girls can chit-chat while we're cleaning up the kitchen," Nina said while looking to Sherri and Colette for approval. "Then we can play whenever you all are finished watching the game" she continued after they nodded in agreement.

"Sounds like a plan," said Frank as Clay and Kevin agreed.

By 8p.m. the football game was over, the after-dinner chores were complete and 2 of the pies as well as a good amount of the other deserts had been eaten and the game of Taboo was in full swing. Rather than play males vs. females as they often do, they decided on a different twist. It was the King siblings against the spouses. That meant Colette, Kevin and Clay were teamed up against Nina, Frank and Sherri. In the meantime all of their offspring had retreated to Abby or Tyler's rooms to partake in more video games. In the past some of these friendly games of Taboo have gotten a little too competitive, but on this occasion the tone of the game had remained friendly and jovial. The margaritas that Sherri had been serving up perhaps had something to do with that as well. By the time she had downed her second margarita Sherri felt a little bit more than a nice buzz. In fact she was borderline tipsy. At about 9:00 she excused herself, saying that she needed to use the bathroom. After exiting the bathroom she tiptoed her way over to the door of the master bedroom. Peeking outside she saw that no one was lurking close by, so she pulled the door towards her until it was slightly ajar.

She then walked over to her nightstand and took a seat on the bed right next to it. After retrieving her Blackberry she started to type a text message, while occasionally looking towards the door.

"Hey you; was just wondering how your holiday has been and if you are back home or still hanging out at your folks?" She then sat there anxiously; waiting to see if there would be any reply.

About a minute later she would get her answer as her handheld sounded off with the familiar tone of an incoming text.

"Hey yourself; you're kind of early tonight. Anyway, yes I'm back home already. What's up?"

"Hi Craig, how was your Thanksgiving with your family?"

"It wasn't bad this year, better than I had feared but I still left at about 7:30. How about yours?"

"It's been pretty good and it's still ongoing. We're actually playing a board game right now; I just snuck away for a bit and decided to check in with you really quick."

"Well that was cool of you."

"And plus I wanted to tell you that I'm really feeling horny right now."

"Oh really?"

"Oh yeah; and I've had a couple of drinks so it's even more pronounced than usual. My pussy is really throbbing right now."

"And I know just what it needs I bet."

"You do? Well tell me."

"You could really use a bit of tongue fu right now, and some lips sucking on your clit."

Sherri stood and turned her back to the door before typing her next reply.

"Oh yes, could I use that right now! That would be excellent," she sent back just before she reached her left hand down her pants and started to finger herself.

"And I'm certain it would be even better than that for me."

She removed her hand in order to respond again. "You have no idea h…"

"Sherri what are you doing? We're waiting for you."

Startled, she dropped her Blackberry to the floor as she quickly turned around.

"Um I was um; I was just sending my sister Mary Ann a message wishing her a Happy Thanksgiving."

"Well I don't know why you couldn't just call her like you do any other time; anyway come on," Clay insisted.

"I'll be there in a second," she promised as he departed, leaving the door just as it was when he entered. She hoped that he wasn't suspicious of anything because of how unnerved she got when he burst into the room. Quickly picking the Blackberry off the floor she then completed the message.

"You have no idea how tempting that sounds Craig; but I've got to go. Bye for now."

As she placed the device in the top drawer of the nightstand Craig read her last message to him. Smiling, he shrugged his shoulders and shook his head a few times. "Oh well, he thought to himself. Sherri then hurried into the bathroom to freshen up a bit before returning to her guests and the game of Taboo. Taboo---how fitting, she said to herself.

CHAPTER FIVE

While she didn't get out there with the early birds determined to get the best bargains, Sherri did manage to get some Black Friday shopping in the next day. She made it over to the Bridgewater Commons mall at about noon, with all three kids in tow. While at the food court having lunch with them, she decided to text Craig to apologize for her abrupt departure the night before, explaining to him that her husband had interrupted their brief but very hot exchange. He assured her that while he would have loved to have continued the chat he understood completely and there was no real need to apologize. Satisfied that he was okay with her, she then continued on with her lunch before resuming shopping. Sherri was old-fashioned enough that whenever possible she avoided purchasing Christmas gifts for her children while they're present. She still loved to see that morning's surprised looks of joy on their faces. Besides, Zach hadn't yet reached the age at which the Santa Claus fantasy for him was no longer. So instead she just purchased some things for her nieces and nephews, both those close by in New Jersey, or the kids of her siblings in Massachusetts. And yes she did manage to squeeze in a few items for herself. A pair of Armani boots, 2 pair of jeans and some bodysuits.

In the coming days things settled pretty much back into the familiar routine. Work for Clay, school for Abby and Tyler, and the drab existence of a neglected housewife and stay-at home mom for Sherri. But at least now she had her little secret diversion to break free from the monotony of the every day, if only for all too brief episodes. Her moments spent engaging Craig had become as much a part of her life as anything else. They refreshed her mind, gave her spirits a much-needed kick and never failed to give her body quite the jolt also.

∞∞∞∞∞∞∞∞∞∞

December 1st was the day that Clay and many others had long anticipated. The official announcement came from Governor-elect Christian that Clayton Alexander King Jr. was going to be the next Somerset County Prosecutor. It had become such a loosely guarded secret that local reporters had taken to regularly trying to reach Clay for comment, in the days leading up to the appointment. Mr. Christian made the announcement in a press conference held on the steps of the county courthouse. Clay was of course in attendance as well as several local and statewide Republican Party officials. Sherri, ever the dutiful wife had also attended at Clay's insistence. There she was smiling throughout; all the while hoping that she wouldn't need to spend too much time standing outside on such a frigid morning. She posed for numerous pictures; that is when she was unable to avoid the photographers; and she stayed right by Clay's side until the proceedings were over. And oh was she glad when it was; not only for the chance to escape the cold, but she was also anxious to return home in order to catch up with Craig. After all it had been 3 nights since she'd had her libido stimulated by his alluring words.

In the days following the announcement Clay's focus had really become divided. His new position only awaited confirmation by the state legislature, something that was considered a mere formality. The timeline was that the vote would take place before Christmas and he would then step into the Prosecutor's chair by mid-January. That left him a relatively short amount of time to clear his docket at the firm as well as start work with the outgoing Prosecutor on a smooth transition. And then there was also the task of putting some names together for a staff. There were assistant Prosecutors and upper level law enforcement personnel to be chosen, as well as clerks and the all-important office staff. Indeed there was much to be done, all without the luxury of an abundance of time. And as much of an afterthought as she was before, Sherri knew just where that left her on the priority list now.

With only ten days left until Christmas, things were in full swing in regards to shopping. There wasn't a whole lot more to pick up, but Sherri was anxious to get it over with; certainly before Christmas week. She hated the stress of last minute holiday shopping. Not to mention the maddening crowds. In order to make things easier for each of them she and her friend Lily took turns babysitting the other's kids so that they could each shop more freely. Lily's children were six and the other three just like Zach, so that arrangement worked out quite well for both of them.

Sherri had every intention of making this one her last trip to the mall before Christmas. Anything else she needed she would have to pick up at stand alone stores like Target or Kohl's. There she was loaded down with bags in each hand when she heard the very familiar notification tone of a new text. Placing the bags down, she reached into her pocket and pulled out her Blackberry. A happy smile creased her face once she saw the message was from her friend, the self-proclaimed tongue fu master. She picked up the bags and made her way over to a nearby bench. There were several people seated on it already, but she excused herself and carved out a little space on the corner and took a seat.

"Hey Sherri; I was just thinking about you and wanted to see how you were today," the message read.

"Hello Craig, I'm doing just fine. Actually a little better now that I've heard from you. So tell me what you were thinking about me?"

"You can probably pretty much guess that."

"Maybe, but I want you to tell me."

"Okay, you know by now that i'm not bashful about much of anything, I was thinking about how sweet and delicious that lovely slit between your legs probably is."

Uncrossing her legs, Sherri peered over her shoulder for any prying eyes. She then smiled widely before starting to type her response."Wouldn't you like to find out for sure?"

"You know I would."

"Well you just might have to."

"So, just what is it that you're saying Sherri?"

"I've said enough for now. Let me finish up my shopping and we'll talk tonight."

"Okay; about the usual time?"

"Yes, about the usual time."

"I will talk to you then."

"Okay bye."

"Bye-bye."

Sherri then slid the unit back into her pocket, picked up her bags and moved on. After the full day of shopping was complete, she was more than satisfied with her haul. And pleased that she got home in plenty of time to not only hide away what things she had purchased for the kids, but to also greet Abby and Tyler when they arrived on the school bus.

By 11:30 that night not a creature stirred inside the house. It was her time; she was ready for her fun and games. But this time she had decided to take a different course. Rather than resorting to texting, she made her way to the computer. She would look to see if Craig was logged into Yahoo messenger first. Gladly for her, he indeed was, so she wasted no time getting to her point.

"Good evening Tongue Fu."

"Good evening to you too tasty."

"Oh that's a new one; you've never called me that before. I like it. But anyway, let me cut to the chase. Are you interested in getting together in person?

"Wow, that is getting right to it; but hold on a second while I pinch myself. Okay I'm really awake, so let me answer that question for you. HELL YEAH!! Just let me know when."

"I'm thinking soon; maybe even this Friday. How does that sound?"

"Like I said, just let me know when and we can make it happen."

"That won't be a problem for work?"

"Well maybe if I wasn't the boss it might, but no, not at all."

"Okay sounds good."

"So Sherri tell me something; why the change of heart? Not that I should even care about that right now."

"You mean about hooking up in person?"

"Yes."

"Well, like I told you a while back, that was up to you; that I would never say never. So you can credit yourself, because honestly I really had no intention of doing such a thing when this first started out."

"But you're ready and willing to do it now?"

" Yep and don't forget able. Listen, I'm 100% ready Craig believe me; or I wouldn't have made the offer. Trust me this is not something I take lightly or would play around with."

"Sounds good to me babe; so what's the game plan?"

"In terms of when and where? Well I'm thinking mid to late morning, because I do have to get the kids off to school and then be back for when they get out. And as for where, I can come to your place. That's not a problem. You don't live too close for comfort."

"Great, let's make it happen."

"Well we don't need to talk too much tonight. Why don't you just email me your address when you can, and then we'll just firm it up sometime tomorrow okay."

"Consider it done. But wow, I can't believe it. Friday— that's just 2 days away. Well less than that when you think in terms of Friday morning. OMG I can't wait."

"Neither can I Craig. I'm really looking forward to it at this point."

"Not as much as I am I bet. I can taste you already."

"And I can feel your tongue inside of me as I lay there with my eyes closed. Both my hands pressed to the back of your head."

"Oh I like the way that sounds," Craig messaged back in a hurry."

"Well let me stop right there before I'm grabbing up my car keys now. I'll talk to you tomorrow sometime."

"Okay and if you don't feel like texting, chatting or emailing me, you can always call me on my cell."

"All right; have a good night Craig."

"You too Sherri; bye."

"Bye."

The next morning Sherri hurriedly sought to schedule a bikini wax for herself. She wanted her nether region to be as silky smooth as possible for what she had been anticipating for some time. That being an up close and personal encounter with Craig's face. She was fortunate enough to squeeze in an appointment for 2:00 that afternoon at the Valencia Day Spa right in town. And that was perfect because it would allow her to pick up her two oldest children from school on the way back home.

But she did still have the issue of what she could arrange for Zach for the next day. The first person she thought to ask was Lily, but unfortunately she had plans for the morning. Next up was Dawn Ricciardi, the 19 year old daughter of the family that lived 2 houses away. She sat with Zach on occasion when she was in high school, but that mattered little now. She was a different person now and let's face it; it was not every teen's desire to spend some of their precious college semester break babysitting a three year old. There were Sherri figured, too many other far more appealing options available to an attractive, outgoing young lady in this day and age. But she decided it was worth a shot nevertheless.

To no great surprise Dawn informed her that while she would have loved to have done it for her with more notice, she had arranged to go shopping and then to lunch with friends in the morning, before later spending some time with her boyfriend. As soon as she hung up the phone with Dawn, Sherri covered her face with her hands in a moment of anguish. She started thinking that she may as well get in touch with Craig and inform him that she would have to cancel their planned rendezvous. She should have known better than to try to make fairly spontaneous plans, she thought. She hoped he wouldn't be too disappointed, though she had had every expectation that he would be. After all that was her feeling. As she started to slowly type up a text message to him, she decided to explore one more long shot option. She put down her Blackberry and picked up the phone.

"I know that Zach, just like all three year olds can be a handful so I was really hesitant to even ask."

"Oh don't worry I can handle it, you just do what you need to do and leave little Zachary to me. It'll be good to see him. I haven't seen him much at all since Clay Sr. died."

"I know, and I'm sorry about that. I'll make it a point of doing better in that regard."

"Well I know it's not all you dear. The relationship between Clay Jr. and I doesn't help matters."

Sherri had called Beth King, Clay's stepmother. Except Clay has never accepted her as such. She had been married to Clay's Dad Clay Sr. for close to 25 years when he passed away 2 years ago from a massive heart attack at age 68. And for every one of those years plus now a while longer, Beth and Clay have had a relationship that could be described as distant at best. She had been his Dad's mistress before Clay's parents divorced, and he has never viewed her as anything but the women who broke up his parents' marriage and as a result his family. Clay Sr. had always attempted to reason with him by maintaining that the marriage to his mother was failing before the affair began, but Clay was insistent. After his parents' divorce his Dad had married Beth less than a year later, and though Clay continued to live with his Mom, he would of course see Beth during visits with his Dad. But that is something he saw no reason to do now that his father was gone.

"Yes, but Clay doesn't necessarily have to be a part of you seeing the kids," Sherri reasoned.

"That's true I suppose, but it would make it a bit more special. And it would probably lead to Clay Sr. smiling down on us from heaven."

"I have no doubt that it would and hopefully that can start to happen sometime soon."

"But I do understand his feelings, I really do," Beth commented before a period of silence which was finally broken by Sherri. She sensed Beth's pain at that moment and decided she should end the conversation.

"Okay, well thank you again Beth and we will see you in the morning."

"All right sweetie, see you then. Bye-bye.

As soon as she hung up the phone Sherri grabbed her Blackberry and erased the message she had started to draft to send Craig. She instead placed a call to his cell phone.

"Hello."

"Hey, good news; we're pretty much a definite go on this end for Friday. There was a possibility that I might have needed to cancel but I pulled something out of my hat fortunately. So unless something else comes up I will see you sometime between 10:30 and 11:30 I'd say."

"Okay that sounds great baby."

"And I will be showing up with a fresh and clean pussy just for you. So don't fill up too much at breakfast," she chuckled.

"Well let me say that I'm very glad you were able to work out whatever problem that may have kept this from happening. And believe me; nothing is going to prevent me from being here ready and waiting for you, with a healthy appetite."

"I can't wait. Did you email me the address?"

"Yes I did. Last night in fact."

"Oh okay, I haven't logged onto the PC yet today and didn't check on my Blackberry for emails. But cool; I guess we're all set then. I will see you Friday morning. I can't wait Craig."

"Yes, I will see you then. And neither can I."

Sherri awakened early Friday morning with a little added pep in her step. Surprisingly she wasn't all that nervous, but rather had a feeling of genuine excitement. The sun was shining brightly and even the birds seemed to her a bit livelier. She didn't bother telling Clay that Zach would be spending some time with Beth later in the day. She didn't want to risk having his reaction spoil her mood. "I'm just feeling good and upbeat because it's that time of year. And besides it's going to be a beautiful day," she answered when he questioned her about her clear exuberance.

After everyone had departed for the day, Sherri fed Zach his breakfast and put on Sesame Street for him before stepping into the shower. She enjoyed a long, leisurely stay in there, relishing the warm jets of pulsating water caressing her skin and removing what little tensions she had. Her soft loofah sponge glided over her body, cleansing every crease and crevice to strawberry-scented delight. After exiting the shower she wrapped herself in a luxuriously soft velour robe before taking a peek at Zach. Seeing that Elmo and Big Bird still had his complete attention, she returned to her room and slowly pampered her skin from head to toe in baby oil topped by creamy shea butter.

Standing in front of the dresser mirror, she slipped into her sexiest, lace push-bra and matching panties, both in black. Next, she dressed herself in a pair of black, fitted slacks topped by a long-sleeved royal blue sweater with a tantalizingly low-cut v-shaped neckline. She placed on her feet a pair of ankle high Louis Vuitton boots. After briefly admiring herself in the mirror she sprayed some Armani perfume behind both ears, just below her collarbones, a bit on each wrist and one little spritz between her lightly freckled sized 36 C breasts. She took one last look in the mirror; but she needn't fret over anything. She was beautiful, she was hot, and she was sexy. She was ready for action.

Sherri had decided to wait to apply her makeup, so she instead quickly went to pack up Zach's backpack with lunch, a couple of snacks and a spare set of clothes. She checked the time just before 10:00 which was good because that meant that she didn't need to concern herself with Zach protesting over her turning off his TV in the middle of Sesame Street because it had ended.

The drive to Beth's home in Bedminster was only be a brief 15 minutes at that time of day so being late was not a concern at all.

Beth gave Sherri a big hug as soon as she opened the front door to the lovely Tudor-style home she had once shared with Clay Sr.

"How are you? It's so good to see you," she gushed. "Oh my God you look great."

"It's good to see you too Beth. Look Zach its Grandma Beth, say hi."

"Hi Grandma Beth," Zach whispered shyly, as she reached out for him.

"Look at you, you've gotten so big," she said before lifting him up and planting wet kisses on the side of his face. "Oh you're not shy are you?" she asked when Zach tried to pull his face away from her.

"No don't worry about that, he's not really shy at all," Sherri assured her as Beth placed him back on the floor. "He just likes to pretend sometimes, right baby," she said before playfully poking Zach in the ribs. He giggled and squirmed before taking off into the living room.

"I really appreciate you doing this for me Beth," said Sherri.

"Oh of course; anytime I can help just let me know; even if it's just to give you a break for a day. How are Abby and Tyler?"

"Oh they're both doing great. Thanks."

"Hopefully I can see them real soon also."

"Yes I hope so too Beth."

"And how is Clay doing?" she asked hesitantly.

"Oh he's doing okay. You know Clay."

"Well if you remember give him my best," Beth asked.

Sherri saw the sadness etched on Beth's face at that point; even through the forced smile. Maybe Beth was thinking back to happier times. And comparing them to the way things were currently. There is not much about her that is as it used to be. In her younger days she was always the type to be the life of any party. Unabashedly flirtatious and outwardly sexual, she was known for sporting the miniest of miniskirts, and most everything she wore was so body-hugging that it may as well have been painted onto her well-proportioned 5 foot 8 inch body. She and Clay Sr. had met when she was hired as his assistant at the public relations firm at which he worked. And as things sometimes happen, their working relationship gradually morphed into a personal one as well. The other women at the firm hated her and the men naturally couldn't get enough of her. Yet it was Clay Sr. who in spite of being married for 21 years at the time, that not only bedded her but eventually made her his own. Beth can still recall when he first told her that he felt they were deeply connected; like soul mates.

But, at age 62 Beth was nothing like she used to be. The one-time center of attention and life of the party had become largely a loner. She was 36 when she had married Senior and she never had children of her own. That was by the wishes of Clay Sr. who was 44 at the time and had Colette, Clay and Kevin by his first wife Maureen. So Beth now lived by herself in the large home she and her late husband once shared. Her long blond hair was now gone; replaced by a short style in her natural brunette color, mixed with a good amount of gray. And though she still carried the same long, lean frame, she is most comfortable in loose-fitting loungewear or simple jogging suits.

"I sure will," Sherri said while knowing that she had no attention of doing so. She was well aware of Clay's reaction whenever Beth's name as much as came up in his presence. "Okay, well let me go. Thank you again Beth and I will see you later." They embraced once again as tears welled up in the corner of Beth's brown eyes. Sherri called out to Zach to come give her a hug before she departed.

"Don't you give Grandma Beth any trouble now okay; be a good boy."

"Okay Mommy I won't, bye."

"Bye sweetie I'll see you later."

Sherri spent a few minutes applying some makeup when she got back in the car. She started by applying a light layer of blue eye shadow, some mascara and eye liner. The only thing else she put on was a coat of pink passion lipstick, and after doing so and checking herself in the mirror she quickly entered Craig's address into her GPS and was on her way. The drive to Craig's place figured to take about 30 minutes barring any traffic issues. She slid Sade's greatest hits into the CD player to smooth her ride as well as relax her mind on the way. When her favorite tune on the disc came on she tapped her fingers on the steering wheel and started to sing along.

"There's a quiet storm
And it never felt like this before
There's a quiet storm
I think it's you
There's a quiet storm
And I never felt this hot before
Giving me something that's taboo

You give me the sweetest taboo
That's why I'm in love with you
You give me, you're giving me the sweetest taboo
Too good for me."

She dialed Craig's cell phone number as soon as she reached the exit for Boonton Township.

"Ready or not here I come," she said sweetly once he answered.

"Oh good because that's what I expect. That you will come and come again and again."

"Well you'd better be ready to put up Craig, because it's too late to back out now."

"Like I'd even consider it. You just get here as soon as you can with that sweet ass of yours."

"Well that's the main reason why I called; before we got sidetracked as usual. To tell you I'm coming off your exit; so I should be there shortly."

"Okay great, I'll be on the lookout for you."

"All right, I'll see you in a bit."

Sherri slowed to 15 mph hour as she turned onto Craig's block; looking intently at house numbers as she crept along. When she arrived at the address she parked her car in the driveway as he had instructed. She immediately started to survey the house and the area around it after she turned off the engine. The house was a modest, well maintained cape cod type with what looked to be fairly new aluminum siding covering the exterior. The lawn was well-manicured, although the grass was as brown as you'd expect for mid-December. Sherri covered her eyes with her Hugo Boss sunglasses before stepping out of the car. Walking quickly around the back of it she climbed the steps and gave the doorbell two short taps. Just as she turned to look behind her one last time the door was opened.

"Hey, come on in," an excited voice prodded her. Turning around, her eyes narrowed and wrinkles quickly formed in her forehead.

"Craig?" she said quizzedly. As her heart sank a bit, she wondered if he could read the disappointment etched on her face.

"Yes, I'm certainly Craig. That is if you're Sherri," he said with a wide smile that showed off some slightly discolored teeth. She slowly walked past him and stepped inside. "So we meet at last, you certainly are what I envisioned. In fact I'd have to say that picture you have on your profile doesn't do you justice."

Sherri forced an uncomfortable smile as Craig looked at her just like she was lunch. But then who could blame him. After all that was all they had discussed of late. "Well to be honest you are sort of different than what I had expected," she admitted. The person she was looking at was quite a bit older than the one in the picture he had emailed to her recently. And that well-defined body was nowhere to be found. 5'11" 175? Don't think so; maybe more like 5'9" and 240 plus soft, flabby pounds, she figured. He had salt and pepper hair and the Marlboro man mustache was now an unkempt full beard. A large beer belly shook underneath his shirt every time he moved. "I thought you said you were 36?"

"Oh that—well I'm sorry about that, but I just thought that if I told you my real age you might bypass me just based on that."

"So you thought it was better to lie about it. I mean really lie about it from the looks of it. What age are you really?"

"I'm 56 but…"

"Sherri ran her left hand over her face and turned away from him.

"I mean it doesn't really matter that much now does it. I mean you're here, and I'm still your Tongue Fu Panda and all that right?"

Well one thing for sure you're certainly more a panda than a tiger she thought to herself as she looked at his wide midsection. She pulled her Blackberry out of her pocket and scrolled through it for a few moments. "But Craig, I mean look at this picture; it doesn't look anything like you. And true the age is not a big issue; only that you lied about it. I thought only women did that supposedly."

Craig looked at the picture before pleading on his own behalf. "Is it the beard? Wait a second I can lose the beard; I'll go do it right now," he said before rushing out of the room. Sherri stood there dumbfounded; unable to believe it. She started pacing back and forth, intermittently staring at the ceiling or the badly-stained carpet. As well-maintained as the outside of the house was the inside was quite the opposite. The walls were a bit dirty and the house in general had a stale odor to it. Her first impulse was to just high tail it out of there. But something kept telling her to stick around. Maybe he would look less slovenly after coming out of the bathroom. She also thought of the many times that he had led to her pussy tingling with desire just by way of enticing her with his words. Yeah sure he lied to me and grossly misrepresented himself, but like he said he had a reason; he was concerned he might have been quickly dismissed if he had been forthcoming. Besides, it's not like I'm going to marry the guy or even have any sort of relationship with him. I just need him to get me off. We won't even be seen in public together anyway. No way, no how. Not even if he had wound up looking like George Clooney. She then started to think about some of the specific things he had said to her recently. How he would make her feel like she was levitating off the bed once he put his tongue inside of her. How they were sure to make a rhythm of their own once she started to do the "Macarena" while sitting on his face. As her mind wandered back to some of their chats, she felt herself getting horny all over again. She took a seat on his living room sofa, but found she couldn't sit there long. She walked in the direction he had travelled until she located the bathroom down the hall. She knocked lightly on the door. "Try not to be too long in there okay; I'm waiting on you. And is there another bathroom?"

"Yes, straight up the stairs and the first door on the right. And I'll be out shortly."

Sherri then walked slowly up the stairs and into the bathroom. She located the light switch and flipped it on. Looking around she noticed that the toilet could use a good cleaning; the sink also. There was no hand soap as well as no hand towels in sight. She didn't even want to think about what that implied. She felt happy that she had only come in there to check her makeup and hair in the mirror. Exiting the bathroom, she returned to the living room and took a seat. But only briefly as she soon walked over and placed her ear against the bathroom door. All she could hear was the sound of the shower running. She stepped away and went back to take a seat. Almost immediately she started fanning her legs open and close in rapid fashion. She placed her hands to her breasts and started to caress them. Moments later the bathroom door opened and out stepped Craig walking swiftly in her direction. He wore a heavy, cotton robe and was still dripping slightly. He was running a towel across his thin hair.

"So, how's that; better?" he questioned. Sherri looked at him intently. His facial hair was once again limited to a mustache, which though not professionally trimmed, now looked at least presentable. I even threw in a shower although I took one before going to bed last night."

"Yes that is much better actually. You look sort of like new money. Now I at least recognize you as the guy in the picture you sent me; just an older version. But that's okay, I'm over that. I was just a little put off by the fact that you weren't upfront about it, but as you said you had your reasons."

"Well I'm glad that..," Craig started to reply back before Sherri cut him off.

"Shhhh, no offense, but I didn't really come here to talk. We've done enough of that over the last couple of months don't you think? It's time to put some of that talk into action now."

She went back to fondling her own breasts and began to gyrate suggestively on the sofa. Lifting herself up slightly, she started to undo her pants. Craig just sat there, his eyes fixated on her. Slowly she slid out of her pants until they were on the floor. She rubbed the moist crotch of her panties before placing her right hand inside of them. Her other hand motioned Craig over to her. As she worked a couple of fingers inside of her pussy he fell to his knees before her. Removing her fingers, she placed them against his lips. He closed his eyes and took in her scent, before hungrily sucking her fingers into his mouth. Sherri then removed her bra exposing her supple breasts to him and he wasted no time going right at them. Cupping his hands around them he flicked her nipples with his tongue. It was her first chance to see his tongue in action and as she closed her eyes and relished the feeling, she was also anticipating what else he would do with it. His lips latched onto her hard nipples like a newborn baby, eliciting low moans from Sherri. He moved his lips to hers for a kiss which she accepted but only on tightly closed lips. Luckily he was not pushy and instead returned his focus to her warm flesh mounds. His circled his tongue around each of her areolas before again teasing the nipples. She felt her pussy lips clapping like a flamenco dancer. "Come on eat my pussy," she pleaded.

She didn't need to ask twice. He climbed off of her long enough for her to quickly remove her panties. Falling to his knees, Craig dove right in. He slowly licked the wet lips, soaking up some of the wetness with his tongue. "You want to go upstairs?" he asked. "No, no right here is just fine," she replied right away. He probed inside briefly before moving up to her clit. He worked it expertly, alternating between running his tongue across it slowly and sucking it between his lips. Her eyes were closed yet her hands easily found the back of his head, and pulled him in closer. He was right. She did feel like she was starting to levitate. Her orgasm rocked her entire body. As she bucked her hips wildly he continued to feast on her undeterred. The sweet sound of her moans as she came turned him on more it seemed. Rolling her over, he placed her lithesome body above him as he fell back against the sofa. Sherri then rocked her hips up and down in a slow, rhythmic dance on his face. His tongue was like an artist's brush creating a masterpiece on canvas. He directed her movements with both his hands tightly gripping her ass. He was insatiable all right, seemingly never needing air. "Oh Yeah, oh yeah I'm gonna come again," she whispered through deep, intense breaths. Sherri fell onto her back on the floor, temporarily spent. As Craig sat there licking his lips, she looked at him intently. The surest sign of her satisfaction was covering his wet face. With heaving breasts she looked at the expression of glee on his glistening face and pondered what was to happen next.

Undressing him with her lust filled eyes; she knew just what else she needed to make this a perfect event. She crawled over to him slowly, never once moving her eyes away. "Have you anything in here for me?" she asked seductively as she untied his robe. MMMMMM, yes you do," she cooed as she opened it wide and got her first look at his full frontal nudity albeit in a flaccid state. At that point Sherri was so horny that it didn't matter to her that she wasn't particularly attracted to Craig. He had a penis and that's what she wanted. And right then she intended to get what she wanted. "I have a condom in my purse, so you don't have to worry about going to get one, but first things first. Let me go to work on your little friend." Never hesitating for a moment, she began to stroke him up and down in order to get him up and ready. "Let me get it nice and hard," she whispered. He seemed far slower to respond to her touch than she expected. "Oh, what's the matter he doesn't like me?" She gently cupped and massaged his balls with one hand while working his penis with the other in an attempt to speed up the process. She also decided on a bit of verbal enticement. "OOOH I want you inside me so bad." In spite of her efforts his penis maintained nothing more than a semi-erect state. "Are you okay," she inquired, drawing no response. "Well let me try a little magic trick."

Positioning herself lower she parted her soft lips and took him into her mouth. She held it there briefly before starting to slide her lips up and down his length. Looking him directly in the eyes she held it in one hand and slowly circled the tip with her tongue, before licking up and down the still soft member. Sherri tried her best to mask her concern as she fondled his balls and kissed them gently. "You like that?" she asked in her best bedroom voice," His reply was strongly affirmative, yet each time she released her grip on his penis it laid down meekly, falling against his round stomach like a strand of cooked pasta. By the time five minutes had passed with no signs of life, Sherri found herself at wit's end. Exasperated, she sat up looking into his face. "I give up. I mean I don't know what else I can do. You said there's nothing wrong with you; I mean physically? Have you had this problem before?"

She felt for Craig as he shamefully hung his head without responding. "Hey it's okay, don't worry about it. It happens," she said as she placed a sympathetic hand on his knee. "Maybe it's just stress or something, but don't get too down on yourself okay. We can try it another time. And believe me what you did for me was out of this world."

He was unable to look her in the eyes as he spoke. "I don't know what happened. I'm sorry. This doesn't usually happen to me, "he lied. The truth is he had been dealing with off and on impotence for several years. And pride and male ego had kept him from even seeing a specialist about it.

"Well again, like I said I'm still very satisfied, "Sherri said in an attempt to soothe him. She rubbed her right hand up and down his leg before rising to her feet. "Well I guess I'll get ready to go." She looked at her watch and noticing that it was only 11:45 decided that she would run home to shower and change and maybe even relax for a little while before going to pick up Zach. After quickly getting dressed she headed out to her car with Craig still seated pensively on the sofa, his robe still wide open.

"I'll be in touch," she said simply before departing.

CHAPTER SIX

As she slowly pulled out of the driveway Sherri began to look back on what had just taken place inside. For the first time in about 16 years, she had been intimate with another man besides her husband. And yet she had no real feelings of shame; nor sense of remorse. She wondered if that was strange, or what that may say about her. But she quickly brushed those feelings aside, thinking what led her to Craig was more about her husband than anything to do with her, she reasoned. After all, hadn't she sent him all kind of signals? Did she need to spell it out any more clearly that she felt neglected? And that her physical needs weren't being met. Not to mention the emotional ones. But what led her to seeing Craig was all about the physical.

Oh yes Craig. What to do about him? Sure, she had told him inside that they could try again sometime. And she assured him before leaving that she would be in touch. But she knew that she had lied when she did. Only a fraction of her needs were being met at home; so why would she place so much on the line for another situation in which only a fraction of her needs were going to be met. Sure he was every bit as good with his tongue as he bragged about, and had taken her to two explosive orgasms. Something Clay never was willing or able to make happen anymore; but what about the rest? She'd also been longing for the feel of her lips pleasuring a rock-hard penis. Which as strange as it may seem, Clay never much wanted her to do anymore either. And God forbid he go down on her; foreplay of that type apparently was too much effort and too time-consuming on the increasingly rare occasions that he made love to her at all. And it seemed her body was forever longing for a good, long, bout of lovemaking. So as she headed home, her feelings about what she had just experienced were where exactly is the beef?

With the way that she was just able to go on with her day as if nothing of note had happened, you would think that Sherri had a lot of experience with sex outside of her marriage. Clay was none the wiser, and in fact that evening she was actually able to seduce some yet again unsatisfying sex out of him as well. As it turned out it was nothing more than a far too familiar reminder of just why she had taken the daring leap into the arms of another man. But she figured she was lucky to get even that. Maybe he was feeling in the holiday spirit or something she guessed. And she was certainly feeling the void for what she had missed out on that morning. The only problem is that in the aftermath, that feeling and want still remained once Clay left her unfulfilled as well.

Around midnight and still feelling restless, Sherri found herself lying in bed awash in her thoughts. Craig—Clay—Clay—Craig and what to do next; fold and throw in her hand and settle, or make another play. Unable to sleep, she climbed out of bed and headed to the computer. As tempted as she was to log onto asudesire she opted for Facebook instead. Maybe she would spend some time playing one of the games like farmville or mafia wars she figured. But she was pleasantly surprised when she noticed a friend she hadn't talk to much lately logged on, so she decided to see if he had some time to chat for a bit instead.

"Hey you, where have you been? I haven't heard from you in a while," she typed to Miguel.

"Well hello yourself. Yes it has been awhile. What's new with you? I've been very busy myself."

Sherri noticed that he had finally gotten around to adding a picture to his profile.

"Oh a little bit of this and a little bit of that," she began. "But before we get into any of that, I see that you now have a picture up. Nice," she said as she clicked on it to enlarge it. "Real nice," she added as she looked at Miguel's full length picture staring back at her. He looked to be well over 6 feet tall and was well put-together. His honey-colored complexion was smooth and his handsome face adorned with a well-trimmed beard. His light-brown eyes were strikingly attractive as she looked at them.

They were topped by a pair of thick eyebrows. His hair was a tightly-wound dark brown mop.

"Wow, you're very handsome. You've should have had a picture up a long time ago. And how tall are you?"

"Thank you, you're too kind. And I'm 6'6"."

"OMG, you dwarf me."

"How tall are you? Or should I say how short?"

"Okay funny man; well I'm not that short. I'm 5'3" but I mean compared to you that's like 4 feet nothing."

"Yeah you're not that short and besides they say good things come in small packages right?"

"That's right and it is so true. Okay let me stop, but back to you; again wow, and you've got some sort of exotic thing going on with the hair and the eyes and all that."

Miguel chuckled before starting his reply.

"Yeah I guess that's a good way to describe me. An exotic blend, sort of like a tropical punch or something I guess."

"Do you mind if I ask you what nationality you are? I mean I don't want to offend you or anything."

"No don't worry, it doesn't offend me. I get asked that quite a bit, well not as much now that I've cut my hair. I have a lot less than when that picture was taken a couple of years ago. But I'm Afro-Brazilian on my Mom's side and my Dad is Thai, French and Puerto Rican. So yes there's a lot going on there."

"Yes there sure is Miguel."

"So really I'm Black, Asian, French, Spanish and Taino Indian."

"Oh God, that's something else. Well it looks like a recipe with a lot of ingredients that turned out just great to me."

"Yep I'm all those things so let's just say I'm the quintessential mutt. No wonder I like doggie style so much."

"Huh, what's gotten into you?"

"Ooops that slipped out, sorry about that."

"Oh please no need to apologize; you don't know me very well I can tell. And besides I love it doggie style myself lol."

"Oh really, so you do, do you?"

"I most certainly do; that and riding it cowgirl style are my preferences if I have a choice."

"Yee haw, giddy up."

"Oh you know it; just call me the rodeo queen. But of course I'll take getting laid any way I can get it these days."

Miguel could feel a little something stirring inside his pants as he responded. "Well this conversation has certainly taken a turn."

"Oh sorry about that I guess I got carried away for a moment there. Whew, I'm alright now."

"Hey it's cool, don't worry about it. I was just saying. Besides, I was the one that started it with the doggie style comment out of left field."

"All right well back to other things. So what is it that's been keeping you so busy? Fun things I hope."

"Nope, it's work. Well actually work is fun for me sometimes. I do enjoy what I do so I can't say that it's like real work. Like a construction worker or a longshoreman or welder or someone like that does."

"Okay, so what line of work are you in exactly if you don't mind me asking?"

"I'm a basketball coach. And right now I'm an assistant at Qunnipiac University up here in Connecticut. So there you have the reason why I'm here.

"Sounds like an interesting job, and at your height I would think you might know a thing or two about basketball."

"Yeah I know a little bit about it," he joked. "And yes it's a nice job. It has its perks but there's also a down side too I guess."

"Really; what's that?

"Well the main thing is that it's leads to a very transient lifestyle. It's kind of hard to put down roots someplace. I've been doing it for seven years now and in that time I've been in 4 different locations, with the longest in any one place being three years. This is my first year at this school. So that part is kind of tough, but it's okay. Like I said I enjoy doing what I do. But there's long hours involved in season and that's where we're at right now. So that's what I mean by having been so busy. During the season it's pretty much 10 to around midnight on game days and that's not to mention all the road trips."

"It seems   like that would make things hard on your personal life if I'm not getting too personal myself.   I mean unless you have a real understanding girlfriend."

"Well I don't have one right now, but if I did yeah she would have to be very understanding. Not to mention very trusting."

"No doubt about that because I'm sure you must have girls falling at your feet, because I can't imagine all of that going to waste," Sherri devilishly replied."

"Oh please, all of what?"

"Oh come on Miguel you know; that gorgeous face. And that body; oh good lord; I'm just imagining what lies beneath?   All those clothes I mean."

Sherri then went back to studying Miguel's photo. He was standing on a beach somewhere with the ocean as a backdrop. His broad shoulders stood out in the black tank top he had on. His well-defined calves were just as obvious in the multi-colored swim trunks he wore. A single, thick gold necklace adorned his neck.

"See—there you go again."

"I'm sorry I know. I can't help it; you might need to take that picture down. Where was that taken by the way?"

"That was actually taken in Brazil; Rio to be exact. I had always wanted to go there and finally made it back in 2009. What a great trip."

"Cool, and what a great shot. That picture does a little something to me. I need to stop looking at it."

"No I think you'll be okay," Miguel replied before deftly changing the subject. So anyway tell me what if anything has been going on with the site?

"Well funny you should ask. Let me see; where exactly should I begin. First of all I can tell you that things went a lot further than I ever imagined it would or even could."

"Uh Oh; how far?"

"Okay, well first of all you have to promise not to judge me for what I'm about to tell you okay?"

"Of course; besides who am I to judge you?"

"All right good; anyway, as I told you way back when, I only intended to check things out to see what the sites were like. You know to satisfy my natural curiosity. But the thing is, that turned into a lot of conversation. I mean a lot; and really enjoyable conversation. It was spicy, fun, exciting—all that. So I started to really enjoy the attention because that's not something I've been getting a whole lot of at home you know."

"Yeah I kind of get that feeling."

"Oh yeah it's been pretty bad to the point where I feel like I might as well just be like another piece of furniture at the house. So when this guy came along and started to feed me all these compliments and tell me how desirable I was and all, I guess I just got caught up in it. I mean I was loving it; I was feeling like I did years ago when I was still single and on the market. I started to look forward to chatting with this guy like you wouldn't believe. And he wasn't shy about telling me about any of the things he would love to do to me. So here I was the sexually frustrated wife, and I just ate that up."

"And so it went I guess," Miguel interjected.

"Yep, and so it went; for just about every day or night or both for weeks. Until it got to the point where I just was thinking about all of the naughty little things he said he wanted to do so much, that hell I decided one day that I was going to take the opportunity to just go for it."

"And I'm guessing you did."

"Yeah I sure did Miguel. I went after it."

"When did it get to that point and has it happened just once?"

"Okay get this, how about just this morning, so it's only been that one time."

"Wow, check you out. Any regrets?"

"Hmm, let me see; well just one I'd say. That it was only half of what I wanted. But what I got was great. It just wasn't enough."

"So there are no regrets about having done the dirty deed?"

"No I can't really say that there are. I mean we'll see if I wake up crying in the middle of the night out of guilt sometime soon, but right now the only regret that I'm feeling is that I didn't get a good, hardcore fucking out of it. Ooops did I just say that?"

"Um, yes you did Sherri. It was you."

"Yep it sure was me; oh what the hell. I guess I found out something about myself today. So anyway, back to you mister long and tall. Oh let me stop, before you start to think I'm some kind of disgusting slut who can't control herself."

"Like I said I won't judge you. Not at all, but having said that let's not go there right now. No offense.

"Not to worry, no offense taken."

"Okay then, well let me reverse field again and run away from that one. So now that's what is done is done; what's next? I mean since it's almost like you got your virginity taken away for a second time so to speak."

"Honestly I don't know for sure. But I can tell you this though, the situation that existed here at home which may have led to what happened; well it's still the same, so I wouldn't say that I'm not willing to do it again; just with somebody else if I do."

"With somebody else? You mean there might be some other guy or guys in the mix? "

"Well there isn't right now, but I could cast my bait out there and try to catch another one. I mean I've gotten a taste of it now."

"So this guy, from this morning he's done, kaput, outta here?"

"Probably so, I mean hey…Well let me be blunt about it Miguel, the guy couldn't get it up. He went down on me like a pro, but beyond that I'm afraid he wasn't up to the task so I can't be bothered. I'm sure there must be a lot of guys out there who can give me the best of both worlds so to speak."

"So now, if you do decide to move on to another guy you have to take the time to get to know him and move things to the point where you're comfortable enough to sleep with him."

"Well not necessarily. I mean don't get me wrong I'm not saying that I would just talk with somebody one time and bam that's it, come and get it if you want it; but I just don't think that I need to invest a whole lot of time like I did with this guy. Not for what it is I'd be looking for."

"Just a good time right?"

"Yep, you've got it, some hot, steamy, maybe even sweaty, wall-pounding sex. Just the way I'm feeling these days."

"Hey like I said I'm not going to judge you. I've been there done that. Just be careful that's all."

"But of course."

"I guess I should blame myself for ever mentioning something about those types of sites. See what we have now, another corrupted wife just like I said. Oh well."

"Hey don't blame yourself. Like the saying goes you can lead a horse to water…"

"Yeah I know. I guess I don't really blame myself."

"That's good; besides, the way things were going I might have very well eventually done something anyway. I mean how long was I going to be able to put up with being pretty much ignored. I might have wound up jumping the mailman. Well the mailman is actually the mailwoman so maybe the UPS man. He is pretty hot in those shorts he wears all the time. Hell I might still offer him to come inside for some refreshment one day, lol."

"Oh Lord, would you look at this I've created a monster. Anyway let me go so I can get some sleep."

"Okay take care and no you haven't created a monster Miguel. Maybe the sex beast inside of me has been awakened but there's nothing that you had to do with that. It was just time to end that long deep slumber. Anyway I will talk to you again whenever I guess."

"All right Sherri. You take care of yourself and Happy Holidays and New Year and all that good stuff."

"Oh yeah, I almost forgot; same to you Miguel. Merry Christmas and Happy New Year."

"Bye."

"Bye-bye. And thanks for understanding and not judging me"

"No problem."

After a restless night of sleep Sherri anxiously logged into her asudesire account first thing the next morning. It was shortly after 8 a.m. and the kids were still asleep in their rooms. As for Clay; well he was doing his own thing as usual, oblivious to her even being around not to mention what she was up to. She just wanted to see if there was anyone else out there who could pique her interest as Craig had. Yet who could also give her the type of complete sexual experience she was craving. She was pleased when she saw that quite a few men had shown interest in her since the time that she had made the decision to focus all of her energy on the willing, but sadly lacking Craig. She was now feeling that if she was going to continue down this path that she may as well explore more varied options. That is to not limit herself to the first halfway decent looking man who raised his hand. This time she wanted it all and would settle for nothing less.

As Sherri perused the messages she had received, and the profiles of the men who'd sent them, she was struck by one in particular. It belonged to a tall, dark-haired man with the username of Hard2please. Besides liking what she saw, Sherri also appreciated the fact that he didn't just send her a wave but instead took the time to send her a personal message. Or maybe it was just the fact that he used the word hard in his name. Whatever it was she made an impromptu decision to send a message back to him reciprocating the interest. She also took note of the fact that he showed up as currently being logged in as well. Hopefully that would lead to a quick reply on his part she thought.

But rather than spend time sitting there waiting to find out, Sherri continued to explore. As 9:00 approached, she then decided that it was time to log off. She had been at it for about 45 minutes and wanted to check and see if the kids were awake and ready for breakfast. Just as she was about to sign out she noticed the little pop-up on the screen. She had received a new message. Shifting in the chair she clicked on her message link and immediately smiled as it opened because it indeed said that the message was from the member Hard2please. She quickly opened up the message and began to read.

"Hello again Stormy; it's very nice to have received a reply back from you. I was starting to think that wasn't going to happen; in spite of how much I've been hoping that it would.

You're certainly a beautiful and sexy lady and I'm still very interested in getting acquainted with you. And now at least I can think the possibility exists that you might feel the same way. So what do you say we see about that? Let's talk soon and find out shall we. I guess this initially plays out sort of like a tennis match so I return serve and place the ball back in your court. But let's not volley back in forth too long before we know if there are any points to be scored. Take care and again; why don't we talk and start to get to know each other soon."

Being in the frame of mind of not wanting to waste time at this point, Sherri decided right then and there to make a proactive move. She quickly initiated a chat session between the two of them and sent out a brief message.

"Hey you, guess who?"

"Well hello there Stormy."

"Oh good guess, you're pretty good."

"Well the fact that your username is showing in the chat window didn't make it very difficult."

"No I guess not. Anyway, let's get the formalities out of the way. How are you?"

"I'm doing well. Very glad to have heard from you I might add."

"Oh really; that's nice. I was very anxious to touch base with you also."

"You don't say."

"Actually I very much do say hard2please."

"Okay then, cool. So what's up?"

"I don't know. I'm hoping you can tell me since you have the word hard in your screen name."

"Well nothing like that at the moment. I hope that doesn't disappoint you."

"No it doesn't since I'm not there with you."

"I gotcha and I must say you don't seem the shy type to me that's for sure."

"Should I be?"

"No not at all. I want you to be yourself and I feel good that you're comfortable enough to do so."

"Oh I've got to be myself. But let me pull back a little bit before you start to think I'm just some easy little piece; even if I am."

"LOL, you are quite funny you know that?"

"Thank you. I think I was joking. I'm not sure. I mean I don't know, I mean that depends."

"Depends on?"

"Well you know; if I meet somebody who does it for me right away who knows? I mean I'm certainly not on this site looking for a romance or somebody to wine and dine me."

"So in other words you're not interested in much more beyond physical gratification?"

"Yes I'd say that's an accurate statement. Let me put it this way, a little wham bam thank you maam would be fine with me right now."

"That's interesting."

"Does that shock you? Or I guess to put it another way does that bother you?

"Oh hell no; not at all. I think a lot of men could get into that kind of thinking on the part of a woman."

"Okay good; it seems like we're on the same page there so that's a good starting point. So where do you live?"

"In Watchung off of Route 22."

"Okay that's not too far; I live in Basking Ridge.

"All right cool. The fact that your profile said you lived in Central Jersey did have something to do with me choosing to reach out to you also. So tell me something. I guess I'm reading between the lines here based on your ad and now this conversation; but I'm thinking you might be married right?"

"Well you're certainly perceptive enough. Yes I do have a husband. What I don't have is someone to handle me sexually the way I want and need it. Oh by the way, you'll have to tell me if I'm a bit too blunt."

"Nope; like I said I'm sure to a lot of men you'd be like a breath of fresh air. Well let me not speak for anyone besides myself, but you sure are for this one."

"Great. So does that sound like something you might be interested in?"

"Ummm, let's see--- I definitely like what I've heard, so unless I really don't like what I see then hell yes; of course."

"Oh I don't think you'll be disappointed at all with what you see."

"Well you may just be right. Probably are. I'd like to find out though; hopefully soon enough."

"Now that won't be a problem at all. In fact I have to go now, but what I can do is this; I have a set of private pictures attached to my profile and I can give you access to those. Sound good?"

"Yep that sounds like a plan to me."

"All right well I'll do that right now. You can check for them in a few minutes okay?"

"Good deal; I'll take a look shortly."

"Okay then and oh yeah by the way; my name is Sherri in real life."

"And I'm Scott, nice to meet you sort of Sherri."

"Well same here Scott. I hope we'll be in touch again soon."

"I feel the same way Sherri."

All right well how about tomorrow some time?"

"That works just fine for me," Scott agreed.

"Great. So why don't I give you my email and then you can get me anytime because I usually have my Blackberry somewhere close by."

"Oh so you have that crackberry addiction also huh, I never go too long without checking in on mine."

"Well moreso when I might be anxiously awaiting a message from someone. Like I will from you," a broadly smiling Sherri typed, along with her email address.

"Why you flatter me. And that will get you anywhere and everywhere."

"Ha, ha, well I was hoping that might be the case. Anyway, let me run. I Hope we can do this again soon."

"Oh yeah, count on it. I've got your email, so for sure. Take care Sherri."

"You too Scott; bye-bye."

Sherri smiled as she rose from the chair and headed into the kids rooms to check in on them. They were all awake and at the moment perfectly content with watching television. That is except Zach who was amusing himself by tussling with the blanket on his bed.

"Yes," he answered quickly when Sherri asked him if he were ready for breakfast.

"Well how about a bowl of cereal and some fruit cocktail?"

"Okay Mommy."

"Well let's go sport," she said lightly as she lifted him off the bed and led him into the kitchen. Tyler and Abby entered a short time later and after greeting their mom, each prepared themselves a bowl of corn flakes with sliced bananas. Next in was Clay who after greeting everyone split a bagel down the middle before dropping it into the toaster.

"I think I want a second cup of coffee this morning, you care for one?" he asked Sherri.

She was somewhat surprised by the question. It wasn't like Clay to make such a gesture; though she did appreciate the offer.

"No thanks. I think I'm just gonna have a bit of orange-grapefruit juice this morning," she answered before turning her attention back to Zach.   Moments later she posed a question to Clay as he stood waiting on the toaster to complete its cycle.

"I was just wondering; if you don't have a whole lot going on this afternoon can we go in search of a Christmas tree today. Maybe take a ride up to Hackettstown."

There was no such thing as an artificial tree in the King household as they've long held onto the belief that for Christmas the tree should be real and natural. With sharp needles that shed themselves all over the floor, Christmas tree smell and all.

"Yeah sure we can do that; it shouldn't take all that long."

"All right, but don't forget tonight is also the Britton's party.

"Oh shit I,"

"Clay!!"

"Ooops I'm sorry kids. I mean oh shoot, I did forget about that. What time does it start?

"Well they've asked that everyone try to arrive by 6:30 so that they can serve dinner by 7:00," Sherri replied. "Is that going to be a problem?"

"Ah, I don't know," Clay hesitated before continuing. "You know what, never mind that's fine, I'll work it out."

"You sure, because if not I'm sure they'd understand."

"No really, let's go. I know how much of a great time the kids always have, right kids?"

"Right Dad," Abby answered for all of them.

"Great, well it's all settled then," Sherri said happily.

"Yep okay then.......well I guess I'd better go get some things done now then with the agenda all set for the rest of the day," said Clay. About what time do you think we should head out for tree shopping," he questioned Sherri.

Turning to look at the wall clock, she answered with her back to him. "Hmmm I guess about 1:30-2:00 will be fine."

"Okay well let me hurry and put in a few hours of work then," he responded as he spread some cream cheese on his bagel.

"Alright we'll see you later," Sherri said before he rushed off.

"Bye kids."

"Bye Dad," Tyler and Abby responded respectively as they went about their business of eating. Clay brushed one of his hands, through Zach's hair before picking up his cup and continuing on with the coffee in one hand and the bagel firmly held in the other.

"Take care, champ."

"Bye Daddy."

A few hours later as she was just getting prepared to slip on something to wear after getting the kids dressed to go out into the cold, afternoon air, Sherri's decided to check her Blackberry and saw that she had received an email from Scott.

"Hi Sherri, just a quick note to let you know that I checked out the pictures and all I can say is WOW! You weren't kidding when you said I wouldn't be at all disappointed. You've really got me excited and anxious about the possibility of hooking up with you now. Anyway, thanks for showing them to me and I really hope to communicate with you again soon."

Sherri smiled widely as she read the message and after doing so immediately started to compose a reply.

"Hey you; so I take it you liked the photos huh? But anyway, how about this; I was wondering if you would shoot me back an email with your number. I'll be out and about in a bit and also tonight and would like to try to squeeze in a call to you if I could. What do you say?"

The selection of a Christmas tree was a quick and easy task and by 3:00 the 7 foot pine was standing in the tree stand needing only to be decorated. That would have to wait until the next day however because there was not enough time for that right then. Not to mention that the kids were now tired and in need of dhort naps before preparing for the party. With the little window of opportunity Clay decided to do a bit a bit more work before they headed out to the party.

With everyone accounted for, Sherri then went about the task of selecting her attire for the evening. She chose a simple black sheath that she would accentuate with a strand of white pearls, a pair of black tights and 3 inch black pumps. With that out of the way she decided to relax on the bed herself for a while. After watching a semi-interesting movie for a while she too dozed off. Upon awakening she immediately glanced over at the clock on the night stand. Four-thirty; time to get up and get going.

CHAPTER SEVEN

The annual pre-holiday party given by the King's neighbors the Britton's placed Clay was right in his element. All evening long he was showered with praise and congratulations on being nominated as the next county prosecutor. And Sherri expertly played the role of the perfect trophy wife; smiling broadly whenever someone mentioned how proud she must be of her husband. She even made it a point of agreeing that it was indeed quite a man she has for a husband on more than one occasion. All while chuckling on the inside. Really it's like I have half a man, she was thinking. Sure he's outstanding on certain levels, but nothing but cold, unfeeling and seemingly uncaring on another more intimate level. And to her, that is what left her with the mindset that she had right then and there. She took a look at her watch which read nine-twenty. She then excused herself in order to escape the drab conversation she was having with another of their neighbors and quickly walked in the direction of Clay. She again excused herself so that she could get past the 3 people that he was engaged in a conversation with so she could have a brief word with him.

"Sweetie, I'm going to step outside for a while for some air. I won't be long. The kids are all downstairs playing with the other children so they're fine, but just keep an ear out okay?"

Half listening, Clay nodded slightly before resuming his conversation. He never even noticed the dismissive look Sherri gave him before turning to walk away.

"I'll be back shortly," she announced to the woman she had been talking to. I just wanna get some fresh air for a few minutes."

"You know, that's sounds like a good idea; I could use some air myself. Would you mind some company," the woman inquired.

"Um well, no, no I don't mind," Sherri hesitated.

"Okay, well let me just go find my husband and tell him where I'll be," the gregarious and somewhat overbearing, middle-aged woman, replied.

"All right," Sherri responded before the woman rushed off.

Acting quickly, she retrieved her overcoat from the foyer closet before quietly stepping out the door. She crossed the street and walked several houses down the block before coming to a halt about 120 feet away. She then pulled her Blackberry from her pocket and plugged the earpiece into it before inserting the other end into her ear. While dialing a number, she occasionally looked back in the direction of the house. The phone rang several times before there was an answer.

"Hello.

"Hello Scott," Sherri said in a deliberately sexy voice.

"Hey sweet lady, how are you?"

"I'm doing great; did I disturb you?"

"Disturb me? I kept looking at the phone hoping it would ring. And hoping it would be you calling it."

"Yeah, sure you were."

"Really I was. Well okay I admit I wasn't exactly standing over the phone trying to coax it into ringing, but I was hoping you'd call. And here you are."

"Yep, here I am. So how are you this evening mister?"

"Oh I'm doing very well gorgeous lady; and what are you doing this evening?"

"I'm just at a party. It's right in the neighborhood. Within walking distance of home. And I decided to escape for a bit to give you a call. Wasn't that nice and thoughtful of me?"

"It most certainly was. But you're like that."

"Oh really; and how can you be so sure of that?"

"Let's just say I have a gut feeling about it. But anyway since you were so kind as to take the risk in breaking away to call me, I guess I should make the most of this time. That is assuming that your husband may also be at this party."

"Yes he is; it's a family type thing. But no big deal there; I would say he's oblivious as is often the case. Probably hardly even took note of me telling him I was stepping outside for some air."

"Okay, well in that case let me be undivided in my attention to you while I have you."

"Please do. I'm all ears. Well that and some other things," Sherri said in her most coquettish tone."

"Oh yes, since I saw the pictures I have no doubt about that."

"So does that mean you like what you saw?"

"Oh I love what I saw." Wonder if I might be able to see more."

"Oh that might be a possibility. Just how much do you want to see though?"

"As much as you want to show me baby."

"Hmmmmm," Sherri purred. "So I guess the ball is in my court then."

"Yes indeed and speaking of balls; maybe I can show you mine soon."

"Oh you are so bad Scott."

"Does that bother you?"

"Well…. no. It doesn't; I kind of like it actually. Honestly it's sort of refreshing with the lame ass stick in the mud I'm married to."

"All right well in that case you can expect more, Scott said after he chuckled at her remark about her husband."

"Okay, as long as you remember that I can give as good I get."

"Of course not, I'm guessing you're the type of lady who lives by the adage that it's better to give than receive."

"Yes I do love to give, but damn if receiving isn't great also."

"Oh yeah the best of both worlds Scott agreed."

"Exactly," Sherri whispered as she audibly smacked her lips together. "So Scott," she continued after a brief pause.

"Yes Sherri."

"It seems that you like me and found me pleasing to the eye and all that."

"Yes."

"And I certainly find you attractive and interesting and funny."

"Why thank you."

"So.........having said that I guess the question is what are we going to do about that?"

"Well I have a suggestion."

"Oh I'm sure you do," Sherri replied, drawing laughs from Scott.

"And you know what? The thing is I would say we're both pretty much on the same page, she added."

"Uh huh, we're both on page 69."

"You're silly do you know that?"

"Thank you I work hard at it. I take being silly very seriously."

"Oh stop it, listen to me for a second."

"Okay Sherri I'm sorry. I'm listening go right ahead."

"Good. Anyway, since we both know what we have here, let me ask you this. What is your availability like for a boring old stay at home mom?"

"Boring? Somehow I doubt that. And definitely not old either."

"Well thanks but how about more bored than boring; is that more like it?"

"Better, even though I hate to hear that. But then I guess that's where I come in."

"Yes, that's right where you come in. Well unless I ask you to come in something else," Sherri said with a mischievous laugh.

"Oh wait a minute, was that a little sexual innuendo?"

"Hey I told you I have my moments too."

"Well go ahead, have your say."

"Well I'll just have to let it come out in little spurts. Don't want to shock you too much."

"Okay if you say so."

"Anyway, back to where I was going. With my situation my play time would pretty much be limited to during the day, so I'm just wondering how that would work for you Scott?"

"Well as far as my schedule is concerned pretty much anything goes. I'm self employed so basically I can usually come and go as I please. And I have my own place so there's no issue there. I mean I do have my kids every other weekend but I assume we're talking about during the week anyway."

"Oh yeah without a doubt."

"Well I'm free and clear; single and ready, willing and able to mingle. Night or day I'm ready to play."

"That's good to know. And not to change subjects but what line of work are you in?"

"I run my own insurance agency. Auto, homeowners, and life; we handle it all; hey maybe I can give you a sales pitch."

"Well Scott I think I've already got your pitch and I'm ready to hit it, circle the bases and slide into home."

"Wow, a sports analogy too; that's impressive. I must say there seems to be a lot about you to like but I'm just going to stay focused on the prize. The pot of gold buried down there between your legs."

"Okay you do that Scott; you crazy man. Anyway, it's pretty cold out here so I should get back inside. Why don't we talk again soon and then try to arrange a little something. Sound like a plan?"

"Sounds like a great plan. And I have your number now so I'll give you a call or you can give me a call or whatever."

"Okay let's talk early next week."

"That works for me."

"All right well I will talk to you soon Scott."

"Okay Sherri, take care and enjoy the party."

"Yeah let me go show my face to my husband. I'm sure he's in there really feeling my absence and wondering where I am."

"He should be."

"Trust me on this. He's not."

"Poor sap. Anyway you go ahead and I will talk to you."

"Okay good night Scott."

"Bye sexy Sherri."

"Bye."

As Sherri walked back down the block and began to cross the street she could make out a figure sitting on the porch as she approached the house. No it can't be. He wouldn't be out here looking for me. He was in his own little world in there; just soaking up all the adulation. As she drew closer a voice called out to her.

"Oh there you are, I was looking for you."

A sigh of relief; It was just Cindi Belson, the free-talking neighbor. On second thought maybe it wasn't such a relief.

"I'm sorry, while I was out I just decided to walk on down to our house and take a peek. I know that not much takes place around here but you can never be too sure."

"Oh I do understand that. So I guess you're headed back inside now then?"

"Yes, I started to get a little chilly so I am going to head back in."

"Okay that's fine; we can chat just the same in there right?"

"Ummm sure, yes we most certainly can," Sherri agreed reluctantly. "But first let me take a trip to the bathroom."

"Okay, go ahead," Cindi said almost as if she was granting permission.

Sherri rolled her eyes as she moved away from her; at one point sneaking a look back over her shoulder to see if Cindi was following behind her. On the way, she passed within a few feet of Clay who was still giving the appearance of holding a press conference. She merely shook her head and kept moving.

By shortly after midnight the King family was about ready to depart the party although it was still going strong. The kids were still having a blast and Clay was perfectly content yet Sherri was all of bored, feeling a bit tipsy and a lot horny. Oh well nothing good will come from that she figured. Clay, who seemed sort of anxious to hang around longer since he was so much the center of attention, was finally persuaded otherwise. He even went as far as offering to just walk Sherri and the kid's home before returning to the party. But Sherri finally convinced him that wasn't a good idea. Unfortunately she was not able to similarly convince him that about an hour after all the children were asleep was the perfect time and opportunity for a little fun in the sack. Instead he actually accused her of pushing for them to come home from the party strictly due to an ulterior motive. That being her desire to get laid. "Okay now I see. How selfish of you to seek to deprive not only me but also the kids of a bit more enjoyment due to your own lust and greed," he assailed her. Heaven forbid she wanted to have sex on more than the occasion of a full moon. "My lust and greed!" she shot back, how about simply my need. It's not like I'm being overwhelmed in the sex department Clay. Not at all."

"You know Sherri I'm a bit fed up with your whining and complaining about that, so you know what; I'm not even going to entertain you right now," Clay countered. Sherri was angry to the point where she left Clay alone in the bedroom while she retreated to the downstairs family room. Once there, she promptly took matters into her own hands; well two fingers of her right hand anyway.Her thoughts as she did so......... I wish I had someone to give me what I want right now; the real thing that I've been missing out on so often.

∞∞∞∞∞∞∞∞∞∞

The following Monday morning, Sherri received an early call from Colette; not long after Clay had departed. She and Frank were going to be hosting Christmas dinner and she just wanted to go over a few of the details with Sherri. Just before they were about to hang up, Sherri asked Colette if she could ask a question.

"Sure, what's up," said Colette.

"I just wanted to get your opinion on something," Sherri began.

"What's that?"

"How would you feel about inviting Beth over for Christmas?"

"Uh---I don't know Sherri. I mean I would be fine with it and Frank certainly would as well, but what about Clay? I'm not so sure he would be on board with the idea. Did you run it past him?"

"No and I don't think I really should."

"Oh you don't?" Colette reacted with surprise.

"Colette, I had the chance to see Beth recently and I can tell you that she feels terrible about the way things are. She's lonely, she's sad and she's just hurting. That much was obvious to me. And I just feel like it's time to let bygones be bygones. I mean nothing is going to change what happened in the past, but I just think that a little forgiveness would be a good thing; especially at this time of year."

"Sherri I understand what you're saying and I can't say I disagree with you. I just hate the possibility of our Christmas dinner deteriorating into a big mess."

"Well I would hope that wouldn't happen."

"But you do recognize there's the chance that it could right?"

"Yes of course I do Colette, but I also feel like there's a chance that the risk could all be worth it; that this could be a changing of the course so to speak. Colette; I looked in Beth's eyes and I could see the pain there. I know she wants so much to be back in our lives. All of ours."

"Yes I understand that Sherri, but I just don't know; I mean………….."

"Please Colette it would mean so much to her, "Sherri cut her off. And I know how much it would mean to the kids. Please."

"Okay, maybe; just give me a little time to think about it," Colette said softly.

"Oh thank you Colette."

"Hey I just said I'd think about it Sherri."

"All right fair enough," replied Sherri although she had already convinced herself what Colette's answer would be. "I'll talk to you soon."

"Okay bye."

"Bye."

Sherri smiled as she hung up the receiver. Pumped up by her conversation with Colette, she took a moment to check in on the kids who were of course home for Christmas recess. Returning to the living room she picked up her Blackberry and immediately placed a call to Scott.

"Hello."

"Hey Scott."

"Hey what's going on?"

"Not a whole lot; are you busy?"

"No I'm in the car headed to the office. What are you up to?"

"Nothing really, I was just thinking about you and decided to give you a call."

"Okay cool I like that. Well come on baby talk to me; what's on your mind?"

"You can probably guess what's on my mind," Sherri cooed.

"Actually I have no idea," Scott said feigning innocence.

"Oh no, well in that case let me share. The possibility of you and I getting horizontal with each other is squarely on my mind. What about yours Scott?"

"Well the day ahead was on my mind, but that's all changed now."

"So do you want to talk about it?" Sherri inquired.

"No actually I want to be about it," was Scott's quick retort.

"Well let's go with it. What do you think would be a good day for you?"

"Hey like I said I'm pretty much free and clear anytime; so the question is when can you break away?"

"Oh how I wish I could right now, but no can't do that, so I'm thinking later on in the week."

"Don't forget Christmas is Friday."

"Yeah I know. Well maybe I can give myself an early Christmas present and get together with you like Wednesday or Thursday; what do ya think?"

"Well I don't see a problem here. Just give me a little bit of advance notice and we'll be good," replied Scott.

"Great; well listen, you go ahead and I'll call you either later today or tomorrow and get your address okay."

"That sounds good Sherri. So do you have any idea as to your game plan? I mean as far as for getting away for a while."

"No but don't worry, I'll certainly come up with something."

"Oh I'm not concerned really. I'm sure you'll work it out. I was just curious. Anyway let me go and I'll talk to you soon."

"Okay have a great day."

"Thanks. I'm sure I will now that I know what lies ahead for later this week sometime."

"Yeah me too; in fact my nipples are getting pretty hard from just thinking about it."

"Oh you bad girl, behave yourself."

"Do I have to," Sherri whispered seductively.

"No not really," Scott responded leading to both of them laughing in unison.

"I thought you'd see it my way. So tell me are you hard at all."

"Maybe just a little," Scott admitted

"I wish I could see," Sherri teased.

"Bye Sherri, let me hang up before I run into a parked car or something."

"Bye Scott," she flirted one more time before hanging up.

As she went about the rest of that day, Sherri spent a fair amount of time thinking about Scott. At least when she wasn't occupied with Abby, Tyler and Zach that is. About 1:00 in the afternoon she retreated to the bedroom where she called him once again.

"Guess who," she said once he answered.

"Oh I have no idea, "Scott joked. I think perhaps you have the wrong number. But I like your voice though. It's very sexy. Mind if we talk for a minute?"

"No I don't, not at all. So what's on your mind baby?" Sherri said in picking up on the game.

"I don't know—let's see, so…what are you wearing?"

"Oh nothing but a pair of panties, and I have my hand inside of those."

"Would you like anything else inside of them?"

"Maybe, what might you have in mind big fella?"

"Well how about something from my tool box?"

"Oooh, your tool box huh? Okay I'll go with it that might work. What do you mean like a screwdriver, a pair of pliers?"

"Actually I have just the thing for the job. I was thinking more along the lines of a hammer."

"What you don't have a nice power drill in there anywhere?"

"Let me check again I might just have one down in there somewhere."

"Yeah look good because you need to get deep down in there for this job."

Unable to keep the game going any longer, Sherri broke up laughing before Scott could again respond. "We are both terrible, you know that right?" she said without any real shame.

"Yeah I guess we are; so what's up babe? What did you really call for?"

"I don't know, I can't remember now," Sherri quipped. "Oh wait I know what it was about."

"Okay what's up?"

"Well I don't even know why I'm the least bit concerned about this," Sherri began. She didn't really want to let on that she had just recently slept with another man outside of her marriage, and that he had turned out to be incapable of performing. "I guess it's kind of ironic after the little game we just played but anyway, I really feel sort of uncomfortable in even bringing this up but you don't, um, um…..you know have any issues I might need to know about do you?"

"Issues, what sort of issues?"

"Oh God this is so awkward." Sherri wasn't about to take the risk of putting herself out there, just to wind up with another man with the physical limitations that Craig ended up having. "You know like performance issues. Like I said I feel strange even asking something like that so please don't be offended."

"Sherri I think I know what you're asking me and no I'm not the least bit offended. But don't worry, there are no problems there. I wouldn't dare waste your time if there were."

Sherri breathed a sigh of relief that Scott had taken the question in stride.

"Well Scott thanks for bearing with me in my own little moment of silliness. I'm sorry for even interrupting your day with this."

"Hey don't mention it, no big deal. None at all," he assured her, though it did give him reason to wonder. Has she had that situation come up with somebody else she's had an encounter with? Or maybe her husband can't get it up. That would explain some things he thought to himself.

"Okay then you get back to work and we'll talk soon."

"You can count on it," Scott replied before they hung up.

Just seconds later Sherri's phone rang. So quickly in fact that she wondered if it was Scott calling her back about something. As she checked the call display she saw that wasn't the case.

"Hey Lina, how are you," she answered the call excitedly.

The call was from Lina DiLorenzo a former co-worker and also good friend from when she worked at Jarman, Klein. Lina had moved to South Florida a couple of years previously and she and Sherri kept in touch, but far too infrequently.

"Hi Sherri."

"Oh my God, Lina what's going on? We haven't talked in months. What's new?"

"I'm doing great, and as for the other thing; you know a little bit of this and a whole lot of that. But anyway I'm in Jersey so you know we need to get together; do lunch or something."

"Oh you are! That's great we definitely need to do that then. When did you get in and how long will you be home?"

"I got here yesterday evening; flew up after work yesterday and I'll be home for a while; until almost New Year's Eve"

"Oh that long? That's great."

"Yes it's been a while since I've been back so I need to spend some real time with my family."

"I know just what you mean because it's been a while for me too and I miss mine. But anyway you know we've got a lot to catch up on so just let me know when you're ready to go hang out."

"Well I was thinking perhaps we can do lunch one day early next week, Lina suggested."

"Yeah we can do that. Maybe mix in a little shopping with it. You know for old time's sake," Sherri chuckled.

"Oh you know I'm always down for that," Lina agreed.

"Okay, so why don't we just talk over the weekend to firm things up and take it from there."

"Yep sounds good, I'll give you a call or you can call me."

"All right Lina talk to you soon.   And have a great Christmas."

"Yeah you and the family do the same, bye-bye."

"Bye."

For much of the rest of the morning Sherri's focus was on what would be her out in order to allow her time to hook up with Scott. In time she did come up with an idea. And she would tell it to Clay sometime that evening.

Clay went to bed about 10:30 after spending some time working in the office.   Sherri was halfway through the 10:00 news when he entered and she wasted no time in taking the next step in her plan.

"Hey, my former co-worker Lina is in town to spend some time with her family for the holidays and she wants to do some last minute shopping for some of her family members. And I told her I would come along with her. We're looking at Wednesday mid-morning or so.   I assume you'll probably be heading into the office so I'll see about finding someone to sit with the kids."

Sherri had already been thinking along those lines, contemplating who might be able to assist her this time around. She had even made a couple of calls to put some feelers out there already.

"Okay no problem and yes I will be working that day," Clay replied flatly.

 Some minutes later as she and Clay had settled into bed and were watching the news, Sherri checked her Blackberry and saw that she had received a new picture mail message from Scott. She snuck a glance over at Clay who was leaning back against the headboard with his hands locked behind his head. Rising to her feet, she went over and stood leaning against the dresser just opposite the bed.

"Just a little something for you," read the subject line. But it was the contents that both surprised and delighted Sherri. Scott had sent her a picture of himself in which he was standing and turned to the side wearing nothing but a sly grin. Extending from his body was his fully erect penis. Sherri's first reaction was to smile broadly as she focused in on the photo. Wow, that's quite impressive was her immediate thought. The smile remained and her pulse seemed to quicken as she continued to admire the photo. Briefly lost in her thoughts she had seemingly forgotten that her husband was in such close proximity. That was until he reminded her.

"What's so interesting on your phone that you had to get out of bed to check out," he questioned, causing Sherri to think quickly.

"Oh Jennifer just sent me some pictures of the girls from their school's holiday play. They're so adorable."

"Oh okay, let me take a peek, I haven't seen them In so long, said Clay. They've probably gotten big as I don't know what."

Sherri was again caught off guard but she believes she certainly responded quickly and calmly enough to not bring on any real suspicion.

"Well there are about 20 pictures in total so I can let you see them after I finish going through them all. Unless you're tired and just want to look at them in the morning or something."

"No it's okay I'll let you finish and then I'll check them out. I'm not that sleepy actually."

As Sherri pretended to be scrolling through a set of photos Clay turned his attention back to the television. But luck was on her side as the next thing he said pulled her out of the fire.

"Oh dammit, you know what, I almost forgot I have some things I need to type up and email to my secretary," he said while jumping up from the bed. I have an early meeting out of the office so I need to get them to her tonight so she can get going on it first thing in the morning. I'll have to check out the pictures some other time I guess."

Sherri exhaled, before turning her gaze back to the erotic photo the moment Clay left the room. Smiling once again, she smacked her lips together as she let her imagination take flight. At least she knew that in a matter of hours her imagination would in this case be replaced by reality. She then noticed that Scott had also written a few words to go along with the photo.

"Smile Sherri; I just wanted to eliminate any concerns you might still have. Hopefully this does it."

"Hey, I just saw the picture and does it ever put my mind at ease," she typed in a return message. Not that I was ever truly concerned. . But thank you Scott and believe me I haven't stopped smiling. Also, I now have the perfect setup for Wednesday so you can consider me green-lighted. Please confirm when you can that it works for you also. And whatever you do don't forget to bring that thing with you. It looks absolutely mouth-watering."

Clay didn't return to the bedroom until after she had fallen asleep, and by the next morning those supposed photos of her nieces that Clay thought was what had bought a smile to her face the night before were the farthest thing from his mind. And she knew him well enough to feel comfortable that he would never bring them up again unless she mentioned them. Certainly something she wasn't about to do. Especially given the fact that the alleged pictures were non-existent. And lady luck continued to smile on Sherri as later that morning her teenaged neighbor Dawn called to let her know that she would in fact be available to babysit the following morning. They quickly settled on 11:00 as a good time for her to come by. With that final bit of business out of the way Sherri texted Scott with the news and the resulting firm commitment of their plans; something that he soon reciprocated.

By 10:00 on Wednesday morning, Clay had departed and after getting the kids all fed and dressed for the day Sherri turned her attention to preparing for her rendezvous with Scott "hard to please" Wesley. After showering, she dressed simply; with a pair of jeans and a turtleneck sweater. But she did have a delightfully sexy, baby blue matching bra and panty set on beneath it. She felt oddly relaxed as she put on her boots. There were no signs of the butterflies she had in the hours leading up to her hooking up with Craig. Oh yes, poor Craig. He still texted or sent her emails from time to time; messages that always went unanswered. She considered that the best way to handle him, thinking that in time he would surely get the hint that she was no longer interested in him. She wished him no harm after all. So as long as he didn't become overbearing or belligerent she decided she'd play it just that way until he just faded away; sort of like a harmless, nonthreatening cloud passes on a mostly sunny day. And this day was indeed one of those. But the only thing blue in Sherri's morning was the beautiful sky. The sun also seemed to smile down upon her as it peeked between the white, puffy clouds as they parted. She drew energy from it as she prepared to set off into the radiance of its far reaching rays.

Dawn was right on time, ringing the doorbell at 11:00 on the button. Sherri told her she would try to be back by 3, but Dawn assured her that it wouldn't be a problem if she were extended beyond that time. She said she was free and clear for the day so there was no need to rush. And of course it didn't hurt that Sherri had agreed to pay her 15 dollars for every hour. And what teenage girl wouldn't love the chance to make 60, 75 or maybe even an astounding 90 dollars for one day of babysitting. Of course Sherri being gone for the 6 hours it would take her to make that much was unlikely, but Dawn certainly wouldn't be too upset if she was.

Sherri had used her as a sitter before so she was completely comfortable with Dawn, but she did still want to go over a few finals details before departing. Once that was handled, Sherri was ready to head out in a matter of minutes. The drive to Watchung was smooth and steady and in what seemed almost like no time at all Sherri was pulling into Scott's driveway. Not that she was nervous or paranoid about anything, but she was glad that his home had a side entry garage. That allowed her to park her car in a manner which made it pretty much unviewable from the street. And she also parked to the left of his SUV, thus further blocking anyone from being able to spot it while driving by. She made one final check of her hair and makeup before putting on her sunglasses and stepping out of the car. Instinctively, she peered behind her just as she arrived at his front door.

Sherri looked at her watch after she pressed the doorbell. 11:20. Time to get this thing going. She took a deep breath as she heard the door being unlocked. Well here I go again was her thought at that moment. She soon found that any worries she might have had about another heart sinking moment like she had at the first sight of Craig were completely unfounded. She greeted Scott with an enormous smile that said hello and excuse me while I throw myself into your arms. Wow, she was thinking; if anything, the pictures don't do this guy justice. Scott looked every bit like the former athlete he had described himself as in one of their discussions. A former lower-level college football linebacker he was a shade over 6'1" and 210 well- defined pounds. At 40 he still sported a head full of bushy, brown hair. Divorced for 2 years, he is the father of two small children himself. He had said that he was at a point in his life where a committed relationship was not something he was necessarily seeking at the moment. Fun and excitement is what he was looking for. And that made him the ideal man to get involved with in Sherri's eyes. Speaking of eyes; starting the moment he opened the door to let her in Sherri seemingly found herself lost in his. They were a striking bluish-gray and looking into them caused a lump to form in her throat.

"Hey, aren't you the punctual one. Come on in," he said with a friendly, welcoming smile of his own.

"Yes I'm usually pretty good about being places on time I'd say. I know that's not something we women are generally known for but I do pretty well at it."

"Well great; less time I had to spend waiting for you," Scott said while still beaming.

His eyes again captured Sherri's intense stare as he spoke. She wondered if he noticed.

"Let me help you with that coat," he said before he started to unzip her waist length shearling jacket.

"Well isn't this something; I've hardly set foot in the door and you're trying to undress me already," she kidded.

"Hey, nothing ventured nothing gained," he replied similarly tongue in cheek. "But anyway, let me hang this up for you."

As Scott exited the hall closet Sherri stood there before him almost like a shy, young, innocent girl who was about to surrender herself for the first time. Her hands were clasped behind her back, her eyes pointed at the floor. As he moved close to her she slowly ran one hand through her long, brown hair.

"Let me look at you. Oh my God, you look out of this world," he said as she slowly lifted her head to meet his glance. He pulled her close in a tight embrace while also playfully stroking her hair. And then came those eyes again. Burning into hers and erasing what little hesitation she may have had left.

"Come on let's sit down," he said softly before leading her by the hand over to his sofa. "Can I get you anything; maybe something to drink?" he asked politely.

"No thanks," she declined. She knew just what it was that she wanted from him at that moment and she hoped she wouldn't need to wait much longer. Some friendly small talk ensued for a few minutes before to her great delight Sherri discovered that Scott too was a man who didn't believe in denying or even delaying the obvious. That they wanted each other, right then, right there, right away. He moved in very close to her and placed his right hand high up on her thigh. And from there it all started with a kiss.

∞∞∞∞∞∞∞∞

Some four hours and an equal number of mind-blowing orgasms later, Sherri was showered, dressed and ready to head home. Scott helped her back on with her coat and kissed her goodbye on the cheek, being thoughtful enough to do it before she was out in the open doorway.

"Can't wait until we get to do this again; that is if you want to," he said as she faced him in the foyer on the way to the door.

"Yes you'd better believe it, and hopefully it won't be long either," she assured him.

"Well in that case you know I'm available."

"And I'll make myself available," Sherri countered. "We'll be in touch. Bye Scott."

"Bye for now Sherri," he said as he flashed an effervescent smile and an all knowing wink.

"Oh yeah; just for now, believe me," she replied.

She made eye contact with him one last time before placing on her shades, stepping outside and walking to her car, his eyes following her every step of the way. As she got into the car she parted her lips and placed her right index finger just inside of her mouth; the same place where Scott's penis had made itself at home not so long before. As she began to pull out of the driveway, her mind continued to wander back to what had occurred inside and a smile curved across her sultry lips. She could feel her nipples immediately harden and her panties moisten slightly. Oh yes I will see you again real soon she said to herself as she looked towards the house one last time before pulling out of the driveway and off down the street.

With the feelings of euphoria that she was experiencing, Sherri may have just as well floated home above the car rather than seated inside of it. For her there was just nothing like a good hard fucking complete with multiple orgasms to take you to that special place; one that to her seemed so far away just mere hours before. As it turned out the tryst with Scott wasn't the only thing that would make her feel good on that day. As she neared home her cell phone rang with a call from Colette.

"Hey I've got good news," she exclaimed after Sherri answered. "I just got off the phone with Beth and she's in."

"Oh that's great Colette.

"Yes and she sounded so excited. I guess you were right. I'm going to call Kevin and let him know as soon as I hang up with you, but I actually wanted to tell you first because you were the one who put the wheels in motion."

"Oh this is so wonderful; the kids are going to be so happy to see her Colette."

"Yes I'm sure they will, but what about Clay Sherri?"

"Oh don't worry about that I'll handle things with Clay."

"Are you sure?"

"Yes I am, don't worry," Sherri repeated.

"Okay, because Kevin might be a little caught off guard when I tell him but I'm certain he'll be okay with it after a while. But Clay's the one who has held steadfast in his animosity towards her. And I just don't want anything to put a damper on the day. And I wouldn't want to put Beth in an uncomfortable position either. So please make sure you do handle it if you say you will."

"Colette, I will take care of it. And if by any chance I feel like its best that we reconsider the invitation than I will call and let you know okay?"

"Okay Sherri but.......".Colette began before being cut off by Sherri.

"So if you don't hear from me than you can take that as a sign that everything is cool. Good enough?"

"Sure, good enough."

"All right, well we will see you all on Friday."

"Yeah Friday it is. Oh and Sherri I'm asking everyone to come for dinner by 4:30-5:00 so that we can get going on the gift swapping fairly early."

"Sounds good; we'll see you then."

"All right bye-bye."

"Bye."

That evening about 9:00 Sherri was busy in the kitchen when Clay entered from the office where he had been going over some things. His docket at the firm was just about cleared up, but he still had some work to put in, in order to be ready to hit the ground running in his new role as Prosecutor in advance of his January 5th swearing-in.

"Hey," Sherri greeted him as she turned in his direction. "Are you hungry? You want me to prepare you something?"

"Yeah I am a little bit. I thought I might grab a little something to snack on that's all."

"Well I can prepare you a sandwich, I don't mind."

"Are you sure? I was just going to grab a few cookies and a cup of coffee. It looks like it's going to be another late night for me."

"Sure it's no problem, I wouldn't mind a bit."

"Okay, well I appreciate it," Clay said as Sherri stopped what she had been doing.

"Turkey and cheese okay?" she questioned.

"Yeah sure, that'd be great."

"You want me to just bring it in to you?"

"No that's okay I can kind of use a short mental break anyway. But thanks."

"You're welcome," Sherri replied cheerfully.   Clay stood off to the side as he waited for her to finish.   Sherri glided around the floor and at one point even broke out into a song.

"You're certainly mighty chipper tonight," he said upon picking up on her mood.

"Well you know what they say, tis the season to be jolly."

"Yes they do say that, he agreed as he watched her pour him a cup of coffee.

"So it's all about the holiday spirit," Sherri stated. But clearly she was far more ebullient due to the happenings earlier in the day.

Clay took a deep breath before beginning to speak again."You know I would love for us all to try to attend midnight mass tomorrow night but I think I'll be so busy working most of the evening that it just won't be possible."

"Well don't worry about it, it's understandable.   Even to God I bet," Sherri quipped while placing the sandwich and cup of black coffee on the kitchen table.

"Yes I suppose he might at that," an exhausted sounding Clay said before sitting down heavily at the table.

Just then Sherri reached down into the pocket of her slacks to pull out her handheld after having felt it vibrate from receiving a new text message. She smiled broadly after seeing who had sent the message. Backpedalling, she leaned up against the countertop before beginning to read the contents.

"Hey sweet lady. I was just thinking about you, and wondering how you were this evening?"

"Hi Scott you sweet, hot and delicious man," Sherri typed in reply while glancing in Clay's direction.

"Oh no I think you're certainly far more sweet than I'm delicious," came her new lover's reply.

"Well that's just your opinion; and one that I just so happen to not share. But anyway what are up too this evening?"

"Oh nothing much; I'm just laying here noticing that my balls are looking and feeling kind of empty. Can I possibly have back some of what you drained out of them today?"

Trying to hold back a big grin, Sherri again looked at her husband before responding.

"Not a chance in hell. In fact I'm going to want a lot more of that if I have my way. So you'd better fill up on the oysters or something if you don't already."

Another peek at Clay gave her the impression that he was deep in thought.

"Well they're not exactly something that are tops on my menu choices but I will do that if need be, because I do want to always make sure you get your fill."

"I certainly did this afternoon but I don't know, I might have a tapeworm or something because I'm very hungry again."

"Well may I interest you in some fine USDA choice beef with a warm cream sauce?"

"Oh that certainly sounds like something I could really sink my teeth into. But anyway believe it or not I have company with me right now. You know who. And he's actually fairly close by. So why don't we pick this up later."

"Well aren't you a daring one. But yes let's hook up later; take care babe."

"Yes I guess I like to live on the edge once in a while but believe me he has no clue. But until later--- smooches sweetie."

"Right back atcha."

Sherri slipped her phone back in her pocket and looked at Clay once more.

How's the sandwich?"

"Oh it's just great, thanks. I noticed you've gotten really attached to that Blackberry. You'd be pretty much lost without that thing. You would think you're still practicing law or something."

"Yeah I do have some chatty girlfriends I must say. And some of the relatives back home also. I can't forget about them always wanting to keep me updated on the latest gossip or to ask about the kids. So yes it is a modern convenience that I've grown accustomed to," Sherri explained before turning away and returning to what she had been busy with before Clay entered. That is removing the clean dishes from the dishwasher.

"Well of course it's no big deal. Just something I noticed that's all."

"All right as long as it doesn't bother you, "said Sherri

"Oh no it's just an observation that's all, but it's not a big deal in the least. Anyway, thanks again for the sandwich. Time to get back to work," said Clay before he rose up from the table and departed the room.

Sherri watched him leave, smiled mischievously and then quickly pulled her phone back out of her pocket. Excited and ripe with anticipation, she immediately began to type on its small keyboard. "Hey guess what, the coast is now clear. And trust me I'm still quite famished. So since you're not in a position to feed me, why don't you at least entice me some more by talking about that prime cut of beef you mentioned before?"

CHAPTER EIGHT

While it didn't exactly fulfill the wishes of those who might have been dreaming of a white Christmas; the night before had left a dusting of powdery snow on the ground. But Christmas morning was quite cold, yet bright, crystal clear and overflowing with abundant sunshine. As expected, Abby and Tyler awakened quite early in anticipation of quite a haul awaiting them under the tree. And they certainly were not at all disappointed when they set their eyes upon the mountain of toys and games they had received. Sherri could clearly hear all of the joyful cries of "oh boy and yes" as she laid in bed trying to gather herself to join them. A pit stop in the bathroom for a morning refresher sure worked wonders in that regard. Obviously not as moved with excitement, little Zach remained in his bed sound asleep as Sherri passed his room on the way to the upstairs version of their home's two family rooms.

After about 45 minutes spent with her two oldest sharing the joy of Christmas morning; Sherri went to look in on Zach once again. And neither the fact that there was more than a small amount of noise from below or that he too had received quite the bounty of gifts himself were enough to motivate Zach to climb out of bed at the ungodly hour of 5 a.m. Sherri wished the other two had been similarly uninspired; but comfortable in their ability to look after themselves while at play, she decided that she would return to the bedroom where she was somewhat surprised to be greeted by Clay as she entered.

Clay had long had a way about him that seemed to want to compensate for whatever failings he may have had as a husband and father by being overly generous with material gifts. This was especially true for birthdays, anniversaries and on Christmas. And certainly this year would be no exception. After they greeted each other with good mornings, Clay reached into the nightstand beside him and pulled out two neatly wrapped small boxes. It was clear to Sherri from the moment she saw them that they must contain some sort of jewelry.

"Hey, these are for you; Merry Christmas," he said softly while placing one box and then the other on her side of the bed. Sherri played it like she was surprised. But her display of open-mouth shock was anything but that in actuality. The only mystery was what exactly was inside of the boxes.

"Oh you got me something," Sherri stated in mock surprise as she slowly opened box number 1. Inside was a beautiful, diamond encrusted Cartier wristwatch. Of course that by itself would have been more than enough in her eyes. Especially in comparison to what Sherri had purchased him. But Clay almost always saw it as necessary to go above and beyond. Seemingly to the point where it would appear that it was an attempt to buy her continued loyalty and steadfast love and support.

"Oh thank you, this is so beautiful," she said to him softly. And it's not even all you got me I see."

"No it's not, so why don't you go ahead and open up the second box."

"Okay," Sherri obliged him, opening the second box in the same deliberate fashion.

This time her surprise was far more genuine. Inside was a set of Roberto Coin yellow and gold, hoop earrings with a gorgeous matching bracelet. Sherri looked at all of what he had bought and then towards Clay. She figured the price tag for everything had to easily be somewhere between 4-6 thousand dollars.

"Wow I don't know what to say," said Sherri. She thought about the monogrammed brief case she had bought Clay. It was marked downed to $300.00 and she had even strongly considered whether that had been way too much to spend. She leaned across the bed and embraced him and gave him a light kiss on the lips.

"Thank you Clay," this was very nice of you, but you didn't have to buy me all this."

"I know, but I just wanted to show you that I appreciate you and all you do; so you're welcome."

While Sherri of course appreciated Clay's overwhelming generosity, she at the same time started to lament all over again that this above all else, was an act of a man so lacking in so many other areas, that he saw this as the best and perhaps only way to curry favor with her. For him, loading up his platinum credit card was so much easier than the priceless costs of attention, affection, passion and romance. But for Sherri the things she desired the most in her life right now could not be purchased at any jeweler, any upscale boutique or luxury car dealership; for any price.

"Well I did get something for you also," she told him. "It's in the garage."

Zach finally awakened at 8:30, just as Abby and Tyler had predictably already grown weary of some of their new play things. So Zach and his toys became their focus as they coached him along in enjoying himself. Something not at all lost on Sherri since this allowed her a little more quiet time. In fact the 3 of them played to their hearts content; all the way through to the mid-afternoon, with the only interruption being for a mid-morning brunch. At 1:00 it became time for Zach to grudgingly take a nap. Once he was finally sound asleep, Sherri prepared a light snack for Abby and Tyler before turning her attention to the upcoming visit to Frank and Colette's home for the holiday gathering. By a quarter past four they were all in the car and on their way.

∞∞∞∞∞∞∞∞

Sherri checked her watch as Clay stopped his Mercedes 550S just in front of the driveway. The time was 4:35. Looking around as she stepped out of the car she didn't notice Beth's car anywhere. She should be arriving very shortly she figured.

It was Frank who answered the door and let them in before the kids quickly rushed past him in a hurry to get to their cousins. However Sherri halted them in their tracks and insisted that they properly greet their uncle before anything else.

"Oh that's okay, I understand. Merry Christmas," Frank said while hugging Sherri before shaking Clay's hand.

They both returned similar greetings before entering the living room area. There stood Kevin and Nina next to the Christmas tree. After the rest of the greetings were out of the way, Sherri turned to Frank.

"Hey Frank, where's Colette?"

"Oh she's running just a little bit behind so she's in back getting showered and dressed. She shouldn't be too long."

"Okay," Sherri responded. Frank then walked off and returned a short time later with a couple of glasses holding rum-spiked eggnog before handing one to each of them. He then proposed a toast.

"Here's to a happy and festive Christmas and all the blessings of the season to us all."

"Here, here," the group sang out in unison as glasses clanged together all around.

About ten minutes later, as everyone stood around engaging in lively banter between sips of the spiked eggnog, the doorbell rang once again.

"Excuse me, I know who that must be," said Frank excitedly before moving swiftly to answer the door.

Knowing that as well, Sherri's stomach began to churn in nervous anticipation.

"Hello, it's so great to see you, come on in. Merry Christmas," she heard Frank say clearly. Right this way," everyone's in here.

"Okay thanks and Merry Christmas to you too. You'll have to excuse me if I seem a bit nervous," she heard in a voice that was unmistakably Beth's. With each word the voices grew louder as they neared the living room.

"Oh please, there's nothing for you to be nervous about. You're here as a welcome guest."

Sherri's heart was now racing as the moment of truth had arrived.

"Hey everybody, look who's here," Frank called out gleefully.

Everything at that point seemed to begin to move in slow motion as the group turned around. Kevin and Nina rushed over to greet Beth as Sherri lowered her head. Eventually she did slowly look up and forced herself to look in that direction also. Everyone gathered around Beth seemed quite pleased to see her. Sherri then forced herself to look at Clay. There he stood, back against the wall and with his face etched in stone. As the pleasantries continued he walked right up to Sherri in a rush.

"Go round up the kids, go get the kids right now, we're leaving," he said in a clearly angry tone. Now Sherri!" he bellowed once it appeared to him that she hadn't reacted to his command fast enough. And wouldn't you know it that just at that moment approaching from behind was Colette. She stood there with her mouth agape. Wondering what the hell had just happened to have Clay seething. Then she looked ahead and saw Beth.

"Sherri what's wrong?" she asked. After getting nothing from Sherri but a shameful look she posed the same question to Clay.

"I think you can figure that out Colette! But don't worry we're getting the hell out of here. You all enjoy each other's company."

By now everyone else had fallen silent; seemingly numb with shock, while Beth could only stand there sad-faced; wishing she had never rang the doorbell, and had never entered the house.

Momenta later Abby and Tyler came rushing into the room holding their coats, sped along by Sherri to the rear of them carrying Zach in her arms.

"But Mommy why are we leaving?" Tyler wondered aloud. "Yeah we just got here,'" Abby complained.

"Abby, Tyler please; we'll talk about this in a little while okay. For now let's just put on your coats okay."

"Grandma Beth," Zach suddenly blurted out as he noticed her standing in front of them. This caused his older brother and sister to then look in that direction. Surprised expressions took over their faces and they quickly made their way over to her. Sherri had by then placed Zach down on the floor and he raced past his siblings to give Beth a big hug. Abby and Tyler smiled through their disappointment over finding out that they would be leaving the gathering as they too hugged her and greeted her warmly.

"It's so good to see you kids. Look I got something for all of you," Beth said. She walked a short distance and retrieved three colorful gift bags which she handed out to each of them respectively. What happened next stunned everyone in the house who saw it. Clay hurried over and snatched the bags from the hands of his children just as they peered inside of them. Dropping them on the floor, he then angrily implored them to head outside. He followed right behind them taking a moment to shoot an icy look into the eyes of Beth as he rushed past her.

"Merry Christmas everybody," he shouted before opening the door and leading the kids outside.

"Sherri what's the matter? You said you'd take care of this," Colette yelled at her. "Sherri! Kevin, go talk to your brother please; can't you talk him out of doing this?"

But Kevin just stood there; either too stunned or too reluctant to say or do anything at that moment.

"Isn't anyone going to try to stop them," Colette demanded before Frank stepped in front of her.

"Honey please, let's just let it go okay."

Sherri continued on, slowly slinking her way past everyone on her way to the door. Just before opening it she turned around to face everyone one final time before also departing.

"I'm very sorry Colette and Frank, and everybody else; especially you Beth; Merry Christmas."

They left in such a rush that they also left behind all of the other gifts that the children had received. Also left behind was a house full of long faces and bewildered looks; from the adults on down to the children.

"I'm sorry, I never should have come. It looks like it's put a damper on the entire evening and the holiday as well," Beth said with sad realization. "Maybe I should just leave."

"No that's nonsense. You're perfectly welcome in this house," Frank assured her.

"That's true Beth. I mean I just don't understand. Sherri told me that she was going to talk to Clay. That she was going to make sure that he was okay with you being here," Colette added.

"Well it's obvious that didn't happen Colette. And just as obvious that he had no idea that Beth was even coming," countered Frank.

"I know Frank," Colette admitted before turning to Beth. Beth listen, I love my brother but this is our house and you are a part of this family. And as distasteful as that may be to him, you are here as a welcome guest of ours. And we'd like for you to stay. But dammit why did I ever place my faith in Sherri's no account ass?"

At that point Kevin approached and touched his right hand to Beth's shoulder. "Listen Beth, I'd just like to let you know that Nina and I feel the same way. That is about you staying and enjoying dinner with us."

Beth looked around at all the still dazed looking faces and took particular note of the expression on the faces of all the children. She swallowed deeply before opening her mouth to speak.

"Okay I'll stay," she announced.

"All right, that's great," Kevin said as all the other adults smiled and nodded in agreement with her decision.

"Well everybody, let's not forget that it's Christmas. Let's get ready to have dinner," shouted Colette.

"Yes let's do that," Beth added as she managed a little smile.

As Beth headed towards the dining room all of the children came over to embrace her one by one. There was now some semblance of joy back in the house.

In the meantime, Clay, Sherri and the kids were now out in the car.

"Okay Clay, so now what?"

"Don't worry I'll figure that out,'" he shot back sternly.

"Yeah I almost forgot. You always do don't you. You always have things completely in control. Or at least in your control; just the way you like it."

"Oh Sherri please, this is so not the time," he said softly but with continued anger.

Sensing his fury, Sherri decided to say nothing else right then and there and instead just sat there with her arms folded as Clay jerked the car into drive and away from the curb. She didn't know where Clay was driving them to and frankly, she wasn't sure she cared all that much. She just wished she was elsewhere. That's how upset she was about the stunt Clay had pulled back at the house. All in all the car ride was silent except for the kids occasionally voicing their displeasure with having been taken away from the good time they were already having and were sure to have continued if they had been allowed to stay. But after some stern admonishing from their father they too thought it best that they protest in silence from there on out. At one point Tyler did complain about being hungry and asked when they were going to eat. Sherri was quick to advise him to seek that answer from Clay.

"Don't worry kids, we'll be eating real soon, and you won't be disappointed with what you have either. Just hang in there a little while longer okay." He then glanced at Sherri who responded by rolling her eyes disdainfully. "I don't know why you're mad at me," if there's anyone that should be angry here it's me," he said. Sherri said nothing but just continued to stare out of the passenger side window. But truthfully she had begun to wonder if it had all been largely her fault. Would it have made a difference if she had forewarned Clay of Beth's invitation? Or actually made an attempt to clear it with him? Hell with it she finally decided. Why should anyone have to get the okay from Clay before inviting someone to their own home? She put the onus right back on Clay; on him and his pigheadedness.

At about 5:30 Clay pulled the car into the crowded parking lot at the King's Cove Inn on Route 22 in Whitehouse Station; one of his favorite restaurants. When they departed the car and arrived at the door, they were hit with the announcement that the restaurant was booked tight and thus reservations were absolutely required. Upon hearing this, Sherri sighed deeply as the kids started to ask why they weren't going inside.

Clay then motioned to the hostess and asked if he could have a word with her in private for a moment. She obliged and they stepped about 15 feet away from the door.

"I'm sorry," he began, "but what is your name?"

"My name is Kate sir," replied the tall, attractive dark-haired young lady. She looked to be in her late 20"s to early 30's perhaps.

"Oh okay, Kate; nice Irish name. Listen Kate, we have a little situation here where our original plans sort of didn't pan out, so this was kind of unexpected. So we of course couldn't or at least didn't make a reservation given that."

"I understand that yes things can happen at the last minute sir, but I'm afraid we're booked solid until at least 6:00."

"And there's no flexibility on that, not only for let's say---- long time, loyal customers?"

"Trust me sir, I wish there were and that we could accommodate everybody. I mean obviously that would be best for the restaurant's bottom line also, but I just can't make it happen today I'm sorry."

"Kate, sweetheart; please don't take offense at me calling you sweetheart by the way."

"None taken Sir."

"Okay good. So Kate what is your last name if you don't mind me asking."

"It's Tierney sir."

"Well it doesn't get any more Irish than that does it? Bless your heart."

No sir I guess it doesn't," Kate replied with a gleam in her pretty green eyes.

"You're pretty new here correct?"

"Yes, I've been with the restaurant about let's see……. 5 weeks now."

"And I guess you never work the weekday lunchtime shift?"

"Rarely; I've done it maybe 1 or 2 times since being here."

"Oh, so I guess that means I probably don't look familiar to you at all."

"No sir I'm afraid not. Not in the least."

"All right well I understand things a little better now Kate. So tell me this then; do you think it would be possible for me to speak to the manager on duty?"

"Okay. If you'll give me a moment I'll see if he's available."

"Hearing that, Clay decided to turn on the phony charm one last time before Kate went on her way. "Thank you gorgeous and do me one more favor would you? Tell him it's Clay King who wants to have a word with him."

"Yes I sure will," she assured him before she walked away.

Clay turned back towards Sherri and the kids who were waiting there impatiently. Sherri held Zach in her arms while

Abby and Tyler had sought and found a respite on a comfortable leather sofa in the holding area. Clay held up one finger signalling that it wouldn't be much longer.

A short time later a tall, mostly bald, heavyset, middle-aged man approached with Kate not far behind him. A smile adorned his face from the moment he was close enough for Clay to take notice of it.

"Clay, how ya doing buddy," he called out once he got fairly close.

"I've been doing real well Steve; life is good," Clay answered before the two men embraced.

"Hey congrats, ya know I heard the news. Go ahead and get em pal. Hey Kate this is Clay King the man who is going to keep the streets of Somerset County safe from the riffraff. I'm sure of that, right Clay."

"Well that's certainly my intention."

"Beautiful just great; ya know we need a good man like you in there Clay. I wish you nothing but the best."

"Thanks I appreciate that Steve. I really do."

"Hey, don't mention it. Anyway I got word from Kate here that you wanted to see me. What can I do for ya pal?"

"Well it's not much and I hate to have disturbed you with this, but it's just that we came here sort of spur of the moment. And as such, you know------well we don't exactly have a reservation. And Kate here, God Bless her, well she's just doing her job."

"Is that all you need buddy. Oh please, let me take care of that right away for ya."

"Thanks Steve I and the entire family appreciate this; really."

"Oh is the family here, well let me go over and introduce myself if you don't mind."

"No don't mind at all, in fact why don't I handle the introductions," said Clay as he led Steve over to Sherri and the kids. Once that was out of the way, Steve then quickly headed over to have a quick word with Kate. After the discussion and them peering around the main dining area, the family was soon seated at a table In the middle of the room. "See how I took care of that for us, "Clay remarked smugly once they were alone; prompting Sherri to look at him dismissively.

As it turned out dinner was delightful. While the atmosphere was nothing like it would have been at Frank and Coleen's and the talking was minimal with all of the hard feelings still remaining, everyone at least left the restaurant perfectly content with the meals they had. Back at home that evening at about 11:00 Clay entered the bedroom where Sherri was reading, having been unable to find anything of interest on television.

"I'm going to prepare for bed now," he said to her without a response of any kind. "I'm just exhausted. I guess more mentally than anything else," he added. "Just still can't really believe that Beth showed up like that. Just like she expected it to be all fine and dandy. Well hell with that."

Now it was those final words that got Sherri to respond. "Well if you ask me I think you were very mean-spirited and unnecessarily cold towards Beth, she said as she placed the book she'd been reading on her lap."

"Oh so you do, do you. Well it's a good thing I didn't ask you huh?"

"Yes I do Clay, regardless of whether you want to hear it or not."

"Exactly how so; care to explain that to me? But when you do so just remember that you weren't the one whose family she ripped apart okay. Just keep that in mind while you're passing judgment on me."

"Believe me I know the entire story of what happened there. And I've always been understanding of that. We just felt like it was about time for you to start to let some of that anger go."

"Hold on Sherri. What do you mean by we just felt like it was time?"

"Nothing; I didn't mean a thing by it."

"Oh you meant something by it because you said it. Are you lying here trying to tell me that you knew something about this? And that you not only knew, but that you might have played a part in arranging it?"

"Look Clay it's been a long time; at some point you just have to let bygones be bygones, or at least try to."

"You know something Sherri, the best thing you could have done and can still do, as opposed to what you did is to just butt out of what is really not your damn business," Clay said angrily.

"Not my business?"

"Yeah that's what I said Sherri; it's none of your god-damned business. I didn't know you then and all that you even know about that entire situation I either told it to you or Kevin or Colette did. And you know what; like I said I'm tired and sort of drained tonight. And I'm dying for some sleep but to tell you the truth I don't think I want that sleeping to take place next to you. Not tonight," he added before snatching his pillow from the bed and bolting out of the room.

"Go right ahead, you think I'll miss you being here? I probably won't even notice the difference," Sherri replied coldly. "And you know what it was my idea too. And I don't regret it at all," Sherri yelled just before Clay was out of earshot.

But in fact she did regret it; at least somewhat. Well at least she had been having 2nd thoughts about it for much of the evening. Not over whether it was the right thing to have invited Beth. But rather if she should have run it past Clay before they had arrived at the get-together. But she didn't and now not only was Clay pissed at her, but she was certain that Colette was as well. She spent about the next half-hour stewing over it before deciding she needed to do something to get her thoughts off of that. Then it dawned on her that Clay had inadvertently done her a favor. With him downstairs for the night she could chat with Scott from the comfort of her bed. Now she only had to hope he was available. She reached into the nightstand and retrieved her Blackberry. She was in luck and her mood instantly changed. She and Scott spent the next hour engaging in their usual spicy conversation. All the way until her eyes would no longer stay open. He left her horny as hell but alas her satisfaction would have to wait for another time.

∞∞∞∞∞∞∞∞∞∞∞

Tuesday arrived and with it Sherri's real afternoon out with Lina. Not the one she pretended to be having while she frolicked with Scott the previous week. Clay left out at about 8:15 that morning. He'd spent a total of 4 consecutive nights in the downstairs guest room and had given no indication of when he might end his self-imposed banishment. And Sherri certainly wasn't bothered enough by it to push the issue either.

"With the amount of under the table cash Dawn had made the last time she was called upon, it certainly wasn't difficult for Sherri to land her as a sitter once again. The itinerary that she and Lina had mapped out called for them to do some shopping after lunch, so the two of them were to meet in front of Bloomingdales at the ritzy Short Hills mall at 11:45 am. Dawn was asked to arrive by no later than 11:00 to allow Sherri time for the drive as well as a margin for error in the event of traffic.

Dawn was once again very punctual which allowed Sherri to get out so quickly that she arrived at the mall 15 minutes early. By the time she valet parked and made her way over to Bloomingdales, another 5 minutes had passed. But Sherri needn't worry about being on time because as it turned out LIna didn't show up until 11:50 or so. She had been looking around from side to side so didn't see Sherri right away as she turned around a corner of the mall walking in her direction. Sherri smiled as she saw her approaching dressed in a pair of flair-legged, black, fitted slacks and a teal sweater. Sherri remembers Lina as someone who never really liked to wear a jacket. Reasoning that she was going to be in the car most of the time anyway, so why wear a jacket and then go through the inconvenience of having to carry it around with you once you got inside. So she was sort of surprised to see Lena sporting a waist length black, suede jacket. Maybe those years in Florida have turned her to someone very intolerant of the cold; even on a relatively mild 43 degree day as this one was.

Sherri rushed over to greet Lina as she got within 20 feet of her. "Oh my God, "she wailed before the two of them hugged tightly.

"It is so good to see you," Sherri said as they prolonged their embrace.

"Oh you too," Lina concurred before they stepped back from each other.

"And check you out, you look great. Have you lost weight?" Sherri inquired.

"Yeah a little bit, not too much; about 8-10 pounds. It's been more about me focusing on reshaping my body. Thanks to my great physical trainer I started working with last spring. Thank you baby," she concluded before placing her fingers to her lips and sending out imaginary kisses to seemingly no one in particular.

"Thank you baby? Oh do tell, do tell," Sherri chirped excitedly.

"Well okay, but we can get into that in a bit at lunch?"

"Sure, that's fine. And what are we waiting for anyway, let's head on inside shall we?"

"We most certainly shall; after you," Lina insisted.

The ladies had decided in a conversation that morning that they would have lunch at The Cheesecake Factory, someplace that the two of them both loved. That was the main reason Sherri had suggested they should meet where they did as the restaurant was located directly adjacent to Bloomingdales. Upon entering the rather sparsely crowded restaurant, they were quickly ushered to a table right in the center of the room by the hostess. An early 20's looking, striking brunette, she appeared to be every bit of 6 feet tall or more with the heels she was sporting. Dressed in a black jacket over a white blouse with a matching black miniskirt, she had legs that seemed to go on for days. She strode quite confidently as she led them to their table, model-like in both build and the way she pranced along.

"Your server will be right with you," she said with a luminous smile once they were seated. She placed two menus on the table before perfectly executing a smooth turn and gliding departure that would have made any world-class supermodel proud. It certainly made both Sherri and Lina take notice.

"Well I wonder if she's just working here while she's waiting for her modeling career to take off," remarked Lina.

"Yeah I could certainly see that being the case too," Sherri said. "I certainly hope so anyway. She's gorgeous and sure has the body and the walk like America's Next Top Model doesn't she?"

"No doubt about it," Lina agreed as she looked over at the young girl whose face beamed brightly as she welcomed more guests. "Anyway," she said while turning to Sherri, "how are things? First of all how are the kids?"

"Oh they are fine, just growing up by the day; literally and figuratively."

"I guess they must be keeping you busy huh?"

"Well they're doing their best. But I still manage to get some me time in on occasion."

"Okay that's good; so how about the hubby?"

"Oh him," Sherri said with a slight grin. "He's doing fine. Basically doing what he does. Except that pretty soon he's going to be doing it on a different scale."

"Oh really, how so," Lina asked

"He's about to become the chief Somerset County Prosecutor. Actually in just a few days now."

"Get outta here Sherri, that's great, good for him."

"Exactly, good for HIM," Sherri said flatly.

"Come on Sherri that's pretty big. You must be excited about it too right?"

"Hmmmm, I don't know," Sherri shrugged. "I mean don't get me wrong I'm happy for him because I know that's the sort of thing he aspired to, but you know I don't expect much to change because of that. Of course he's going to be more visible and more in the public eye, but by the same token this is Somerset County not Manhattan or Brooklyn or something. But yeah I'm happy for him. Whoop de doo. Can't you tell?" Now he's really got some clout down there. It'll do wonders for his ego. And God knows he really needs help in that department," Sherri concluded in her most sarcastic tone.

Lina turned her head sideways slightly yet said nothing. She just looked at Sherri with a puzzled expression on her face. A bit surprised at what appeared to be Sherri's overall lack of enthusiasm since she had begun speaking of her husband. She wondered if this was a sign of something being slightly amiss.

Perhaps sensing that Lina was beginning to read into things, Sherri quickly changed the subject.

"All right so what about you Lina; look at you, I still can't believe how great you look. So what was that you mentioned outside about your personal trainer? If that's the reason you look like that you need to send him this way for a few months."

"Oh please Sherri you look great yourself. If I ever have kids, not to mention three, I should be so lucky to look like you afterwards."

"Thanks Lina, but really; what's up? Talk to me."

Lina did indeed look stunning. Dressed in her black form-fitting pants and short-sleeved knit sweater, her attire did justice to every part of her now 5'8" 138 pound frame. Her arms were tanned, taut and toned, her abs perfectly flat, and her more than ample bustline on full display in her sexy scoop neckline. She always had been blessed with a nicely-rounded backside and her new workout regiment only accentuated it more now that she had trimmed a few inches off her waist. Her almost jet-black hair danced around her shoulders in a lovely spiral of curls; the ideal complement to her stunningly beautiful face which also happened to be perfectly made up. Not overdone but simple, understated and just right. She had moved to Florida two years earlier; making the move in the aftermath of the breakup of her engagement to a verbally and physically abusive jerk named Tony Arreondo. Things had gotten to the point where at the time when she finally made the bold move to break free, many of the people close to her (including Sherri) had been somewhat fearful for her safety. So moving so far away was actually good for her in their estimation. Sherri certainly shared that sentiment; though she missed having Lina close by.

"So tell me how life is treating you down there in South Flooreeda," Sherri asked in an exaggerated fashion.

"Oh everything is great right now. I think I've really settled in; finally."

"And work is good?"

"Oh yeah work is fine. Pretty much settled in there also."

Lina was on her 2nd job since having made the move. After working at another law firm she had made the transition to an executive assistant position at a large consulting firm about 7 months ago; something that had also come with a nice bump up in salary.

"Well in addition to looking so good you also look happier also. Hmmm, anything you want to share," Sherri said playfully.

Before Lina could respond, their server arrived at their table. He was a young, Hispanic male, about 5'10" with dark hair and a thin, nicely trimmed mustache and a patch of hair on his chin.

"Good afternoon ladies," he began; my name is Jacob and I'll be your server today. So what can I get you ladies to drink?" he asked after they returned his greeting.

"I'll have just a glass of water with a slice of lemon," Sherri said before the server turned his attention to Lina.

"And you Miss?"

Lina looked at him squarely as she pondered the question. In addition to his dark hair, he had very dark, penetrating eyes. And at that moment those eyes were seemingly trying to penetrate Lina's cleavage his eyes were so focused there. He made no effort to hide it either. Sherri noticed his lips curling into a slight smile yet Lina somehow seemed oblivious to it as she turned away for a second, continuing to ponder the question.

"I'll have a diet coke with a slice of lemon, wait no; make that a white wine spritzer. What the hell I'm on vacation; sort of," she smiled, again looking him in the eye. Too bad he never noticed it with his pupils fixated squarely between her two breasts.

"Yeah sure, why not," he offered before slowly licking his lips. Okay I'll be right back with those drinks," he added before starting to pivot away from the table only to be stopped in his tracks by the voice of Sherri calling out to him.

"Excuse me; Jacob."

"Yes maam," he answered offending Sherri slightly, but not enough for her to speak on it.

"You know what; let me have a glass of your house champagne."

"Okay that's the spirit. No problem, coming right up," Jacob said as he made the correction on his notepad. "I'll be back in a few minutes." He then smiled and stole one more glance at Lina's goodies before departing.

Sherri smiled and shook her head before speaking. "So, where were we? Oh yeah I had just asked you if you had any news of note that you wanted to spill to me."

"I don't know Sherri. Nothing you might find too interesting," Lina responded coyly.

"Try me. Okay for starters why don't you tell me about this new and improved body of yours? Not that you didn't look good before, but now........wow, you look like one of those NFL cheerleaders. You sure you're not shaking your pom poms on the sidelines on Sunday afternoons now?"

"Oh please I don't look that good I don't think. Those girls don't have an ounce of fat on them. I don't think they're allowed to," Lina chuckled. "Believe me that's not me. But thanks for the compliment."

"Trust me Lina, you do look great and I'm not just saying that. Hey if you don't believe me just ask our waiter when he comes back. It's a wonder that his eyes didn't pop out of his head and fall into your cleavage."

" I didn't notice all that," Lina said as she straightened up slightly.

"Really; I mean he was zoning in. But anyway what's the story there?"

"Well, after living down in Florida for a while I just started to feel like I wanted to see if I could get that typical Florida beach body look?"

"Well you've certainly got that and the tan to go with it."

"You think so? I don't know but I'm still trying."

"Oh please Lina," Sherri groaned.

"Seriously; I'm still trying to get there."

"So what's your program like and who did you get it from? Because trust me it is working."

"Well I did some asking around. At work, at the nail salon, at the place where I get my hair styled you name it."

"Oh and your hair and nails look perfect too," Sherri interjected. "But I'm sorry go ahead."

"Thanks. But anyway, I did some researching and came up with nothing that sounded too great, but one day I struck up a conversation with this girl named Anna who I met while shopping at the supermarket. She had this t-shirt on advertising this place called Donte's Fitness Emporium. And girlfriend looked real tight. I mean like a Sports Illustrated swimwear model. So I decided to ask her about the place. Well as it turned out she worked there. So she gave me a business card and suggested I stop in one day. Well I did and it turned out to be this huge store that sold everything from fitness equipment to workout clothes, all types of vitamins and supplements and so on. I mean this store was almost the size of a supermarket itself. But that's not all that surprising because there's just a huge market down there for that sort of thing."

"Oh yeah I would think so," Sherri chimed in.

"Oh trust me its crazy. You wouldn't believe the number of places that cater to diet and fitness, skimpy clothing, tattooing, swimwear you name it. But anyway, this place is owned by this guy; yes his name is Donte; who used to be a football player in the area. He played for Miami University and then out on the West coast for Seattle and Oakland in the NFL before coming back home to start this business after his pro football career was over."

"Wow, you seem to know a lot about his background for someone who I've never known to be that into football or sports in particular for that matter."

Lina just smiled; an all too knowing smile, before continuing on.

"Well I'll get into that in a bit," she said proudly but with some reserve. "So like I said I stopped in one day and as I'm just browsing around I see Anna there. And while we were talking this time, I asked her if she knew anyone she could recommend as a good personal trainer I could work with for a while. Well as it turns out the guy Donte who owns the place is also one of the top personal trainers in the area. I mean he has some fairly high-profile clients but I won't get into any name-dropping. Many of them are just local high school or college athletes trying to get to the next level. But there are a few entertainers and model types also. Now he just has his name and his money behind the store. He stops in there once in a while to check on things, but he really focuses a lot of his time and energy on training. So anyway, Anna gives me his business card and tells me to just give him a call one day and take it from there. So long story short I call him one day, we set up an appointment for a consultation and next thing you know I have a personal trainer. And the cool thing is you might think that with the clientele he has he might be priced out of my reach. But he really wasn't. His opinion was that it made more sense to be reasonable in what he charged in order to be able to draw in business from across the spectrum."

"Makes sense to me. Sound like a guy with a lot of business savvy," Sherri opined.

"Oh yes he has a bunch of that, among his many other outstanding qualities," Lina beamed.

Sherri cut her eyes at Lina and narrowed them into slits. "Why I am getting the feeling that there are certain other things you're not telling me about this guy?"

"Because there are," Lina answered. She then attempted to look away from Sherri while trying to keep a straight face.

"Lina," Sherri said probingly, while Lina looked towards the ceiling. "Lina," she repeated.

"What," replied Lina as she tried unsuccessfully to keep a sly smile off her face.

"You know what; come on spill it. I mean you've hinted at enough already."

Lina looked at her with that innocent looking smile but saw that Sherri was having none of it.

"Okay, okay," she finally relented. Donte became my personal trainer back in March of this year. He became much more than that a few months later."

"Uh huh, see I knew it; I've known you too long not to be able to pick up on that. Well good for you sweetie."

"Thanks Sherri," Lina said with a deep sigh before breaking into another big smile.

"So.....tell me a little about this; is It Donte?"

"Yes it's Donte. Donte Trent Ellison to be exact."

"Donte Ellison," Sherri repeated. "Why does that name sound familiar?" Sherri was a bit more into sports than Lina had always been. "Anyway go ahead."

"Well you already know that he has a football background and a good business sense. But he's also tall, very handsome, obviously in real good shape being a personal trainer and just an overall good person. Very respectful, very sincere and romantic and I just adore him."

Sherri could tell how Lina must feel about Donte by the way she practically gushed as she was speaking about him.

"So is it pretty serious?" she questioned.

"Well I believe it's exclusive. And I can see it working its way towards serious. Donte's been talking that way as of late. In fact that's' the reason I'm flying back tomorrow. So we can bring in the New Year together."

"Mmmmmm it does sound like it's headed that way. That's great Lina; you deserve it after what you went through in the past."

"Thanks honey," replied Lina before the two of them stretched across the table to embrace each other.

"So do you have any pictures of your beau? Wait, what am I asking; of course you do. Come on show and tell time."

"Yes I do have some in my phone," Lina responded before reaching into her purse and retrieving her cell phone. "Okay let's see," she said softly as she toyed with the phone for a bit. "All right here's a good one," she decided before handing the phone over to Sherri. The picture she had chosen to show her was one of her and Donte seated side by side at a restaurant. He had his right arm curled around her waist as she leaned in towards him. It had been taken fairly recently; within the last month actually.

Lina watched very carefully for any reaction from Sherri once she looked at the photo. But she didn't notice one in particular. In fact the first reaction she received from her turned out to be a verbal one.

"Oh you were right, he is very handsome. And you two look so good together. Not to mention very happy. And I'm so happy for you too."

"Thank you Sherri," Lina said appreciatively as Sherri handed the phone back to her. "Mind if I say something?" she asked after a brief period of silence.

"No, go right ahead," Sherri said.

"Okay, well I must say Sherri you are one of the few people from whom I didn't see any immediate visual reaction when they first saw a picture of my boyfriend or met him face to face. I mean some friends or so-called ones and the few family members who have seen him yes; but from you nothing. No wrinkled brow, no stunned expression, eyes bulging out of their sockets. Not a thing. And I appreciate that."

"You mean to tell me that people sometimes react that way when they see Donte?"

"Oh please; like you wouldn't believe."

"But why," Sherri asked plainly.

Before Lina could respond mister subtlety returned to the table with their drinks.

"Okay ladies, here you go," he said as he placed the glasses on the table. He then quickly turned his focus towards Lina. But having been clued in by Sherri, Lina this time cleverly blocked his view by rubbing her left shoulder in a manner that placed her forearm in front of her bustline and then held it there. She even made a point of smiling at him as she read the look of disappointment on his face.

He quickly turned his attention towards Sherri instead. "Are you ladies ready to order?"

"Yes please," Lina answered without him turning to look her way. With that Sherri ordered first. They both got a nice chuckle out of the entire exchange once he left this time.

"Okay, that was cute," started Lina moments later. "But let me get back to your question. Yes you should see the look on some people's faces once they see Donte for the first time."

"All right, well maybe it's just me because I don't see why that happens."

"Come on Sherri it's because of you know; his race."

"Because of him being a part of the human race you mean?"

"No dear, actually it's because of him being Black."

"Get out of here Lina. You mean to tell me this boyfriend of yours is Black!" Sherri said, feigning surprise. Let me see that picture again."

"Stop kidding Sherri, I know you had to notice that?"

"No really I didn't," a now grinning Sherri replied.

With a surprised expression on her face, Lina prepared to hand her phone back to her."

"Stop, stop, stop," Sherri chuckled, pushing Lina's hand holding the phone away. "Sweetie, of course I noticed he's Black. I just wasn't going to make an issue of it because it's a non-issue as far as I'm concerned. You said he's a great guy, he certainly seems like one from what you've told me and I can tell that you're happy. That's all that matters whether he's white, black, blue, green or purple."

"Awwwwwww, see that's why I love you so much," a clearly touched Lina said to Sherri in response before the two of them clasped hands across the table.

"I am so happy for you and I hope it just continues to grow and ends up wherever you two decide to take it. You deserve a ton of happiness after what you went through with Tony."

"Thanks mama, you know I really appreciate that."

"You know I almost got involved with a black guy myself once. Back when I was in school at B.C."

"Really; so what happened?"

"I just got intimidated that's all. It was right around the time I was about to pledge and I was just worried about how it would play amongst the members of the sorority. But you know what was funny. One of the top girls in our on-campus chapter had this habit of really making these vicious bigoted remarks sometimes. Mostly towards Black people which is actually kind of typical of some of the crowd up there at the college. So the funny thing is that I have it on good authority that this same girl took a ride on the choo choo train with about 4 Black guys from the football team during her senior year. Apparently there was a tape of it circulating around campus and everything. Unfortunately I never got to see it though."

"Wow, really; senior year huh. Talk about going out with a bang" Lina quipped before the two of them broke out into laughter.

There was then a prolonged period of silence once the two of them settled down; one which was eventually broken by Sherri.

'So Lina, tell me something."

"Uh huh."

"Is it true?"

"What's that?"

"You know about black men."

"What about them," Lina answered innocently.

"Oh come on; you know what the word is or the perception or the myth or whatever you want to call it."

"No actually I don't."

"Really you've never heard that?"

"Sherri; never heard what?"

"Please Lina, you know; about black men being nicely packaged. You know; down there," Sherri attempted to whisper while looking all around her.

"No actually I've never heard that. I guess I'm just that naive," a now slightly embarrassed Lina replied.

"Okay well is it true?" Sherri pressed while she looked at Lina with inquisitive eyes.

Lina hesitated at first before she finally caught on to where Sherri was going.

"Oh you're asking me about Donte," she said softly. "You know I can't tell you that Sherri."

"Come on now Lina, you can tell me. As far as we go back? If there's anybody you can tell it's me."

"Well that's just it. What if I feel like there is nobody I can or should share something like that with. I mean that's personal."

"Oh please; I'm sure he wouldn't mind. Guys brag about that all the time and most often they're lying about it. But you know what they say. It's not boasting if you can back it up. So can he? I mean is he?"

Lina just looked at Sherri; shaking her head while doing so. But the look on Sherri's face told her that she was still very intent on receiving an answer.

"Oh come on Lina it's not that big a deal; or is it that big a deal?" Sherri said with a lascivious grin.

After another period of silent prodding from Sherri and more hesitation on her part, Lina finally relented.

"All right, all right," she began. Now I can't speak for all black men. In fact I can only speak for mine but yes."

"Yes what?"

"Yes it's big. Actually it's very big, bordering on humungous," Lina said in a hushed tone.

"Well just how big is big?"

"Sherri please, I don't know. I can't put a number on it or anything."

"Well can you give me an idea?"

A seemingly worn down Lina sighed deeply before looking around the restaurant, checking to see if any eyes were fixated on the two of them. Feeling secure enough she then held up the forefingers on her two hands apart at a distance that Sherri estimated to be between 9 and 10 inches. Sherri's eyes immediately grew wide and her mouth fell open slightly. Not finished, Lina then circled a finger around to her thumb in an attempt to show the circumference. As soon as she did so Sherri covered her mouth with her right hand.

"Oh my God Lina; long and thick? No wonder you're glowing so much. I would be too," Sherri chuckled.

"You are still crazy you know that. Anyway I told you so can we talk about something else now?"

"Oh sure we can, but wow. I mean that's all I can say. Wow," she repeated. That was all she said but in her mind Sherri was thinking much more. Like I wonder if there's one of those out there for me someplace. As she squirmed in her chair Lina made her push to change the subject.

"So what are you guys going to do for New Year's Eve?

"But Sherri would have none of it just yet. "Lina, what is it like with one that big? Is it ever too much?"

"Okay, I'll entertain you with this just a bit, but I'm not going to go into any great details about our sex life together. I'm sure you understand."

"Of course I do and neither would I. I'm just a little bit curious that's all."

"All right, well I must say this. It did take some getting used to. I mean I'd been with well-endowed guys before; Tony is pretty well endowed in fact; just nothing like Donte. So like I said it just took some adapting to; but after a while you do just that and it's fine. You know our hardware can adjust to about anything in time," Lina chuckled. "Besides you learn which positions work the best with that type of size. You have to because honestly, yes some are a bit uncomfortable but when you find one that works, then girl; oh my goodness."

Sherri looked on as Lina shook and quivered in her seat as if a small electrical charge was going through her body.

"Uh huh see there, and you call me the crazy one."

"I know, I know, please forgive me. I was just having a moment."

"Well do you need a towel or a cold pitcher of water?"

"No I think I'll be fine; especially when I get back home to my man."

"Yeah but that's just part of the equation, "Sherri said sheepishly. "I'd be concerned about getting lockjaw too. I mean my lord."

"Well on that I'll just say you'd be amazed what you can achieve with a little concentration and a lot of determination."

Truth is, it was Sherri who was starting to feel as if she could use a pitcher of ice water. Her body temperature had started to elevate in response to Lina's words. And she had to swallow a big gulp of saliva.

"Okay now I agree we need to change the subject," she admitted.

"Okay; well again, what are you guys going to do for New Year's Eve?"

"As soon as she absorbed the question Sherri's mind went to what she knew she'd like to be doing at the stroke of midnight on December 31st; taking some long, deep thrusts from a nice hard dick; and certainly one much bigger than the barely over 5 inches her husband had to offer. As she sat there daydreaming of just such an occurrence and thus not answering the question, their lunch arrived. It was delivered by two kitchen hands, who it was obvious from the way they were ogling Lina, had engaged in a little discussion with Jacob before arriving at the table.

Once the two young men departed Sherri was then able to gather herself enough to answer the question. "Okay, as for New Year's Eve, we usually just get together at one of the neighbor's or either some of them come by our place for a few drinks. Something real light and casual and also that doesn't involve being on the road. "What about you two?"

"Well Donte rented a suite down on South Beach for the night. So I think we're just going to have some dinner someplace and then take a little stroll before bringing in the New Year back in the suite with a little of the bubbly."

"Sounds good," said Sherri while she also thought about what Lina hadn't mentioned. That she no doubt would also be getting close to a foot of dick at some point in the night. Her thoughts then turned to Scott. She wondered what he was going to be doing for New Year's.

The two of them then turned silent for a while as they turned their attention to their lunch. Sherri had ordered the herb crusted salmon salad while Lina went with Louisiana chicken pasta. They were both delicious and yet they each managed to save some room for some dessert also. After all having some cheesecake was almost like a requirement when dining at the Cheesecake Factory. They split a slice of the highly decadent red velvet cheesecake savoring every single morsel.

As they departed the restaurant Sherri looked back in the direction of their table just in time to see Jacob and two other guys engaged in some lively conversation as they cleared the table; slapping palms together and everything. There was little doubt in her mind who the topic of discussion must have been from some of the gesturing that was taking place. She wondered if they had to be speaking in Spanish with all of the English speaking patrons at nearby tables. In any event, she just shook it off, turned back towards Lina and headed out of the restaurant. Off to the main event of the day, shopping.

As she was driving home from the mall a few hours later, Sherri decided to place a call to her newest bed buddy.

"Hey how are you?" she asked once Scott answered his cell phone.

"I'm good, just finishing a few things at the office before heading out. How are you doing?"

"I'm doing okay, could always be better though."

"Oh yeah, how so?"

"Well you should know one of the ways it could be better."

"Yeah I kind of think I do and I wish I could help you there."

"Oh believe me so do I. But I've been out with a friend for several hours today so I have to get on home now."

"Oh too bad; I might have had a little something for you."

"Oh you might have huh?"

"Well take that might out of it. I would have."

"Okay well that's more like it, but don't you mean a big something for me?"

"Mmmmm well I'll leave that up to you to judge."

"Oh I made my judgment on that the other day. That's why I made the correction."

"Well I'll certainly take that as a compliment sweetheart."

"You should because it's not one that every man is able to receive. Trust me I know firsthand."

"Well I'm not getting into that," Scott replied with a bit of laughter. But thank you."

"You're welcome, but why don't you thank me in person when we see each other again."

"I'll be sure to do that; profusely."

"And I hope that won't be too long from now," Sherri cooed.

"You and me both," Scott agreed followed by a period of silence which was finally broken by Sherri.

"It's getting close to New Year's Eve, what are you going to be doing with yourself?"

"Well actually I'll be heading down to Atlantic City for the weekend. I'm going to hang out at the Borgata with a couple of buddies. Play some poker, have some drinks, stuff like that."

"Oh okay, that should be fun. Certainly better than what I'll be doing."

"Why what's on your agenda?"

"Trust me nothing exciting; just the usual. Hang out with some friends from the neighborhood, have some drinks and a little champagne and then call it a night. Sounds like a blast right?"

"Yeah well it all depends on what you're into. Not everybody would want to go anywhere near where I'm going to be either."

"Yeah you have a point there," admitted Sherri. "So," she continued after a pause, "I guess there's no chance we can get together before the calendar runs out on 2010 huh?"

"Hmmm, I don't know. I mean there's always a possibility. It depends on your availability and if it lines up with mine of course. It would be nice."

"Yes it certainly would be. I thoroughly enjoyed the last time that's for sure.

"So did I," Scott concurred before more silence. "Well Sherri I have to make a few calls before I finish up today but I'll tell you what; I can toss some things around in my mind and see if I can come up with a way to possibly make that happen. And then I'll reach out to you and see if it might work for you; that sound okay?"

"Yep, just let me know whenever and we'll see. Hopefully we can work something out."

"All right well I'll call you."

"Okay I'll be waiting."

"Cool."

CHAPTER NINE

By Wednesday afternoon it had been firmly established that Lily and her husband Peter would do the honors of hosting the modest gathering for the neighborhood group to bring in the New Year. As always it was to be kids friendly, so there would be no need to go through the difficult task of obtaining a sitter. No one wanted to have their social life seem so lacking to where they had nothing more interesting to do on New Year's Eve than to babysit. At least not anyone that Sherri knew of. Not even for the premium prices a sitter could command for the evening.

When Thursday morning arrived Sherri was somewhat disappointed that she still hadn't heard any word from Scott. Clay had been working from home all week and Abby wasn't due back for several more hours from a sleepover at a friend's house. So with Tyler about to be dropped off at the arcade at 10:00 for a few hours of play with some classmates it was going to be just Sherri and Zach for a while.

"Okay honey I will pick you at 1:00," Sherri once again told Tyler while also reminding the mothers of 2 of his 3 classmate's mothers of her timeline. Trading off on chaperoning whenever they wanted to do this sort of thing was a neat little arrangement that the parent's had worked out. Next time around the responsibility would rotate over to Sherri and the mother of Tyler's friend Ryan.

"Okay Mom," Tyler said politely before reaching his arms out to accept the hug offered up by her. But Sherri knew better than to embarrass him by attempting to kiss him. Although he was not quite eight such a thing still might have been enough to cost him some serious cool points if occurring in front of his friends.

"Now remember I will meet you right over by the exit okay," she repeated.

"Yes I remember Mom, bye see you later."

"Okay and what else did I tell you little smarty pants?"

"That if you're running a little late and not there by 1:00 that I should not wait for you there. That I should go back to where the worker's are and wait for you there."

"That's right don't mix back in with the crowd; very good. Now you have fun; all you guys have fun, Sherri said to all of the boys before loosely hugging Tyler once again before he managed to wiggle his way out of her embrace. Turning to the mom's of Tyler's other two friends Jeff and Eddie who would be doing the chaperoning this time around, Sherri posed a question to them as well.

"So you guys have my home and cell numbers as well as those for Ryan's mom Claire right?"

"Yes we do and don't worry Sherry, if you happen to be running a few minutes late we'll wait with him of course," they answered almost in unison before Sherri thanked them in advance and headed on out the door.

"All right well that's done; I guess it's just the two of us for now Sherri said to Zach as she placed him back in his car seat. As she walked around the back of the car before climbing inside, her thoughts again turned to Scott. As soon as she fastened her seat belt and began to drive off she dialed his cell number.

"Hey," she greeted him once he answered. I just decided to give you a call and see what you're up to today, since I hadn't heard from you."

"Oh I'm sorry babe; it's actually been a bit hectic around here. You know just trying to tie up some things before the long weekend commences. But I've been thinking about you."

"You have," Sherri exclaimed. "That's nice," she continued after a brief pause. "So....... I'm just assuming there's no chance of us seeing each other before the New Year arrives then."

"Hmmm I don't know; maybe. Let me think for a second. Well," he said slowly, while seemingly gathering his thoughts. Sherri could almost feel his mind processing ideas as she heard the sound of him sucking his teeth into the mouthpiece. "Any chance you can swing by my place a little later on? Like 2 to 2:30; before I have to get ready to hit the road for AC."

"About two, two-thirty? I don't know, I'll have my kids possibly coming and going around that time. Well I guess more coming actually. I have to pick up one of them at 1:00, and my oldest will be coming back home from a sleepover sometime this afternoon also. So the bottom line is that timeframe is real iffy for me. I mean my husband is home but I'm not really able to count on him to pick up the slack with the kids so I can run out. And let's see, ………well what time would you be leaving to head down to Atlantic City?"

"I figure about 5 or 6. Gonna try to beat as much of the traffic heading into the city as I can. It can get kind of crazy if it gets too late with everybody trying to go ahead and get settled in their rooms so they can hit the streets later on."

"Oh well," Sherri sighed deeply. It looks like we might not be able to make it happen today. It would have been nice but both of our itineraries are sort of tight it looks like. I mean for me to get the kids all squared away and then head down to Watchung; hmmm, I just don't know. We're talking about a narrow window. But hey that's okay we can take a rain check right?"

"Now Sherri let's not close the door completely just yet. Why don't you give me a little while to think about it and see if I can come up with something, and then I'll call you back."

"Okay good enough. Call me as soon as you have something one way or the other."

After she and Scott hung up from each other, Sherri turned around and took a glance at Zach to see if he had fallen asleep by any chance. He was actually quietly staring out of the side window as the car moved along at a steady pace on the 15 minute drive back to the house. Just as Sherri was pulling into the driveway her cell phone rang. Upon checking she saw that it was Scott calling. Hmmm that was pretty quick, I wonder what if anything he came up with she was thinking before answering.

"Hey what's up," she said upon answering the phone.

"Check it out I might have an idea. Well no might in it I do have a plan; let me just see how you feel about it."

"Okay shoot."

"Well I'm closing the office at noon today and allowing my staff to leave at that time."

"Uh huh," Sherri replied anxiously.

"And so here's what I thought up, let me know what you think?"

"You know I will; what do you have in mind?"

"Hope it's not too crazy an idea but anyway, here goes. Like I said everyone will be getting out of here at 12 noon so; if you want you could come by shortly after that. I mean like 12:15 or so. You could pop on in once they leave, and then maybe we can get a little something going once you got here. What do you think?"

"Do you mean a little afternoon delight in the office?"

"Yeah; at least that's what I'm thinking."

As Sherri hesitated to respond, Scott set out to let her know he understood if she didn't cater to his idea.

"Hey it was just a thought; you don't have to say yes or anything."

"I know but; okay, yeah sure I'm game, why not."

"Say what?"

"I mean I'll come. It sounds good to me."

"For real?" Scott asked excitedly.

"For real, I'm not kidding. It seems like it could be a fun time."

"Okay then great. And with the office being just over from Basking Ridge in Bedminster it won't be that long a drive for you to get here either."

"Oh yeah that's right your office is pretty close," Sherri said cheerfully. You know I like your idea even more now. I will be there. Just let me get the address so I can jot it down."

Before exiting the car Sherri took a glance at her dashboard clock and took note of the time. It was 10:20. She actually had a little time to kill before heading out once again. Once she and Zach were inside, they popped into the office to say hello to Clay. He only had a minute to spend chatting with either of them as he explained that he was in between phone calls, and was in fact awaiting a conference call at any minute. While she didn't care all that much that Clay didn't have much time for them, Sherri did feel for Zach however. Too often it seemed that their youngest child has been pushed to the background by his father. Abby and Tyler being a bit older were of course a bit more capable of shaking off any feelings of disappointment whenever their Dad was not there to share in the joy that often came with the activities they were involved in. But a three year old naturally takes it more to heart. And as much as Sherri attempted to make little Zach understand, she realized that there was only so much she could do to comfort him in those times that he longed for those special moments of bonding with his Dad.

Sherri took Zach into the family room where the two of them watched television and chatted until 11:15, at which time Sherri decided to give him his lunch. In no more than a half hour's time she had managed to have him fed and prepared for his late morning nap. Once he was sound asleep she then took a few minutes to freshen up before slipping into a pair of comfortable jeans and a long-sleeved sweater. It was 11:55 am when she approached Clay in the office this time.

"Hey listen," she began, "Zach is down for his nap. I need to run an errand or two so can you just keep an ear out for him."

She started to repeat herself once he didn't respond back to her, but he quickly cut her off.

"Okay I heard you the first time," he snapped.

"Well since you didn't respond I just assumed you must not have."

"I'm just running through some things in my mind but yes I heard you loud and clear. Go ahead I've got him," he assured Sherri.

"Oh and Abby might possibly be dropped off while I'm out also," she called out as she headed for the door.

"Either unable to make out what she had said or having tuned her out, Clay called out to her just as she was opening the door to exit.

"What's that?"

"Seemingly a bit perturbed, Sherri sighed deeply before stopping dead in her tracks.

"I said Abby could get here before I get back," she said with a hint of frustration.

"Well next time you might want to spit it out clearly instead of mumbling it with your back to me."

"Okay fine Clay, whatever," well I guess you heard me the second time."

"Yeah I heard you the second time but," he started to reply but he never got to finish whatever else it was he was going to say as Sherri slammed the door shut behind her after stepping outside; saying only a brusque "goodbye" before doing so.

Minutes later Sherri arrived at Scott's office. She parked her car in the back of the building as she had been instructed. She then put her dark glasses on before exiting the car and swiftly walking over to the door where she knocked three times in rapid succession.

Scott smiled from ear to ear once he looked through the blinds and saw that it was her. He quickly opened the door to let her in. It was 12:07 as he looked at his watch.

"Hey sorry, I know I might be a bit early. Hope it's not a problem and that I didn't catch you off guard," she said as she stepped inside.

"His only response was a non-verbal one. He grabbed her around the waist the moment he turned to face her after drawing the blinds shut. Pulling her close, he kissed her passionately with one hand caressing her hair while the other rubbed her back before working its way down to her backside.

"It's just that I'm supposed to pick up my son back in Basking Ridge by 1:00 so I don't have a whole lot of time I guess," she managed to blurt out in between kisses.

"Well in that case we'd better not waste any time," he smiled as he pulled off her coat. He took a moment to hang her coat on the coat rack in the corner of his office before returning to where she stood waiting for him. They stepped into another kiss before Sherri aggressively tugged at his belt while running her other hand across his crotch until she rested it on his rapidly swelling penis. Scott responded by exploring her entire upper body with his hands. As their breathing intensified, his hands circled and gently squeezed her breasts as his lips softly kissed the nape of her neck. He briefly placed his hands on her backside, rubbing and squeezing it with a light touch. She helped him in removing her sweater and bra before he attacked her breasts feverishly with his mouth. She ran her hands through his hair as his tongue delicately teased and then licked her hardened nipples. With her head thrown back Sherri moaned out in sheer ecstasy.

"Oooooh," she purred as he worked on them. Her hand again found his dick, squeezing it through his pants and leading to him squirming noticeably. He suddenly reached down and picked her up from the floor, sitting her squarely on the desk. He then stood over her and removed her jeans and panties before taking a seat in his chair and instantly burying his face between her legs. She wiggled her hips as he tore into her, licking her pussy lips and sucking her clit feverishly. Her juices ran onto his face, seemingly spurring him on further. As she bucked wildly on the desk he placed a finger inside of her as he continued to feast on her soaking wet pussy. At the brink of going over the edge she suddenly moved away from him and moved into a seated position on the desk.

"I want some of that dick right now," she whispered between heavy breaths. As she undid his belt he stood before her rapt with anticipation. As soon as she had his pants open she attacked his erection, taking it into her mouth and sucking it with abandon as she kneeled before him. He placed his hands behind her head and pumped himself into her eager mouth. Saliva poured from her lips onto his throbbing penis as she submissively dropped her hands to her sides. She gasped for air each time he removed his dick from her mouth before sliding it back in repeatedly, filling her with delight.

"Wait, hold on a second, I want you to go deeper" she said before she quickly stood up. Clearing his desk of the few things on it she climbed on top it and laid on her back before positioning herself so that her head was hanging slightly over the edge. She did all this so fast that Scott could do nothing but watch in amusement until she lied there looking up at him. Knowing just what to do, he moved in behind her and placed his dick into her waiting mouth. He helped in supporting her head with his hands as he thrust himself into her mouth over and over. He altered the speed of his pumps, at times slowly burying the entire length inside until his balls came to rest against her nose. Sherri loved every moment of it as he toyed with her, at times taking his penis in his hands and moving it around to different areas of her mouth before suddenly allowing it to go deep down her throat once again. Her gasps were in unison with his low groans. As he released her head and played with her breasts her chestnut-colored hair fell almost to the floor, swinging wildly each time his hips pushed his dick into her mouth.

"Look at you, you love this don't you?" he questioned. "You just love it," he repeated.

"Oh yeah I love it. Put it deep in my throat," she managed to reply between rapid breaths. Her face had by then become a sloppy canvas, a mixture of her own saliva and his pre-cum

"Not wanting to cum as of yet, he removed himself from her mouth, moved around her and helped her to feet before leading her over to the front of the desk.

"Come on, I wanna fuck you now," he said to her before reaching into one of the desk drawers for a condom.

"What do you do this frequently or something," she asked with her breasts heaving up and down as she caught her breath in the aftermath of the pulverizing Scott had just given her mouth.

"Nope, it's called just being prepared for anything," was his reply. "Now turn around please."

Sherri instantly bent over the desk, allowing Scott to enter her easily. He began to work his way in and out of her hot hole intently; the sounds of his dick thrashing her soaking wet pussy filling the room, along with the even louder sound of their bodies slapping together repeatedly. He fucked her hard, long and strong leading to her having a body-rocking orgasm from the incessant pounding. As he continued on, her body jerked noticeably as the explosion of ecstasy shook her to her core. Not quite done with her he guided her down to the floor onto all fours. Climbing over her he placed his feet at her sides and straddling her, used the leverage to penetrate her even more deeply. She folded her arms in front of her before resting her shoulders on them with her head tilted to the side. With her ass pointed up at him, he drilled her eagerly, throwing his arms around like a rodeo cowboy before pressing them into the small of her back. He continued until she climaxed once again, her hips thrusting back at him as he pounded away at her hungry pussy.

"Hey, she struggled to call out to him. "Do you remember something I said to you in jest a while back?"

"Which time was that?" he answered quizzically as he ran the back of his forearm across his suddenly heavily perspiring forehead, trying to catch the sweat before it began to fall down onto her back.

"You know about you cumming somewhere in particular," she groaned.

"Yeah sure I recall that, but is this the proper time to worry about that sort of thing?"

"I don't think you're getting what I'm saying."

"As a sexually mature woman Sherri has a knack for pretty much knowing when a man was about to cum. His dick begins to feel different inside of her, swelling to its maximum size just before spilling over," she had discovered over the years.

"Just think about that conversation we had one day before that first time," she explained before also feeling a few beads of perspiration starting to appear on her brow. A few minutes later she sensed his moment and then stated her desire.

"Cum in my mouth baby; can you do that for me?"

"Okay, now I've got you, and you bet your sweet ass I'll do just that," he murmured before pulling out of her and quickly sliding off the condom. She turned over in a hurry, sitting in front of him as he his slid his hand up and down his penis. His legs quivered and his entire torso rocked as his climax built, ending with a rush of warm fluid exploding directly into her wide open mouth. Sherri puckered her lips as the cum ran from them and dripped down to her chin. "Mmmm," she said softly as she licked her lips. "This is so good," she added as she used a finger to wipe some away before placing it into her mouth. As Scott collapsed into his chair in a heap, she fell to the floor guffawing, leading to a similar response from him as he too slid down to the carpeted floor before slowly crawling over to her. As they sat there relishing the aftermath of what had just happened, they began to chat while she huddled in his arms comfortably. Several minutes into their talk Sherri thought she heard a faint sound; once and then again. She soon recognized the sound as that of her cell phone vibrating inside her purse. At first hesitant to react to it, she moved quickly once something eventually dawned on her.

"Oh shit, what time is it?" she yelled as she leapt to her feet. Looking around for a clock, she found one on the wall to the left. "Oh my God it's 1:10. That was probably one of the other parents calling about my son Tyler," she said as she rushed over to her purse before reaching inside for the phone. A quick check of her call log confirmed just that. She had gotten caught up in the stolen moments and lost track of the time. "Quick, I need to get to a bathroom to freshen up," she said in a slightly panicked voice.

"There's one outside in the hall just to the left once you go out the door."

She scrambled to her feet and threw her clothes on before reaching inside of her pocketbook for what she's began to call her emergency kit. It was actually just a bag containing a toothbrush and toothpaste, a small bottle of mouthwash and a little pack of wipes.

"I'll be right back," she said before dashing towards the door.

"Okay and don't worry about running into anyone out there. None of the building's other occupants were even here today."

"All right thanks. I won't be long." Before she could depart however she turned back to face him. "You know something; I may as well reapply my makeup while I'm in there too. That way I won't have to do it in the car."

"Makes sense to me. The last thing that's needed is another woman trying to put on makeup and drive at the same time," Scott joked.

"Oh be quiet. I'll have you know that most of us are more than capable of that sort of multi—tasking when needed," Sherri responded as she retrieved her purse.

"Okay whatever you say."

"Glad you see it my way. All right, now this time I'll really be right back," she said before half running out the door.

Scott watched her as she rushed past him, smiling at the thought of what had just happened; her being naked and him completely having his way with her.

A few minutes into her time in the ladies room Sherri decided that she'd better call about Tyler. She phoned back the number of the person who had called her, which turned out to be Tyler's friend Jeff's mom Laura. The lie that she used to excuse herself was that she had to stop and get gas on the way."I guess everyone must be filling up before heading out tonight because the pumps are lined up three or four deep at each one. I can't believe it. I'm so sorry.

"That's okay", Laura replied in a pleasant tone. "Everyone probably figures all the stations might be closing early also. We just wanted to make sure everything was okay."

"Yeah I still could have called earlier and let you guys know what was going on. But I should be there shortly. I'm next in line, so unless I run into traffic I won't be long."

"Well like I said its okay and Tyler is fine. We'll just see you when you get here."

"All right and thanks again Laura," Sherri replied wistfully.

"No problem, bye-bye."

"Bye."

And that was that. You've got to love these carefree suburban housewives, Sherri thought as she went back to the task at hand. Nothing seems to upset some of them.

By the time Sherri was ready to bid goodbye to Scott it was nearly 1:25. He had also fully dressed by that time.

"Wow you look just as stunning as you did when you first walked in here," he exclaimed when she returned.

"You mean before you wrecked my face with that loaded weapon between your legs," she smiled.

"Yes I guess so, but it's not like you didn't ask for it."

"You've got that right and I can't wait to ask for and receive it again."

"And believe me you wouldn't have to ask twice," Scott said before wrapping his arms around her waist.

Sherri locked her eyes on his.

"You promise?"

"Oh I can do more than promise. I can guarantee you that," he answered while his hands rested squarely on her ass.

"Let me get out of here before they have to call me again," she said as he squeezed her buttocks gently. "I could be here until 3:00 messing with you."

"You sure could if I also didn't have someplace to go."

"Oh yeah that's right. Well until we meet again, bye," she said teasingly.

Their lips touched softly before she brushed past him, running her right hand across his dick on the way."

"Look at you. You are so bad."

"That's because you are so good," she called back to him.

He sighed deeply as she looked back at him and smiled one last time before placing her sunglasses over her eyes. And just like that she was out the door.

The rest of the day was pretty status quo for Sherri. She returned home with Tyler about 2:00 after stopping briefly at the local pharmacy to pick up something. She at least wanted to give the appearance that she was really out running some errands, just in case Clay happened to see her coming in. Abby was dropped off a short time later, telling anyone who would listen how she had been allowed to help prepare breakfast that morning. Sherri's only thought as her daughter proudly told of being a part of making pancakes and scrambled eggs was that she couldn't wait until Abby would be ready and willing to perform the same tasks at home.

At about 10:30 the entire family headed across the street to the Chiang's for the night's celebration. Peter and Lily had prepared a spread of both American and Chinese dishes and it wasn't long before everyone had their fill of the delicious fare. Sherri particularly loved Lily's homemade spring rolls. She also made generous use of the punchbowl which was filled with Peter's special recipe. She drank to the point of feeling more than slightly tipsy as it neared midnight. As the New Year arrived there was the standard champagne toast and even the obligatory kiss between her and Clay. Sherri didn't know if it was the effect of the deliciously sneaky punch that she'd had before midnight but she thoroughly enjoyed the kiss and allowed it to linger for several seconds.

Who knows, she was thinking, tonight might even be a lucky night for him and her. That was if he felt like getting lucky; certainly no given there. She hoped so because in spite of what had taken place with Scott just hours earlier she felt herself getting horny all over again.

After concluding the kiss with her husband, Sherri then shared New Year's greetings with her children as well as several other persons in attendance at the gathering. That was when she found out that it had to be the effects of the alcohol because she even felt a little tingle between her legs when she shared a firm hug with the 22 year old son of another neighbor. A kid named Darren Asbury whom she had watched grow up from his early teens. And grown up he had indeed, as he was now a strapping 6 foot 4.

Later that morning about 2:30 a.m. Sherri did manage to wrangle a round of what was for once, more than just straightforward sex out of Clay once the kids were asleep. He must have been feeling slightly intoxicated himself she figured. But rather than focusing on the issue of their infrequent lovemaking at that point, she decided she'd be better served by not looking a gift horse in the mouth so to speak. So she just went with it and enjoyed it for what it was worth. A chance to feed her hunger for giving head and actually even receiving some in return for one of the rare occasions. Although no amount of prodding was enough to convince Clay that just a couple of minutes down there was enough to give her an orgasm. He blew her off by arguing that it was late and he was getting sleepy. So of course when all was said and done she was left wanting her own orgasm after Clay had his while making love to her; in the missionary position as usual. Oh where is Scott when I need him, she was thinking as she lay there staring at the ceiling afterwards, her husband already sound asleep by her side. But not before he had made some comments to the effect of him really going to town on her. As she listened to that she chuckled on the inside but kept it right there; not wanting to deflate the only big thing Clay had; that being his ego.

Monday arrived and with it Clay's big day also. The swearing in ceremony was set for 10 am on the steps of the Somerset County Courthouse. The weather Gods had certainly cooperated, for although it was a very chilly morning as you might expect for early January in New Jersey, there wasn't a cloud in the sky. After spending a great deal of time watching football on New Year's Day, Clay had devoted much of his waking hours Saturday and Sunday to preparing the remarks he would give after he took the oath of office.

The itinerary was that the family would be picked up by a limo at 8:30; whisked away to a breakfast with several local dignitaries and their families, and then make the trip over to the courthouse. Abby and Tyler were quite excited for their first ever ride in a limo, and the fact that they'd be missing the first day of school after the holiday recess didn't bother them too much either. As for little Zach, he couldn't care less about either of those two things. All he knew was that his mommy had told him that it was a very big and important day for his daddy so he was merely pleased with that.

The biggest challenge that Sherri faced that morning was getting all the kids up, alert and then them as well as herself suitably dressed for the occasion. But she pulled it off quite nicely and was all dressed in her royal blue Oscar de la Renta dress with matching shoes by 8:20. The limousine driver was very prompt and off they went ten minutes later. The breakfast was at the ritzy Somerset Hills Country Club where they dined on an assortment of fruits, fresh juices, Belgian waffles, Canadian bacon, salmon cakes, almond croissants and omelets made to order. And of course they also had a selection of cereals for the kids.

The swearing-in ceremony was from Sherri's perspective, thankfully fairly short with just some brief words by the county executive and then Governor-elect Christian who in turn introduced Clay. Sherri had to admit that he looked very handsome as he took to the podium in his crisp, navy blue suit. The podium was also ringed by several mayors and chiefs of police from towns within the county. And she played the part of the good wife by smiling throughout as she stood there holding the bible on which he took his oath of office, surrounded also by their three children.

Clay too kept his remarks relatively brief at just under 15 minutes. But in those 15 minutes he did manage to stir up a modicum of controversy. Some; most particularly the mayors of both Somerset Township and New Brunswick objected to what they saw as Clay laying blame for the bulk of the criminal activity in Somerset county on the citizens of their largely minority communities. This was after Clay in his speech stated that he would be focusing most of his crime fighting efforts towards those two areas. One quote in particular raised the ire of many. That was when he said "that to the citizens of Somerset who live on the wrong side of the law I would like to say no more soiling the reputation that the rest of our fine upstanding residents have given our county through our hard work and values. And to those of you from New Brunswick who seek to overrun our streets with your poison and have your immoral and indecent conduct affect the quality of life of our citizenry, I also say no more. We will hunt you down and lock you away."

The press took little time in seizing upon the comments to make headlines locally. They noted that several local African-American and Hispanic community leaders had taken umbrage with the comments. Some had even gone so far as to label the comments as racial fear-mongering. Of course when asked if he agreed with this opinion Clay seemed indignant. When asked the next day why it seems that his remarks singled out people from Somerset Township and New Brunswick, Clay's retort was, "that he was only referring to the "ones who seek to perpetrate crime not the decent ones." When pressed further by being asked point blank if he was saying that those two areas were largely responsible for breeding most of the crime that affects Somerset County, Clay was succinct in his reply, stating…"well you can be sure that not too many people from other parts of Somerset County are out there robbing and stealing and dealing." That of course did nothing to stem the tide of controversy, but Clay was undeterred. In fact that evening he confided his true feelings about the whole tempest to Sherri.

"So do you see that already the loudmouth Leroy's and Jose's," as he tended to refer to Blacks and Hispanics on occasion, "are upset with me. I guess I struck a nerve. Well you know what they say. The truth hurts. But you know what; the bottom line is this. If they toe the line—fine. But if they step out of that line I will bust their asses faster than they can say It's hell up in Harlem," he said in a mocking voice, before chuckling at his own idea of humor. Actually it was more than that. More like a big, deep belly laugh that left Sherri a bit sickened. Sure she knew of his deep-seated racism for years and generally overlooked it; simply chalking it up to a personal flaw that every human being possesses. But it did bother her more now that he was in such an authoritative position.

CHAPTER TEN

Sherri and Scott's sordid affair only intensified over the course of the next couple of months; yet she always took measures to insure that it wasn't going to go beyond the point of mere physical gratification with no emotional attachment. There was of course no seeing each other than when they wanted to do the old bump and grind. And when they were together extended kissing and any other non-sexual affection such as prolonged cuddling or even holding hands was very limited. In fact they didn't even talk all that often except when they wanted to arrange their next time together. This was her call and of course Scott didn't need much prodding to agree to it. After all he was living a lot of men's dream. Regular, adventurous sex with a beautiful woman with no strings attached, no commitments and no financial burden of any sort placed upon him. No dinners, movies or any other type of dating included. Basically none of the time, hard work and effort required to build and maintain a relationship. Not when the mutual desire was for nothing more than simple, hardcore sex.

Sherri even enlisted Beth's help to make it possible for her to get together with her lover regularly. She asked if she could keep Zach for a couple of days out of the week because she had signed on for some volunteer work at a local senior center. But of course the only thing Sherri was really volunteering to do was whatever freaky, outlandish things she and Scott could come up with. Her well thought out alibi did however require that she play it out even on those days that she was unable to see Scott due to mother nature or another commitment for either of them. But other than that the two of them would get together every Monday and Thursday from 10 in the morning until 2 p.m. Their trysts generally occurred at his place but on a couple of occasions Scott got them a room at a nice hotel. And it had to be him because Sherri took great care to make certain that her name wouldn't be attached to any statements or receipts that could possibly come back to haunt her by uncovering her dirty little secret.

But sure enough Clay was in the dark about all of it. There were even times when Sherri decided it was worth the risk to get a little more daring. Like on the nights she slipped out after dinner and the evening chores were complete for a little nightcap with Scott. This most often took the form of her going out under the guise of needing something from the market and would end with them having raw, uninhibited sex right in his car after they rendezvoused someplace under the cover of darkness. She recalls it with a smile now, but remembers being petrified of getting caught at least one time. That was when they went at it in the backseat of his car while it was parked behind the local K-Mart store well after it closing. She thought long and hard about not agreeing to such a thing before she eventually gave in to his desires to as he said; take a walk on the wild side. That was all well and good as far as she was concerned yet; she was more than a little concerned over what the fallout would be if the wife of the county's head Prosecutor were to get caught engaging in oral sex or getting fucked in the backseat of a car by a man who was certainly not her husband. But, while she was initially hesitant she as always gave in to her own carnal cravings and they would tear into each other like a couple of sex-starved kids some twenty years younger.

At the same time it did seem that Clay was putting a bit more effort into at least connecting with her. Still, she had been unable to communicate to him that while making love was nice and sweet and tender and all those things, there were other times when her being a mother as well as the wife of an up and coming public official aside, she simply lusted for hot, slutty sex. But she struggled internally with the idea of how you even go about telling your husband such a thing. So she continued to fill that need elsewhere. Yet as much as Sherri relished her interludes with Scott there were still times that she felt desires for more. For new and different experiences; as if there were so much that she hadn't yet tried but longed to. As much as she fought against these feelings, they at times simply overwhelmed her, distracted and even frightened her. One thing they did not do is lessen her determination to fulfill them. She was once again about to become a woman on a mission.

It was early March and while the entire Northeast had been in the throes of a very cold and inclement winter, there had actually been some fairly mild days as of late. Temperatures had reached the mid to upper 50's for the last few days. On this particular day Sherri was returning home after dropping Zach off at Beth's and then picking up some things from the supermarket. It was a Thursday yet Scott would not be able to accommodate her on this day. He was home with his sick daughter so that his ex-wife who had stayed home with her the previous two days could go to work. But as usual she had to follow through with the charade in order to keep up appearances. As she pulled the car into the driveway Sherri caught a glimpse of Darren, the young man from next door. He was in the driveway taking advantage of the relatively mild temperatures by finishing up a quick washing of his car. Sherri paused to look at him for several seconds before exiting the car.

"Well it's a good day for something like that," she called out to him.

"Oh good morning Mrs. King," he replied as he turned towards her. Yes it's a very nice morning so I decided to take advantage of it. They say it might even reach 60 today.

"Well you're better than me. I still only take mine to the car wash when I want to get it washed or detailed," Sherri said drawing a polite smile from Darren.

She then walked to the back of her BMW and opened the trunk before lifting a couple of bags out.

"You need a hand with those Mrs. King?"

"Sure thanks, that's very nice of you Darren."

He took the two bags from her hand as well as a third leaving her with but one light bag to carry inside. Once she opened the door he followed her inside to the kitchen where they placed the bags down on the table. "Well thanks again Darren," she repeated as they headed back towards the door.

"You're welcome Mrs. King, don't mention it."

"So what are you doing with yourself these days Darren?"

Sherri knew that he had graduated from Rutgers in December because they had gotten an announcement from his parents in the mail.

"Well right now I'm just taking a little time off, but I'm going to be going down to Emory in Atlanta for Med School starting in August."

Darren had stopped in the foyer and turned to face Sherri as they chatted. He was dressed in a scarlet Rutgers sweatshirt and a pair of black sweatpants with a black cap adorned with the school's block R logo. As he stood there towering over her the conversation continued.

"Emory; wow, that's a great school. I know its years down the line but any idea what type of medicine you'd like to specialize in?"

"I'm not 100% sure but I'm thinking it might be obstetrics and gynecology."

"Oh okay, you mean follow in the footsteps of your Dad." His father Hale was a highly regarded ob-gyn with an office in Bridgewater.

"Yes I guess so," he grinned.

"Well I'm sure you'll make him proud."

"Thanks, I hope I might one day."

Sherri paused briefly to look him directly in his hazel eyes; holding the stare until he turned away.

"All right, well let me go so I can finish up with the car. Have a good day Mrs. King."

But rather than letting it end right there Sherri sought to keep the conversation going.

"Well you certainly look just like your father too. And I can't believe that you were once this scrawny little 12 or 13 year old kid when I first met you. I mean look at you now; so tall and handsome and all filled out. You're a man now that's for sure.

Darren stood there taking in her words while trying not to look at her. When she did catch his glance he quickly cast his eyes downward. Okay well, I'll see you around," he said nervously as he reached for the doorknob.

She stopped him by reaching around his body and placing her right hand on top of his.

"Wait a minute Darren, you are all man aren't you?" she whispered. She guided his body around until he again faced her with his back up against the door. As he looked past her in an attempt to avoid eye contact she inched even closer to him. Placing her hands against his chest she began to slowly run them over his upper body, particularly his arms, shoulders and chest. "Oh I think you are all man Darren, but I'm not completely sure yet. So let me find out won't you." With that she placed both of her hands down to the front of his pants, probing all around his crotch area.

"Mmmmmm just as I thought, you are all man and becoming more and more manly by the second. I've felt that way in my mind for a while and now I feel it for sure in my hands."

Darren stood there quietly as she fondled him, his member growing ever larger from her touch.

"Let me see it," she purred as she began to slowly slide his sweatpants down his waist until they stopped mid-thigh. Smiling seductively she took his dick in her hand and began stroking it up and down slowly. Seconds later she inched her way down his body until she was at the desired level. Looking up at him she opened her mouth and slowly slid out her tongue until it made contact with his tip. As much as he in his mind had wanted to move, to get out of there, he found himself frozen in that spot. As he looked down at her all he could see were her lips slowly wrapping themselves around his now fully erect penis. When she firmly sucked on the head for the first time, his body shook from head to toe. And then it was like he suddenly snapped out of whatever trance he had fallen into. Pulling back he placed his hands on her shoulders and pushed her so hard that she fell backwards onto the floor as his dick slid from between her lips.

"Wait no, you can't do this! We can't do this!" He quickly pulled his pants back up, opened the door and hurriedly made his way outside.

Sherri could only sit there on the floor; at once both stunned and embarrassed. It's one thing to be rejected, but to have it happen at that point in time only served to add insult to injury. She slowly dragged herself off the floor and made her way over to the big picture window in the living room. From there she saw no sign of Darren and figured he must have practically run back to his house and made his way inside. She would occasionally see him in passing over the course of the next few weeks, and noticed that he was now going out of his way to avoid any eye contact with her. Oddly enough she had no concerns over whether he had told anyone what had transpired that day. She figured that he would be in no hurry to tell his circle of peers what had happened due simply to the fact that he, for whatever reason literally ran away from her and what could have been. And that was something that would probably make him more the butt of jokes than seemingly a young man of honor. But he was about to find out just how determined Sherri could be when she wanted something or in this case someone.

At the beginning of April, Sherri snuck over to the Asbury's driveway one night and placed a short handwritten note under one of the windshield wipers on Darren's car. She made certain to seal it completely inside of an envelope to lessen the chance that one of his parents would read it if they happened to retrieve it before he could. As it turned out that did not happen and the next morning he noticed it from inside the house and proceeded outside and grabbed it off the car. It was a plain white envelope that had been placed face down so that he couldn't see his name written on it until he grabbed it and turned it over. He opened it as he made his way back towards the front door of the house, pausing in front of it to read it.

"Hello Darren; guess who? Now I believe you could probably make a very good ob-gyn one day except for one thing. How are you going to pull it off if you're afraid of a little pussy? But if you're not you can still show me as much. Anytime you're ready; just once and done. Not a soul to be any the wiser." He immediately balled up the sheet of paper and placed it his pants pocket. He of course knew right away who had written it. He slowly turned and looked in the direction of the neighboring house where he saw Sherri's BMW parked in the driveway, before continuing back inside. It was a few days later when they just so happened to be leaving their respective houses at the same time; Sherri to check the mailbox and Darren on the way to the gym to get in a workout. But this time was a little different because their eyes immediately locked onto each other's. Only on this occasion Darren did not shy away. Instead he returned the stare until it was actually Sherri who broke it as she continued down the walkway leading to the mailbox. By the time she had retrieved the mail Darren was already seated inside his car. Sherri was walking slowly back towards the house, her head down as she looked over the mail when she heard him call out to her.

"Mrs. King; Mrs. King, do you have a minute?"

"Oh hello Darren, how have you been? I haven't seen you around much lately," she said coyly.

"I've been fine Mrs. King." There was a pause as they stood there just looking away from each other for a few moments before he decided to speak up again. "Listen I uh, you know, I got your little note," he said nervously.

"Oh you did," Sherri replied before folding her arms across her chest. "So what did you think of it?"

"Well I know what you've been thinking, but it's not really like that." He grew more relaxed the more that he spoke. "It's just that I've known you since I was a little boy as just Mrs. King. I mean you and your husband; I mean Mr. King. And to go from looking at you as the lady next door to you know...."

"But that's just it Darren. I'm still the lady next door; I'm still Mrs. King and all that. But you're not that little boy any more. I mean look at you, you're a big, grown-up, young man now. I mean really big as I recall," she chuckled. "And you're certainly young and probably strong to boot. And I've been noticing that for a while now; definitely for the last few months. So I've been wondering what it would be like to be with someone like you. But who knows if you even find me attractive," she concluded before locking her eyes onto his once again. "Do you Darren?"

"Oh I do Mrs. King I most certainly do, but there's more to it than that. I've been dating Dawn Ricciardi from down the block for a while now. About 6 months now in fact."

"Oh really; I know Dawn. In fact she did a fair amount of babysitting for me while she was home for semester break over the holidays. She's a sweet, sweet girl; good for you Darren. But---It can't be that serious. First of all what is Dawn 19?"

"Actually she's 20 now," Darren answered.

"Okay, so she's 20 you're 22 and she's still at Rutgers for another year or two while you'll be heading South in the fall. But anyway it's not like any of that matters Darren. Like I said this would just be a one-time adventure. Maybe a little fantasy fulfillment for both of us wouldn't you say?"

Darren did not respond but instead stood there biting his lower lip.

"All right Darren, I don't know where your head is at right now in terms of this happening or not, but I'm willing to make it real easy for you. I know that your dad is at his office and your Mom at the hospital." Darren's mom works as a critical care nurse at Overlook Hospital in Summit. "And the only one here with me is my youngest Zach. It's about noon now and when I head back inside I'm going to give him his lunch and then put him down for his nap around 1:00. By 1:30 he should be deep into sleep for sure. So why don't you do this, that is if you want to of course. Come to the back of our house and tap on the sliding glass door. I'll be right there in the family room waiting to let you in. That's it, pretty simple and straightforward, so hopefully you'll decide to take me up on what I'm offering you this time."

With that Sherri continued inside the house, looking in Darren's direction before closing the door behind her. He still hadn't muttered a word in a while but simply climbed back into his car and headed off to the gym.

By a few minutes after 1:00 Zach was already asleep just as Sherri had stated he would be. At that time Sherri hopped in the shower, feeling quite confident that she would soon have every reason to be as clean and fresh as could be. A short time later she emerged from the bathroom and wearing nothing but a robe, made herself comfortable on the sofa in the family room. A glance at the clock told her that it was 1:17. As the minutes slowly ticked away she tried to avoid peering up at the clock every few minutes. 1:30 would be here soon enough and the answer to the question of whether her little ploy had been successful would be apparent.

It was 1:45 when Sherri started to figure she may as well get up and find something else to do. Maybe make a phone call while she waited for Zach to awaken from his nap. She hadn't talked to Lina more than once since she saw her over the holidays. Maybe she could catch her at work. She stood to head upstairs but then decided what the hell I'll give it a few more minutes.

"Okay then," she sighed a short time later, "I guess this wasn't meant to be. Well it's his loss right?" She had reached the top of the short steps leading out of the sunken room when she stopped in her tracks. A light tapping on the sliding door leading out to the patio had grabbed her attention. She quickly turned and glided down the steps and over to the door. The clock read 1:50. An ear to ear smile instantly appeared on her face once she peered outside. Wasting no time she quickly unlocked the door.

"Hey come on in," she said softly. As she let him past her she took a quick look around outside where she could see nothing but the trees ringing the edge of the acre of land in the back of the spacious home. Satisfied that she saw no one or more importantly that no one saw her visitor entering, she slid the curtain closed.

"I had just about given up on you," she said once she turned to face him. A quick look at Darren allowed her to take notice that he was wearing the same sweatshirt, sweat pants and cap that he'd been sporting the day she made an unsuccessful pass at him last month. Talk about your irony," she was thinking.

"I'm sorry. I know it's quite a bit past 1:30 but hopefully not too late."

"Well Zach should be asleep until at least 3:00 and the other two don't get out of school until 2:55 and still have to catch the school bus after that."

"Cool, then I guess I'm not too late then."

"You are later than I expected but trust me you're still right on time."

"Oh yeah, am I?"

"Yes you are," Sherri said in a throaty voice while slowly sauntering over to him. "You look very comfortable," she told him once she stood right in front of him. She placed her hands on the front of his sweatshirt before slowly moving them down to where she could begin to slide the shirt up and over his head. After tossing the shirt aside she stood there admiring his well-defined upper body.

A former three sport athlete at the township high school, Darren packed 220 muscular pounds onto his 6'4" frame. Sherri ran her hands across his shoulders, upper arms and chest before slowly circling her tongue around both of his nipples. Backing away from him she lowered herself onto the sofa and opened the silk robe she wore, exposing her body to him for the first time. He followed after her, kneeling on the carpeted floor in front of her. He then hungrily sucked on her breasts for several minutes before burying his face between her legs. Sherri had no idea how sexually experienced Darren was, but it certainly seemed to her that he knew his way around a pussy. He ate her like a seasoned veteran; so well in fact that she came in a relatively short time; thrusting her hips wildly as he lashed away at her with his tongue. After coming down from her feelings of ecstasy, she guided him onto the sofa where she removed his pants and proceeded to kneel between his legs and take his more than adequately sized dick into her mouth. Sherri's impression was that his penis had now surpassed Scott's as the largest she had yet seen. She sucked him in that position for a few minutes before she decided that she wanted him standing. Once Darren was in the position she desired, Sherri took a seat on the sofa, leaned forward and again took him in. At that point she began to really do a number on him. Placing both of her hands on his backside she pushed him forward in order to drive his dick further into her mouth. She braced herself with her hands on the sofa as he began to rock his hips back and forth at her request. She gasped deeply in an effort to suck him like she was certain no other girl had before. Sherri knew this would be enough to take him over the edge if it continued much longer, so before he could cum she stood and walked over to the arm of the sofa where she bent herself over it.

"Come on, get a condom on and fuck me with that big, young, hard dick. Give it to me right now." Being the highly intelligent future Doctor that he was, Darren was quick to oblige. One thing that was certain to Sherri by now was that Darren was indeed all man. Once inside of her, he literally drove that point home even further as he pounded away at her pussy until she let loose with a couple of explosive orgasms. After the final one, and as he continued to drill his way deep inside of her, Sherri started to ponder whether she wanted to taste his cum. Before she could decide he provided the answer for her as he removed the condom and unleashed himself all over her lower back, leaving her with only the remnants to suck out of him as best she could. Once she had drained him completely, Darren collapsed on the floor in a heap, grinning from ear to ear. As she reached over and begin to gently tug on his still semi-hard member Sherri looked up at the clock.

"Okay sweetie, you have to go," she said calmly but matter-of factly. "But my Lord; you apparently had a very good teacher at some point." Darren said nothing but smiled politely as he quickly got dressed and prepared to creep back to his home next door.

"Well I guess I should say thank you," he said on his way to the door.

"Okay that's fine as long as you allow me to say the same. Thank you Darren, and remember this is our little secret."

"Yes of course; our dirty little secret. Anyway, I'll see you around; goodbye Mrs. King."

"Goodbye Darren."

Once he departed Sherri spent a few moments mulling over things. She figured that there was little chance that he wouldn't tell at least some of his friends. She doesn't believe there's any young man his age that wouldn't want to beat on his chest at least a little bit about having bagged a so-called cougar. So she pinned her hopes on the thought that Darren might at least want to keep it away from their local area with Dawn living so close by. In any event, it was now 2:50 and Sherri quickly got to work. She wiped down the sofa and sprayed the room with a generous amount of air deodorizer. This has been a hell of a Friday she was thinking as she did so. No this has been a hell of a Thursday and Friday she corrected herself as she looked back on yesterday's usual Thursday morning romp with Scott as well. She had truly spent the last 48 hours in penis heaven. Yet it wouldn't be long before her desires would lead her on another wild ride; a journey to a place previously unexplored by her.

CHAPTER ELEVEN

Life continued on with what had by now become a familiar pattern for Sherri. Juggling her responsibilities as a mother and housewife, while also gladly remaining the sexual plaything of another man. And if she were being honest, she would admit that it was the latter which she derived the most joy from. That is besides the satisfaction she got from being the best Mom she could be. As mid-April rolled around so too would Sherri's milestone 40th birthday. She didn't mind it all though as she felt she was a good place in her life. She had three wonderful children; financial security, one man who provides her with stability, albeit without much in the way of passion, and another man in her life who gives her that needed fire and passion, but without the complications of love. You might say she had the best of both worlds. Yet sometimes it still felt to her as if that just wasn't enough. That though her heart and mind were filled with contentment, she constantly felt the burning desires for something more; for new experiences, for more fantasies to be fulfilled. And as much as a part of her may have wanted to slam on the brakes and stop right where she was, she could not deny those urges. So she soon found herself back in the fast lane; speeding along in search of her next adventure. On another journey of discovery on which she would ultimately reveal more of herself than she'd ever imagined even existed.

Just as they had done on Clay's birthday a month before, the family enjoyed a quiet dinner out at a restaurant followed up with a birthday cake back at the house to celebrate Sherri's special day. And although it was neither Monday nor Thursday, Scott had also provided her with his own outstanding gift earlier. That morning he had taken her to a small, secluded inn in rural Hunterdon County where they had engaged in wild, uninhibited sex for hours. That pretty much sent her into a state of euphoria that would last throughout the day. A mood that not even the lack of any special attention or affection from Clay could spoil. All that really succeeded in doing on this evening was sending her in search of an outlet with which to share the effervescent spirit that was still flowing through her once night had settled in. And that quest would again lead her to the vast wonderland which is the World Wide Web.

It was just past midnight, and Sherri was sitting at the computer just doing some routine surfing when feelings of curiosity began to crash over her like waves at high tide. She had spoken to Lina earlier that day when she called to wish her a happy birthday. As they chatted for a while Sherri was reminded of the feeling of excitement that had surged through her body when Lina had told her about the amazing anatomical gift that her boyfriend was blessed with. With her mind drifting back to visions of such a thing, she again started to wonder how it must feel to be made love to by such a man. Or rather to be soundly fucked by one. She sat there staring aimlessly into space for several seconds. When she snapped out of it she jumped up from the chair walked into the master bedroom and headed over to the night stand where she immediately started rummaging through the desk's right side drawer. She made sure to be as quiet as she could since Clay was sleeping just a few feet away. Once she found what she was in search of she quietly returned to the office.

As she placed the large yellow post-it note in front of her on the desk Sherri thought back to some words that were said to her by Miguel months ago. That one of the sites largely catered to people who were married or otherwise involved. Sounds perfect, she said to herself as she placed her hands on the keyboard and began to type in the address bar. She took her time in order to make sure that she correctly typed www.redhot2trot.com. As soon as the page loaded she jumped right in with both feet. Her first impressions were that she found it very similar to asudesire in that it featured members with rather imaginative and often humorous screen names. One other thing was that she was limited in just how much she could view as a guest, so she decided right then and there that she was going to change that. A site like this was tailor made for her she figured. After all she damn sure was redhot2trot. And as soon as she woke up the next morning she was going to let the male members know just how much so.

∞∞∞∞∞∞∞∞∞

Clay was off to the office, the kids were in school and Zach was perfectly content in his room. It was time for Sherri to go to work. She had laid awake in bed for some time the night before thinking of just what she wanted to convey in her newest profile. By the time she sat down in front of the computer, all that was left for her to do was to put it out there. Of course the first step was selecting a handle that she would be known by. Even that came to her quickly this time around.

SATIN DOLL
Silky Smooth and Sexy

Interested in spending some nights in white satin? Sweet-looking, yet naughty, little White girl seeking a strong, dominant and well-built Black man to rock and roll me with his rhythm and blues. Melt my inhibitions away with your words, seduce me with the touch of your powerful hands on my soft, alabaster skin and I will be yours; giving myself to you completely. Total discretion is a must as is being a non-smoker and sincere.

There; she had done it. She had taken a bold step to move not so much out of her comfort zone, as her familiarity zone. She was totally comfortable with what she was about to embark on. She had decided that since you only live but once, she wanted to explore life as much as humanly possible. Step outside of the box to try new and different things. Especially when you're someone who has as much a zest for life as she does. Sure it's risky but she was willing to again take the chance. After all, in her eyes the excitement and potential benefits far outweighed any risk. She only hoped that when all was said and done she wouldn't look back on this period in her life with regret.

As appealing as she considered her words to be, Sherri knew that to complete the process the right way that there was one task left. That was presenting to those she hoped to attract, an eye-catching profile photo. She waited until Zach was lying down taking his nap before she went to work on it. She dressed in her sexiest, black lingerie ensemble. It featured a lace bra, matching panties and a garter belt with a pair of sheer stockings. She completed the look by adding a pair of black pumps. She placed the camera in the tripod and was then ready to go. But just before taking the photo she decided she first wanted to include one more thing to add to the mystique, while at the same time increasing her level of discretion. She placed over her eyes a black blindfold she had recently purchased to add even more spice to her encounters with Scott.

Taking no chances, she chose to pose using a blank wall as a background, so she removed all decorations from a wall in the spare bedroom downstairs. After setting the timer on the camera she got into position; posing with one foot resting on a chair. Her hair was down but she teased it with one of her hands to add to the allure just that much more. Trying her best to look natural she smiled in the direction of the camera. She was pleased with the way the photo came out on the first try so that's the one she was prepared to go with. But her mind was still churning, thinking up ways she might be able to make it even sexier. She quickly dismissed most of them as she began the process of uploading the picture to her profile. That was until one idea really grabbed her and bought a sly smile to her face. She quickly removed the 3 1/2" pumps and dashed upstairs and into her bedroom where she retrieved something from the bottom of her lingerie drawer. She returned downstairs, slipped back into her shoes and after resetting the camera's timer posed in the same exact position as she had before. But this time as she caressed her hair with her left hand she tilted her head back slightly before parting her lips just enough to slide what she had raced upstairs for in between them. She closed her eyes as she worked half of the eight inch dildo into her mouth. Now, it was a wrap, and Sherri felt that her profile and especially its accompanying picture would be as attention grabbing as anyone out there. All that was left for her to do now was to sit back and wait for that attention to come her way.

She hoped they were as ready for her as she was for them. Sherri King was again a lady on a mission. Ready or not here she comes; just as hot as she wants to be. As she admired her photo some clichés came to her mind. Life begins at 40, forty is the new 30 and, if it's true as they say that a woman reaches her peak sexually in her forties; then she was venturing out in search of that mountain. And once she found it she could see nothing stopping her from reaching its summit. Not any sense of wrongdoing, not any overriding morality and certainly not being married to a man who did very little to indulge her intensely sexual side. She was going to do her and continue to allow some lucky others to do her as well.

If Sherri had any minor concerns that her new profile might not have made her the hot commodity she had hoped for. then she needn't worry about that. By half past midnight when she decided to first check in, she discovered that she already had grabbed the attention of an astounding 55 potential lovers. Some had sent messages, while others showed their interest by merely winking at her. Her first order of business was to begin to go about narrowing down the interested parties to ones who match her criteria. That is their being at least fairly local, attractive enough and of course Black. After all the latter was the entire reason she joined this site; to pursue an experience with a man of color. She already had Scott and occasionally Clay. What she wanted now was to try something new and different.

She decided to start with those who had sent messages. Rather than read all of the messages she figured it would be less time consuming to view their profiles. By the time she dismissed the White ones who apparently didn't even take the time to read her profile she had cut that number to 38. By eliminating the ones who didn't even reside in New Jersey she was down to 25. Now she felt like she had a manageable number to work with. As she continued to click on the profiles of the members who had sent her messages she was disappointed to discover that while within the state many of them were from nowhere close to where she lives; so down to 16. She would get back to the messages. It was time to check out some of those who had winked at her. Maybe that would go a little bit better she hoped. She started to work her way down the list from the top. The first was okay but lived way up in Bergen County. Next up was yet another White guy who was immediately dismissed; nothing personal buddy. The following one made her chuckle just from the sound of his username. "Mandingo Swing." Interesting name at least she said to herself. Okay Mr. Swing let's see about you. As she clicked on his screen name to enter his profile page, she leaned back in the chair, preparing for another letdown. It was getting late and she couldn't stop yawning. Her mind and body were both telling her that it was about time to shut it down for the night. After all it wasn't as if this was going anywhere. But did that all ever change in an instant. Sherri focused her tired eyes as she moved in towards the monitor. She wanted to make sure she was seeing clearly. Her mouth fell open in amazement once it became clear that she was indeed. Staring back at her from the screen was the largest, most majestic piece of manhood she had ever seen or imagined. Of course there was more in the picture than that but she had hardly even noticed that. Her attention was squarely focused on the monstrous member. "Oh my word," she mouthed softly. In time she did begin to study the picture in its entirety. It was of a tall, dark-complexioned, Black male standing next to a table. A towel was draped across the edge of the table and stretching out onto the towel was what looked to her like a good foot long of hard, shiny manhood. The picture was cut off from the shoulders on up, but she could tell by the length of the torso that the person in the picture was on the tall side and slender to athletic in build.

As she stared at the picture, Sherri began to realize that she hadn't stopped smiling for a while now. And once she began to read the profile information her smile grew even wider if that was possible. The man possessing the 3rd leg was in New Jersey, and not only that right within her county in North Plainfield. "How could this get any better?" she thought aloud. She figured there was only one way it could but first things first. Rather than merely reply back with a wink in return, she decided to take it just a little bit further and send a personal message. She kept it fairly brief and to the point, and yet made her interests and intentions clear.

"Well hello, hello and hello again. I just looked at your profile after seeing that you had winked at me, and I was floored to put it mildly. I'm just going to go ahead and say what I'm thinking. And that is that I think we should talk. And that's just for starters. But yes I like, no make that LOVE what you bring to the table (no pun intended) so by all means let's get acquainted. Talk to you soon. At least I sincerely hope so."

The moment Clay started backing his car out of the driveway the next morning Sherri went rushing to the computer. It was only around 8:30 and fortunately for her Zach was still sleeping. She couldn't wait to see if she had heard back from the latest target of her lust. Her excitement only grew when she saw that he had indeed sent her a return message. One that was even shorter and more direct than the one she had sent him the night before. It read simply, "Hey sexy, I got your message and I wholeheartedly agree, we need to talk, and soon. I have to go to work this morning but I will be home by about 3:30 and I will look for you then because I definitely hope we can do a little something too; so later, for now.

While she was very much pleased with the fact that her dark man of mystery had reached back out to her, Sherri also lamented the fact that she would have to wait until later that afternoon to connect with him. It turned out to be the typical day of her hanging out with Zach; with the big difference being how much the time seemed to drag along. She attempted to pass some of time by chatting on the phone once Zach was napping, but was unable to reach any of the handful of persons she tried. She listened to the radio for a short time and then navigated through all 100 plus channels available via satellite TV without finding one single thing that held her interest for very long. Just getting to 2:00 took so long that it felt like it should have been 7:00 by the time that hour arrived. An earlier attempt to settle down for a nap herself had proven futile. Even something she enjoyed as much as reading left her unable to concentrate. She finally found something that helped to pass the time when she decided to go into the kitchen and start dinner.

It's not that she didn't enjoy cooking, but it would be fair to say that Sherri seldom approached it with the zeal that she did on this occasion. And it paid off for her as by the time she had finished preparing a meal of meat loaf, au gratin potatoes and green peas with pearl onions a check of the time revealed that is was 3:15. It was about time for her to lose the apron and make herself comfortable at the computer. All of that nervous energy and anxiety had reached its zenith and she was so ready to do this. It was time for the vixen side of Sherri to come out to play once again.

She logged into her account and upon seeing that the one person she was looking for was not as of yet showing up as online, she minimized that window in order to open another to browse through some of her Yahoo emails. Well more like do some housecleaning as she mostly deleted many of the useless emails she receives on a regular basis. Once done with that she stood up and began to pace around; all the while not straying very far from the computer. That is until his plaintively calling out Mommy, let her know that Zach had awakened. As quickly as she could she escorted him into the bathroom before bringing him a snack of animal crackers and grape juice and turning on the television to keep him occupied.

Just then it dawned on her that Abby and Tyler were a bit late in getting home. Normally the school bus drops them off in front of the house at three-fifteen, three twenty at the latest, and here it was almost three-twenty-five. But she didn't allow herself to get too worked up over it as she instead returned to her seat at the computer. No sooner had she done so when she heard the sound of the bus pulling to a stop out front. Moments later they came rampaging in through the front door led by Tyler as usual who always entered with the appetite of a typical growing lad.

"Mom," she heard him calling out almost as soon as he entered before he began stampeding through the house in search of her.

"I'm back here in the office," she shouted to him while keeping her eyes on the screen in front of her. She didn't need to wonder for even a second why he had entered the house eagerly looking for her.

"Hey Mom," he said upon entering the room, before she cut him off; knowing very well what he was about to ask.

"You can have some of those crackers with the cheese spread. If you want anything else eat an apple or an orange."

"Okay thanks," he said before retreating quickly.

"How was school," she called out to him before he managed to get out of earshot.

"It was good."

"Get started on your homework as soon as you finish with your snack okay."

"Okay Mom."

All the while Sherri had continued to keep much of her attention focused on the monitor, refreshing the screen every 20 seconds or so. After about the fifth time doing so her patience paid off when she saw that the man she had been waiting for had made an appearance online. She broke into a big smile before sliding the chair closer to the desk and selecting to initiate a chat session.

"Well hello Mister, how are you?"

"I'm doing well Miss, Mrs. or Ms. How about you?" he replied seconds later.

"Doing just fine thank you, and we can get into which one of those titles applies to me in time, but not just yet.

"Oh that's cool, I was just trying to be polite more than inquiring actually."

"Okay no problem."

"So what's going on?"

"Oh not a whole lot; I was just waiting for you to pop in and here you are, as promised."

"Well I make an effort to be a man of my word."

"And I can appreciate that. But first of all thanks for showing interest in me."

"Don't mention it, thank you for reciprocating by going as far as sending me a personal message. That was really nice of you."

"Well I checked out your profile once I got the wink from you and I decided at that point that I definitely wanted to talk to you," Sherri informed him.

"Oh you did; well I'm glad that you apparently liked it."

"It certainly got my attention that's for sure. Especially that profile picture; wow!!

The conversation between them had just began and was already on the verge of taking a turn towards the raw and edgy side of things and Sherri was all for it.

"LOL, oh that."

"You're probably not the bashful type. That much I can tell."

"No need to be on a site like this. But still and all I'm happy that the picture didn't offend you.

"Offend me? No way, it was real nice. That's quite a package you have there."

"Well since you referred to it as a package should I have wrapped it and put a bow on it?"

"Actually that would make it more like a gift, and I can just imagine the joy receiving such a gift would bring. But be that as it may I liked it just like that; unwrapped and ready to enjoy. And the things I could do with that."

"Oh yeah, well do tell."

Before Sherri could begin to type out her next reply message Abby came bouncing into the room already plugged into her MP3 player listening to whatever it is that nine year old girls would be listening to just minutes after arriving home from school.

"Hey Mom," she yelled out rather loudly clearly in an attempt to hear herself over the music blasting into her ear drums.

Sherri paused and sat up straight, backing away from the keyboard slightly. "Turn that thing down she yelled out just as loud. "My God you're gonna be deaf before you become a teenager at this rate," she said once Abby lowered the volume. "Do you have homework?"

"Yeah I have some, but I already did most of it on the bus on the way home so I don't have much left."

"Well do what you have left and if you're going to eat anything keep it pretty light. Dinner is going to be whenever your Dad gets home."

"Okay Mom."

Sherri could hear that Abby turned the volume back up to an insane level before she even left the room, but she decided that she wasn't going to deal with that right now. She had other things on her mind at the moment. She slid the chair back in and turned her attention back to the chat.

"Sorry for the delay. I had an interruption."

"No problem."

"Anyway, where were we? Oh yeah I was just about to comment on your thing there. Well first I'd wrap my lips around it and get it nice and wet with my mouth. And then I would bob my head back and forth until it got harder and harder. After that I'd run my tongue all around the head and lick up and down the shaft before putting it back in my mouth and sucking on it like a woman possessed."

"Oh so you like to suck dick then?"

"Say what? Hell no, and please watch your mouth with me. What do you mean I like to suck dick? See now you've offended me."

"I apologize; really. I didn't mean any offense."

"Ha-ha, I gotcha; actually I LOVE to suck dick. And I bet I'd really enjoy sucking that one hanging from between your legs."

"Okay you kind of got me with that one alright. And hey, I'm sure that could be arranged."

"Oh you think so?"

"Oh I know so. But tell me, can you do that deep throat thing?"

"Well I usually can but I must admit it would be a challenge with that huge dick you have. But then I've never been one to back down from a challenge." Sherri then smiled before adding more. "And to tell you the truth it looks like taking you deep would mean getting only halfway down your shaft." She suddenly felt herself getting aroused from the hot conversation that had already stirred up between the two of them. Her nipples had grown erect and she placed one hand between her legs as she felt a little stirring down there also.

"You know something; I think I'm going to like getting to know you, he typed."

"Well that's nice, same here. I'm sorry but you live down in North Plainfield right?"

"Yes that's correct, off of Route 22."

"Okay cool, that's fairly local since I'm in Basking Ridge. Oh and by the way I am a married woman. I just wanted to get that out there."

"Well anytime somebody lists their status as "I'll let you know," then it's not too hard to figure that they're probably either married, shacking up or close to it."

"Yeah I guess it's not."

"But anyway that's fine. Not a problem for me if it's not a problem for you. Besides I have a girl myself. Kind of the way this place rolls."

"Huh? You'll have to excuse the White girl if she's not up on all the latest slang."

"Lol, okay I got you. Basically I'm just saying that this place is sort of geared towards attached people looking for a little action on the side."

"Yes that's very true. A friend told me about this site and told me all about it also."

"So in your case can I assume that your husband isn't serving it up right then?"

Well, let's just say that's he's really been skimping on his service. Let me put it this way. Say you have this great restaurant that you've always liked to go to. But then all of a sudden they start slacking in the service department. What can or should you do?"

"Ummm, I guess complain about it?"

"Right; and then if nothing is done to address it what next?"

"You need to consider looking into another restaurant to give your business to."

"Ding, ding, ding, ding; exactly; but anyway I don't want to get too deep into that. It is what it is."

"And so here you are."

"Yes here I am, ready, willing and able."

"And with all your cards on the table."

"Cute, nice rhyming; you seem quick on your feet. Wonder how you are on your back."

"Well I wouldn't skimp on you that's for sure. I'll serve you all you want; all you can eat like a buffet. I just hope you're not a vegetarian because it's 100% pure, prime cut beef."

"That sounds good to me. And no I'm not a vegetarian so I wanna eat it all."

"Be my guest baby, dinner is served."

"Cool; and I take it to the limit too."

"Break that down for me if you would."

"I mean that I like to swallow; either that or to take it on the face. How do you like the sound of that?"

"Damn, let's just say you've got me hard as hell now."

"Mmmm, I wish I could see."

"Well you can soon if that's what you want."

"I think we can make that happen. And I think we need to make that happen," Sherri quickly typed back before again pressing her fingers against her pussy through her pants.

"Well you're married, so how available are you to get out?"

"We can talk about that soon."

"Sounds good to me; let's do that."

"Okay I've got to run; I have some things to take care of."

"All right; well until next time, take care."

"You too and I guess I'll look for you on here?" Sherri asked.

"That'll work; you can look for me anytime. Sometime early in the morning, other times around this time or maybe late at night. It depends on my work schedule. We can get more into that next time."

"Sure, and I suppose we can exchange real names next time too."

"Oh yeah we can do that too."

"Okay talk to you soon then."

"Yep, you take it easy."

"You do the same, bye," Sherri responded.

"Bye."

Sherri immediately shut down the computer before beating a hasty retreat to the master bathroom where she pulled down her pants and her panties before masturbating while seated on the edge of the tub. She of course had to muffle her screams as she bought herself to an intense orgasm; no doubt in large part due to the hot online chat session she had just finished up minutes earlier. By the time she was done the eruption had actually led to her sliding down to the floor where her body convulsed as pleasure overcame her. I have got to meet this man soon she was thinking as she laid there with her legs spread wide apart; imagining him deep inside of her. She wished that she could be with him tonight, though she knew better than to think it possible. But she had already determined in her mind that she would do whatever it took to make it a reality soon.

CHAPTER TWELVE

Not even a day had passed since Sherri had spoken to the tall, dark stranger Mandingo Swing for the first time, and all she could think about were him and the possibilities. Of what it might feel like to have her body taken by him. Her mind visualized it clearly enough that she felt herself unable to settle into sleep that night. After a good amount of tossing and turning, she decided to quietly climb out of bed. She first walked to the kitchen before seeking out the computer and what had certainly become her favored form of entertainment. She found no one of interest logged in to either of the sites she was now a member of; not surprising given that it was close to 1:00 am. She pondered what she might do to occupy herself until she felt ready to attempt sleep again, and an idea soon hit her. A quick search led her to one of several free internet porn sites, where she then entered the search criteria for Black men. Watching adult videos was not something that she would normally take part in, but then so much of her life of late has been lived outside of her norms. After selecting a clip of interest based on the still photo which accompanied the link all she had to do was sit back and prepare for what was coming her way. The action commenced the moment the video began. One of the participants was a very pretty and petite, dark-complexioned, Black female with long hair styled in braids. Her build was not all that dissimilar to that of Sherri except she appeared to be slightly taller. But the star attraction for Sherri was of course her partner, a tall, dark chocolate man. He was dressed in only a pair of dark lounge pants as the clip began. He moved towards the woman who was dressed in but a bra and panties. Removing her bra, he immediately went to work on her full breasts as she stood before him. After about a minute he backed her over to a sofa where she took a seat. He then slid down her panties and wasted no time burying his face in her pussy. The close ups really put into focus just how expertly he ate her out. Just as it appeared to Sherri that the feeling must have gotten really good to her, the girl hooked her legs around his torso and started to squeal in delight. With her hands pressed to the back of his head, he fucked her with his tongue as she thrust her hips upwards in a perfect rhythm. Next he stood up, before helping her into a seated position on the sofa. Once she slid his pants down to the floor she wasted no time in taking his large piece of meat into her mouth. The camera angles used were perfect in showing not only just how well-endowed he was but also that the girl was a beast when it came to giving head. She was able to take him deep without much effort, gagging only when his balls came to rest against her chin. Sherri had to admit that as big as the guy was she was impressed by the girl's skill in pleasing him. She used a open-mouthed technique that many women could only dream of mastering. Sherri might have been most impressed by the fact that she never stopped; only taking a break from sucking him off when she took some time to attend to his scrotum with her full, sexy lips as well as her tongue. When it came time to enter her, he positioned her on her knees on the sofa before mounting her from up above. As the man began to sweat from his brow while fucking her with zeal, Sherri felt her own body temperature start to skyrocket. She knew she had never seen and certainly not felt anything like what she imagined that must feel like. She needed to lower the volume on the computer's speakers the girl's screams were so loud. A few minutes more and that was it for Sherri; she had reached a point where she couldn't stand to watch any more of the action on the monitor in front of her. That was her first actual look at a black dick in action and she was thinking that she'd certainly have one of what the lucky girl in the video was having. Quickly powering off the PC she beat a hasty retreat downstairs where she again pleasured herself before exploding with a volcanic orgasm. Returning to the bedroom shortly thereafter she was soon sleeping like a newborn baby. The next day was Friday, and from the time she awakened Sherri was thinking about when would be the next chance for her to engage her new friend. As it turned out, good fortune was on her side and she did not have to wait long. She discovered him online that morning about 8:00. And she wasn't about to pass on the chance to get a little more acquainted, even though Clay hadn't even quite left for his office as of yet.

"Good morning, what a pleasant surprise to find you on here so bright and early," she typed.

"Good morning to you too; I'm going to work a little later today so I have a little downtime this morning. What about you? Why are you on the computer at such an early hour?"

"Well they say they say the early bird gets the worm so here I am looking for that worm. Lucky for me that instead of a worm I happened to run into something a little bit bigger. More like a huge snake actually; one that just so happens to be attached to your body."

"You're something else you know that?"

"No you're something else. I've never seen anyone quite like you. That is with anything quite like yours. By the way my name is Sherri; what might yours be?"

"Nice to meet you Sherri, my name might be Garrick. Or it might be just Gee because that's what most people call me, and I guess you can too."

"Okay Gee it is. So why don't you tell me a little more about yourself Gee?"

"What would you like to know?"

"I don't know; I guess just enough to make me feel comfortable enough to think that you're not a crazed killer, or that you don't have a girlfriend that might be a jealous stalker. That's a good place to start."

"No my girl isn't a jealous maniac and she's oblivious to all of this anyway so no worries there. But I might be a crazed killer, I haven't decided yet. Just kidding; but no you'd be safe from her; and me.

"So you say right?"

"Hey trust me, I mean I don't know what else I can say, except that I wouldn't be on this site if I felt like it was high risk for me or whoever I might hook up with."

"Okay I'll trust you, it's just that I can see how your woman might go crazy if she thought you were giving away some of that."

"No we're good there; really."

"All right then moving on; what else interesting is there to know about you Gee?"

"I don't know, let me see. I'm thirty-two, I work for Continental Airlines, have no kids, love to get my sex on. I mean there's not a whole lot interesting about me."

"Well I can tell you that the fact that you mentioned that you love to get your sex on as you put it, is quite interesting to me. So why don't we just focus on that?"

"Hey you know that works for me."

"Okay, but let me ask you something first."

"Shoot."

"I'm a bit older than you. In fact I just turned 40 yesterday actually. That's not a problem for you is it?"

"First of all happy belated Birthday, and to answer your question, no, it's not a problem at all. Older women tend to be on point with theirs."

"Sorry you lost me again."

"Ooops I forgot. I mean that older women know what they're doing in bed. Pretty much have been there done that and don't need any instruction manual.

"Yes I guess you can say that. And don't forget one more thing Gee."

"What's that Sherri?"

"A woman is considered to be at her sexual peak in her 40's."

"Now that's what I'm talking about. So when can I get in on some of that?

"When might you want to is the question?"

"Well I want to right now lol, but let me know what works for you."

Sherri paused to think for a moment before responding back.

"How about next Monday morning? That works for me if it does for you."

"Well that's cool with me. I work nights mostly so that's not a problem at all."

"Okay that's fine. Oh and Gee let me ask you one more thing."

"Go right ahead."

"You wouldn't be uncomfortable being with me so soon would you?"

"Oh hell no, "I'm cool with it. I mean we're both grown, so why not. We're not trying to get into anything serious, just kick it with each other right?"

"You're absolutely right and I was hoping you'd say something like that because for me it's all about the sex. You definitely have something I want a piece of and hopefully I have something that you like, so hey, why not. Life is short."

"Hey, you know you're preaching to the choir here; I'm ready for whatever sweetheart."

"Hold on for a few minutes if you don't mind Gee," Sherri asked after taking a glance up at the clock on the wall which then read 8:20. She then went into the bedroom where Clay was finishing up his preparations to depart for the day.

"Hey; I know you'll be leaving in a little while so I just wanted to come and give you a kiss," she announced as she approached him.

"Okay, well thanks, but you didn't need to get up I would have come in to say goodbye to you."

"That's okay I wanted to look in on Zach anyway," she said just before their lips briefly came together.

"Have a good day, I'll see you later," she said.

"You do the same, see you this evening."

Sherri indeed did pop in on Zach next. "Hey sweetie, are you doing okay in here?"

"Hi Mommy."

"How you doing honey?"

"I'm good Mommy."

"All right that's good; Mommy will be making you breakfast in a little while okay.

"Okay Mommy," her son replied sweetly.

As she was departing the room she crossed path with Clay who was just coming in to say goodbye to their son himself. She continued on back to the office and again took a seat at the desk. She sat there listening as Clay said his goodbyes to Zach and headed towards the front door. "Okay see you later," she shouted back as Clay again called out a goodbye before heading downstairs and out the door. She sat there watching him until he started to back out of the driveway at which point she quickly turned her attention back to the pc.

"Sorry about that Gee, I just wanted to see my husband off to work so that there would be no chance of him coming in here and spoiling my fun."

"My aren't you a brazen one."

"Well believe me I'm always careful to keep myself one step ahead of him," Sherri said proudly in response.

"So what about you then; do you have to head out to work?"

"No I have the day off. Well actually I have every day off from that type of working. I'm a stay- at- home mom."

"Oh that's cool, good for you. How old are your kids?"

"One is almost ten, one is eight and the youngest is three. He's the one who's here with me while everyone else is out at either work or school. But it's okay; it affords me this opportunity to play that I really wouldn't have if I was working a nine to five, which in my former line of work often turned into nine to eight or nine or occasionally later. I certainly do not miss that part of being out there in the workforce."

"I hear you there; especially because I might be about to benefit from that myself."

"Yeah you might be if I like you, but; I don't know so far," Sherri joked.

"Well don't give up on me yet, just tell me what I need to do to impress you and I'll do it."

"Okay, okay let's stop kidding because trust me on this, the only thing you need to work on is my body. Use that big magic wand on me and abracadabra, I might fall under your spell in no time."

"Oh I see you have a little sense of humor too."

"Yeah I do; in fact it often seems like the only type of sense I have."

"Remember it was you who said that."

'Hey it's fine, I readily accept that. But anyway Gee, let me run in and prepare my son's breakfast. As for you and me; why don't we do this? We can touch base over the weekend and see if we're firm for Monday."

"Well I will be beyond firm for Monday. I'll be rock hard."

"Okay silly, that's good to know. Anyway, here's my cell number. You can call me or text me. And don't worry about anything. If you text me he'll never know because that function is on silent, and if you call me my phone will only vibrate and I could always pass it off as somebody else if necessary . Not that he has reason to suspect anything anyway. I mean he does, but he doesn't know that. And that's my aim; to keep him in the dark."

"Believe me Sherri, we're on the same page as far as that's concerned; trust me."

After Sherri sent him her number they said their goodbyes and she went off to continue on with the rest of her day. By midday Saturday her Monday morning tryst was all but set in stone after Gee sent her a text confirming his availability. All that was left for her to do now was to let Scott know that she wouldn't be seeing him that day. Now that was something that she knew she must handle carefully because that's a tie that she certainly didn't want to completely sever. It just might be a matter of juggling the two of them, assuming that things with Gee clicked to the point where they want to make it a semi-regular thing as well.

An hour after hearing from Gee, Sherri had worked out just how she was going to handle things with Scott for now. She called him up and arranged a drive out to see him late that afternoon. She simply told Clay that she was going to get her nails done and then pick up a few things from the market. She knew that she could just self-apply any different color polish to her nails and then make a brief stop at the supermarket before coming back in, and he'd be clueless to her actual whereabouts. But she did want to return as quickly as she could because she was not 100% comfortable with him having complete responsibility for the kids for too long. It was probably very silly of her to think that way. After all as much as he made her feel like an afterthought at times, Clay was a very doting father; whenever he was around to be one that is.

"I'm surprised that you wanted to get together today, but I mean pleasantly surprised," Scott explained after letting her in.

"Well you've been on my mind since I woke up this morning so I just decided to take a chance and call you. I mean the worst that could happen was that you'd say no. But I had faith that you wouldn't if I could reach you."

"Oh you know me too well, because I would never turn down the chance to be with you."

"Yes that is what I was counting on," Sherri said sexily as she backed him up against a wall. Tearing at his belt she soon had his pants undone. You know I always want some of you don't you," she said as she dropped to her knees before him.

"And believe me I'm always willing to give it to you," he replied as she took him into her mouth and started to slowly suck him. Mmmm," she groaned while opening her eyes and looking up at him, prompting him to place his hands on the back of her head and begin to slowly pump back and forth in rhythm with her lips as they worked on him intently; taking him to complete hardness before finishing him off in no time.

"I have something to tell you, "Sherri said minutes later as she sat on the floor below him. "I'm afraid I won't be able to see you on Monday. One of the kids is sick so I'll be keeping him out of school and home with me. I'm sure you understand."

"Of course I do Sherri; don't forget I have kids also, so I understand completely. I just appreciate you coming by to see me today."

"Well I can't stay long today either, but hopefully I'm leaving you with something that'll keep me on your mind for a while," she said with a grin."

"Oh believe you me you certainly are. I'll be thinking about you for sure."

"Let me ask you a favor if you don't mind Scott," Sherri interjected quickly; I told my husband that I was going to get a manicure and pedicure. Now I don't believe I need to go that far but; if I could just hang out here long enough to apply some polish to my fingers and toes and allow it to dry, then I'd be good."

"Sure that's not a problem at all, go right ahead."

"Thanks I appreciate it. If he pays any attention at all he won't know the difference between what a professional manicure and just some self-applied polish looks like anyway.

"I have to give it to you Sherri, you are a sharp one."

"I'm just trying to make certain that I touch all the bases that's all. I don't have a lot of practice at being with someone other than my husband, so I'm sort of just feeling my way along here. I'm relying on my guile to a big extent."

"Okay, well just be careful that's all. This is not something so deep that you want to jeopardize what you have at home," Scott implored her.

"Oh no worries there, if nothing else my marriage is and will remain priority number one."

∞∞∞∞∞∞∞∞∞

When Monday morning arrived a very excited yet slightly nervous Sherri tried her best to maintain her same level of focus while handling the normal tasks of getting Abby and Tyler off to school. After all the day would follow a now familiar pattern she had followed for the time that she'd been enjoying her stolen hours with Scott; except this time it would just be a different man she'd be hooking up with. And that undoubtedly is what had her stomach doing flips almost as if she was about to experience her first time making love with anyone. She was due at Gee's place at the same 10:00 time that she always arrived for her sexcaspades with Scott. Unable to eat due to the case of butterflies she was experiencing, she instead downed a couple of cups of coffee with one being decaffeinated. The last thing she wanted was to be too over the top with excitement and jitters when she arrived to meet Gee. She had gone out the day before and purchased a sexy, cherry red lace baby doll with matching panties. She admired herself in the mirror briefly before slipping into a pair of fitted jeans with a simple, blue long-sleeved tunic. Once she got into the car she texted him to let him know she was on her way as he had requested, and then she was off. Just before leaving Beth's place after dropping off Zach, she punched Gee's address into the car's gps and took off towards North Plainfield.

She had spent much of the last couple of days trying to visualize what Gee would look like. He had been no help in that regard, refusing to even give her a clue when she had asked. Even as she had emailed him a picture of herself without the cover of a mask as she was pictured on her profile. All he would say is that she wouldn't be disappointed. Maybe he looks a bit like the actor Denzel Washington she thought as she cruised along on route 287 southbound. She'd always thought of him as handsome. Or perhaps his appearance is similar to the r&b crooner Maxwell; another man of color that has always tickled her fancy. In any event the time was near when that question would finally be answered.

Sherri checked her watch one last time before exiting the car. The time was 9:58 a.m. when in spite of the very overcast sky she placed her dark sunglasses over her eyes before stepping outside. One thing she was always very cognizant of was not taking any chances in being recognized when she was getting together with one of her lovers. Of course her car being spotted was just a risk that she often had to take, and one that she took without hesitation. She peered all around her just after ringing the doorbell, another habit she had developed since becoming involved in her illicit lifestyle. Gee's two story townhouse was one of about 15 that were all attached and ran the entire length of the block on which they stood. It's in the middle of a former industrial area which had been converted to residential as well as commercial dwellings. Directly across the street were a string of businesses constructed in a classic European style. Included among them were a combination bakery-coffee shop, a hair salon, a deli, a store that sold sporting goods and a woman's boutique. A small parking lot was located on each end of the tree-lined block from which customers walked to whichever business they were headed. All in all the area was quite attractive and growing moreso by the day as the building occupancy took off both for the shops and the townhomes. Each of the townhouses had its own driveway and 2 car garage, which was definitely a strong selling point in an area where going forward on street parking figured to be at a premium as the traffic to the area continued to grow. Sherri was still looking up and down the block admiring the area when the door was opened. She had actually been so preoccupied with the picturesque surroundings that she was no longer focused on how nervous she was as she'd rung the bell.

"Hello Sherri," came a deep voice from over her shoulder as she stood there facing the street.

To him it must have seemed that she had intentionally set out to avoid coming face to face right then; almost as if she wasn't quite prepared for that moment, though she'd arrived there as planned and not a second late. In actuality she had become so taken by her surroundings that she hadn't even heard the door being opened. But that all changed in an instant as the voice sank into her consciousness. And in that instant the rush of adrenalin mixed with a heavy dose of nerves returned.

"Hi, she replied quietly after turning to face him.

"Come on in it's starting to rain a little bit," spoke the voice again. Sherri hadn't even noticed the raindrops landing on her head and face. He held the door open and allowed her inside where they then stood motionless. Her and the man of so much mystery; right there in the entryway. She had not so much as heard his voice until now, and yet he had so intrigued her that this moment was all she could think about for the last couple of days.

"Oh I guess I should formerly introduce myself now that we're meeting face to face huh? I'm Garrick but of course you can still call me Gee."

The voice seemed to move her a bit more each time she heard it, though it had only been a few times. It was a deep, rich baritone. The type of voice you'd expect to hear doing voiceovers for commercials or movie previews.

"Hello Gee and yes I'm Sherri, nice to meet you," she said almost timidly in response before extending her hand to him.

"Come on now, what is that; a handshake?" he chuckled deeply in that stirring tone. "Oh I don't do handshakes with ladies. Not unless it's in a businesslike setting. And this is certainly not that," he added. He then moved in closer to her before hugging Sherri tightly, pressing her head firmly against his chest. One she could tell was a firm, strong chest. At that moment she looked up at him and they made real eye contact for the first time. Her immediate impression was that while no he was not Denzel Washington or Maxwell he was nonetheless a very attractive man in his own right. He had coffee-brown skin, penetrating brown eyes and a goatee. His head was completely shaved and seemed to glisten even in the relative darkness of the vestibule with the gloom of the morning's cloudy sky.

"You're a very attractive woman you know that; even more than in the picture you sent me."

Sherri looked up at him briefly before darting her eyes away.

"Oh don't tell me you're acting shy on me in person. I know better than that," the voice called out.

"No I'm not shy, and thank you for the compliment," Sherri responded with a bit more assuredness in her voice. It's just that," she began before her voice trailed off.

"It's just that what?" Gee attempted to complete her thought before stopping. "Come on lets go upstairs."

He then took her by the hand and led her up the flight of stairs to his entrance. The townhouses had an unusual configuration in that the entrance for each unit was on the 2nd floor at the top of a shared stairwell, but there was also an interior set of stairs that led down to the ground level floor of every one of them.

"Have a seat and make yourself comfortable. Can I get you anything? Something to drink maybe?"

"Maybe some water if you don't mind," Sherri answered.

"Okay sexy coming right up."

"You have a really nice place," she called out to him once he was in the kitchen. "This entire area is nice in fact."

"Yeah I kind of like it around here," the baritone shot back at her. "it sort of suits me at this point and time."

Moments later he came back into the room and handed her a bottle of water as he opened one for himself. He took a sip before placing the bottle down on a table. Heading over to his stereo he placed a cd in the player and started it up. Sherri immediately recognized the voice as the one and only Luther Vandross. As she took another sip of her water she felt her anxiety slowly melting away in his presence.

"I hope a little Luther is okay with you," he said in as soft a voice he could probably muster up with his naturally deep tone.

"How could it not be? You know you really can't go wrong with Luther Vandross," she acknowledged.

As he stood with his back to her, Sherri took the time to admire Gee's frame. He was 6'3" and 215 pounds of solid muscle and she began to imagine it all over her as she looked at the way his perfectly contoured frame wore his jeans as well as the muscular arms and shoulders that stretched the limits of the black tee shirt he was wearing. She stood and walked over in his direction; so close that he almost plowed right through her as he turned back around.

"Oh I'm sorry," he attempted to apologize as if he was at fault.

"No I was the cause of that. I think I got a little too close."

"As they stood there close to each other, Sherri without hesitation placed both of her hands first on his chest, before running them along his arms and up to his strong shoulders.

"Oooh," she purred. "You must work out a lot."

"I used to at one time but not so much anymore; just enough to try to maintain I guess."

"Mmmmm hmmm," she continued on as she slid her hands down his back to his backside, squeezing firmly as she did so. "Well I'd say however much it is, it's working because you're as hard as steel all over."

"Am I?"

"Well let me see for sure," she whispered before she placed her right hand onto his crotch. "Oh yes I think you are," she said with a smile as he instantly grew erect from her touch.

"Oh, so you really are a naughty little vixen aren't you?"

"I told you I wasn't shy. I just act that way at times, but that's all it is, an act. Something that comes out for brief appearances. This is who I really am. I just hope the real me doesn't scare you too much."

"No not in the least; be yourself baby," Gee grinned.

Sherri also laughed lightly before their lips came together briefly in a kiss. All while her hand remained squarely pressed against the front of his pants.

"I've been dying to see it in person rather than just in a picture. Can I see it now?"

"Oh yeah, go right ahead, "Gee answered, though he had no real need to. Sherri had already taken it upon herself to start undoing his pants; an easy task since Gee wasn't wearing a belt.

"Oh my goodness gracious; I just can't believe it, "Sherri said in amazement once Gee's member stood out before her. She began to stroke it back and forth in her small hands. "This isn't a dick, it's really a diving board for little people right," she joked.

"You're crazy you know that," Gee said with a big bellowing laugh.

"Well some women might think I'm crazy for what I'm about to take on, but I beg to differ because I want this dick."

"You want this dick baby?"

"Yeah I do."

"You really want this dick?

"Yes."

"You're sure you want this dick?"

"I'm damn sure."

"You're damn sure huh?"

"Hell yes I am."

"Well, then take it."

Once Gee was done with his little game, Sherri slide his tee shirt up and over his head. She took a moment to admire his bare torso before running first her hands and then her tongue across and around his nipples, leading to even more hardening of his dick. Dropping down to her knees, she opened her mouth as wide as she could before leaning forward and taking his missile into her mouth. She moaned deeply as she felt it fill up her oral cavity and tickle the back of her throat for the first time. It didn't take long for Sherri to find out that Gee was a major talker during sex. As she sucked him; first slowly, and then with vigor; he continuously shouted out encouragment to her. Or maybe it was more like instruction. Either way it didn't seem to bother her at all. If anything it spurred her on since she certainly had no intention of allowing him to think she wasn't up to the task.

"That's it, suck that dick, come on get it baby," he blurted out more than once in his booming voice. The voice that melted away what little inhibitions she may have had left from the moment she'd first heard it.

"Go ahead and go deep on it; make that shit nice and wet," he bellowed.

Sherri paused briefly for some needed air before taking him as deep into her throat as she could. She couldn't take nearly it all, but she felt no shame in that, because she couldn't imagine there were many women around who could.

"Mmmmm, oh yeah; you are a nasty little one aren't you?" he asked just as he began to tug on her long hair.

Initially somewhat taken aback by some of the things he said to her, Sherri decided that there was nothing at all personal about it. Probably just his way of expressing his excitement at what she was doing. So she took it as a voicing of his approval and nothing more.

"Oh yeah, I'm a nasty little slut," she groaned in between breaths after he had repeated the same question.

That seemed to turn him on even more as Gee then began to thrust himself into her mouth with even more force, undeterred by the amount of saliva that had started to fall from her mouth.

"Are you ready for me to put it inside of you? You want to this dick inside you?"

"Yes," Sherri answered in an almost childlike voice.

He jerked his dick out of her mouth so quickly that it made a loud popping sound as it fell from her lips.

"I'll be right back," he said to her before leaving the room. He returned a short time later unrolling a condom onto his penis. Sherri was seated on the floor leaning back against his leather sofa with her right hand down her pants, toying with her clit. She smiled once she saw him approaching.

"Take off your clothes," he ordered before she stood up and immediately complied.

Gee gave her nude body a quick once over before he moved in close to her. He then kissed her briefly before pushing her face away from his. Next he wrapped his lips around each of her breasts, sucking on them for a short period of time. Just long enough to send sensations throughout her entire body. The feeling of his warm breath against her skin bought moisture to her eager pussy.

"You know you have a real nice body," he said as he placed his hands on her ass, rubbing and then firmly squeezing both of the cheeks.

"Get up on the sofa," he commanded.

Sherri loved the way he took control of her, and she intended to submit herself to him completely. For the first time in a while she felt her insides start to dance a little as she realized the time was near when he would be entering her. The feelings she had were a mixture of excitement, nerves and what if? In particular, what if she was unable to receive him fully? And to satisfy him completely? But they were only brief concerns that she was soon able to chase from her mind.

She sat and leaned her back against the back of the sofa with her legs spread wide apart. Her heart raced in antcipation of what was coming next.

"Come on, put that big dick inside of me," she said with a sudden confidence as she once again fingered her pussy.

Gee knelt before her and while holding his dick in his right hand, started to tease her opening with it. That only served to heighten Sherri's anxiety.

"Come on, don't tease me," she pleaded. "Give it to me baby."

He smiled yet continued to do the same for several more seconds. Finally he entered her slowly, careful to place only some of himself inside of her at first. Sherri tensed up noticeably at the moment he first went inside, but quickly relaxed as he penetrated her further. She was pleasantly surprised at how well she was able to adapt to his size in short order. And her excitement only grew as she felt him in places that she had never felt any man before. He climbed off his knees, placed his pelvis over hers and after entering her again, started to fuck her with a purpose. Sherri screamed loudly as he drove his huge dick into her pussy over and over. Raising her legs in the air, she placed her hands on his buttocks, pressing down on them in time with each of his intense thrusts.

"This is what you wanted right? You wanted to get fucked just like this didn't you.

"Ooooh yes, just like this, oooh, oh yes baby, fuck me, that's it, harder," she groaned.

It was really sort of amazing the way he spoke to her without her even as much as flinching. He said some things which if they had come from her husband's mouth, would have probably caused her to freeze up immediately and put a halt to things. Yet she welcomed and encouraged it from Gee; even responding in kind more often than not. The naughty back and forth banter only served to turn her on more coming from him.

He was pulling almost all of the way out of her before slamming back inside of her as deep as he could with every stroke. The sound of his oversized penis pounding away at her wet pussy filled the room.

"That's it, get it, deeper," she implored him.

As soon as she experienced her initial orgasm he climbed off of her and directed her to get on the floor in front of the sofa on her knees. He then stood behind her before entering her from behind. Using his height as leverage, he buried his dick into her rapidly. Her juices started to run down her thighs as he fucked her like crazy, pushing her breasts into the softness of the leather sofa with each determined stroke. Powerless to move, Sherri just froze there, enjoying the feeling deep in her loins. Her second orgasm came quickly, her thighs quivering from the sensation as he drilled away at her without pause. When he was ready to cum, his deep baritone-infused groans resonated loudly. She slid him out of her and rolled over onto her back in anticipation of where he might shoot his load of fluid. Hoping he might cum on her face, she was midly disappointed when he instead took aim for her tits. In the aftermath she sat there leaning up against the sofa, rubbing her breasts together as his semen ran down them onto her stomach. It was over; she had received her super-sized dick initiation. But it was over just for then, because Sherri felt her adventures had really just begun. And she had no idea just how prophetic that would be.

CHAPTER THIRTEEN

Over the course of the next 6 weeks Sherri continued to deftly juggle her affairs with both Scott and Gee. But if anything she started to display a clear preference for spending time with Gee. This was in spite of the fact that unlike Scott, he declined to ever go down on her. His reasoning was that he was not going to be eating off another man's plate as he put it. He was referring to Clay because Sherri made it a point of not even allowing Scott and Gee to know about each other. Gee also stated that eating pussy was something that he reserved for only the main lady in his life. When Sherri tried to complain that she gave him oral favors eagerly and quite often, he remained unmoved; merely stating that it was her decision to get involved with him and hers to decide if she no longer wanted to continue to see him. So for Sherri the implication was clear; either they'd continue things on his terms or he would gladly cut ties with her without missing a beat. She recalls the day that they first had that discussion that she provided him with an answer the best way she knew how; by again sucking his dick like it was the last one left on Earth.

In the meantime, as Clay settled into his position as Prosecutor, he had started to delegate things more and more, thus allowing him additional time out of the office whenever he wanted it. That's not to say that he had started to devote more of this time to Sherri however. While he remained steadfast in his role as a Dad, the other real beneficiary of his increased leisure time was his golf game. He had taken to playing at least twice a week on average, give or take. So while Sherri continued to see no reason to doubt that he loved her just as she still loved him, she knew as she had known for some time that love doesn't always equate to passion. That two hearts, though connected don't necessarily burn with the same heat or desire. She had come to accept that, albeit sadly, as a fact of their life together.

During the first week of May, Sherri received a pleasant surprise when she received an email from Miguel. She hadn't heard from him in a few months and she had really started to wonder if she ever would again. Not that it rested on just him to maintain contact; it's just that with her life being so hectic, she figured it might be something that he could spend more time focused on than she. In the email, Miguel mentioned that he would be in Jersey the next weekend and asked her to let him know if there was a possibility that they might be able to get together for lunch one day. She was very happy to have heard from him and wasted no time replying that she would love to meet him for lunch someplace. In his next message to her in this brief game of email tag, he left her a number at which she could reach him. When they spoke later he told her that he would be coming to the area on a scouting trip at a weekend basketball tournament and that they could hopefully meet for lunch that coming Friday afternoon before the games commenced that evening.

∞∞∞∞∞∞∞∞∞∞

Fortunately Beth was able to keep Zach and the two of them met at the Spanish Tavern in Mountainside at noon. Miguel had arrived first and called Sherri to let her know that the restaurant was pretty sparsely filled, so rather than grab a table he would just wait for her in the lobby. They had told each other what they were wearing so between that and the fact there weren't any other exotic looking, bearded 6'6" men standing in the vicinity it was pretty easy for her to spot him. He broke into a big smile as she headed in his direction after seeing him.

"Hey Sherri, it's nice to meet you after all this time," Miguel said as they came together in an embrace; her head nestled into his chest.

"Yes same here; finally," Sherri concurred.

"Let's grab a table shall we," he suggested.

"Most certainly," Sherri replied.

"So Sherri, what have you been doing with yourself? Wait let me re-phrase that; what have you been doing with yourself that you can tell me about?"

"Well in that case that won't leave much for me tell you at all," Sherri grinned.

"Come on now, it can't be that bad can it?"

"Sherri lost herself in his eyes as she thought about what she might say next; eventually deciding that it was best she not go down that path.

"Well Miguel I have to tell you that picture didn't quite do you justice because you actually are even more handsome in person," she said in changing the subject.

"Thank you, I was thinking the same thing; I just didn't say it that's all."

"You were thinking that you're more handsome in person also," Sherri said jokingly.

"No of course not," Miguel laughed. "I was thinking that you're much more beautiful in person silly."

"Thank you, that's very nice of you to say."

They were enjoying a very nice lunch with the conversation easily flowing between them when Sherri finally asked what she had been thinking for quite a while.

"So where are you staying while you're here," she interjected while they were busy talking about something else.

"I just got a room at the Sheraton at the airport for a couple of nights. The tournament is being played at Kean University in Union so it's nice and convenient."

"Oh okay, you're right that is a good place to stay if you're going to be travelling back and forth to Union."

"Yeah the school loves it when you can keep those expenses down, so the less distance to travel the better as far as they're concerned."

"Well I hope you're not charging the gas you used to get here to your expense account," Sherri kidded.

"Oh no believe me, that and this meal will be strictly out of pocket."

By this time Sherri was hanging on his every word as she stared at his face. Her eyes penetrated so deeply that he began to feel slightly uncomfortable. It was almost as if he could feel what she was thinking. It was not a look he was unfamiliar with. So he was braced for what came from her next.

"But anyway the reason I asked where you're staying is because I have nothing planned for tonight or tomorrow night."

Miguel said nothing but picked up his soft drink and took a long sip out of it.

"I could probably easily get out and come spend a few hours with you. That is if that's something that would interest you," she continued. The words flowed from her lips so easily. It was as if they were a couple who had been together forever rather than a man who while they had become fairly well acquainted, she had just met in person for the first time less than an hour ago.

Miguel let it all sink in for a moment before he responded to her bold offer.

"Sherri listen; I don't want you to take any of this the wrong way, but that's not why I asked if you wanted to meet while I was going to be in the area. I mean like I said you are a beautiful and sexy woman but,"…………………………………..

"But, you're not interested," Sherri interrupted. Hey you don't need to say it; I get what you're saying.

"I don't know if that's the way I would put it exactly. So let me say it like this Sherri; I think that's the last thing that we need to do. I don't think that would be helpful to you at all with what you're dealing with. I think you and I could possibly become really good friends though."

"So if I'm reading this right, what you're saying is that I seem to be some sort of out of control slut and you want no part of that."

"No that's not what I'm saying Sherri. Look, like I hinted at back when I first mentioned the websites that are out there; I got caught up in that sort of thing at one time myself. See when you work in the profession that I'm in one of the hardest things to do is to maintain a relationship with someone. Between the schedules, all of the travel and last but not least the fact that you often have to move around a lot just to stay in a job; it can be very difficult. But I got lucky. I mean I had found someone really special and I think things were really going someplace. But you know what; I got caught up in some of all that was out there. I mean I got hooked on the excitement of constantly coming into contact with someone new and then having it turn into the sort of thing where both I and the other parties could just be free and open with each other. I mean it was easy because of the anonymity of the internet. And then what happens after a while; you start to get so comfortable with each other that you decide that you want more. Why not meet in person and see if the chemistry you have online can translate in an in-person meeting. And sometimes that does happen; and what do you have then? Yep a situation where you wind up cheating on that wonderful person you have in your life. And that's what happened to me. I lost her Sherri; all because I got caught up. I was caught up in the excitement, caught up in the easy thrills, caught up in the boost to your ego that comes from the chase, and ultimately the capture. And even though it wasn't a chase in the traditional sense, it felt just the same in the end. So I say that to say that since it appears that's where you are, I don't want to be a part of it, because that wonderful lady I'm referring to; well I still haven't been able to find anyone else like her to this day."

"Well Miguel thanks for the great speech but there's only one problem with your little scenario as it relates to me. I don't feel that I have someone so wonderful and deserving of better at home. You see most of the time I'm made to feel like nothing more than just another piece of furniture. Just a decorative object to display to everyone once in a while; like a car you keep in the garage just to show to some of your friends on occasion. But I do appreciate your concern; really I do," she stated in a sarcastic tone.

"Sherri's reaction both shocked and disappointed Miguel. The conversation slowed to a crawl from that point on and it wasn't long after when she suggested that they ask for the check from their server, although neither of them had even completed their meals. The way they parted company was far different from how they had greeted each other when Sherri first arrived. There was no hug and very few words even exchanged.

"Well thanks for lunch," Sherri said flatly as they stood up from the table.

"It was nice meeting you Sherri and hopefully we can talk again sometime."

"Sherri said nothing for several seconds before eventually responding with a terse, "we'll see as they walked slowly towards the exit before going their separate ways.

∞∞∞∞∞∞∞∞∞∞∞∞

The 3rd week of June meant not only the final week of the school year but also marked Clay and Sherri's 14th wedding anniversary. It would fall on a Saturday, the date being June 19th. Some weeks ago, largely at Sherri's urging, the two of them had booked a long weekend getaway to mark the occasion. She always loved to go down to Pompano Beach but it had been years since the two of them had gone. The kids last day of school was on Thursday and the very next morning they dropped them off at Kevin and Nina's and took off for a little bit of what she hoped would be fun in the sun in Florida.

They were staying Friday through Monday with a Tuesday midday checkout. While they did go out for a nice dinner on the evening of their anniversary the rest of the trip was pretty much business as usual__literally. Clay spent much of Friday and Monday conducting business. He was either in contact with someone from his office via email or over the phone, or tracking the stock market online. Sherri hadn't really allowed herself to think that things were going to be any different so that lessened the disappointment somewhat. But she figured that at least she wouldn't be dining alone; something which incredibly enough happened a couple of times while there. So naturally any chance at even a romantic stroll along the beach was way out of the question. She figured she was lucky for the sliver of passion and romance she got from him on the night of their anniversary. A quickie in the missionary position was better than nothing she supposed but tough to swallow nonetheless. But the expensive, 14K white gold, diamond encrusted, solitaire necklace she'd received from him at the restaurant earlier that evening did show that he had some appreciation for her she had to admit. At least in the way that he best knew how.

Sherri had waiting for him back at the house a set of nickel-plated golf clubs. And she was certain, that if she had given them to him before they'd left, he would have come hell or high-water found some way to use them down in Florida. So she thought it best that she hold off on those. The last thing she wanted to do was to give him even more incentive to leave her to entertain herself. But on the other hand it was nice of him to leave her plenty of chances to communicate with both Gee and Scott throughout the weekend. And she felt it was particularly nice of Gee to fulfill her request to drop his pants and send her a picture of the 'Loch Ness Monster' as she'd taken to calling it. This happened while they were in the midst of a text session one afternoon while she was lounging out by the pool. With her being slightly tipsy at the time, it took all she had not to start fingering herself right then and there once she took a look at it hanging from between his legs along with the words, "a little something that will be waiting for you when you get back."

"A little something my ass; if it were any bigger it would need its own apartment," she quickly typed back as she recalled having recently measured him at just under 11 inches. "And yes it's been a little while so believe me I can't wait." Sherri had just come off of her period before leaving home, so she hadn't been with him in over a week and closer to 2 weeks by then. So while she was more than ready, she would have to wait it out until the Thursday after her return. After they had said their goodbyes she sighed deeply before taking a long sip from her pina colada.

Late Monday afternoon Clay took off for a short drive up to Boca Raton to spend some time with his Mother, so Lina came up from Miami to pick up Sherri in order for them to do some shopping. They headed to the huge Sawgrass Mills shopping complex out in Sunrise. The mall features well over 300 stores so they had to carefully pick and choose which ones they wanted to hit, because the place was far too large to navigate fully. It was during their time spent walking around that Lina informed Sherri that things between her and Donte had indeed moved into the serious category. They had in fact recently decided that she would be moving in with him. Sherri was ecstatic for her friend and told her as much. But while she considered Lina a very good friend one thing she never let on was that she too had a man of color in her life; not to mention another one in Scott as well.

"Wow Lina it sounds like there could be wedding bells in your future."

"Well to tell you the truth Sherri I can't say that the possibility hasn't crossed my mind also. I just don't want to jinx it that's all."

"I understand that, believe me I do," Sherri replied. "Just be patient and if it's meant to be it will surely come."

"Thanks Sherri, I feel exactly the same way."

Meanwhile up in Boca Raton, Clay was engaged in conversation with his Mother. Maureen King was a smallish, gray-haired 71 year old, with a vibrant, full-spirited nature and an ongoing zest for life. She still led a full social life which included a boyfriend ten years her junior who resided in the same upscale, seniors' condominium community as she did. She and Clay had been talking for about thirty minutes about not much more than work and the kids etc, when he decided to take things in another direction. There were just some things he was dying to know and he figured now was as good a time as any to ask.

"Mom," he began, "can I ask you something? I mean it may be kind of personal or even painful for you to talk about but, it's something I feel like I would really like to know."

"Sure Clay, just fire away and if it's something I'd just as soon not get into then I'll let you know son."

"It's about you and Dad," Clay said somewhat hesitantly.

"Okay, and what is that?"

"Well it's a bit more also actually. I'm curious about the circumstances around the time that he became involved with the woman whom he eventually married after you."

Maureen shifted in her seat before responding back to him.

"I noticed that you apparently didn't even want to say Beth's name, but its okay Clayton. Hopefully the fact that I have no problem with addressing her by name will show you that it's okay for you to do the same."

Clay knew from experience that his Mom only called him Clayton when she was about to get serious about something. Usually it was when he had run afoul of things as he grew up.

But since he knew that not to be the case in this instance he merely braced himself for whatever she had to say.

Listen son; at the time that your Father and Beth became let's say, really cozy; Clay Sr. and I were going through a little rough patch. Well more than a little to tell you the truth. There was more like a divide if not a full-fledged canyon separating us at that time. I mean honestly we had been discussing divorce for a couple of years. It was just that divorcing wasn't something that people did so quickly back in those days; especially not if you had a family.

So we decided to stick it out. To try to hold onto whatever it was that we had; which really was more of a charade at that point than anything else. But then Beth happened, and while it hurt at first, I came to understand. I understood why he would seek out more than what we had at that time. I mean I wanted more too, much more actually. It's just that in our case we decided that it would have to wait for the day when I might be free. That was if it was truly ever meant to be."

At that point Clay stood and started pacing around with his hands on top of his head. He was trying hard to digest just what it was that he felt his Mother was saying to him. What he had just heard was pretty much a confession from her that she too had her own outside dalliance. Just that she and whomever it was that she spoke of apparently made the decision to keep things at arm's length for at least as long as she was married to his father. As he walked around dumbfounded Maureen continued on slowly.

"So that's we decided to do; even after Beth came into the picture and the divorce proceedings eventually ensued. We waited it out and finally one day we were able to be together the way that we had wanted to for so long."

At that point Clay decided he had heard enough and interrupted her suddenly by telling her just that.

"Now Clayton, I know that some of this may be difficult for you. I mean it was difficult for your brother and sister also."

"What," Clay snapped. "You mean to tell me that they knew all of this?"

"Don't be upset with your brother and sister Clay. I asked them not to tell you anything."

"But why Mom?"

"You were the one who took the divorce the hardest. So I just decided that things were better off that way. I mean you never warmed up to Beth in the least. I knew that from your Father. Yes it may come as some surprise to you but we were able to remain on reasonably friendly terms even after we went our separate ways. But I realize that what happened may have in some way affected your relationship with your Father and the way you viewed him. So I didn't want to have anything hurt our relationship also son."

"I understand that Mom, and yes all of that did have some affect on the closeness between Dad and I."

"I know Clay and I'm truly sorry for that. Not to mention the fact that it also hurt the chances of you having a good relationship with your stepmother," a now teary eyed Maureen confessed.

Clay slowly walked over and gave her a hug. "It's okay Mom; I don't blame you for doing what you felt was right. You were trying to spare my feelings."

"Yes but look what's happened in the process. But there is one thing that it's not too late for. You can still have a better relationship with Beth. Please try not to be so hard on her Clay. She was just a part of what was going on at the time. And I hold no ill will against her myself. So can you try for me to forgive her; even if you feel you can never forget?"

"Yes Mom I promise to you that I will try."

"Thank you Son, that would make me feel a little bit better."

"But just one more thing if you don't mind Mom."

"Sure, what is it Clay?"

"This individual that you've alluded to; whatever happened to him?"

Maureen dipped her head before she started to answer slowly. It was clear that whatever her answer would be, it was somewhat painful for her to talk about.

"His divorce became final about six months after Clay Sr's and mine did. And," she continued hesitantly; "He and a couple of his buddies went out one night to celebrate together. They had all been drinking pretty heavily before they climbed into one of his friend's car headed back home. But they never made it back that night. They ran off the road someplace and down an embankment. Ironically enough the guy driving was the only one to survive the crash."

"I'm so sorry Mom, I had no idea."

"So as it turned out we had only a few short days together while we were both single."

"Well I guess I should get going then," Clay announced.

Tears again fell from Maureen's eyes as they embraced before Clay departed.

∞∞∞∞∞∞∞∞∞∞∞∞

Upon their return home from Florida, Clay didn't wait long at all to call on Beth. It was Wednesday, his first day back in the office when he decided to try to catch her at home around midday. He was pleased when he was able to reach her, because this was something he was ready to get over with in order to move on from there.

"Hi Beth, this is Clay; do you have a few minutes to talk," he asked her once she answered the phone.

"Sure Clay," she replied with more than a hint of anxiety in her voice. She was understandably concerned that he was calling just to chastise her some more. But those fears would soon be alleviated to her great surprise.

"Listen Beth, I had a talk with my Mother just recently and she made me aware of some things that I had no clue about previously. By that I mean some circumstances that were present at the time you and my father began seeing each other."

"Okay well," Beth started to cut in before Clay stopped her.

"Please Beth let me finish. Like I was saying, she made me aware of the fact that things between her and my Father were headed way south before you even entered the picture. So all these years that I've looked at you as being a home wrecker and the person solely responsible for my parents splitting up, I was wrong. I was very much wrong, and for that I apologize. And I'm very sorry that I never really respected you as a stepmom or gave you a chance to build that sort of relationship between us."

Just like his Mother a couple of days before, Beth too was very emotional when she finally was able to respond. "It's okay Clay, you were very young and I know that none of that could have been very easy for you. It wasn't easy for any of us at the time."

"No it wasn't, not at all, but let me say this. I know that it's been a lot of years and a lot of feelings have been involved, but it's never too late; so if it's okay with you I would like for us to be cordial to each other."

"Clay I would like that very much," Beth replied tearfully.

"Well I guess it's more like me starting to be cordial to you. I don't think you being nice to me has been the problem," Clay said with a bit of a chuckle.

"No I guess it hasn't," a smiling Beth agreed.

"Well I guess that's settled so let me say just one more thing."

"Yes what is it Clay?"

"The very next time we host a gathering at our home you'll be at the top of the invitation list."

"Okay I will look forward to that," Beth said cheerfully.

"All right well let me go so I can get back to work."

"Okay Clay but before you go let me say how much of a thrill it's been for me to be seeing little Zach so often. He's just a joy."

"You've been seeing Zach?" Clay responded with surprise.

"Ooops, I guess Sherri didn't want you to know given the way things have been between you and me. But I suppose it's okay now right?"

"Yeah sure it is Beth; that's great that you've gotten to spend time with him."

"And you know what's also great is the volunteer work that Sherri is doing. Not everyone will devote their time to that sort of thing."

"Oh yeah that's very good of her to do that. Well okay Beth let me go, and I'm sure we'll be in touch soon. You take care of yourself."

"You too Clay; bye-bye."

"Bye."

After ending that call Clay immediately called home. Sherri answered quickly and he cut right to the chase.

"How come you haven't told me that you've been doing some volunteer work outside of the house? I just found out from Beth."

"From Beth," Sherri said with surprise.

"Yes we just finished speaking before I called you, but that's neither here nor there; back to my question."

"Clay the reason I didn't bother telling you is because I felt like you wouldn't approve of it. I know how you feel about me doing any work outside of the home. You've made your feelings abundantly clear on that."

"Well that's true but apparently my wishes only carried so much weight as far as you're concerned."

"But that's only because I've started to think more about what I want and this is something that I've really wanted to do. I relish the feeling of getting out of the house a couple of days out of the week and not feeling so cooped up. Not to mention that I really enjoy it also and would like to continue with it."

After a noticeable pause Clay offered up his response.

"Okay, that's fine."

"Huh, did you say it was fine Clay?"

"Yes that is what I said. I mean I haven't seen where it's had any adverse affect on Zach or anything else and; being that you say that you really like doing it, then I say go right ahead. Besides, it's given Beth the chance to really get acquainted with Zach and vice-versa. So that's also a good thing. But where are you volunteering though?"

"At a senior center down in Lyons; I do everything from helping with serving meals to taking the residents' on walks or just engaging them in conversation or playing cards or board games with them. I really enjoy it; you'd be surprised how many older people just really don't have anyone there for them."

"Well I think it's good that you're giving of yourself like that Sherri, so I just want you to know that you do have my blessing."

"Thank you Clay, that means a lot to me."

And that was that. Sherri had pulled it off like a pro. It was quite a convincing   performance she had put on when one considers that the only volunteering she'd been doing was to voluntarily give herself completely to her two lovers on a regular basis. But there was one thing about the conversation with Clay that left her confused.

"So Clay, are you telling me that you and Beth had a normal, friendly conversation?"

"Yes we most certainly did but I won't get into that at this moment. I'll fill you in later but right now I need to take care of some things down here."

"Okay fair enough. And thanks for being open minded on this."

"No problem and I will see you this evening. Bye."

"Alright see you later."

Sherri was very proud of Clay after he told her all about the events of the last couple of days later that evening. She saw a somewhat sensitive side of him that he very rarely put on display. Not for her or anyone else for that matter. It moved her to the point that she genuinely desired him at that moment. But yet she was not all that disappointed when he rebuffed an attempt by her to seduce him. He brushed her off by instead promising her a rain check for over the weekend at some point. But of course she wasn't all that bothered by this once she remembered that she would finally be seeing Gee the next morning. And she kind of liked the idea of unleashing all of her horniness on him, figuring he would best be able to quell it. And in that he did not disappoint her in the least as they spent a rollicking four hours simply tearing into each other. When she left his place that afternoon she was amazed that she could stand upright, not to mention drive home, he had rocked her body so hard.

As for the rain check with Clay she decided to cash that in early that following Saturday morning. But although she did feel somewhat more connected to him as they made love, the bottom line was that for her, it again fell far short of the ultimate. She figures that would not have bothered her so much if he hadn't failed to respond to her not so subtle attempt to get his face between her legs for a change. That was the one frustrating thing for her. That he knew just what she wanted and still moved things along like he was in a rush. So what did she do in response? After quickly showering she told him a lie about wanting to go to the gym for a workout rather than use the one downstairs. She really stepped out to see Scott; someone who she knew would take care of her just the way she liked it. And once again Scott showed that he was indeed of some very good use to her. He came through like he always did when he ate her pussy like a professional. But in spite of that they would not see each other very much from that day forward. She could feel in her gut that their fling was close to running its course. Simply a casualty of the limitations of time and opportunity as well as the hold Gee had taken over her.

CHAPTER FOURTEEN

The first official day of summer couldn't have been more of a picture perfect day; a clear and sunny 82 degrees with a light breeze and very low humidity. Now Sherri wouldn't go as far as to say that factored into it, but she did notice that for some reason Gee was unusually affable and especially frisky on that day.

From the moment she entered his place he'd been smiling, and he even greeted her with an extended hug. And no sooner than had she walked past him, he came up behind her and wrapped his arms around her waist and again pulled her close to him. Brushing her hair aside he began to kiss her softly on her neck and shoulders. Using her left hand, she pushed and then held her long brown hair up on her head, giving him easy access; thus allowing him to seductively brush his lips against her soft skin.

"MMMMM, you smell so good," he whispered, his breath warm on her neck.

"It's a new perfume called Intense by Prada. I'm glad you like it."

"Oh yeah I love it," Gee replied as he moved his hands down to her breasts and begin to circle them slowly.

Sherri's legs started to quiver slightly and she felt a hint of moisture in the crotch of her panties. As his large hands continued to gently caress her breasts, Sherri reached one hand behind her seeking out his manhood. He grew hard in an instant from the touch of her fingers rubbing on his dick through his pants.

"Oh my, I see you have something for me. That didn't take long at all," she said before she turned and faced him and began to undo his belt. Just as she started to slowly lower his zipper while inching her way down to her knees, he abruptly stopped her.

"No, no hold on, "he said as he backed away from her slightly. He then walked around her and grabbed his keys off of the cocktail table. "Let's go," he commanded.

"Let's go? Gee what's going on, I don't get it."

"Nothing," he assured her while helping her back up to an upright position.

"Come on, just follow me; it's cool, I'll explain in time," he added.

Sherri threw her hands up slightly but placed her sunglasses over her eyes and trailed him out the door. As they climbed into his car and took off all Gee would tell her was that they were going for a drive.

"Listen; Gee, I know we have this great thing going on between us, but that doesn't mean that I'm comfortable with you just taking off and driving me God knows where. Come on now, tell me something."

"Relax baby, just chill for a minute. I just feel like a little something different that's all. Trust me; can you do that for me? Please?"

"Okay sure, I'll trust you. But just let me in on whatever you have up your sleeve soon okay?"

"You know I will, besides; it'll be clear enough in just a little while," he assured her as he reached over and patted her on the thigh.

They rode along, mostly quietly until they reached the entry ramp for Route 287 South. Gee quickly accelerated onto the heavily travelled highway and settled into the center lane. Cruising along at about 60 mph, he turned in Sherri's direction.

"Okay, are you ready?" he asked.

"For what?" she questioned in response.

Gee didn't answer with any words but instead placed a hand on his zipper and started to slide it down as a mischievous grin spread across his face.

"Are you serious?" Sherri responded with a somewhat uneasy smile.

"Oh yes, very serious. Come on, it'll be crazy; and fun, and certainly different.

"Yeah but…"

Gee knew just where her mind was at that point so he cut in before she could get all the words out.

"Oh don't worry, I've got this. I wouldn't put us at risk would I? I mean I don't know about you but I don't have a death wish."

"Well, I guess not, but I'm telling you, at the first sign of any weaving around or anything I'm stopping."

"Okay fair enough. But like I said, I've got the wheel, you just get this," he said while placing a hand on his crotch.

"Oh yeah, I can certainly handle that for you," she grinned.

Sherri quickly undid his pants, reached inside of his boxers and pulled out his already rock hard penis. After brushing her hair away from her face she leaned across his lap and slowly took him into her mouth.

"Shame on you Gee; you knew how bad I wanted it before we left your place and you made me wait so that you could set up your little scenario. Just for that I'm really gonna do a number on you."

"You're gonna make me pay baby?"

"Uh huh," she grunted between deep strokes down his shaft. "I'm gonna suck the hell out of this dick. Not to mention every drop of something else."

"Hey you've gotta do what ya gotta do," Gee quipped. He then twirled a handful of her hair around his fist and used it to guide her head up and down in a steady rhythm. "That's it baby," he moaned in his low, gravelly tone.

"You like it?" Sherri gasped when she came up for a bit of air.

"Oh I'm way beyond just liking it believe me, go ahead and do your thing."

"You just make sure you keep your eyes on the road," she insisted before taking him well into her mouth again.

"Come on now, I told you not to worry."

Convinced he could handle himself, she sucked firmly on the head while gripping him tightly with one hand.

"Whooooah," he cried out when she flicked her tongue all around the ultra sensitive tip of his penis.

Taking a glance to his left, he suddenly lowered the driver side window. He spent the next several seconds, honking the horn and then pumping his fist outside of the window. With the attention drawn to the car, several truckers began to sound their horns loudly after getting a bird's eye view of the action.

"Hey Sherri, I think we have an audience."

"Oh yeah," she replied dryly.

"Yep we sure do. Go ahead and wave at the nice people."

Sherri raised one hand overhead and waved it slowly as she continued to suck on Gee with abandon.

"Woo hoo, hey buddy you the man," someone shouted from one of the trucks Gee cruised alongside of.

"Go ahead, suck that dick baby," yelled out another.

Sherri responded with double thumbs up signal while steadfastly bobbing her head up and down.

"Okay this is getting too good, show time is over," Gee said while closing the open window. Glancing in his right outside mirror, he veered into the right lane before slowly coming to a stop on the shoulder of the highway.

"All right, now I have to admit; I had to stop. This shit was starting to get me shaking. But don't you stop though. You go ahead; that's right, do it baby," he groaned.

"There are some napkins in the glove compartment," Gee told Sherri after he had shot off in her mouth.

"What do you stay prepared for things like this or did you have them there because you had this pre-planned?"

"Neither. I just had them in there. Probably from some drive thru I went to."

"Can you imagine if a trooper had come by a few seconds ago?

"Oh please no big deal, I would have seen them coming way before they could have gotten close and pulled you off it if need be. Besides that's part of the thrill and excitement."

"I must admit I do sort of feel like a 21 year old again," Sherri stated as she sat there wiping the fruits of her labor from around her mouth with one of the napkins.

"You did something like this when you were 21?" asked Gee curiously.

"No, but I would have if I were ever given the chance to. You were right it was fun."

Gee was so appreciative of Sherri being so open and willing that he immediately took her back to his place where he gave her a robust fuck that left her both completely satisfied and fully spent. A short time later, as they laid there chatting about this and that, she ventured to ask him something that she had been wondering about for a while.

"Hey do you mind if I ask you a question," she said as she lightly stroked his still semi-erect penis."

"Go ahead shoot," he replied.

"I'm just curious about something. What's your girlfriend like?"

"Come on now, why would you ask me something like that? That's like me wanting to know about your husband."

"It's no big deal, I would tell you about him."

"Yeah but that's just it, I don't give a damn and neither should you."

"It's not so much that I care, it's just that I'm curious as to what type of woman managed to capture your heart that's all."

"Yeah okay; whatever."

"Hey that's fine, you don't have to tell me, sorry I asked," Sherri complained before she rolled over onto her back, folding her arms across her chest.

After several seconds she realized it worked when Gee relented. "Okay, okay I will tell you if you want to know that badly," he began. Well first of all she's tall, about 5'8" and slender yet with curves if that makes sense. You know I need some curves in the right places. I don't want any straightaway unless it's when I'm driving," he chuckled. "I mean what else? I don't know; she's certainly very pretty. The first time I met her she reminded me of Tyra Banks facially. She has shoulder length hair, she's both smart and intelligent and just a sweet hearted person overall.

"What type of work does she do?"

"Well damn what are you planning to write an autobiography on her?"

"Oh never mind then, if it's that much of a secret."

"Alright damn; she's a Flight Attendant."

"Oh really, and you work at the airport; is that where you two met?"

"Actually no, I guess that's what most people would think but we met at a function we were both attending."

"I've always thought that being a Flight Attendant might be a cool job except of course that you have to be away from home a lot."

"Yeah and I guess that's something that I had to come to accept over time."

"Oh I would think so. Do you think that has anything to do with you wanting someone on the side?"

"I don't know, maybe a little; it's more about me. I mean I love my girl no doubt. And I'm definitely planning to marry her. One day. It's just that I don't think I'm exactly a one-woman man just yet. I still enjoy some variety. But anyway enough of that right now. Why don't you come over here and serve me up some more of that good and plenty."

"You are such a horny man do you know that?"

"Yes I am and don't you like me that way? I mean if I wasn't would you be here right now?"

"Maybe, I don't know. I guess I would just get to enjoy you far less often if you weren't such a stud."

"Well if that's the way you look at me then take some more of this dick."

"You know you don't have to tell me twice," Sherri said as she started to roll over. She straddled his body and started to lick and suck his nipples until he was again standing at attention. "You know we're both crazy right?" she inquired to him.

"Yep, I'm crazy about pussy and you're crazy about dick."

"What am I gonna do with you Gee?"

"I don't know, I kind of like what you're doing with me right now to tell you the truth."

Sherri merely shook her head. "Pass me a condom please. She then proceeded to roll the condom onto his dick before riding Gee all the way to ecstasy; both his and hers. "Oh my God!" she exclaimed when it was over. That was out of this world. You're absolutely right; I damn sure love that dick. I just can't get enough of it. So I'm just going to enjoy as much of it as I can for as long as I can."

"You know that's all right with me," Gee offered.

Several minutes later they were engaging in more idle small talk once again when Sherri showed her curiosity hadn't yet waned; at least not completely.

"Hey, I know how you apparently feel about it Gee, but do you mind if I ask you one last question about your lady friend?"

"Okay go ahead; and I might even answer," he said with a smile that hid just how he was feeling about her increasingly probing inquiries.

"Well I was just sort of wondering about something. Does she make you want to climb the walls like I do?"

"Oh you think you're all of that with your sex skills huh?"

"Oh no I know I am. I have no doubts about that." But again I'm just curious."

"And you don't think you're overstepping your boundaries with a question like that?"

"No, not particularly, but if you see it that way you can always decline to answer. I'd understand."

"Yes I know that, but its okay. Now I'm not about to go into any sort of details about the sex life my girl and I have, but I will say this---I have no and I mean none, concerns in that department. It's off da chain as they say. If that wasn't the case we wouldn't be together. I mean could you see me with somebody who doesn't like to get it as well as give it?"

"No I guess I really can't," Sherri admitted. "But I suppose the one thing different is that you go down on her often huh?"

"Oh you better believe I do. Every chance I get, which really isn't often enough to suit me. Don't get it twisted now; I love to go downtown. Eating pussy is an extreme pleasure of mine. It's just that like I said hers is the only elevator I choose to ride down on."

"Yes I know, you've made that oh so clear," Sherri replied sarcastically.

"Hey I told you the deal on that almost from the door, so there's no need to act like you've got an attitude about it now.

Besides, you can stop getting down on mine anytime you want to. I'll still be alright."

"Okay, like I can just do that anytime with no problem. Like it would really be that easy."

"Oh trust me baby, I know what's up. Attitude or not right now; you'll be right back here on Thursday sucking this dick like a popsicle."

Sherri's wry smile told him just how correct he was.

It's the truth; we both know that; anyway that's as much as I'm going to say."

"That's okay Gee, at least you're always straight up with me; how I take it is up to me."

"It's nothing at all personal baby, just the way it is."

"Don't worry about it Gee I don't take it that way at all."

"Alright, so we're good then?"

"Yeah we're good."

"Okay cool, that's what I like to hear," Gee said. "Now why don't you go on and get ready to get outta here before we wind up doing that shit one more time."

"Well you know I wouldn't mind that."

"Yes I know with your little hot ass, but I need to try to get some rest before I have to go to work today."

"Okay I guess I'll see you in a few days," Sherri said just before departing. Gee was already comfortable and seemingly half-asleep when she left, not even bothering to see her to the door.

CHAPTER FIFTEEN

"I'm going to go on home and get some rest. Maybe I'll feel better in the morning. Hopefully that's the case anyway."

With that Clay left the office and headed home. It had been a while since he'd had a migraine this bad. He was hoping that taking something and getting some added rest would help it to go away. "If you have a need for anything just give me a call at home or email me," he said to his administrative assistant Jeri. "I should be home in less than 30 minutes."

∞∞∞∞∞∞

Gee had pretty much taken over as Sherri's boy toy, so unfortunately that didn't leave a lot of time for her to spend with Scott. In fact she hadn't seen him in a few weeks. He'd tried to pin her down on a few occasions but she was completely dicknotized by Gee and just wasn't leaving much opportunity for Scott to fit in someplace. That was really sort of a pity for her too because that man knew how to eat her pussy and was never reluctant to do so. He was fairly decent at everything else also, but he was so good with his tongue that it sort of overshadowed the other skills he had in the bedroom.

On this day she was chatting with Scott on Yahoo in an attempt to at least keep the lines of communication open. She never knew when she might want to break that emergency glass and line up that talented tongue to take care of her in a pinch.

"Hey babe, how have you been?" she had asked him as an opening.

"I've been doing okay."

"Oh, just okay?"

"Yeah that's about it."

"I wish I could do something to make things better."

"Oh really, you don't say."

"Yes I do. So, have you missed me?"

"I guess I have a little but I've been getting by."

"You know I have nothing but good thoughts about every time with you."

"Me too, I suppose."

"Come on you can do a little better than that can't you?"

"I could, but I'm just choosing not to right now."

"Is there any particular reason why that is?"

"Not really; at least nothing other than that I can sense things are different between us now."

"I'm sorry it's just that I've been really busy."

"Hey it's okay; I know how things change. This isn't my first rodeo; I just have to make some adjustments myself."

"If you're patient with me I can promise you things would get better on my end really soon."

"Hey I'll still be around so we'll see, but I'm certainly not limiting myself."

" I wouldn't expect you too, but I'm happy you're at least keeping a door open."

"But anyway, I have a call to make so let me get going."

"Sure go ahead babe. I want to take a shower anyway. Perhaps we can pick this up after we both finish what we have to do."

"Hmmm I don't know; maybe I'll talk to you later; or maybe not."

"Well we can if you want to; I'll check when I get out of the shower to see if you're still around anyway; but bye for now."

"Bye," Scott said simply in closing.

Thinking like an optimist, Sherri decided to leave the chat open so that they could possibly pick up where they were left off once she completed her shower and Scott took care of his business. But unbeknownst to her and certainly completely unexpectedly, Clay arrived home a short time after Sherri had gotten up from the computer and climbed into the shower. His first stop was in the bedroom where he kicked off his shoes. He could hear the sound of the shower running so he knew Sherri was in there. He wanted to lie down right away but he decided to check in at the office one last time and also check his email. He figured he would use the phone in the office to call Jeri so that he could sit at the PC and also check the stock performances thus far for the day, rather than do it from his handheld. He picked up the phone and started dialing the office as he took a seat at the computer. He was peering in at the monitor in front of him just as Jeri answered.

"Hey Jeri it's me; any messages?

Jeri informed him of the one message that he had and asked if he wanted the number that was left for him to call back. But he never heard any of that. He couldn't believe his eyes as they focused in on what was on the screen in front of his face.

"Jeri, let me call you right back," he whispered into the phone.

"Are you feeling any better?" she then asked.

"I'll call you right back," he repeated slowly before placing the cordless receiver on the desk. The more he read the more astonished he became over what he appeared to have just stumbled upon. He took his time and read it back from the beginning. Now convinced, he slowly rose from the chair and walked back into the bedroom where he peeled off his pants and walked into the closet to hang them up before replacing them with a pair of sweatpants. He then made himself comfortable on the bed, lying on his back staring at the ceiling. With his head now hurting a little more he got up and retrieved a single extra strength Advil and quickly ingested it.

About five minutes later Sherri emerged from the bathroom wrapped in her black silk robe.

"Hey what are you doing home," a very surprised Sherri said when she saw him.

"I came down with a pretty bad migraine so I just wanted to come home and lie down."

"Can I get you anything?" Sherri offered.

"No thanks, I just took something. I'm just gonna lay here and relax for a while. Hopefully I'll feel much better after that."

"Well if you're sure I can't get you anything I'm gonna go and let you get some rest."

"Yes I'm fine, you go ahead."

"Well feel better."

"Thanks," Clay replied while he studied her face intently, paying particular attention to her eyes. As she turned and departed the room his eyes followed her until she was completely out of his sight.

As Sherri stepped into the hallway she suddenly remembered what she had been doing before she went into the shower. She paused in her tracks, wondering but not sure. She looked back in the direction of the bedroom where Clay now was. She would never know if she didn't ask, she was thinking. But what if he had in fact stopped at the computer before heading into the bedroom? To ask him would have been almost like an admission of guilt or something. So instead she went into the kitchen and got herself a glass of cold water before quietly making her way back to the office. She was a bit shaken, but knew she needed to play it cool. She immediately closed the chat window. Even without checking to see if Scott was there waiting on her. She would explain later if need be. But now she just had to hope. She went into the living room and stared at the wall as she pondered things. Next, she picked up a magazine and thumbed through it in an attempt to divert her attention elsewhere, although she knew it was unlikely to help. Again, hope was all that she could use to push away what was in her mind and now dominating her thoughts. Damn, she thought to herself as she ran her hands along her face in a worrisome fashion. How could he happen to come home just then out of all times? She got up and went back into the kitchen where she poured out the glass of water and replaced it with some Chardonnay which she stood there sipping while leaning against the counter.

Meanwhile in the bedroom, Clay laid on his back staring at the ceiling for about 10 minutes before he reached for the phone. The first call he made was another one to his office in which he retrieved the message that Jeri had for him. Next up he dialed the cell phone of his Chief of Detectives for the prosecutor's office. He and Roland "Rollie" Celini were former high school classmates and Clay had plucked him from the state police where Roland was a Sargeant, to be the head of his investigative unit.

"Hello," Rollie answered in his deep baritone when Clay dialed him.

"Hey Rollie it's me Clay, how you doing?"

"Good buddy," what's going on?"

"Well I just wanted to ask if you could come by my office sometime tomorrow. Got a little something I want to ask you. Just a little favor, nothing too major."

"Sure Clay I can come by; any particular time?"

"Nope, whenever you can make it; you just might want to give me a heads up just in case of the unlikely possibility of me not being in."

"Okay I'll give you a call about an hour or so before I would be showing up; that good?

"Sure, that sound good Rollie, I'll just wait for your call."

"Okay buddy, take it easy, have a good day."

"You do the same, bye."

"Bye."

Clay hung up the phone and rolled back over; again staring blankly at the ceiling. A short time later, Sherri came in to check on him.

"Hey, I thought you might be asleep. I just came to see how you were doing."

Or maybe you hoped I would be sleeping so you can comfortably go back to your little chat you had going on before I apparently spoiled it by coming home unexpectedly, Clay was thinking, though he answered differently. "I feel okay, just waiting for the pain relief to kick in some more. Either that or for me to go to sleep," he said softly.

Sherri tried to get a read on where his head might be by looking him straight in the eye, but she couldn't get a real feel for it one way or the other. "Well try to get some sleep," she suggested.

"I've been trying but I've had a lot on my mind," Clay let on.

"Sherri paused before responding. "Oh yeah, such as what?" she asked a bit nervously.

"Oh nothing in particular; just things," was all that Clay would say.

"Okay well I'm going; just let me know if you need anything. And try to get some needed rest," said Sherri.

"Thanks I'll see you in a bit. You know it feels strange to be home this time of day on a weekday."

"Maybe I'll close the door," Sherri said as she walked away.

NO, leave it like it is," Clay snapped. I mean how will you hear if I do call out for you," he then said in a much calmer tone.

"Okay never mind," a confused sounding Sherri responded before trudging her way out of the bedroom slowly. "Geez it's not like you're suddenly an invalid," she thought aloud as she made her way back to the living room, pausing for only a quick look in on Zach who was still content in his room.

∞∞∞∞∞∞∞∞∞∞

"Clay's cell phone rang about 9:00 the next morning with a call from Rollie.

"Hey are you in the office yet," he asked once Clay answered.

"No but I'm on the road; I should be in by 9:30 at the latest."

"Well in that case why don't I shoot by about 10:15 or so? That would give you some time to get settled in. That work for you?"

"Sounds perfect, I'll see you then."

"Okay see ya in a bit," Rollie said in response.

Jerilyn Barnsworth was a top notch administrative assistant. But she was also a notorious slacker when afforded the opportunity. And this particular day fit the bill as she was surfing on the Orbitz.com website when Rollie entered. She was so engrossed in checking out resorts down in the Caribbean for her upcoming honeymoon that she hadn't even heard him nor seen the shadow of the 6'2" 250 lb. man until he was practically hovering right over her desk.

"Hey what's going on sexy lady," he growled causing Jeri to react noticably.

"Oh my God, you scared the you know what out of me," she said. Her next reaction was to hold one hand up at the top of her blouse in order to keep it from falling too far open. Rollie always had a way of making her feel uncomfortable in his presence and that day was no exception.

"Hey sorry, but it's not my fault that whatever you're looking at on the internet had your attention to the point where you had blocked everything else out. Anyway I'm here to see Clay sweetheart."

She loathed the way that he always called her things like sweetheart or sweetie, sexy lady, baby etc. But she knew that he was one of Clay's top guys so she never wanted to make much of an issue out of it because she figured that would probably lead to her being out of a job sooner than anything else. Sure, she could then file suit for harassment but why go through all that, just because of some occasional rude comments tossed her way by some jerk.

"I'll let him know you're here," said Jeri. As she stood and walked as quickly as she could into Clay's office, she tugged at the hem of her skirt in a futile attempt to somehow make it longer. Jeri had a penchant for wearing short skirts and the highest of heels and right then she was regretting that combination. As she walked away from him she could almost feel Rollie's penetrating stare all over her 5'10" inch frame.

"He'll be right out," Jeri said when she returned a short time later.

"Thanks, honey buns," a leering Rollie replied.

Oh today its honey buns; that's actually a new one Jeri was thinking as she took a seat. But she said nothing; only pushed some of her short, neatly- styled, blonde hair off of her face and refocused her attention on the computer screen before her. After several seconds she noticed that he hadn't moved and was just standing over her; even annoyingly tapping his fingers on the ledge above her desk.

"You can go have a seat and I'm sure Clay will be right with you," she said hopefully.

"No that's okay; I don't mind waiting here, but thanks anyway."

"Yes but I might mind," she protested to no avail as he insisted on staying put where he was.

Jeri let out a deep breath and tried not to let his presence bother her. She would just have to live with his invasion of her personal space for a short time. Thankfully Clay appeared a few moments later albeit very, very long moments in Jeri's eyes.

Hey bud come on in," Clay said the moment he saw Rollie standing by Jeri's desk.

"Well pick out someplace nice to go on your honeymoon," Rollie whispered as he started away from the desk in order to follow Clay into his office. "You are getting married aren't you; next year I believe right?" he added after he noticed the stunned expression on Jeri's face.

By this time Jeri was fuming and Rollie only added to it as he turned back and winked at her as he departed on the heels of Clay. She would deal with how he knew all this later.

Clay and Rollie embraced the moment, they entered his huge office.

"Good to see you Rollie," Clay said to him.

"Same here, how's the family and everything?"

"Well I guess that's sort of why I asked you to come by today. I'll explain in a bit," he said upon noticing the confused look on Rollie's face. "In the meantime, have a seat," Clay insisted as he went over to close his office door.

Clay took a seat at his desk while Rollie made himself comfortable in one of his 2 guest chairs. He took a moment to study Clay's face and took no time in determining that something heavy was laying on his mind.

"Wow Clay I can tell there's something bugging you. Is everything good with the kids?"

"Sure the kids are fine, no problems there."

"Okay well, how about the wife?"

Both Clay's head and his heart sank a bit at the question but he could come up with no words with which to respond, so he instead said nothing.

"Clay come on, talk to me buddy; is everything good with Sherri? I mean with the way you reacted at the mere mention of her I guess there must be something you need to get off your chest. Unless," he paused; "she's not sick or anything is she?"

"No Sherri isn't sick; she's just fine; maybe a little too good actually. Look Roll I'm just going to give it to you straight. I have some concerns about something that Sherri may and I do mean may, be involved in."

"Well come on give it to me straight Clay, just like you said."

Clay stared off into the ceiling for a brief moment before turning to Rollie and again starting to speak. "Okay here goes. I left work early yesterday and went home because I had a major headache. I didn't call to announce that I was coming, I just left. I mean I was going home, not to visit a friend or associate who I needed to check with first to see if the timing was right. So anyway, when I arrived home I immediately went into the bedroom to get comfortable and I guess say hello to Sherri; but that's when I discovered that she was in the shower. So then I decided to check in with Jeri for any calls that may have come in for me, and also to check my stocks on the home computer," Clay continued before pausing.

"Alright I'm with you, go ahead," Rollie said before Clay continued.

"Well when I sat down at the PC I couldn't quite believe my eyes. Couldn't believe what was staring back at me Roll. Clearly Sherri had been chatting online with some guy before she jumped in the shower because the conversation was still on the screen in plain view. I mean I started to read through what was said up until that point and it was crystal clear to me."

"Come on now Clay, are you sure?"

"I'm very sure. I'm telling you Roll, it was full of suggestive dialog. I mean I can't recall verbatim what was said but things were along the lines of asking have you missed me, wish I could do something to make you better and referring to the other party as babe; I mean it doesn't get more obvious."

"Clay could you be reading too much into that? I mean are you certain she was even chatting with someone of the opposite sex? That's stuff that could just as well be said to a relative or friend."

"Well I can't say that I'm 100% sure and it certainly wasn't a good time for me to be questioning, but if it walks and talks like a duck…"

"Then it's more than likely a duck," Rollie finished the statement. And let's say that it is a fucking duck; what's your thought on how you're gonna deal with it and how I come in. I mean I'm here for you, but I would just hate to see you make something out of nothing."

"Well I'm getting to that but first let me also tell you this; I found out recently that Sherri has been dropping our youngest off at my stepmom's twice a week so that she can go out and do some volunteer work."

"Some volunteer work?" Rollie repeated with a smirk. "Hmmm that's a good one. I mean if it's really just a front."

"And she didn't even tell me about this volunteering until I asked her about it. I heard it from my stepmom first."

"Wow. Well I must say I see where you're coming from now. I still hope you're wrong and all because in spite of my personal feelings about marriage I've always considered Sherri to be like the salt of the Earth," the long divorced Rollie commented.

"I hope so too Rollie, but at least now you understand my concerns here right?"

"Oh I certainly do Clay. But the question is how are you going to get a clear answer?"

"Well I have been doing some thinking and that brings me to why I asked you to come by. I'm wondering if maybe you could help me out with this."

"Sure pal, you know I will if I can; what is it you have in mind?"

"I'm hoping maybe you could just keep an eye on Sherri for a little while."

"You mean like put a tail on her?"

"Well not exactly. Not like around the clock or anything crazy like that, but more on those days when she's supposed to be doing this volunteer work."

"I see what you're saying, because on the chance that there is anything going on, that's more than likely when it's going down."

"Exactly; I mean I just don't see any other possibility with the kids and all of her other responsibilities."

"I hear you loud and clear buddy."

"So are you on board with my idea?" asked Clay.

"Come on now Clay, you know I am. My feelings about Sherri as a friend aside, I feel far more loyalty towards you. So if she is stepping out on you, I want nothing more than for you to know so that you can handle it however you would see fit."

"Okay, well let me fill you in on some particulars then shall I."

Clay then went on to tell Rollie the days on which Sherri said her volunteering was taking place. They also briefly discussed what the modus operandi would entail. The conversation ended with Rollie telling Clay that he would get back to him in 24 hours once he'd had the chance to think on it. As he prepared to depart once Clay walked him back out to the reception area, Rollie couldn't resist stopping for a little more ogling of Jeri. As it turned out she was just returning to her desk from getting a drink as Rollie was headed out. As she walked past him on her way to her desk he stood there nearly salivating at the sight of her long, sleek, sexy body.

"My oh my," he snickered while coming to a sudden halt in front of her desk once again. "Now I have no idea how religious you may or may not be, but Lord have mercy; that is one heavenly body you've got there."

"Goodbye, it was nice seeing you. Wish you could stay but I'm sure you must have some things to do," Jeri replied dismissively.

"Yes and I'm hoping you might be one of those things I have to do one day," Rollie grinned at her.

At that point Jeri stood up from her desk and walked away while throwing an angry look in his direction.

"Hey, I'm just trying to help you out here baby," he called out to her. "Give you a chance to come to your senses before you make the mistake of getting married."

At that point Jeri decided she'd had enough. She slammed shut the file cabinet she had started going through and quickly walked back over to him. "You know something I've never complained to Clay about you, but if you keep this shit up I assure you that's just what's gonna happen. And if he doesn't do anything to put a stop to it than I'm more than ready to take it to someone else who will."

Rollie looked at her intently, incredulous that she was threatening to take it that far.

"Come on now sweet thing, it's not that serious, I just like to have fun with you that's all. But if it that's much of an issue with you I'll leave it alone okay."

"Good and you might want to start by not calling me sweet thing or honey buns or whatever else might come to your mind."

"Okay, okay fine, no problem. I'm getting out of here. Enjoy the rest of your day," Rollie muttered before leaving.

Jeri hoped that her words alone would be enough to shake him to the point where he would stop his harassment and unwanted comments. Because again, she knew that she had no real intention of complaining to Clay due to the closeness of his friendship with Rollie.

Rollie called Clay that evening while he was driving home from the office.

"Hey buddy I have a thought in regards to what you would like to do as far as keeping tabs on Sherri for a bit."

"Okay, I'm all ears; what do you have in mind Rollie?"

"Well I like the idea of watching her for a while, but the only problem is this. Sherri is very familiar with me, so if something were to ever happen where she might spot me at any time while I was tailing her, well that could just tip her off, you know."

"Yeah I guess that's a possibility, but if you were to be careful that probably wouldn't happen."

"True, but the way I see it why take that chance. So here's what I'm thinking. I could just hand over the task to somebody else."

"All right I get what you're saying, but somebody like whom?"

"Oh don't worry I have somebody who'd be perfect for the job. I can bring him by in the morning and the three of us can sit down and discuss it."

"Okay that's fine. And you feel comfortable with this person?"

"Yes I am; completely," Rollie assured Clay. But I won't say anything to him until we're both in front of you," he added.

"Okay, but instead of you bringing him by the office why don't we all meet someplace for lunch."

"Sure that'll be fine; you have any place in mind?"

"How about Carmichael's?"

"Sounds good; one o'clock work for you?"

"That works fine, we'll see you then," Clay responded before they said their goodbyes.

∞∞∞∞∞∞∞∞∞∞∞∞

"I just think I need to lay low for a while until the heat goes down a little bit," Sherri was reasoning with Gee.

"Well just how long are we talking here?"

"I don't know Gee, we'll just have to wait and see. I'm thinking at least a couple of weeks and then I can see what feel I have for things. Just be a little patient with me, that's all I'm asking."

Gee sighed deeply into the phone before speaking again. "Okay I can give it a couple of weeks. Besides my girl will be off all the week after next so it's gonna be all about her that entire week anyway."

"Oh so I wouldn't have seen you that week regardless?"

"Nah baby it's gonna be me and her that week; a chance for us to catch up on a lot of things. I'm sure you would have been alright. Shit, you could have hung out with your hubby that week. You still can."

"Yeah okay, whatever," Sherri said as if she was put off by the mere thought of it. "Anyway; what about next week; you'll be fine with that right? I mean you won't abandon me just like that will you?"

"Come on, you know I won't do that to you. I'll just let you make up for it whenever we get together again," he chuckled while being dead serious.

"Oh trust me, you know I will do that," Sherri flirted.

"Oh believe me, I'm gonna see to that," Gee promised.

Strangely enough as much as Sherri made certain to inform Gee of her desire to stand down for a couple of weeks she had no inclination to make a similar call to Scott. It was as if she was just prepared to simply let that go if that's what was in the cards. Like que sera sera, whatever will be will be. She hadn't even reached out to him in an attempt to explain what had happened when Clay came home unexpectedly the other day. Maybe she shouldn't allow that door to close completely, a part of her thought. But yet that seemed to be just what was about to happen. She could only hope it wasn't something that she would come to regret in time.

Carmichael's is a popular and well known sandwich shop located on Route 22 in Bridgewater. They're famous for their overstuffed deli sandwiches featuring everything from pastrami, corned beef and ham to chicken salad and chopped liver.

And in Clay's estimation they also make one of the best Italian hotdogs he has ever tasted. In fact he was dying to order one, but as the first one to arrive there he wanted to wait for his lunch companions just in case they were running very late rather than just by a few minutes. So he instead stood just inside the entry door. He took a glance at his watch and noted that the current time was 1:07. He had come from home rather than the office and he figured that Rollie might be running late due to either he, or whomever he was bringing with him having to pick the other one up. But that notion was dismissed when they stepped out of separate cars and approached the restaurant some 10 or so minutes later. They walked side by side, Rollie and a bearded man of average height and weight. Clay stepped outside to greet them when they got close to the door.

"Hey I was starting to think I was being stood up," Clay blurted out as soon as Rollie saw him.

"Oh yeah sorry about that, it was entirely my fault, I had to stop and get gas and a pack of smokes," Rollie admitted.

"Well you're here now so let's head inside shall we?"

"Sure pal, but first let me do the honors. Clay this is Michael Marciniak; he's one of my detectives."

"Hey good to meet you Michael; Clay King," was the response before the two of them shook hands.

"Same here Sir, but you can call me Mike."

"Sure no problem Mike," Clay said as he held the door open for the other two men. "Oh and by the way, none of that Sir stuff here; call me Clay."

"You've got it Clay."

The three of them took seats at one of the booths in the rear of the sandwich shop.

"We're really lucky to get a booth during this time of day," Rollie noted. "I mean with the lunchtime crunch and all."

"Well actually I asked them if they could hold a booth for us after I first arrived here and introduced myself," said Clay. "Anyway let's hurry up and order so that we can get right to why we're all here."

Clay already knew what he was going to have so Rollie and Mike quickly browsed through menus before also deciding on something fairly quickly.

"Okay I'll be right back," Rollie announced before he went up to the counter to put the sandwich orders in for the three of them.

"So Mike, how long have you known Rollie?" Clay asked once they were seated at the table alone.

"About 9 years, I'm also a former trooper and we served out of the same barracks."

Clay took a moment to study Mike further as he answered the question. He looked to be in his mid to late 30's. He sported a military style haircut and a few tattoos adorned his bare forearms.

"You former military?" was Clay's next question.

"Yeah special forces; I did a tour over in Iraq."

"Cool, good man; I commend you for that. I have a great respect for what you guys have done and continue to do."

"Thanks, we appreciate that, believe me."

"Anyway I don't know if he told you at all but Rollie and I go way back. Grew up in the same neighborhood in Brooklyn and even graduated high school together," Clay noted just as Rollie was returning to the booth.

"Yeah and Clay was the neighborhood bully," Rollie quipped.

"Really," Mike responded with a look of surprise.

"Really; I was not to be fucked with," said Clay. But hey, I was an Irish guy in a mostly Italian neighborhood. I had to learn to walk the walk or get walked over."

"Wow," Mike said with a raised brow.

"Hey but its okay I was the neighborhood romeo who stole all the girls virginity," Rollie noted. "I was a lover not a fighter."

"Okay now that I really don't believe," Mike quickly replied.

"Smart man and obviously one who has a nose for bullshit," Clay interjected before they all laughed. "Anyway let's get to the matter at hand shall we?"

"Yes by all means, let's do that. Clay let me handle this for starters," Rollie insisted.

"Sure go ahead buddy."

"Okay Mike I'm just going to get right into it. This is the deal. Clay has a wife and three kids. They've been married what about 15 years Clay?" he asked as he looked to Clay.

"Close, we just passed fourteen."

"Alright I was only in the wedding, you'd think I might remember but hey I'm getting old, but anyway—Mikey like I was saying Clay has a wife and just recently some things have come to his attention that have given him pause. And these things have started to make him wonder if perhaps his lady hasn't been straying a bit. Now we don't need to go into any details about what these things are but let's just say they're there okay," Rollie concluded in his deep-voiced New York accent.

Mike nodded his head while passing his glance back and forth between the two of them.

"So anyway there you have it in a nutshell. And next is where we come in. I mean first me, and now hopefully you if you're up to it," Rollie continued before pausing briefly. "So what Clay would like to do is to have his wife watched for a while. Sort of kept tabs on if you know what I mean.

"You mean put a tail on her?" Mike questioned, seeking clarification.

"Yes that's exactly what we're talking about Mike," Clay chimed in.

"And you see Clay's wife Sherri and I know each other pretty well. So we're thinking that might lead to a problem somewhere along the line; make it more difficult for me to pull it off. And that's what brings us to you.

"In the meantime, the next call that Sherri placed after Gee was to Beth. She informed her that she wouldn't need her to keep Zach for a couple of weeks. That the senior center was experiencing a reduction in the number of residents as of late and thus wouldn't need quite as many volunteers for the time being. That particular lie was an easy sell as there was absolutely no reason at all for her honesty to be questioned by Beth.

Back at Carmichaels the three men were trying to iron out some details of what they'd been discussing. "Mike I told Clay how confident I am that you'd be able to pull this off," Rollie informed him.

Mike looked at Clay, who nodded in agreement.

"Yeah sure, it's something I can handle with no problem."

"Good, it's nice to know that you have the confidence that Rollie's belief in you is not misplaced."

"Yeah well I certainly have every bit of confidence in that," Mike reiterated.

"Well here's what you'll do," Clay began as Rollie looked on intently. "My wife supposedly volunteers at a senior center on Mondays and Thursdays. On those days you'll stake out a position on the block where our home is located and wait for her to leave. And when she does you'll simply track where she goes. I mean hopefully I've been reading too much into things and she's been going just where she says she has. But if not, what you'll do is report your findings to Rollie. Where she's going and how long she's staying there. Simple enough right?"

"Yes I would think so," Mike concurred.

"Okay, now listen Mike," Rollie instructed. You're going to have a pair of binoculars and a camera. You know what to do with those. Now what we'll do is give it a couple of weeks to see what you come up with. And you'll report anything directly to me first understood?"

"Yep, completely," answered Mike.

Clay handed Mike a piece of paper on which he had written something down as Rollie was speaking. "Here's my address, you can get started on this next Monday," he told him.

"Sounds good and hopefully things are not as they seem," Mike said.

"Well we'll see, but yes hopefully that is the case," Clay seconded.

Spending so much time at home during the week was something that Sherri had grown unaccustomed to, but she had no doubt that she had done the prudent thing when she made the decision to keep a low profile for a bit. With the school year over Abby and Tyler were by then fully immersed in their daily summer camp schedule. The township places a heavy emphasis on using the summer to further enrich the lives of its youth with interesting activities that exercise and develop them not just physically but mentally as well. So with just her and Zach left behind Sherri was able to balance time spent playing, with trying to get him a head start on the fall when he would begin preschool. It was nothing too overwhelming, just some basic work on the alphabet, numbering, various shapes and colors. Zach took to it right away and seemed to genuinely enjoy it. All in all Sherri felt like she did a good enough job of remaining busy during those couple of weeks that she spent little time dwelling on the break she felt compelled to take from Gee. And on the rare occasions that she did, she simply took the time to relieve herself via masturbation.

It was 2 weeks from the day they'd met at Carmichael's when Clay received a call from Rollie.

"Hey I just wanted to give you a call because I heard from Mike today."

Clay's pulse quickened and a lump formed in his throat as he braced himself to hear the words he wasn't necessarily prepared for. He stood and started to walk towards the window and looked outside into the gray sky. "Okay let me hear it," he said slowly.

"He says he's got nothing buddy."

"What!" Clay exclaimed as he hurried over and took a seat in his chair.

"That's right; says he's been there not just on the past two Mondays and Thursdays but every weekday and Sherri hasn't been going much of anyplace. She's been making the occasional trip to the supermarket or the drug store and such but nothing more than that."

"Are you, I mean is he sure Rollie? There's no possibility that she slipped away from him at all?"

"No. I'm telling you Mike is good and what he does, so if he's says that then I certainly believe him."

"Wow. I can't believe it. I mean that's good news and all but I just was so sure there was something."

"Well let me just say this Clay; it still may be that you weren't wrong. I mean it could be that she started to have a feeling you might be on to something and just decided to cool it for a while. I have a friend who's a Private Investigator and he says that's a pretty common thing; for the guilty party to try lesson any suspicion that may be placed on them once they get a sense of it. But only for a while; just long enough for them to think that the heat is off. But it seldom lasts for long if an affair is ongoing."

"You know that's a good point. So what are you suggesting I do Rollie?"

"Well nothing really, just keep things as they are. Let 's have Mike stay on it for a little while longer and then we'll see."

"Okay let's do that and I guess you can update me in another 2-3 weeks."

"Yeah that should be more than long enough to see if your gut was right or not."

"Yes I guess it would be. Thanks Roll and I'll wait for your next call."

CHAPTER SIXTEEN

"So, are you ready to do this again?"

"Yes of course I am. It's been a while now."

"Well I hope your girlfriend saved me a little bit."

"Oh you know I was going to see to that," Gee responded.

"Great, well I guess I'll see you tomorrow then?"

"I'll sure be here waiting for you."

"The regular time?"

"Yep, that sure works for me."

"I don't know about you but I can't wait. It's all I've been thinking about for the last week," Sherri confessed.

"Cool; then I'll have to make sure that I really put it on you."

"Oh you'd better, because I'm really counting on that. I need a good fuck in the worst way."

"Don't worry I'm gonna give it to you in the best way. The only way I know how."

"Damn I wish I could come over there and get some right now."

"Come on, what's stopping you?"

"Oh you know I can't do that; as much as I would love to."

"Yeah I know but hey, tomorrow will be here before we know it."

"Yes but not soon enough, trust me."

"Well I hear you, but it is what it is."

"That's true. But anyway let me get back to preparing Sunday dinner and I will see you tomorrow morning okay."

"Okay little lady, see you then. Take care."

"You too, bye-bye."

With a little added pep in her step Sherri got out of the house a little bit early the next morning. She and Zach arrived at Beth's home about 15 minutes earlier than had become the norm. She really wanted to just be on her way quickly, but thought it might be best that she linger for at least a short time so that she wouldn't arrive too soon and too unexpectedly at Gee's place. As she and Beth engaged in idle chit-chat with Beth really doing most of the talking, it was clear that her mind was already out the door. Having killed as much time as she felt she could, when 9:30 arrived she managed to squeeze in a word long enough to say that she was headed out, using the excuse of having heard traffic reports of a bit of a tie-up on the interstate. In reality, Sherri was glad that wasn't the case. That's the last thing she wanted to see when she was so anxious to get to her destination. And was she ever overjoyed once she did. She pretty much threw herself into Gee's arms the moment he opened the door to let her in. A big part of her wanted to tear off his pants and have at him right there, but she managed to refrain from doing so for the moment at least.

"My if you aren't a sight for sore eyes; and a pretty aching pussy too," she said as they started up the stairs."

"You are too much you know that," Gee replied with a laugh.

"No, you are too much, yet you're just enough," Sherri grinned.

"I must say it is very good to see you too."

"Oh really, you don't say. Why did you miss me?" she teased.

"Maybe a little bit," he playfully admitted as he led her over to the sofa where they both took a seat. "Can I get you anything?" he offered.

"Well nothing from the kitchen thanks, but I'd love one full serving of chocolate dick if you have any."

"Gee threw his head back in laughter at her comment. "You're certainly in rare form today aren't you?" he said.

"Did you expect me to change in a couple of weeks? Now come on, why don't you show me how much both you and the Loch Ness monster have missed me?"

"Sure, with pleasure," said Gee before he opened up his robe exposing his nude body to her.

Wasting no time whatsoever, Sherri got down on her knees and quickly engulfed him, breathing heavily as she bobbed her head vigorously. Gee threw his arms over the back of the sofa as he looked on, enjoying the sight of her lips stretching to take him as fully as she could. Then suddenly looking to his left he made a motion with his left hand as the right gripped her hair lightly. Sherri abruptly stopped pleasuring him as she sensed the presence of something. Then she quickly lifted her head from his lap.

"What the; who the hell are you?" she yelled as she jumped to her feet. "Gee who is this?"

"Relax sweetheart it's all good," the stranger said cockily.

"Relax my ass, where the hell did you come from? Gee what's going on;" she demanded to know," as she looked in his direction before again eying the stranger warily.

"Sherri come on, chill out okay."

"What! What are you talking about? Who is this Gee?"

"Come on baby; let me talk to you for a second."

He then led her back to his bedroom where they stopped just inside before he closed the door.

"Okay I'm listening. Are you gonna let me know what this is all about? And who the hell that is out there?"

"Yeah, yeah sure I'm about to tell you; just hold up for a second. That's my homeboy Damon alright."

Sherri folded her arm across her chest, before responding back. "Your homeboy Damon huh; okay, and just what is he doing here?"

"Well you know," Gee began hesitantly before Sherri cut him off.

"No I don't know actually, so why don't you tell me. Why is he here?" she asked angrily.

"Again baby, you need to just chill out, it's not that serious."

"It's not; then exactly what is it when a total stranger comes out of nowhere while I have your dick halfway down my throat?"

"Like I said that's my boy Damon so he's not a stranger."

"Well he's a stranger to me Gee. So I'm just not getting why he's here and I'm not getting any real answers from you either," Sherri said in a loud voice.

"Come on now, do I need to spell it out for you?"

"Obviously you do, and the quicker the better too," she snapped.

"Alright, alright, damn baby lower your voice a little bit. Damon's my boy from way back and you know I; well I guess we really; you know we just figured you might be down with a little something to spice things up a little bit that's all."

"A little something to spice things up a little bit?" And that's what you come up with?"

"Yeah you know, like double your pleasure," a grinning Gee said.

"Oh I see. And so you decided to just spring this on me like that? Like right then and there by having your so-called "homeboy" creep up while I'm sucking your dick? Sure, there's a plan if I've ever seen one."

"I don't know, maybe I was wrong but it seemed just as good a time as any. Listen baby, the bottom line is I just wanted to give you another different experience. One that I assume you've never had before."

"Well I do appreciate the kind gesture and all Gee, but why can't it be just you and me? Especially when it's our first time together in a little while."

Gee could sense some softening on her part so he decided to push it further.

"I know I know and like I said maybe I was wrong but I just figured you might enjoy it. It has been only you and me every time and it'll be like that going forward. I guess I was just thinking about how it could be a once in a lifetime experience; one that not every women will have the chance at. But I'm sorry okay."

He then walked up to her and kissed her lightly on the forehead while placing his hand under her chin. "Okay, you can wait here while I see Damon out," he said before stepping towards the door.

"Wait, hold on Gee. Let me get a good look at this friend Damon. I was so stunned before that I didn't even take much notice."

He turned and walked back to her and took her by the hand before draping his arm around her shoulder. He smiled broadly enough that it compelled Sherri to do the same as they started back towards the door.

"Come on," he whispered as he looked down into her eyes.

Sherri took the opportunity to really check Damon out once she and Gee re-entered the living room. He was standing over by the window with his back to them before turning to face them once he heard them coming in his direction. The long expression he wore on his face gave every indication that he had heard some of the exchange that had just taken place in Gee's bedroom. As he stood before them wearing nothing but a pair of blue jeans, the first thing that jumped out to Sherri was how toned and muscular his upper body was. He even sported a full six pack. He was about 6 feet tall with a short haircut and a youthful looking face that was clean-shaven outside of a thin mustache.

"Hey man I know the deal, let me just go in your room and put the rest of my stuff on and then I'll be out."

Gee looked in the direction of Sherri without saying anything and she soon returned the glance before stepping away from him and towards Damon.

"Hi," she whispered once she got close to him. "I'm Sherri, sorry that I was so cold to you before."

"Oh I understand so it's okay; nice to meet you anyway."

"Yes it's good to meet you too Damon."

He looked at her with some surprise before Sherri informed him that Gee had told her his name during their animated discussion that had just taken place.

"Well I guess we weren't talking so loud that you heard all of what we were saying huh," she said with a little smile."

"No I didn't hear all of it but I did hear enough. So I'm gonna go ahead and get out of here so you two can do your thing."

"Excuse me, he said as he started to step around her before Sherri stopped him in his tracks.

"Hey listen," she said after grabbing a hold of his right hand. "You don't have to go if you don't want to."

Taken by surprise, Damon looked over at Gee who was grinning like a Cheshire cat.

"You mean that?" he asked as he looked back at Sherri.

"Yes I do, I'd like for you to stay," she said assuredly while locking her eyes onto his.

Gee quietly crept away and back into his bedroom as Sherri and Damon stood close to each other chatting away. He was gone less than 2 minutes and thus was shocked at the sight before him when he returned. Damon was seated on the edge of the sofa with his legs spread out in front of him. Perched in front of him on her knees was Sherri, her head slowly bobbing up and down on his dick as he ran both of his hands through her hair.

"Well damn, what the hell happened? I didn't think I was gone that long."

Sherri lifted her head briefly before turning and winking in Gee's direction.

"You weren't, but hey I work fast," she said with a smile before picking up where she had left off.

"I just went to use the bathroom and grab the condoms just in case something was to go down, and I can see something did go down. And it's you baby."

"Yo Gee, you weren't kidding. Honey here has some skills, go ahead, get it girl."

The sight of Sherri gorging herself on Damon's dick got Gee instantly aroused.

"Oh hell no, you know I want in on this shit," he said as he hurriedly got out of his clothes.

Grabbing a condom out of the package he rushed over and lifted her onto her feet. Sherri bent at the waist and took Damon into her mouth once again. He wasn't as lengthy as Gee; it's not likely very many men are she figured, but he was certainly plenty long and thick enough to suit her. She always got nice and wet just from giving head so she was perfectly ready when she spread her legs apart in anticipation of Gee entering her from behind. She was soon grunting and groaning non-stop as she enjoyed the pleasures of the double serving of dick. She had already had her first orgasm by the time they switched positions with her now standing with Gee in front of her pumping in and out her mouth as Damon banged away at her pussy from the rear. Gee had his hands placed along the sides of her head but removed them long enough for him and Damon to exchange a high five over the top of Sherri's back.

"Damn Gee this chick is a major freak."

"See I told you. I knew she would be down. She just loves her some dick."

"Yeah I see that," Damon remarked as he intensified his strokes inside of Sherri's soaking wet hole.

"Yes I do, especially big fucking ones like the two of you were blessed with," Sherri pointed out when she took a brief moment to grab some air.

Saliva dripped from Sherri's lips each time Gee's giant tool went back and forth inside of her mouth. When it was over her face was a mask of cum from the double loads she received. Damon was first, making his deposit before stepping away as Gee immediately positioned himself over a prone Sherri before emptying himself with a series of loud moans as she urged him on. Exhausted but plenty satisfied she then collapsed onto her back before breaking into a huge smile.

"Wow that was amazing; thank you both. I know one thing for sure; I will never forget this day."

"Oh trust me neither will we," Damon responded as he and Gee again slapped hands as they stood a few feet away before Damon started to get dressed and Gee retreated into his bedroom.

∞∞∞∞∞∞∞∞∞∞∞∞

A few days later marked Independence Day and as usual it was celebrated with a backyard barbecue hosted by Clay and Sherri. The guest list included among others Kevin and Colette, their spouses and their kids, some of Clay's friends from his former law firm, some employees from the Prosecutor's office as well as some of his old college buddies who lived in the area. Also there from the neighborhood were Lily and her family along with Dawn's parents Steve and Maria, and the Asbury's from right next door. And of course no guest was more pleased to be there or more welcomed than Beth. Sherri couldn't help but wonder if Dawn and Darren might also come by together, thereby creating a potentially awkward scene for the two fo them. But any concern over that was alleviated when Maria informed Sherri that Dawn and Darren were spending the day together down at some friends' summer house at the shore.

Clay always had a love for entertaining guests throughout the course of their marriage; whereas Sherri for her part could take or leave it with all of the extra work that came with it; both before and after. As was always the case when they entertained outdoors, Clay deferred most of the grilling duties to his brother in order to allow him more time to do what he does best. That being schmooze it up with the guests. But on this day he seemed a bit more reserved than usual, something that did not go unnoticed by Sherri.

"Are you okay," she asked him as they sat across from each other at one of the many circular tables placed throughout the yard. "You're usually the life of the party. Working the room like it's a political fundraiser."

"Well maybe it's because this isn't a room," he quipped.

"Oh you know what I mean. Anyway, I'll be right back I want to go get that bottle of wine that I've been chilling in the fridge."

"Well I'll be here," Clay replied flatly.

"You know you don't seem like yourself at all today and it's pretty noticeable," Sherri stated at that point.

"Believe me I'm fine, but thank you for your concern," he replied just as Sherri stepped away from him.

She emerged from the house a few minutes later and placed the bottle of wine inside of one of the large ice-filled coolers placed on the edge of the patio closest to the house. She stopped to say something to the kids who were running around on the grass playing before continuing on towards the table at which she had been seated with Clay. As she closed to within 25-30 feet of him she stopped to retrieve her cell phone from her pocket as she felt the vibration in her pocket as a call came in.

"Hello."

"Hey, how is Little Miss Good Time doing today?" the unmistakable voice on the other end boomed.

"Hey yourself, I'm doing just wonderful how are you?"

"Everything is good so I can't complain. I have the holiday off so that's good. Can you talk for a quick minute?"

Sherri snuck a glance in Clay's direction and noticed that he was in turn looking directly at her. He held the stare briefly before getting up and making his way over to one of the coolers where he retrieved a beer.

"Umm yeah sure I can talk for a bit," she said as she sought out an isolated area away from anyone."

"So what are you doing for the holiday?" Gee questioned.

"Well actually we're entertaining a bunch of people at a backyard barbecue as we speak."

"Oh really; well I guess my invitation got lost in the mail," he joked.

"Oh yeah it must have because I certainly sent it," Sherri reciprocated. "Anyway, what are you doing with your big, sexy self today lover of mine?"

"I'm just relaxing for now. My girl is out of town working so I'm just chilling out. I am going to a cookout later though."

"Sounds good, enjoy yourself."

"Thanks, I will; but speaking of enjoying yourself it sure seemed like you did on Monday."

"Oh yeah, I told you I had a blast. It was incredible."

"Incredible? Wow, that's strong praise."

"It's well deserved; you two worked me over real good. Both of my jaws were still sort of tender up until yesterday and my pussy hurt for two days afterwards, but it hurt so good," Sherri chuckled.

"Well glad to be of service. Would you do it again?"

"I don't know. As great as it was it still seems like one of those things that is best left as a once in a lifetime experience."

"Hey I hear you," Gee replied. "That's understandable."

'I'll tell you what I would love to do though; a threesome with a man and another woman."

"Oh really," Gee exclaimed.

"Hell yeah; now that's the one I've fantasized about many times."

"Okay well I've already got that one filed away in the memory bank just in case."

"Cool; maybe that'll be another sweet surprise you spring on me one day."

"Well if I ever can I will, how's that?"

"Sounds good to me; anyway babe let me go okay. You enjoy the rest of your holiday and I will see you next Monday."

"You sure will and yes it will be just the two of us as usual this time."

"Great I'm looking forward to it already."

"See you then, bye."

"Bye-bye."

Sherri had turned her back to everyone while she was chatting but now turned and walked back over to where her husband was seated. He looked away from her from the time he saw her returning and even as she sat down.

"Hey, I'm back," she announced as she got comfortable.

"I thought you were just leaving me here by myself since you were so wrapped up in your phone call," he said as he shifted his body towards her. His head dipped slightly and he made no eye contact with her.

"Oh I'm sorry, my friend Ingrid called to tell me she wouldn't be able to make it."

"That was a pretty long chat just for her to say that."

"Well Ingrid can talk with the best of them that's for sure. But I don't think it was that long."

"Yeah maybe not, just seemed like it I guess," said Clay.

Just as he had gotten the words out of his mouth Sherri leaped to her feet. Zach who had been playing with Tyler and some other kids had just taken a spill while running from the grass onto the concrete patio. Ever the worried Mom, Sherri quickly raced towards him placing her cell phone which had been in her hand, down on the table. Clay watched her as she ran towards Zach even as he quickly decided that it was an overreaction on her part. Just as she neared the patio he turned and began to eye Sherri's phone while also looking in her direction. He didn't know her friend Ingrid all that well. He had met her once at a party he and Sherri attended at her place up in Hoboken.

As his eyes quickly scanned the yard, Clay slid Sherri's phone close to him and began to press a few keys on it. He had a Blackberry himself so he was well acquainted with its functionality. In a matter of moments he was looking at the phone's call history. Just long enough to view the one thing he wanted to see. The most recent call received wasn't listed by a name but rather merely the description of Sprint cellular caller along with the number. But what he did take instant note of was the fact that the call came from a number with a 732 area code, thereby designating it as being from a Central Jersey caller. Armed with the information he sought, he slid the phone back over to where Sherri had placed it, again being careful that he wasn't seen by anyone. With that done he stood and walked over to where Sherri crouched chatting with little Zach.

"You okay little buddy?"

"Yes Daddy," was the soft response from his now almost 4 year old son.

"I didn't think it looked like anything to be too concerned about," Clay said to Sherri.

"No it's not but you know how I am, I guess it's how all of us mothers are."

Clay then turned to Tyler and the other children who had been involved in the horseplay and now stood close by. "Alright you guys just be careful, try to stay on the grass okay."

"Okay Dad, we're sorry," said Tyler.

"It's okay, just be careful with your brother. Now go on and have fun," Clay said before the bigger kids took off running with Zach in pursuit.

Clay and Sherri stood there watching them briefly before starting back in the direction of the table at which they'd been seated.

"Oh well boys will be boys," Sherri remarked as they moved along slowly.

"Oh so you were saying that your friend Ingrid wasn't going to be able to make it?" Clay questioned as they moved along.

"No, she gave her regrets. I was really looking forward to seeing her too. It's been a good while."

"Does she still live in Hoboken," he asked curiously.

"Yeah she does."

Clay's eyes narrowed and his jaw tightened before he replied. "Well maybe the distance played a part in her decision not to come."

"Could be I suppose, I mean with tomorrow being a quick turnaround to go back to work and everything."

CHAPTER SEVENTEEN

It was almost one in the morning before all the guests had departed and the initial cleanup was complete. Kevin and Nina, along with Lily and Beth helped a great deal in either disposing of or storing away the extra food. As much as Sherri had attempted to distribute it to the guests to take home, there was still an abundance of leftovers. As usual Clay stayed out of sight as all the work was being done; having retired to the bedroom a couple of hours earlier. The fact that he didn't even step forward to assist with what was going out into the garbage disappointed Sherri somewhat, although she can't say that it surprised her at all. Beth was actually the last one to leave, with Sherri escorting her to her car.

"Again, thank you so much for the help Beth. I really appreciate it."

"No problem, I was happy to help. I can remember how it was entertaining so many people back when Clay Sr. and I used to do it fairly often. It doesn't get much worse than the cleanup after it ends. Especially when you're already tired."

"Isn't that the truth," Sherri lamented.

"Okay, well I guess I will see you when you drop off Zachary on Monday," she said as she stepped into her car.

"Yes you sure will," Sherri concurred. "You drive safely, have a good night and thanks again for coming."

"Oh thanks for having me. You have no idea how great it was for me to be here with all of you like a part of the family."

"Well it was just as good for us Beth," Sherri said.

Once she had freshened up a bit; Sherri climbed into bed as quietly as she could in order to not disturb her sleeping husband. Or so she thought.

At almost the moment she laid down he rolled over to face her, his eyes wide open.

"Hey I see you finally made it to bed," he remarked in either a possible attempt at humor or an incredible moment of poor judgment.

"Excuse me; you must be kidding, you know somebody had to actually do some work once everybody left. Thankfully Kevin and Nina along with Beth and Lily chipped in to help. More than I can say for some people around here."

"Hey I was tired. Feel like I had done enough beforehand," Clay stated.

"Oh really, well I guess it's a good thing I'm a machine because at least I don't have to worry about little things like getting tired," Sherri fired back sarcastically. "Anyway good night," she added.

Several minutes later Sherri was roused awake by a nudge in her side from Clay.

"I'm sorry, but can I ask you something?" he said in a voice slightly above a whisper.

Sherri sighed before answering him. "Yes what is it?" she said as she rolled onto her back slowly.

"If I was umm, you know, being a little less to you than I could be; would you bring it to my attention?"

"I'm sorry Clay but I'm not quite getting what it is you're asking me."

"Okay, okay I'll rephrase the question. If I was not being as attentive, romantic and affectionate and all those sort of things towards you as you would like, would you let me know?"

"Haven't I?"

"Okay now I'm lost," said Clay.

"You are? Well just think about it. All the things you mentioned in your question and whether or not I would bring my complaints or concerns to you? I ask you again, haven't I? Like I said, think about it. And on that note, once again good night," she said before again rolling over onto her side.

A short time later she laid there not having yet managed to go back to sleep when she felt Clay nudge in close to her. His left hand first resting on her side before he slid it onto her lower stomach before inching it downward.

"Nope don't even think about it," Sherri said without flinching.

"Huh; but what about what you just said?" Clay wondered out loud.

"What I just said? Oh yeah what I just said. Well let me repeat it. Don't even think about it!"

"No I meant before that; about not enough affection and attention."

"Well now is so not the time Clay," Sherri chastised him in response.

It was not as if Sherri wasn't at least a bit horny. She almost always was those days. Plus the wine she had been consuming earlier probably only added to her libido a bit. But she was intent on unleashing that passion on Gee in a few days rather than waste some of it on Clay. She figured it wasn't worth the time or the effort, even if he were deserving of it, which he certainly wasn't.

"Okay just forget it," Clay fumed before he rolled onto his side in a huff, his back to her.

Having gained a little bit of satisfaction, Sherri smiled before she again drifted off to sleep.

Two weeks later on a late afternoon, Clay was in his office going over some case material when his phone rang. It was Jeri dialing into his office.

"Yes Jeri," he answered as he pressed the button to take the call via the direct hotline between the two of them.

"I have Roland Cellini for you."

"Okay put him right through thanks, Clay replied before pausing for a moment.

"Hey Rollie, what's up?"

"Hey how you doing Clay?" Rollie replied in a tone somewhere between sullen and downright somber.

"I'm okay Roll; what's going on? You sound like you just lost your best friend."

"We need to have a sit-down ASAP; you, Mike and myself. When would be a good time for you?"

At that point Clay picked up the handset rather than continue the conversation on speakerphone. "I don't know, about any time I guess. Is everything status quo? Or is there something new you have for me in terms of information."

"How about tomorrow morning," Rollie countered while avoiding providing any answers to Clay.

"Sure that's fine. I was going to take tomorrow off to hit the links but I can cancel of course. But come on Rollie if you have anything to report you can just tell me now right?"

"It's best that we see you in person. Is ten o'clock okay?"

"Yeah that works," Clay confirmed, before starting to continue on. "Roll come on don't do this to me man."

"We will see you in the morning," Rollie answered; quickly hanging up before Clay could object any further.

"Shit," Clay said as he looked at the receiver in his hand before placing it back down on its base. He then stood and started pacing intently; having been rendered a nervous wreck by the brief conversation that had just ended. A short time later he walked up to Jeri's desk, interrupting her game of online solitaire in the process.

"Listen, I'm going to go ahead and take off. Any calls just direct them to my voice mail. I mean any; even from my family. I'll be checking it later on."

"Sure no problem," Jeri assured Clay. She couldn't help noticing a bit of angst on his face. "Will you be in tomorrow?"

"Yes I will be in by nine-thirty or nine-forty-five at the latest I'd say. Have a good night."

"You too; see you in the morning."

Clay didn't arrive home that evening until 7:30 because he stopped at a local pub for a few drinks when he left the office. Three double shots of bourbon on the rocks.

"Hey you didn't tell me that you were going to be coming home late? I called both your office and your cell phone and nothing back from you," Sherri said when he entered the house.

"Guess it slipped my mind."

"Oh you guess it slipped your mind; that's your reason for not calling to let me know?"

"You do catch on quick."

"Okay well whatever; I can see you're in a bit of a mood so I'm not going to take it any further. Dinner is on the top of the stove. I'm going to tend to Zach and then go do a load of laundry."

Sherri noticed that as intently as he looked at her, Clay didn't respond, so she just slowly slid away towards the back of the house. He also didn't come to bed that night until 1:00 in the morning, saying that he had fallen asleep while watching television down in the family room. When he awakened the next morning he had two cups of black coffee before getting dressed. But he said little to Sherri beyond good morning, as she came into the kitchen for her own cup of coffee. He answered a simple yes and not one word more when she asked if he would be going into the office that morning.

Clay arrived for work about 9:30; stopping for a word with Jeri before heading into his office.

"Good morning Clay," she said as he approached.

"Good morning; listen I'm expecting Mr. Celini and Mr. Marciniak this morning. Call me the moment they get here okay."

"Sure no problem; what time are you expecting them?"

"I'm not certain exactly, but sometime by ten for sure."

"All right, well I'll be looking out for them."

"Thanks and hold off on putting any calls through until after they leave. Just take messages."

"Okay," Jeri said before getting back to what she had been doing before Clay had arrived. That being chatting with one of her friends on the phone.

"Great, I just found out that this creep who seems to get off on harassing me will be coming into the office to meet with my boss shortly," she said into the phone with a deep sigh. "And the way I feel this morning I'm so not in the mood for his crap right now," she added.

At 9:55 Rollie stepped off the elevator followed closely by Mike. As they slowly trudged over to her desk Jeri finally ended her phone call which by then had gone on for about 45 minutes. Rollie was empty handed but Mike carried a large manila envelope in his right hand. The first thing that jumped out at her was the blank expressions they both wore on their faces.

"Good morning, we're here to see Clay," Rollie said plainly.

"Yes, he's expecting the two of you. Hold on and I'll call in and let him know you're here," Jeri said before reaching for the phone.

"Your visitors have arrived."

Seconds later she hung up and turned back to Rollie and Mike. "Okay, you two can go on in."

"Thanks," was all that Jeri got as a response before they stepped away from her desk.

Jeri had never before seen Rollie appear so pre-occupied, but she had to admit that as much as she wondered what might be wrong, she quite enjoyed the difference. Better than him salivating at the mere sight of her she figured. As for Mike, he hadn't as much as cracked a smile from the moment he emerged from the elevator, so that made her really wonder just what the deal was. Maybe they screwed something up and are here because they're about to get chewed out, she guessed. Whatever the case, she shrugged her shoulders before turning her attention to her computer. Time for a little game of solitaire, she decided.

Rollie entered Clay's office first followed closely by Mike. The serious expressions they wore sent Clay's stomach into a little tizzy from the moment he looked at the two of them.

"Have a seat," he said in a tone matching their demeanors. As he looked in their direction, Clay noticed the large envelope that Mike held in his lap. "Okay what do you have?" he asked as he slowly lowered himself into his large, leather desk chair; his face now a steely mask that matched theirs.

Mike looked at Rollie who responded with a slight hand gesture. He then leaned forward slightly before slowly rocking back into an upright position. He ran his right hand across his face before opening the envelope and placing the contents on top of it as it rested on his lap.

"I just want you to know that this is not at all easy for me but I know what you called on me to do," Mike began as he looked at Clay stoically. "Now these first few pictures were taken Thursday of last week," he said as he handed them in his direction."

As his eyes focused in on the photos, Clay placed a hand to his forehead; the result of the sudden feeling of a headache coming on.

"And these were taken this past Monday; the first few about 10 in the morning and the other two about four hours later."

Rollie looked on, feeling very much uneasy at the sight of his friend's anguish.

"And I have one last set from just yesterday; again covering the same timeframe," Mike continued.

"That's okay I don't need to see anymore," Clay said somberly without even lifting his head.

"Clay, I'm so sorry that we had to bring this to you," Rollie lamented. "And I just want you to know that I'm just as shocked as you are. I just really can't believe it to tell you the truth. But if you need some time to absorb all this I certainly understand because…"

"Do you have any idea who he is?" Clay interrupted him in a barely audible voice.

"I'm sorry what's that?" Rollie replied.

"Do you know who the Black bastard is?" Clay then yelled out. "Who the fuck is he?" he demanded.

"If I may answer that," Mike stepped in. "Well I don't have a name or anything, but I also took some photos of what I believe to be his car, so I can run the plate and get back to you within an hour."

Clay looked at Mike before nodding his approval. "Yeah get back to me as soon as you can with that," he said softly. "Thanks."

"Hey Mike if you don't mind why don't you give Clay and I a few minutes," Rollie then said.

"Sure no problem."

"Thanks, you can just wait right outside for me."

Mike gathered up all of the pictures, placed them back into the envelope and stood up to depart. As soon as the door to the office closed, Rollie turned towards Clay.

"Hey buddy I know this has probably not all sunk in for you yet, but I'm just trying to get an idea of your mindset right now."

"My mindset? I'm not sure I follow you Roll."

"I mean you know, in terms of how you may be looking at Sherri right now."

"Well," Clay began with a sigh, "you're right it hasn't really hit me yet. Probably won't hit me fully until I see her this evening."

"Well whatever you do just try to keep your head about things. I know that's easier said than done and all that, but hey at least try. Really try."

Clay looked right into his face but had no response so Rollie went on.

"In your heart of hearts, do you feel like you'll ever be able to possibly forgive her for what's been going on?"

"I don't know Roll; really I don't. Not at the moment anyway. But I can say that she's tarnished forever in my eyes. I mean the fact that's she's been sneaking around sleeping with another man at all is one thing. But to have it be with a goddamn spook; what the fuck? How am I supposed to even begin to understand, let alone accept that and move on?"

"Well I don't see it as something to accept at all Clay. As much as I've always liked Sherri she really took the low road here. I would have never believed any of it if not for the photographs. A fucking darkie? I'm still dumbfounded as to how she could do that, not to mention then look you in the face, and lay down next to you at night as if nothing was going on."

Clay reached for his phone and snatched the receiver off of the hook. "You know I sort of feel like I should call her and confront her with this right now."

"No, no, no Clay; not a good idea. You're way too on edge about this right now." When you confront her with this you need to do it low-key and just very matter of factly. That's the best way to do it if you ask me."

Clay held the receiver in his hand for a few moments before angrily slamming it back down and sweeping the phone off the desk onto the floor. "Sonofabitch," he yelled out," before Rollie made an attempt to calm him.

"Hey you know I can't blame you one bit for going nuts over this. But the best thing you can do is to just take a deep breath and approach this rationally. That way you're less likely to act out of anger and do something you might come to regret later."

Clay pushed back from his desk and hooked his hands behind his head.

"You know you're probably right. And to take it a step further, it might not be a good idea to let on to Sherri that I know about this at all right now. I mean think about it; I tell her what I know and bring the proof of it to her. So what happens then? She ends it and that's it. And her lover boy just goes on about his business. He probably just moves on to soil another White woman out there someplace. So what does he care? No Roll, this Black mother fucker needs to pay big time."

"I agree, but how?" Rollie questioned.

"Give me a couple of days to think it through and then I'll get back to you."

"Okay," Rollie said while rising to his feet. "Just give me a call in a day or two."

"Alright, will do; by Monday sometime at the latest."

"Okay. And Clay; whatever you decide I want in on it because like I said I agree that this nigger has to pay a price for what he's been doing to Sherri."

"Rollie and Mike left just as quietly and stone-faced as they had arrived with neither of them as much as really looking in Jeri's direction. With the loud crash and yelling that she had heard coming from Clay's office a short time earlier she just figured that he must have been going off and ripping them a new one. Something that she can personally attest to him being quite capable of at times. After the two of them departed Clay did his best to just go on with his day as normal but he just couldn't shake the image of his wife and the dark, mysterious man out of his mind. Before noon he had indeed heard back from Mike. He now had a name.

∞∞∞∞∞∞∞∞∞∞∞∞

That weekend was Clay's time to put up a front. He had to play it as if he had no clue what Sherri had been involved in. He did get a funny feeling in the pit of his stomach when he saw her for the first time that evening after having received the news earlier that day. But as much as he burned on the inside he managed to pull off a cool exterior as they just went about things as they normally do; though he did find himself staring in her direction numerous times, but almost always when she could not see him.

It was about 3:15 Monday afternoon when Clay called Rollie who was in his office rather than working the streets.

"Hey I think I know just how I can make this Garrick Andrews wish he'd never put his hands on my wife."

"Okay let's hear it, I've been waiting to see what you'd come up with."

"Now you and Mike both said this homeboy is as clean as a whistle right?"

"Yeah squeaky clean; not even as much as a parking ticket showing anywhere."

"Well he won't be once we get through with him. Pretty soon he's gonna be sought on felony charges and facing a stint behind bars."

"Hey, you weren't kidding when you said you were going to go after this guy hard," Rollie said. "That's really harsh, but you know what; I like it. Let's get the Black bastard. But just what are you thinking about in terms of a plan?"

"Well I have a scenario in mind, but that's where I'm looking to you to help make it happen."

"Sure buddy, just tell me what I can do to help?"

∞∞∞∞∞∞∞∞∞∞∞∞

The two men were already seated at a table in the middle of the bar when Rollie and Mike entered. Roberto Torres and Jimmy Klevans were a couple of small timers that Rollie had a bit of a history with going way back to his days as a plainclothes detective down in South Bound Brook. Both of their rap sheets were sprinkled with things such as petty larceny, possession of stolen property and breaking and entering. And Rollie had personally been in the middle of busting them on a few of those occasions. But this time they were about to team up as strange as that seemed.

They were both having beers when Rollie and Mike approached them.

"Excuse us for not getting up," Roberto quipped as the two of them sat down.

"Yeah don't take it personally, it's not at all that we're not honored by your presence," added Jimmy.

"Trust me that's quite alright; anyway, let's get right down to business shall we?" Rollie suggested.

"You mean you guys aren't gonna join us in having a drink? I feel insulted," Roberto said tongue in cheek.

"Oh we would but it's just past noon on a Friday, so we're kind of still on duty ya know," Mike interjected.

"Okay I understand whoever you are," Roberto stated. "Hey who is this guy?" he asked while turning to Rollie.

This is one of my top, if not my very top deputy. That's all you need to know right now."

"Well does he have a name?" Roberto, obviously the more talkative of the two inquired.

"All right I'll give you that; his name is Mike. Mike this is Roberto and Jimmy," Rollie said in doing the formal introductions. That was followed by an exchange of nods of the head but no handshakes.

Rollie locked his fingers of both hands on the table and leaned forward, peering across the table as he did so. Returning his glare was Roberto who was in his late thirties, and about 5'7" with dark hair and several missing teeth to go along with the ones that were slowly decaying inside of his mouth. Rollie also deftly cut his eyes in the direction of Jimmy a tall wiry man with dirty blonde hair pulled into a ponytail. Tattoos covered all of his arms that were visible under the short sleeve shirt he wore. He was older than Roberto by a few years, probably about 40 or just beyond.

"Okay if you two don't mind let's cut to the chase okay. This is the deal. What we're looking for is pretty straightforward and simple. There's this little situation that has arisen and as a result we need to have something taken care of."

"What exactly do you mean something taken care of?" Roberto wanted to know.

"Taken care of as in having a person removed from a situation," Rollie told him.

"Hey man we don't do any murders," Roberto shot back.

"Relax, we're not talking about killing anybody. Let me explain just what we'd like you guys to do. It's basically just a break-in plus a little something more. We'll provide you with the address of course. Now what you're to do from there is this; gain entry to the premises and leave a little something behind." Rollie noticed the way that the 2 hoods were looking back at him and decided that some clarification was needed. "Listen, we're looking to take somebody down; so what we want you guys to do is to go in and plant some stuff that's gonna set up a bust somewhere down the line."

Jimmy took a long swig from his beer before placing it down on the table. "All right, so basically you want us to break into somebody's place and instead of taking stuff out, bring something in," he said while glancing in Roberto's direction before the two of them smirked at each other.

"Exactly; sounds pretty simple right?"

"Yeah; it's a little unusual but sure it sounds pretty simple," Roberto concurred.

"Now it's real important that there be no traces of a break-in," Mike chimed in. "Are you two able to pull that off?"

Roberto glared at Mike before looking over at Jimmy. "I'll let you handle that one."

"That won't be a problem. I'm more than capable of pulling that off trust me," Jimmy said with conviction.

"And Detective Celini here knows that better than anyone," a smiling Roberto added, prompting Rollie to nod in agreement.

"That's good to know. Well I guess there's only one thing left to discuss," Mike said.

"Six-thousand dollars; that's what's in it for you two; half now and the rest once the job is done," Rollie announced.

"Roberto and Jimmy looked at each other briefly before turning back towards Rollie and Mike. "Alright you've got a deal," Roberto said.

"Very well then. Now we can tell you this much; this guy works a night shift but we'll leave it up to you too to work out when you want to get this done," said Mike.

In the meantime Rollie handed over a sheet of paper on which he had written down the address of Gee's townhouse. Next Mike pulled a folded up white envelope out of his pocket and handed it over to Roberto who opened it and looked at several bundles of neatly rubber-banded dollar bills.

"It's all there," Mike assured them. "But feel free to count it if you want."

"Just get in touch with me a few days before you're ready to make it happen so that I can get the stuff to you," said Rollie.

"Sure no problem," said Roberto.

With that Rollie and Mike stood up and turned and left the premises.

"You don't have any concerns about these two guys just taking off with the cash do you?" Mike asked once they were back in the car.

"None; they know better believe me," Rollie assured him. "Besides I know these guys and they're nothing but a couple of small-time wannabes, so trust me they want that other three grand for completing the job."

CHAPTER EIGHTEEN

"Stop it, I have to go; really," Sherri protested mildly. But Gee seemed insistent on breaking down her already weakened defenses. He went from softly caressing her neck and shoulders with first his hands and then his lips to an all-out attack.

"Come on you have time for once more," he argued.

"No I really don't. I have to get going," Sherri repeated. But her strong lust betrayed her will as she again fell prey to their continued desires for each other.

Her eyes danced in her head before closing tightly as his mouth clasped down on one of her breasts and then the other.

"Ooooh," she purred as the sensations tore through her body. "Stop it please," she pleaded, though the fact that her hands were now pressed to the back of his head made her argument seem invalid. As her legs spread apart involuntarily, his right hand found her paradise. Her hips wiggled about as his fingers probed her; his lips now loudly sucking away at her excited nipples. She pulled away from him, rolling onto her stomach in a final meager attempt to escape him. But as much as her mind was telling her that she should be getting up, getting dressed and getting out, her pussy at the same time was saying differently. She turned her head to face him. "Quick, get a condom on."

He took her just that way, climbing atop her prone body as she spread her legs in order to receive him. The weight of his body seemed as if would drive her through the mattress as he rose up off her; supporting his weight on his hands, then dropping his hips as his pelvis began to slam against her backside over and over. There was nothing gentle or tender about the way he fucked her yet Sherri loved every single moment of it, alternating between screaming out "yes" and "oh yeah fuck me" with each determined thrust from Gee. Her head remained turned to the side with her face pressed to a pillow thereby muffling the volume of her screams somewhat. A good thing as she sounded off like a mezzo-soprano when she came. So caught up in the passion and intensity of the lovemaking, Sherri never heard her cell phone as it vibrated repeatedly. Nor had she reacted to the tone emanating from the device with the numerous voice mail messages that had been left. Being left extremely drained from that latest round of steamy sex with her lover, she'd fallen into a deep slumber, his large frame cradled beside her. She had no idea how long they had been asleep when they were jarred awake by the ringing of Gee's house phone. And while he was slow in reacting to the sound, Sherri on the other hand leapt to her feet in a panic the moment she realized that she'd been sleeping.

"Oh shit, what time is it," she screamed as she stood next to the bed trying to get her bearings.

Gee looked over at the clock radio on his nightstand just as he let out a loud, lengthy yawn. "It's 2:20," he said in his trademark deep voice which in this instance came out more like a growl.

"Two-twenty; you must be kidding! Please tell me you're kidding," she said hopefully.

"Nope I'm not kidding it is 2:20," he replied calmly as he slowly rose to his feet.

"Dammit, I can't believe this. How could I fall asleep?"

"Well I think I have a good idea. I know why I fell asleep," Gee chuckled.

"No this is very serious Gee. I'm usually picking up my son by now and I haven't even left. Haven't even gotten dressed yet," Sherri explained as she rounded up her clothing.

"Well just call his Step-Grandma and tell her something happened. You can tell her you ran into bad traffic. Tell her just about anything. Well anything except that you fell asleep after getting an extra good fuckin that is."

"Well I'm glad you can joke about this because I sure don't find it too amusing," Sherri complained as she hurried towards the bathroom. "Wait where's my cell phone, she said as she came to a halt; briefly forgetting that it was in the pocket of her jeans.

Once she retrieved it and took it in her hands, slight panic turned into a sense of impending trouble. Before she could place a call to Beth, she saw that she had numerous missed calls that had come in as well as several voice messages. Three of the calls and an equal number of the voice mails were from someone who identified themselves as being from the day camp that Abby and Tyler attended. There were also five calls and two messages from Clay. Upon listening to the messages from the camp, what Sherri found out was this. Tyler had taken very ill during the day so they had been trying to contact her for that reason. The two messages from Clay were both similar in terms of wording, with the exception of the latter being more angry and profane.

"I've been trying to reach you. The camp called me because they said they haven't been able to reach you. Tyler is sick and they need one of us to go pick him up. Call me back ASAP."

The next message from her husband came in just a few minutes later with more detail and yes, more venom attached to it.

"Sherri, where the hell are you? The camp called and said Tyler is very sick. That he apparently has some sort of stomach virus or maybe food poisoning or something because he's been throwing up all over the place. But yet for some reason you're nowhere to be found and neither them or now I can reach you and you're not even returning God damn phone calls. So let me know what the fuck is going on will you?"

The final and most recent message was from Beth and markedly less intense in nature by comparison.

"Hello sweetheart I just wanted to make sure everything was okay because you're usually here by now. We're fine but again I'm just checking on you. Call me back if you can or I'll just wait until you get here." Sherri knew just from that, that it was apparent that Clay hadn't reached out to Beth in an attempt to get a hold of her, because Beth clearly knew nothing of what the situation was with Tyler.

Sherri then took a moment to inform Gee what was going on.

"Listen, there's something wrong with my seven year old son and my husband as well as the day camp he's at have been calling me like crazy. I have to call him back right away. So I'm going to step outside into your living room okay?"

"Yeah sure that's fine. I just checked and that was my girlfriend calling me a little while ago. But I'll wait until you get squared away and take off to call her back."

"Okay I'll be right back," Sherri said before dialing Clay's office while walking out of Gee's bedroom. After Jeri informed her that Clay had taken off in a rush, she instantly called his cell phone.

"Where the hell have you been? I've been trying to call you like crazy," he screamed into the phone without even as much as a hello preceding it.

Thinking quickly, Sherri responded as fast as she could; knowing that to do otherwise would raise even more suspicion than there might have already been on Clay's part.

"I'm very sorry Clay. My phone's battery had run down and I didn't even realize it because it was in my purse. And then when I did discover that it had died I had no charger with me. I usually charge it at night but I guess things have been so overwhelming of late that I just forgot last night. When I wanted to call and check on Zach was when I found out it was dead. You just wouldn't believe that no one else at the senior center had a charger that was compatible with my Blackberry. And of all days for this to happen. Anyway; where is Tyler, and how is he?"

"He's lying down in his bed getting some rest; he seems okay for now. He hasn't thrown up in a while anyway. So where are you now?"

"I just picked up Zach and got back in the car. We haven't even pulled off yet. It's a little later than normal because I agreed to stay behind at the center for a while to help out with something. But if I had any idea what was going on…"

There was a period of silence as Clay didn't respond right away. Though Sherri did detect what sounded like a slight sucking of his teeth along with a sigh.

"Okay let me talk to Zach for a moment. Just say a quick hello to him."

"I'm sorry he was sound asleep when I picked him up so I decided not to wake him. We'll be home before too long."

"So tell me how did you get your phone charged up to call me now?"

"It's plugged into the car charger. But anyway, let me go because it hasn't charged all that much yet. Just enough for me to power it up, check my messages and then call you; we'll see you in a bit okay."

As soon as they ended the call Clay stood there shaking his head incredulously at the gall displayed by Sherri; his emotions were a mixture of sadness and anger. His sadness over the length to which she was now apparently willing to go in an attempt to hide her deceit; coupled with anger over her continued betrayal. He knew he could easily call Beth to confirm his suspicions, but really felt no need to.

Sherri dashed out of the room and quickly moved past Gee into the bathroom.

"I have to get out of here as fast as I can," she explained on the way.

Rather than taking her customary full shower she merely washed her face, brushed her teeth and freshened up the area between her legs before taking off. As she drove towards Beth's home to collect Zach she took time to ponder all that was. For the first time she had to admit to herself just how much of a hold that Gee had over her. Just how easy it was for him to get her to act against her better judgment.

By rushing, Sherri managed to make it home 30 minutes after having spoken to Clay. Tyler got better over the course of the next couple of days with the help of some over the counter medications as they decided that simply letting things run their course was preferable to a trip to a Doctor. They were not quite able to pinpoint exactly what may have caused him to fall ill but they suspect it might have been something he ate at the travelling carnival they had attended the day before the illness hit him. And Clay continued to play his part well also, never letting on even a hint of suspicion of Sherri having been less than truthful to him the day Tyler first fell ill. So as far as she was concerned he remained completely unaware of her ongoing transgressions.

Mid-August signaled the time for the King family's annual summer vacation. This time around the destination of choice was the Atlantis resort in the Bahamas where they had booked a spacious three bedroom suite. The weeklong trip was filled with fun and adventure for the kids centered around the resort's renowned water park, organized children's activities and a game room geared towards young ones. Zach's 4th birthday was also celebrated during the stay. And for Sherri it also meant a break from Gee for a while; something that she had managed to convince herself that she needed. And she did just fine with that. That was until the next to last night there when she suddenly felt compelled to make an attempt to communicate with him.

It was about 11:00 Saturday night. Worn out from a long day in the searing Caribbean sun, the kids had fallen asleep not long after the family returned from dinner. Clay joined them about an hour later, dozing off while he and Sherri were lounging on the bed watching a movie. It was not exactly the type of movie that was to Sherri's liking so once he was asleep she saw little reason to continue watching it. In fact she didn't feel much like television at all any longer. Climbing off the bed, she retrieved her black silk robe and threw it on over the matching nightie she was wearing. She walked out of the bedroom and after looking in on the children, stepped into the kitchen and poured herself a glass of Chardonnay that had been ordered from room service the night before. After turning on a single small lamp for lighting, she took a seat in the living room and kicked her feet up on the sofa. As she slowly sipped her wine her mind began to wander in an instant. Picking up the glass, she walked over to the sliding glass door which led to the balcony and quietly opened it before stepping outside. After placing the glass down on the small table out there, she made herself comfortable on one of the cushiony chaise loungers on either side of it. As she relaxed and stared out into the starlit sky, Sherri's imagination quickly began to run wild. She slipped back inside just long enough to retrieve her Blackberry before again stretching out to enjoy the wonderfully pleasant night. Tropical breezes washed over her body like the gentle waves along the beach a short distance away. The sound of the calm water kissing the sand gave the atmosphere an added feel of peace and tranquility. It felt like the perfect backdrop for romance; the ideal setting for passions to explode. Again raising the glass to her lips, she reached over to the table for her Blackberry. After placing the glass on the table, she began to type on the phone's small keyboard.

"Hey, are you around?" As she laid there hoping and waiting for a response, she twirled her long brown hair around the fingers on her right hand. A few minutes later the flashing light on the phone told her that indeed a reply had arrived. She smiled as she lifted the phone close enough to her face to read the message.

"Hello there; this is a surprise. What are you back home already?"

"Nope, still in the Bahamas. But I was just thinking about you."

Gee grinned before sending his next reply back to her. "Oh really, and what were you thinking about me?"

"Oh you can probably guess that. I'm pretty horny tonight."

"You don't say. Well in that case it's too bad that we're not even in the same country. Speaking of which, you must have some real good cell service."

"Yes I do. I should, I pay enough for it. But don't go trying to change the subject on me."

"Now would I do that? I was just making an observation that's all. Anyway, what was it that you were saying?"

"Oh nothing; just about how horny I'm feeling right now."

"So where is your husband while you're in such a way?"

"Oh please, useless to me as usual. He's sound asleep, without a care in the world about how I'm feeling right now believe me."

"My girl is here spending the night tonight also."

"You know, you're getting almost as bold as me, but you should go. I don't want you to have any problems."

"Don't worry she's asleep for the night also. She has been for a couple of hours in fact. Not like her to go to bed quite so early; especially on the weekend, but she said she was tired so I wasn't going to make an issue out of it or anything."

"Well you must have given her one of your special love injections as only you can do. I can personally attest to the fact that a wrestling match with the Loch Ness monster can be very sleep inducing."

"Oh please; anyway, how is the vacation going?"

"See there you go trying to change the subject again."

"No, I was just inquiring."

"Whatever Gee," Sherri typed as she smiled. "I'll tell you all about it when I get back home okay. Anyway, I'm out on the balcony, but hold on. I want to step inside for a quick moment," Sherri said before lifting herself up to her feet and heading in. She returned a short time later and immediately resumed the conversation.

"Okay I'm back and I feel much better now. So much more comfortable."

"And why is that?"

"I just took off my panties. That's why I went inside. I have a short nightie on and now when I spread my legs this tropical breeze feels really good on my pussy."

"Well don't catch a cold down there. But that's really nice. And you know that if a breeze could talk that it would be saying the same thing."

"Haha very funny; anyway, what same thing?"

"That this pussy feels real good."

"You are crazy do you know that?"

"Yes I have been told that."

"Good because it's true. Anyway, since we won't be getting in until Monday afternoon I guess you won't be able to see or feel my pussy until Thursday."

"Well I'll have you know that I can see it anytime I want to log onto my computer and look at the pictures you emailed me. But as for feeling it, yes I suppose I'll have to wait until Thursday for that.

"Oh yeah those pictures; well you'd just better make sure that your girlfriend doesn't see them. The last thing I want or need is an angry woman coming after me with a butcher knife."

"Hey it's my personal computer and my email so I don't see any need to worry about that."

"All right Gee, if you say so. Anyway, Thursday is like an eternity away. I could go for some of your good, chocolate dick right now; but I guess I'll have to settle for lying here playing with my clit."

"You know I wouldn't mind that either if it was somehow possible. But maybe you can fantasize about it while you're fingering yourself."

"Yeah I guess that's the best that I can do right now. Oh and you know what, the following Monday I have a Doctor's appointment; so that day is out too."

Just as Sherri sent that text she was startled by the sound of the sliding door being opened behind her.

"What are you doing out here? And why are your panties on the floor in there?"

"Oh my God you scared the crap out of me!"

"I'm so sorry, but that wasn't my intention," said Clay with a hint of sarcasm as he slowly moved towards her.

"I just came out here to have a glass of wine and soak in the atmosphere. It's beautiful out here, and so peaceful. You wanna join me?"

While looking at her, Clay couldn't help but notice the little red flashing light coming from an object Sherri held in her hand. From that it was easy for him to figure out that it was her Blackberry phone and that she had likely been engaging in a text conversation. And he had no doubt in his mind who the other party must have been.

"No thanks, I think I'll pass," he replied coldly. Just make sure you pick up your damn panties before the kids see them in the morning," he added as he stepped away from her.

"Sorry that the sight of them bothers you so much. Anyway, don't worry I'll get them when I come in."

"Good you do that," Clay responded just before he opened the door and stepped back inside.

After allowing a couple of minutes to pass, Sherri turned her attention back to her phone and the last message she had received.

"Well in that case we'd better make sure we get enough in on Thursday to hold us for a while," Gee had sent.

"Oh I'm sure we'll do that; the more the better. Anyway lover I have to go. My husband snuck up on me a couple of minutes ago; scared the crap out me. He went back inside now but no telling if he'll come back so I'm gonna go ahead and go back in myself. Hopefully I'll talk to you sometime Monday?"

"Sure thing, have a safe flight home."

"Thanks, you have a good night Gee.

"You too; bye."

The moment Sherri crawled into the king-sized bed beside him Clay slid several inches away from her. But he did so in such a subtle fashion that it was barely detectable to her. She laid flat on her back for several seconds before turning onto her side facing him.

"Clay," she whispered, with him not responding back right away. "Are you awake?"

"Yes, what is it," he finally answered her.

"I still don't have any panties on," she said seductively.

With his back remaining to her he quickly replied that time. "That's nice Sherri, have a good night."

"But honey," she began before he cut her off in mid-sentence.

"Go to sleep Sherri."

She did eventually do just that. But not before staring into the darkness of the room for what seemed like at least an hour to her. Sure her mind had been elsewhere; on a man hundreds and hundreds of miles away. But her body was there for the taking by the man to whom she was married. But as it often had happened, he turned her away. So she again went to sleep wanting. Wanting a man she couldn't be with on that night; and sleeping with a man who apparently didn't want her. At least not in the way she needed; neither at this moment or on many other occasions. Thursday just couldn't arrive fast enough for her.

∞∞∞∞∞∞∞∞∞∞∞∞∞

With vacation now over, life in the King household quickly settled back into what was more or less the familiar routine. And that was certainly true for Sherri. It was the kids, cooking, cleaning and Gee. Yes Gee. He was just as much a part of her existence as many other things. Sure, in Clay she had a husband, but in Gee she had a dynamic lover. Basically her only lover by and large if you took away the occasional exercise in frustration with Clay. But it was far from that with Gee of course. And with all of the pleasure she also had to sometimes endure the pain; the pain that came with realizing just how much of a hold he had on her. It wasn't emotional. No she didn't love him at all. But rather it was like a constant longing. One that left her vulnerable to him and his sometimes overwhelming demands for her to service him in any way he desired. Except she didn't see it as merely serving him; she came to see it more as him allowing her to serve as his ever willing sexual plaything, as she also fulfilled her own strong desires. She also got off on the control he took over her. Even as she often felt that she lost just a little bit of herself each time he manipulated her to his liking, and to her possible detriment. Even if her lust for him didn't always allow her to see it that way in those moments of unbridled passion. It was in the aftermath when it would hit her if it did at all. And one of those moments slapped her dead in the face just a week to the day after her return from the Bahamas.

"Hurry up, let's go," Sherri shouted to her two oldest children Abby and Tyler. Seconds later they hustled down the stairs and reached out to grab the jackets their mother held for them.

"Mom are you sure I have to go," a forlorn sounding Abby pleaded. "I just don't feel up to it."

Sherri cut her eyes sharply at her daughter. "Yes you have to go. Now get outside. Wait on the porch, I'll be right out."

"Uggh, I hate Mondays, Abby replied as she walked out the door.

"You're ten; that's too young to hate Mondays," Sherri countered.

With that she turned her attention to her youngest, the just recently turned four years old Zach. She buttoned up his shirt after guiding his arms into the sleeves. Eight year old Tyler then brushed his hands through Zach's hair on the way past him, drawing a predictable response.

"Hey, cut it out," he said in his soft voice. "Mommy tell Tywer to stop it."

"Tyler please leave your brother alone. Let's not get him started okay."

"Okay I'll leave the baby alone. And my name's Tyler not Tywer."

"I'm not a baby, you're a baby." Zach fired back, before his Mom cut off the exchange.

"Tyler, outside!" she snapped. "Let's go. I have an appointment this morning so I have to hurry back."

She pulled up at the kids' day camp at 8:55, just 5 minutes before the 9 am start to the daily activities.

"Okay you two, hustle on in," Sherri said before giving both Abby and Tyler a quick kiss on the cheek. "I'll see you guys later; have a good day."

"Okay Mom bye," Tyler said as he hurried out of the car.

"Bye Mom, said Abby. "Bye squirt," she said to Zach, after kissing his forehead lightly.

Tyler on the other hand, wasn't quite as endearing in saying good-bye to his little brother.

"Bye little baby, he quipped.

"Mommy," Zach complained in a whiny tone.

"Don't worry about it honey," Sherri said in a comforting voice before turning back to the front.

"Go," she commanded Tyler. Just as the car doors closed, her cell phone beeped twice, signaling that she had received a text message. Pulling the phone out of her jacket pocket, she began to read the brief message on the phone's screen.

"What are you doing?"

"Good morning to you too," she quickly typed in response.

"Oh my bad; good morning. Now, what are you doing?

"I just finished dropping two of the kids off at camp, why?"

"You feel like swinging on by and doing that little thing for me this morning before I start my day?"

Sherri knew that in his own indirect way he was requesting an early morning blowjob. She shook her head from side to side before typing her reply.

"I'm sorry but I can't. In case you forgot I have that Doctor's appointment this morning so I need to get back home."

"You can't? You can't or you won't?"

"I mean I can't Gee."

"And why not?"

"I told you I have an appointment. Don't you remember me telling you about it while I was on vacation? Once again I'm sorry."

"What time is your appointment?"

"10:45. And I have to get dressed because I just threw something on to drop the kids off. So I have to get home, get showered, and then get dressed.   And of course drop my youngest off at his sitter and then drive there."

At that point Sherri decided that she needed to call rather than continue with the texting.

"Hello."

"Hey, listen, I can try to come by tomorrow rather than not seeing you until Thursday. If I can work out a sitter for my youngest I'll do that. Does that sound okay?"

"Nah forget all that; I need you to set this Monday off right. Whatever you're going to the Doctor for can wait for another day I'm sure."

"No it can't wait. It's a pretty important office visit actually."

"So in other words hell with me huh?"

"Listen it's not like that; you know I would if I could but I just can't this morning, sorry."

"Yeah you keep saying you're sorry and you know what, you've got that shit right. You're getting to be about one sorry ass bitch if you ask me.   But you go ahead; I've just about had enough of you anyway." His words cut Sherri like a knife but she said nothing.

"That's right. There are a lot more hoes out there that can fill your shoes. And probably better too."

"Please, don't say that. Give me a break. I'll make it up to you, I promise."

"Oh bullshit, whatever. Take your ass on home then."

"Don't be mad okay, I…"

Sherri held the phone to her ear for several seconds while saying hello before she accepted what had happened. That he had hung up on her. A bit shaken, she placed the phone back in her pocket, put the car in drive and pulled away from the curb. About 5 minutes or so later she made the turn onto Ridge Valley Drive, the street on which her home was located. Moving along slowly, she pulled her phone back out of her pocket. She stared at it briefly before tossing it onto the seat beside her. Once within 50 yards of her driveway she suddenly slammed on the brakes, paused and then turned into one of her neighbor's driveway. Reaching over to the passenger seat, she snatched up her phone and started dialing numbers.

"Hello."

"Great, I'm glad you answered. Don't go anywhere; I'm on my way, bye."

She took a brief moment to look at Zach who was quietly staring out the window from his car seat, and then quickly executed a K-turn headed back in the opposite direction. Her new destination—Route 287 South.

CHAPTER NINETEEN

The light post-rush hour traffic enabled Sherri to make good time on the interstate. She was able to cruise along at or slightly over the 65 mph speed limit all the way to the exit. She knew from the fact that he had gone silent that Zach had fallen asleep somewhere along the way. As she made her way closer to Gee's place, she suddenly remembered her appointment. "Oh shit," she said softly as she moved along on Route 22. A short time later she was fortunate to be stopped at a light. Quickly fumbling through her purse, she retrieved the number for the doctor's office and dialed the number.

"Good morning, Mid-state OB-GYN Associates; Melissa speaking how may I help you?"

"Good morning Melissa my name is Sherri King. I have a 10:45 appointment with Dr. Felder."

"Uh huh," the young lady replied.

"Well I'm afraid something has just come up so I won't be able to make my appointment this morning. I apologize for the late notice."

"That's okay, would you like to reschedule?"

"Actually," Sherri began, "I was wondering if there are by any chance any openings for early this afternoon perhaps? I'm only tied up this morning."

"Hmmm, not likely, but if you hold on I will certainly check for you."

"Sure no problem, thanks."

After about 75 seconds or so later the young lady returned to the phone.

"Ms. King."

"Yes, I'm here."

"Thanks for holding. Anyway here's what I have. We shut down for lunch from twelve thirty to one thirty and then he's solidly booked right after lunch. Now we do have another cancellation at four o'clock, so we could work you in there."

"Four o'clock; really that's all? Four o'clock won't work for me because I have to pick up my kids by then," Sherri lamented.

"I'm sorry Ms. King, but I'm afraid that's the best we can do today."

"No it's okay, I'm the one that's not gonna be able to make the appointment I had. I do appreciate you checking though."

"No problem. Would you like to reschedule?"

"Yes please."

"And are there any specific timeframes that you prefer?"

"Yes another early to mid-morning preferably," Sherri answered.

"Ummm, let's see. He's pretty much booked solid for a while; especially at that time of day because that seems to be everyone's first preference. That and late afternoons"

"I understand, well just whatever you have."

"Well we have a ten o'clock on September 17th. That's a Wednesday."

"Sure that'll be fine."

"Okay you're all set then Mrs. King; we will see you on the 17th at 10 a.m."

"Yep sure will, thank you Melissa."

"You're welcome, have a good day."

"You too bye-bye."

Sherri sighed deeply as soon as the call ended; blowing air out through her pursed lips. Now I have to wait almost a month. Damn you Gee, she was thinking to herself as she continued along on her way to him. A few minutes later she pulled right behind his car. She turned and took another look at Zach who was still sound asleep. The day already had all the makings of a typically hot and humid August one so she certainly didn't want to chance anything. Therefore she left all four windows down slightly and quickly departed the car, trying not to awake him with the sound of the door closing as she exited before rushing over to ring the doorbell.

"Hey baby; what a surprise. I'm happy to see you. I'm glad you changed your mind, "a smiling Gee said as he opened the door to let her in.

"Whatever;" Sherri said as she quickly pushed her way past him and started up the stairs.

"Hold up sweetheart, slow done for a second. What happened with your appointment?"

Sherri stopped and turned to face him just as she reached the top step.

"Oh so now it's baby and sweetheart. What about all that disrespect you showed me on the phone?"

"Aww come on now, you know I didn't mean any of that stuff. Come here let me give you a hug," he said once he also reached the top of the stairs and opened the door to let her inside.

As Sherri folded her arms across her chest and rolled her eyes without moving at all, Gee slowly walked toward her before wrapping his arms around her neck and pulling her close to him. "MMMM, there you go," he whispered to her. "You better now?"

Sherri unfolded her arms and looked up at him. "I don't know, maybe a little. Anyway, I rescheduled my appointment."

"Oh okay; well I sure do appreciate you doing that and coming by."

"Yeah sure you do. Anyway, I came straight here after talking to you and my son is in the car sleeping, so that means I still don't have a lot of time."

"Don't worry this won't take a lot of time," Gee said with his by now familiar, mischievous smile.

Sherri undid the belt on his robe allowing it to fall open. He wore nothing beneath it except a pair of solid colored boxer briefs. "Come on," she said as she grabbed his hand and started to lead him over to the sofa in the living room.

"Hold up, I've got an idea; follow me," Gee said.

"Well what is it your mind has cooked up this time?" Sherri questioned as she trailed behind him.

He led her back down the common stairs he shared with his neighbor until they reached the midway point. There he stopped, turned to face her and placed his hands on her shoulders.

"Have a seat."

"What; right here? What about your next door neighbor?"

"Oh she's gone already. Besides if she was home she could just come out here and get some of this too."

"Oh whatever mister ego, let's just do this."

"Hey you know I'm ready. Do your thing baby."

Sherri sat on one of the steps and Gee positioned himself one step below facing directly towards her.

After he removed his robe and let it fall to the step below she pulled his boxers down and slowly leaned in towards him with her mouth opened as wide as she could get it. She took him in and immediately began to work her head back and forth as she sucked him vigorously.

"Come on feed it to me," she implored him as she clasped her hands behind her back.

Gee then grabbed her by both sides of her head and started to quickly pump his dick into her wide open mouth.

She gasped for air and her eyes danced as he gripped her by the bun she wore her hair in, thrusting hard all the while. After about a minute had passed she pulled away from him long enough to ask him a question.

"Were you really ready to break it off with me if I hadn't come this morning?

"Nah, you know I wouldn't have done that to you. Now come on, lean back on the steps."

Sherri used her right hand to wipe away some of the saliva that had spilled from her lips and covered both the area around her mouth and her chin. She then rested her upper back against the stairs before Gee quickly straddled her with his nude body. He then started to slowly pump deep inside her mouth, leading to her making loud, gurgling sounds with every up and down stroke of his penis. As promised he seemed focused only on working his way towards an orgasm as quickly as he could.

Being careful in an attempt to avoid both the stairs and her clothing, he covered as much of her face with his cum as possible. He shook out every last drop that he could before she took him back into her mouth in order to suck out any that might remain. Having gotten the release that he was after, he yanked his meat from her mouth and raced up the stairs. He made a stop in the linen closet where he grabbed a washcloth, hurried into the bathroom to moisten it and hustled it back down to her.

"Here use this," he said as he handed it to her.

"Are you okay now," she asked as she used both sides of the cloth to wipe her face clean.

"Yeah I'm good; real good. I do appreciate this baby. Thank you so much."

"Well let me go now okay."

"All right I'll talk to you soon," Gee replied

"Bye," she said as he opened the door to let her out.

As she quickly walked around the front end of her car to reach the driver's side, Sherri could see that Zach had awakened. His eyes were wide open and looking all around at nothing in particular.

"Hey sweetie," she called out as she climbed into the car. "You woke up I see."

"Mommy, where were you at?"

"I'm sorry honey; Mommy was just visiting a friend. Let's go home now okay."

"Okay Mommy," he replied in his soft, high-pitched voice.

Sherri ducked her head in shame, softly leaning it against the steering wheel for a few moments before straightening herself back up in order to drive. As she pulled back into the street, tears welled up in her eyes and one eventually fell.

About 5 minutes after Sherri had departed and left him in a much better frame of mind, Gee picked up the phone to make another, different type of call.

"Hey, I called you earlier, but I didn't leave a message; is everything okay over there?"he asked.

He posed this question to Alicia Tolliver, his girlfriend of the last three years. She had been feeling under the weather to the point where's she'd had to miss a few flight assignments as of late.

"I'm sorry honey; I had to run to the bathroom. It's as if my bladder is tired also because I've been going like crazy all morning."

"So you're not feeling any better then?"

"No, not at all," she sighed. "I just can't wait to go to the Doctor this afternoon so I can get a better handle on what's wrong with me. I just feel like I've been on the wrong end of a beating that just won't stop. And also, I apologize for the way I've been acting towards you lately. I think it's just because I'm so tired and worn out all the time, but I know I've been a bitch to deal with the last couple of weeks. So please just bear with me sweetheart."

"Yeah we have been getting into it a little more than I'm accustomed to. It was pretty bad last night. I think we both probably said some things that we wish we hadn't so I apologize too. And I understand that you haven't been yourself lately. But don't worry baby I'm not going anywhere. We've been through too much and I love you too much to even think about my life without you."

"See that's why I love you so much Garrick Andrews. You know just what to say. But anyway, why don't I call you later after I get back from my appointment. I feel like lying down for a while."

"Okay love, call me later."

"All right I will. Bye baby, I love you."

"Love you too, bye."

Sherri hadn't been able to chase away her blues from the time she had left Gee. As much as she loved pleasuring Gee and got equal pleasure from it as well, what had just occurred was still troubling her deeply. That she had so greatly altered her plans in order to go out of her way to suck a man's dick; and a man who wasn't even her husband at that. A man to whom she by all that is right should not feel beholden to at all. And to do this while her child was left just outside in the car was beyond crazy. Forgoing her shame for mainly his satisfaction, and ignoring her better judgment simply for the sake of their desires. Even as she knew that Gee was likely feeling far different emotions. Probably feeling just that much more empowered over her. Knowing that she was his to do with whatever he wanted, whenever he wanted and however he wished. If there was any way out of this twisted situation she knew she needed to find it quickly.

"Hey sweetheart, thanks for coming by," Alicia said after she opened the door to her apartment in Summit.

"Well you said it was important, so of course I was going to come right by," said Gee after they exchanged a kiss. "Now you said the Doctor told you to just get a lot of rest for a few days, but that you were going to be fine right?" he added.

"Yeah pretty much, but there's a bit more to it also and that's actually the reason why I wanted to see you in person," she said as she grabbed Gee by a hand and led him over to her living room sofa. "Have a seat baby."

She couldn't help but notice the confused look on his face as he slowly lowered himself to the sofa; never taking his eyes off of her in the process.

"I can see that you're wondering what the hell I'm talking about, so I'm just going to come out with it," Alicia assured him. She then reached out and grabbed a hold of both of his hands before exhaling deeply. Gee's anxiety increased by the moment as he waited for whatever she was about to hit him with. "Baby, I did go to the doctor today but it wasn't just a regular doctor like a general practitioner; I went to my ob-gyn. Garrick I'm pregnant."

"You, you you're wwwhat," Gee said with his eyes big and lit up like neon saucers.

"I'm pregnant. Garrick we're gonna have a baby."

Gee leapt to his feet, beaming with a smile that spread from ear to ear. "Woo hoo, you're pregnant. Pregnant as in gonna have a baby. I'm going to be a father," he said excitedly.

"Yes, all of the above," Alicia chuckled, relieved that he was so ecstatic over the news.

Gee's display continued with him placing both of his hands on top of his head with a look of disbelief before breaking into a little impromptu dance; stopping long enough to kiss her firmly on the lips and hugging her tightly before slowly helping her to her feet.

"You know I was actually a little worried that you might be upset to find this out."

"Are you kidding; baby this is great news, I love you lady, do you know that?"

"Yes and I love you too Garrick, I love you so very much."

They locked lips again for what seemed like forever before Gee pulled away from her slightly, a huge grin still covering his face.

"You know what, I feel like we need to celebrate; don't you have a bottle of champagne around here someplace?"

"Gee!" Alicia said incredulously.

"What? Oh you mean because it's daytime, why should that matter, this is a joyous occasion."

Alicia turned her head sideways, stretched her eyes at him and cleared her throat while pointing to her stomach, hoping that he would then get what she was trying to say.

It was at that point when the light finally came on for Gee. "Oh that's right, sorry baby. Do you happen to have any sparkling apple juice here?"

"No not right now, but feel free to pick some up today."

"Okay and then we can celebrate with a nice toast."

"Yes that would be nice," Alicia agreed, just as Gee placed a hand to her stomach.

"Sweetie I don't think you're going to feel anything in there right now, I'm not even quite a month along," she laughed.

"Oh okay; wait, have you told your folks? I have to call my Mom and Dad and tell them the news," Gee said excitedly.

"Baby, baby hold on a second; the general rule of thumb is that you keep it to yourself until you've passed the first trimester. So no I haven't told a soul. The only person who has any inkling at all is my sister Rhonda because she's the one who suggested that I might be pregnant when I kept telling her how I've been feeling. But I haven't even confirmed it with her now that I know. But I guess I'll have to and then just trust her to keep it to herself."

"Okay, I see where you're coming from. We can keep it on the low for now. But i'm just so happy right now; it's like I'm on could nine or something."

"And believe me I'm just as happy to see you take it this way as I was excited about the news itself."

"You're gonna be such a great Mother, I just know it."

"And you're gonna be a great dad Garrick."

As they embraced once again, Gee whispered softly to her. "This is going to change so many things baby; but only for the better."

"I know it is and I can't wait to have your baby Garrick."

"Make that our baby."

"Yes of course; our baby, our little bundle of joy."

"I love you Alicia."

"And I really and truly love you Garrick Andrews," she replied before their lips came together. As the kiss lingered, he guided her back to the sofa where they sat down. As the kissing continued Gee placed his hands on her torso, first around her back before making his way to her breasts. As his hands caressed her his lips moved downward. She tilted her head backwards as he planted soft kisses all over the soft skin of her neck. They took turns helping the other out of the t-shirts that each of them wore before Alicia leaned forward, running her tongue across each of his nipples. Pushing her back gently, Gee unhooked and then removed her bra before taking one of her firm breasts into his mouth. She squirmed in delight as he attached his lips to each of them in succession, teasing her excited nipples with his tongue. Raising his head back up their lips quickly found each other's once again. Heavy breaths passed between them as their passions soared. He returned his attention to her lovely flesh mounds, delighting in sucking them once again. After several more minutes his lips slowly made their way down her stomach, delicate kisses left everywhere they found themselves. Now kneeling before her, he helped her out of her jeans and then her panties. They kissed again just before he lowered his head to her paradise. He started by softly sucking and kissing her inner thigh area.

"Mmmm," she moaned softly. Not only in response to that but in anticipation of what was to come next. "Oh yessss baby," she cooed as she first felt his lips come into contact with her by then throbbing pussy. Her hips wiggled as he licked up and down slowly. From the moment he turned his focus to her swollen clit, she went into almost a state of delirium; driven wild with pleasure from him first licking and then delicately sucking on her magic spot. She threw her hands up to her head, relishing the feeling of his loving tongue. "That's it baby, right there. Oh, oh, oh," she whispered repeatedly. Gripping her hips, Gee then flipped her over in one smooth motion until it was he on his back with her goodies hovering above him. Pressing down on her lightly, he laid back in comfort as she began to grind on his happy face. Now wanting something herself, Alicia insisted that he then remove the rest of his clothes also. Once he complied, she again straddled his face as he now lay on the carpeted floor. Only this time she wrapped her lips around his rock hard tool in return. Testing her limits, she took in as much of him as she could, going deeper with each downward stroke; stopping only when she felt the beginning of her gag reflex. It was as if they were trying to outdo the other in dishing out oral delights, with him exploring every inch of her sweetness; wielding his tongue's like an artist does his brush. She felt as if she might be ready to explode at any moment, yet she climbed off of him; rolling onto her back in one smooth motion. She wanted him inside and didn't hesitate to let him know that. Lying flat on her back, she spread her legs to receive him, beckoning him on with gesturing hands. After initially tensing up slightly as Gee entered her slowly, she gripped him tightly; allowing him to feel every bit of her wet, tender pussy. They kissed passionately as their bodies melted into each other's; warm lips drawn together by passion as strong as a magnetic force. Climbing to his feet, Gee backed up to the sofa, sitting himself down as he pulled Alicia by the hands. She wasted no time in mounting him before riding his towering penis to delirium, both his and her own. Her orgasm seemed to come like waves crashing ashore during high tide, his lips again caressing her heaving breasts as she cried out in ecstasy. Gee's own explosion came just moments later, filling her up as he too found himself unable to stifle the feelings that accompanied his own release. As he moaned loudly, they fell to the floor, locked in an embrace; another lingering kiss soon following.

"Baby I know I haven't always showed it or told you so, but do you have any idea how much you mean to me. I just need to make sure that you know that," he whispered as they cuddled on the floor.

"Yes I do sweetheart and I love you too. So, so much. But I've never doubted your love for me no matter what we've been through."

Gee sat up, just enough to allow him to look directly into her eyes.

"That's so great to hear Alicia, and I promise you right here and now that the best is yet to come."

CHAPTER TWENTY

In what had of course become her regular Thursday morning routine, Sherri had just dropped Zach off with Beth and was now headed for yet another tryst with Gee. She had at least temporarily gotten over her discomfort with the entire convoluted situation she was caught up in, and was genuinely looking forward to being with him again. Wearing what had become his favorite piece of lingerie and lightly splashed with his preferred aromatic scent, it was with hormones raging and her libido soaring that she cruised in his direction; ready to submit to his every desire and surrender all she had to him yet again. Turning up the volume on her car's radio, she pressed hard on the accelerator, anxiously anticipating the feel of him inside of her, and smiling at the mere thought of it.

But Sherri got an eerie feeling the moment that she saw Gee as he opened the door to let her in. His stoic demeanor was far different than what was normally the case when she arrived at his place. There was no smile from him, nor a hug or any other show of affection. He was instead downright stone-faced as he greeted her.

"Hey, come on in; thanks for coming by," he said plainly.

"You make it sound as if I came for a business meeting or something," Sherri replied. With that comment she was at least able to draw out a half smile from him. "Is everything okay? You don't seem like yourself at all."

"Yeah I'm fine," he assured her. "In fact I'm a little better than fine, I'm feeling great actually. Let's go upstairs."

"Oh really; if you're doing great you could have fooled me, she said as she walked towards the sofa once they were upstairs, coming to a halt just in front of it. You've had almost the expression of a mime from the moment you opened the door. Anyway, I have your favorite piece of lingerie on underneath these clothes. You want me to show you?"

"Have a seat Sherri; please."

"Have a seat? Okay now you're scaring me; what's up with you Gee?"

"Sherri please; sit down."

"Okay, okay I'm sitting; what's going on?"

After taking a deep breath he opened his mouth to speak. "Okay listen, I know we've had this thing going on for a while now," he began deliberately. "And believe me I've enjoyed every moment of it; as I hope you have. I mean usually we would be all over each other already as you well know. But the circumstances have changed now," he added before a long pause. "Sherri I'm not going to be able to see you any longer."

"Okay Gee, why are you playing around this morning?" Sherri chuckled.

"I'm afraid I'm not playing; not this time. I'm dead serious," a straight-faced Gee replied.

Looking at him intently, Sherri inched a bit closer to him. "Come on, stop it; give me what I came here for," she pleaded while at the same time reaching down and tugging at his belt.

"Sherri no; stop it," Gee snapped. "I'm being for real here; it's over between us. I'm sorry."

Suddenly reality seemed to hit Sherri flush in the face. And like a well-delivered punch it rocked and then staggered her much the same way. "You're sorry? What do you mean you're sorry? How can it be over just like that Gee," she said pensively. "No, I refuse to believe it. This has to be a prank that you're playing on me right?" Standing up, she quickly walked away from him and over to the nearest window. After a few moments he stood and followed her.

"Why don't you come on back and sit down; let me explain. Please, I owe you that," he said while placing a hand on her shoulder.

Slowly lifting her head, she looked up at him with moist, reddened eyes before allowing him to guide her back over to the sofa where they both sat down.

"Okay I'm just gonna just come right out with this. Sherri, my girlfriend is pregnant. I just found out a few days ago. So I wanna do the right thing by her. I think i'm going to marry her. She deserves as much."

"She's pregnant? But I thought she was on the pill?"

"Yeah me too, so I don't know what happened."

"So how do you feel about it," Sherri asked as she dabbed at her eyes with the back of her right hand. She hated that he must know that what he'd just told her had bought her to tears.

"Well it wasn't planned, and yes she was supposed to be on birth control, but you know what, I'm absolutely ecstatic."

"Really? So you're ready to be a Dad?"

"Yes I am. I've always wanted to be a Father. I mean I didn't expect it to happen like this or at this time, but I'm taking it as a blessing from above. So yes I am very, very happy about it. And I'm ready for all of the responsibility that comes along with it."

"Well in that case I'm very happy for you Gee. I just feel bad that I was acting so selfish a little while ago."

"That's okay Sherri, you didn't know."

Sherri's entire disposition had by now changed as she was now able to share in his joy."

She looked at him and smiled as she thought about it. "In any event I should have been able to handle it better than that. I mean I knew what this was and that it was never really going to be a long-term thing. But I guess I just got caught up in it over these months."

"I understand, so don't worry about it," Gee said with a warming smile. "And let me say that although it might not have always seemed like it, it meant something to me too."

"As Sherri smiled again, she wondered if he could read that behind this one was a feeling of skepticism. It wasn't that she didn't appreciate him making the effort to soothe her feelings; she just questioned how genuine he was in the process.

"Well I guess I should be going then," she said.

She picked up her purse and headed to the stairs with Gee following right along with her.

"So I guess one final blowjob here on the stairs is out of the question huh," she said half-jokingly," as they started down the steps slowly.

"Well as tempting as that may sound and it does sound plenty tempting; it's not a good idea. But how about a nice big hug," he offered as they reached the front door.

"Bye Sherri, you take care of yourself."

"You do the same Gee," she countered as they held each other tightly in a lingering embrace. "And congratulations on everything, I'm sure you'll be a great Dad."

"Thanks, I really appreciate that," he responded. "And I hope you understand why I had you come all the way over here just to deliver this news. I just felt like it would be better to tell you such a thing in person than over the phone or in an email or something."

"Yes I agree with that and I appreciate it Gee. Anyway, goodbye and good luck to you two."

"Thanks Sherri, I'll always remember you, and what we had."

"Maybe you can let me know when the baby is born."

"Sure I can do that, no problem," Gee promised her.

As he opened the door to let her out she took one more glance into his eyes before lowering her head. And with that she was gone. Out of the door and out of his life.

It was a good thing that she now had several hours before she had to pick up Zach from Beth's home. And Sherri needed every bit of it. As she returned home; alone and much sooner than she had planned; she threw herself across the bed. For much of the next couple of hours her only companion was her aching heart; carrying with it a bucket full of tears.

∞∞∞∞∞∞∞∞

In the aftermath of the demise of her intense affair with Gee, Sherri struggled to adjust without him being a part of her life. She thought about him a bit on each and every day; sometimes longingly, other times with a small amount of contempt. But there he was every day; memories of him lingering over her like the thick haze of the August heat. She had thoughts of how she had over and over again submitted herself to him completely. Way beyond where she had ever gone for her very own husband even. When he mentioned that he was a little short and couldn't make his car payment, she stepped up and wrote a check for him no questions asked. Not as a loan but rather as a gift. But even with all of that she was surely able to understand things from his perspective. One thing that helped her to cope was the impending start to the school year and all the time she had to spend prepping for that. And she realized all too well just how important it was for her to maintain a solid exterior, even on the days that she had to fight not to crumble on the inside.

But in no way could she make it appear to Clay that she was hurting in some way. To do so would be to invite an inquiry into her state of mind. Something she obviously wanted to avoid at all costs. So she wore a mask; to hide what was sometimes pain and at others bitterness; but was always confusion. Over how the man who at times seemed so poisonous to her, was also the one man she still often longed for.

It was mid-September when Rollie got back in touch with Roberto and Jimmy in order to let them know that everything was a go. All that was left was for the two of them to get in to do the plant and then get out clean and without any signs of them having been there. Jimmy gave reassurances to Rollie that this in itself would not be an issue. They just needed to pick the proper time to make it happen.

As each day passed Sherri's hurt feelings eased, replaced more and more by the return of the kind of desires that had led her down that previously travelled path in the first place. She even thought about Scott from time to time. Although he wasn't blessed with the same anatomical gift as Gee, he was a very giving lover. The way that he would feverishly attack her pussy with his tongue reminded her of a hungry kitten lapping away at a saucer of milk. But she had burned that bridge behind her and sadly, ravenous lust was once again searing through her flesh, her mind once again given to thoughts of lurid encounters and fantasies of complete submission. She knew that hers was a losing battle and that she could not for much longer fight her urges. It was accepting this that led to the first in a series of fateful events that would turn her world completely upside down.

"Hey, just calling you like you requested. It's a done deal; in and out within an hour."

"Great; and were you careful to plant it someplace very hidden away just like we had discussed," Rollie asked.

"Sure did," Roberto assured him. One bundle is underneath the fridge and the others behind the bottom two drawers in the dresser in the master bedroom. Places where he'll never come across the stuff believe me."

"Nice job, I'll call you back within an hour to let you know when we'll pass the rest of the payment off to you boys."

Sherri had recently seen a segment on daytime television focused on how people use the popular all-purpose website Craigslist to arrange casual meetings for sex. And although she found it a bit eye-opening, she otherwise didn't think much of it at the time. And surely never thought that there was a snowball's chance in hell that here a short time later, she would be on the verge of doing that very thing. But as they say, desperate times call for desperate measures. And with Gee having dismissed her, much as she had previously allowed things with Scott to fade away in favor of Gee, Sherri did feel all of that and more.

With Clay scheduled to travel to San Antonio for the national convention of the National Law Enforcement Officials Association, Sherri decided the upcoming weekend would be a good time for her to play. So to that end she too had decided to make use of Craigslist to find a potential lover. The process was remarkably easy and fast in producing the desired results. Since Gee had turned her completely inside out, she now had a strong preference for another Black man. She was so taken by his confidence, and could in no way deny that she had been driven wild by the sheer power and dominance he so often displayed during their many times together. And the raw, uninhibited manner in which he took her to the brink of complete ecstasy, before always taking her over that edge each and every time he fucked her. Maybe there was some truth in that old myth. All she knew was now that she'd had Black she didn't feel quite ready to go back.

She placed a brief but straightforward ad on Saturday afternoon and by early Sunday morning she was in business, discovering once again just how with all of the other purposes it serves, that the internet was also a huge supermarket for illicit sex. Out of the dozen or so men who responded to her, she quickly settled on a guy who went by the rather humorous moniker of Brick City Booty Bandit. What else she found out about him was that his name was actually Derrick and that he now lived in West Orange which is about 12 miles west of Newark aka Brick City. They exchanged emails frequently during the course of the week leading up to Clay's departure, as well as swapping explicit photos at her request. Derrick was 36 year old, medium-complexioned, about 5'11" and stocky with a closely-cropped haircut. And while Sherri perhaps didn't see him as overly attractive initially, she favored him largely because he was both local and readily available as opposed to most of the others. And she upped her opinion of him considerably once she got a look at what he was packing down below. She decided at that point that he would certainly fill the bill for what she was looking for. That being more of the same type of no-holds barred sex that she had always had with Gee. They agreed to meet on Friday at the after work mixer which is held weekly at the lounge which is part of the New Jersey Performing Arts Center complex in Newark.

Sherri dropped Clay off at the airport early Friday morning and her thoughts then immediately turned to that evening. She had arranged for the kids to stay overnight at Kevin and Nina's, telling them that she was going into Manhattan to have dinner and attend a play with an old friend. After dropping the kids off at about 6, Sherri arrived at the lounge at 8:30, or about thirty minutes later than expected. That was largely because after leaving her in-laws dressed in a conservative pant suit she had returned home to dress in something just a bit more provocative. She was sporting a scoop-necked red bodysuit underneath a very short Black skirt; both of which she had picked up at the mall earlier in the day. Before departing her car she checked her hair and makeup one final time and sprayed on just the right amount of perfume.

It would not be very long before Sherri would come to the realization that the evening was not going to go as planned; at least not as she had planned in her mind. She figured that she and Derrick would have a drink or two, chat for a bit to get more comfortable, and then take off someplace to be alone. They were quite familiar with each other's appearance from the photos they had exchanged,so she figured it shouldn't be too hard for her to spot him once she walked in. The lounge had a stage to the front of it and a long bar that sat to the left. Below the stage were 8-10 small, intimate tables and to the right and the rear there was some booth seating. They had exchanged emails earlier in the evening detailing what each would be wearing and to make it even easier, arranged to look for each other in the area of the bar closest to the stage. As she approached the bar she looked around for any signs of him in the crowded area. Seeing no sign of him initially, she decided to turn towards the bar and order herself a drink. After ordering herself a cosmopolitan she turned around again in the hope that she might now see Derrick milling about. And she did see him, but he was doing anything but milling about. There he was seated at one of the tables. Sharing the table was another Black male along with two very attractive ladies. One was a medium-complexioned Black girl with a stylish, short haircut. She was flawlessly beautiful; dressed in a gold-colored sheath and matching pumps. Her oversized hoop earrings stood out even from halfway across the room. The other girl was no less gorgeous. Dressed in a black skirt and what looked like a satin dark- colored blouse, she was a tall, leggy Latina with trademark long dark hair. The group was engaged in an animated discussion which included a lot of laughter. It appeared for the entire world to Sherri that there was some sort of double-date going on. She looked at them for a while before turning back to the bar before he could spot her.

While slowly nursing her drink she did allow herself the occasional glance back at the group enjoying themselves at the table some 40 or so feet behind her. Just as she was downing the last of her cosmo, Sherri noticed that Derrick had stood and walked towards the rear of the building; just past the far end of the bar. After glancing at the table, she stood and headed in that direction. She soon found out that was where the rest rooms were located. Hatching a plan, she sat there at the edge of the bar, biding her time. Looking around she noticed that the place had filled up quite well on this evening. The crowd was largely African-American and Hispanic with more than a few White faces sprinkled in as well; certainly enough that she didn't stick out in the place like a sore thumb.

She turned back in the direction of the rest rooms just in time to see Derrick headed her way. Leaping to her feet, she quickly stood and walked directly into his path so that they were sure to bump into each other.

"Excuse me," she said softly as they brushed against each other with her placing her hand against his torso as if to deflect him away.

"No problem, excuse me," he said in return as they made brief eye contact.

As he started to move on, she called out to him. "Wait, you don't recognize me?"

"Excuse me," he said once again, this time with a bemused look covering his face.

"Derrick, it's me Sherri. Do I look that different than in the pictures I sent you during the week?"

"Oh; hey how you doing," he said with a big smile. I see you made it."

"Yeah I did. I got here about 15-20 minutes ago I guess. I spent some time looking for you, but from the looks of things you certainly weren't doing the same."

"Why do you say that," he asked while cocking his head sideways.

"Well I saw you up front at one of the tables, and it looks to me like you're on a little double date or something."

He then looked over his shoulder for a quick moment before turning back towards her.

"Hey let me talk to you for a second," he said as he guided her over to the corner of the bar. "Nah, it's not even like that. Me and my boy just met those chicks here tonight."

"Oh, so we were supposed to hook up here, but instead you decided to pick up some other girl. Okay I've got it."

"No that wasn't my intention, but hey, I thought you weren't showing so you know, I had to do what I had to do."

"Okay, so I was a little late, sorry about that. But I didn't think I was that late. But apparently I was too late as far as you're concerned."

"No not necessarily. Listen, why don't you hang out, have a drink and just chill for a little while. We can still do this thing."

"Oh so you just want me to wait in the background while you finish up with your date?"

"That's not what I'm saying and like I said it's not a date," sighed Derrick. He then pulled a bill out of his pocket and reached it out towards her. "Listen, why don't you buy yourself a drink and just wait on me for a little while okay?"

"Sherri looked up at him before turning away slightly. "Okay I'll do that, but I'll pay for my own drink. Save your money to spend on that pretty little thing you're trying to pick up."

"Okay whatever Miss Independent do your thing, but just give me a little time. You're looking damn good too. So you know I still wanna get with you just like we talked about," Derrick said with a disarming smile.

"All right, I'll wait for a while. Just don't expect me to wait all night."

"Cool, I appreciate that baby," he said before brushing her lightly on the arm. Moving away from her, he headed back towards the stage and the table he had been occupying; sneaking a look back in her direction as he did so.

Sherri had already turned her attention towards the bar and never saw his final look back at her however. She decided to remain at that end of the bar rather than return to the end close to where Derrick sat making time with the beauty in the gold dress. A second cosmo soon turned into a third and still no sign of Derrick headed back to spend time with her. But she had attracted some attention while seated there at the bar however. One guy in particular had taken two shots at her with Sherri rebuffing him each time by telling him that she was waiting for someone. She checked her watch just before heading into the ladies room and noted that the time was approaching 9:45. She stood in front of the mirror checking her hair and makeup before turning towards the exit. Just as she opened the door she was met by a person entering at the same exact moment.

"Excuse me," she said as she started to make her way past her.

"Oh excuse me; I'm sorry, the woman said as she looked Sherri in the face. Oh my God; Sherri is that you?"

Sherri turned, look and saw a very familiar face. It belonged to Amanda Stuart a past colleague at her former place of employment in Manhattan. They had been together at the firm as associates until Sherri departed to become a stay at home mom.

"Amanda, how are you doing," Sherri replied before they hugged each other lightly and Amanda stepped outside of the ladies room to continue the conversation.

If there was one thing that Amanda always had it was the gift of gab and it didn't take Sherri long to find out that hadn't changed a bit, as Amanda start to pepper her with questions, many coming before Sherri could even began to answer the previous one.

"How have you been?

"I'm fine, just great how about you?"

"I'm good, what brings you here? This place is not bad; it's sort of a meat market, but I like coming here to see the live bands. They have a great cover band playing tonight. They play some Earth Wind & Fire, K.C. & the Sunshine Band, some Motown stuff and even a little Michael Jackson. They're really good; should be coming back on around 10:30."

"Oh okay cool," Sherri managed to squeeze in before Amanda started up again.

"Are you still at home? I'm with one of the firms down here In Newark now. I got tired of the whole Manhattan commute thing. How are the kids? They must be so big now huh?"

"Oh they're great and yes they are getting big and I'm still a stay at home Mom."

"By the way you look great Sherri."

"Thanks."

"Who are you here with? I'm on a little date with this guy I've been seeing. Are you here with your husband? Hey maybe you guys can join us, we have a booth up front. Not too far from the stage. Speaking of your husband I read that he's the Somerset County Prosecutor now. That is so great; I know you must be so proud of him. I came in here to check my hair but never mind, let's go; why don't I show you where we're sitting so you guys can join us. The guy I'm with works with the Essex County courts so he and your hubby might have a lot to talk about. Well as much as either of them is at liberty to discuss that is. This is so cool. I can't believe I ran into you."

As Sherri smiled politely something began to dawn on her. She couldn't have Amanda knowing that she was there; at an obvious meat market by herself. Not only would that lead to Amanda drawing God knows what sort of conclusions but probably taking those conclusions and spreading them around to whatever common friends they shared from their years spent working together. Sherri could just hear it now.

You won't believe who I ran into? Sherri King; remember her? But the weird thing is, she was at this place that's sort of like hookup heaven but she was all by herself. Hmmm, I wonder what that was all about.

As they stepped a little further away from the ladies' room Sherri began to ponder just how to sidestep the situation.

"Come on we're over this way. Where's your husband?" Amanda asked, not even realizing that Sherri hadn't even answered the question of who she was there with. Amanda hadn't given her a chance to. As she walked with Sherri alongside her, she suddenly stopped in her tracks. Reaching into the pocket of her slacks she pulled out her cell phone. She looked at it before turning to Sherri.

"Uh oh, it's the ex; he has our daughter tonight. So I have to take this. Why don't you wait here for me and I'll be right back. I'm going to step outside to make sure that we can hear each other."

"Okay I'll be right here," said Sherri with a smile. But as soon as Amanda stepped completely outside she sprung into action. Sauntering up towards the front, she had her attention squarely focused on finding out just what the deal with Derrick was. As she appraoched him she noticed that Derrick and his male companion were the only ones at the table. She hadn't seen if the two heavenly bodies had come in the direction of the ladies room while she was standing close by the entrance talking with Amanda. Nor did she have any idea if they had possibly left the premises. In truth she didn't particularly care at that point. All she wanted was to find out what Derrick's intentions were. And she had to find out right then and there.

As she drew closer her pace quickened, with her wanting to get answeres before the young ladies possibly returned. She walked up behind Derrick before coming to a halt almost right beside him. It was his friend who actually saw her first, his eyes then drawing Derrick's attention towards Sherri.

"I need to talk to you for a second," she said loud enough for both of them to hear.

"Damn baby, where'd you come from," a stunned Derrick replied.

"You know where I came from, now can we talk or not?" Sherri was even surprising herself with how demonstrative she was being. It was probably attributable to the three drinks that she'd had.

Derrick glared at her for a few seconds before turning in the direction of his friend. "I'll be right back man," he said before rising to his feet and leading her over to the front of the bar. Before they walked away Sherri took a look at Derrick's friend long enough to note the confused expression on his face; him no doubt wondering who the hell this chick was.

When she and Derrick came to a halt, Sherri immediately turned to face him, her arms folded across her chest. "So what are we doing?" she asked him sternly.

"Well we're not necessarily doing anything, But I'm going back to my table in a few minutes and you can do whatever the hell it is you're gonna do," he answered to her great consternation.

"So what is it you're trying to say Derrick? That you were just playing a game; just stringing me along in case things didn't go as you hoped with that other girl? What the fuck is that?"

"Listen sweetheart, I realize you've probably had a few drinks tonight but you really need to check yourself right now. I mean you're not my girl or anything. Shit I don't even know you to tell you the truth. I mean that little playing around thing during the week was cool and everything, but don't be going overboard because of it."

"Oh so basically you really didn't have any intention of being with me tonight. What did you have this double date thing lined up and just have me as a backup if needed in case that wasn't going well."

"See now you're wrong. Like I said we just met those girls here tonight. I mean I really had the mindset that if things went as well in person as they had during the week that we could do a little something tonight. But like I said I met this other chick and we just clicked that's all. Nothing against you, not at all; truth is I think you have it going on yourself. It's just that she's a little more my speed that's all."

"Well forgive me, because I thought it was all about what we might be getting into before the night was over. Not me trying to make a claim on you or anything. But I can tell you one thing; if you really did meet those girls just tonight, good luck dipping into that later on. At least with me you know you had close to a sure thing unless you blew it. And from the looks of things more than blowing it you just passed on it, and me. But those chicks don't look like the types that are gonna spread their legs for you tonight."

"Why not, it certainly seems like you were ready to doesn't it?"

It was at that point that Sherri who had been trying to keep an eye out for Amanda during this conversation, saw her moving through the crowd towards her. Her eyes were darting all around as she navigated her way around numerous people; clearly in an attempt to locate her. Sherri knew it was just a matter of time before Amanda would spot her standing there. She quickly moved around Derrick and with her back now in the direction, from which Amanda was approaching, nudged him closer to the front of the bar where she was then hidden by several persons who surrounded her.

"Yes you're right Derrick; all things being equal, I was ready to fuck your brains out tonight. And I probably still would, but you have to give me an answer right now."

"He paused for a few seconds, clearly uncomfortable with being put on the spot in such a way. He looked in the direction of the table, at which his friend remained seated, their companions still having not returned. He then turned back to her and uttered five words in response to her.

"It was nice meeting you."

And with that he was off. Leaving Sherri standing there feeling a bit stunned as he headed back to the table. She took a moment to gather herself; swallowing deeply before quickly ducking out the door to the rear of the bar.

CHAPTER TWENTY-ONE

Sherri had to make her way around the entire building in order to arrive back in front of the lounge. The first persons she saw there were none other than Derrick and his friend's two lovely companions. The Hispanic one was puffing on a cigarette while her friend paced around holding a conversation on her cell phone. They hardly noticed Sherri as she passed them before stopping at the curb in order to cross the street. It was right then that she heard a somewhat familiar voice. At least it had become familiar during the course of this evening. Rushing up from behind and calling out to her was the guy who had been making advances towards her all night. Just as she turned to look at him he was upon her, standing right by her side.

"Hey, how you doing sweetheart?" he asked her softly.

"I'm doing just fine; just leaving in fact," she said as she continued to walk rather briskly.

"Well I don't know where you're from, but this here is Newark, so maybe you shouldn't be out here walking by yourself."

"Thanks for your concern but I think I'll be okay."

"Oh, you're so sure about that huh?" he asked as he struggled to keep up with her stride for stride.

"That's what I said didn't I? Besides I don't have all that far to go to get to my car."

With that he broke out into a smile. "Whoa, you're a feisty little one, aren't you? I'm just trying to be nice. What's your name anyway?

Sherri then stopped in her tracks long enough to make a little eye contact with him; holding the stare for several seconds before cracking a little smile of her own.

"I'm sorry; I don't mean to be rude. My name is Sherri."

"And I'm Chulo; it's nice to meet you Sherri.

"It's nice to meet you too. So, I guess you must be wondering what happened to the person that I kept telling you that I was meeting inside."

"No actually I wasn't. It's none of my business or my concern to tell you the truth. But what I am wondering is why you're calling it a night so early? It's barely ten o'clock."

"Well you know, I just wasn't having a very good time in there, so I just decided to cut my night short rather than just staying just to be staying."

"And the guy who decided to hang out with the girl in the gold dress rather than you has nothing to do with it right," he said with a grin.

Sherri stopped dead in her tracks and looked right into his face before responding.

"How on Earth did you know about that," she said with a straight face. Is he a friend or acquaintance of yours or something?

"No not at all; it's just that I was observing things with you for a while. And game recognizes game, so I was able to read between the lines, connect the dots and all that. And your body language spoke all the words I couldn't hear."

"Yeah as it turns out I guess he was all about games. But I wasn't interested in playing any longer."

"Hey I don't blame you one bit for that."

As they stood there talking in the well-lit area across from the complex, Sherri decided to take a moment to study the fellow next to her more fully. He was about 30, approximately 5'10" tall with a wiry, athletic build. He had a stylish haircut and about two days worth of growth on his face. Her impression of him then was that he was the ruggedly handsome type.

"I'm sorry what did you say your name was again?"

"It's Chulo. Well actually it's Armando but everybody pretty much calls me Chulo. That's C-H-U-L-O he spelled out for her.

"Okay Chulo I think I've got it. So tell me something Chulo, you said that my body language spoke the words that you couldn't hear. Well what might it be saying now?" Sherri asked in a soft voice.

"Well right now it seems to be saying that you weren't really ready to leave when you did. But you just felt like it was in your best interests to do so. Also, that while you have a real feeling of disappointment over how the evening went you wish it could continue, because you agree that's it kind of early to be going home."

"It's saying all of that huh?" Sherri asked as she unfolded her arms from across her chest and placed them on her hips; a smile now curving her lips.

"Yep it sure is," Chulo replied without hesitation.

"Maybe you're right. It's just that I'm not from around here at all so I don't know the first thing about anything, anybody or any places to go. I just came here tonight at someone's suggestion."

The expression on her face told Chulo that she was talking about the guy she was supposed to be hanging out with tonight. Well one man's loss is another's possible gain he was thinking as he spoke up next.

"Well you're in luck sweetheart, because I know several places that are fun to hang out at. That is if you're interested."

Sherri took a few moments to ponder the offer before responding. "Oh, I don't know, maybe I should just go ahead and call it a night."

"Yeah maybe you should, but then you might wind up wishing you hadn't soon after you've arrived back home. Now stop me if I'm wrong but you appear to me to be the type that probably doesn't get out all that much. So you came out tonight looking to make the most of it." Being that Sherri didn't interrupt him, he continued on. "And I don't think it's worked out that way. At least not up to this point. But what I'm saying is that you can still turn that around and make something out of it. And I can help you in that regard."

Sherri studied him further before looking away as she took in all that he'd said.

"Okay I must admit that I did come out tonight looking to have some fun and that the night hasn't gone at all like I'd hoped for."

"Not yet anyway," Chulo said confidently.

"Yes that's correct; not yet," she concurred.

"Well then, what do you say we make it better together?"

"Sherri turned away from him once again, this time with her back completely facing him; she was obviously in conflict between her better judgment and her thirst for more excitement. After several seconds she turned back around and looked at him poker-faced before answering.

"These places you mentioned, are they in the area?"

"Oh yeah, they're no more than ten or so minutes away tops."

As they strode along on the sidewalk, Chulo told Sherri that she would need to drive, explaining to her that he had come out with a buddy of his who had done the driving.

"Well don't you need to tell him something?" Sherri wondered aloud.

"No not really. He knows the deal, but I'll call him in a little while anyway.

They found a place to park on a little side street before walking a couple of blocks to their destination. As they walked along chatting casually, Sherri looked around at her surroundings. She took notice of all the small shops, restaurants and bars. They were lit in such a way that they gave the entire block a festive appearance almost reminiscent of the holiday season. Plenty of people were still out and about on the mild fall night, strolling in and out of the various establishments with looks of glee and voices full of excitement.

"This area seems to have a nice vibe to it," she offered.

"Oh this is the famous Ironbound section of the city," Chulo told her. "Home of the best Spanish, Portugese and Brazilian restaurants you will find anywhere outside of those countries. If you were ever want a good, plentiful meal this is the place to be in the city."

"Oh I see; well I'll certainly have to keep that in mind," Sherri said.

It was something how the person who had been so wary of ever being seen out in public with her two previous lovers, was now walking around in full view with another man. Feeling the effects of the alcohol she had consumed, she was clearly oblivious to any concerns over who might potentially notice the two of them.

Chulo led her into a small, quiet bar near the end of a long block. It was a simple little place with nothing distinguishing it at all. As soon as they entered they walked over to the far end of the bar. It was fairly well occupied but they managed to find a couple of empty stools on which to sit.

"What'll you have to drink?" he said directly into Sherri's ear in an attempt to be heard over the din of the music that dominated the place.

"Oh you're buying me a drink? Okay, I'll have a cosmopolitan thanks."

"Okay, coming right up."

While Sherri was slowly sipping on her cosmo, Chulo quickly downed three shots of scotch with a beer chaser. At the same time they somehow managed to keep a fairly steady conversation going over the music as well. As the effects of this latest drink began to creep up on her, Sherri started to get into the music that was being piped in. It was Latin-tinged with a very lively beat. "The music they've been playing is really good," she said as she leaned in towards him. "Do you dance Chulo?"

"I'm Latino, of course I dance," he answered jokingly. "I mean I'm not the best but I do okay. I dance a pretty mean meringue I think."

"Oh really; so you're a pretty good dancer huh?"

"Well since you're putting me on the spot here; yes I think I am."

Sherri then smiled and leapt to her feet. "Well come on then. Show me what you've got; let's dance."

"Now? And here?"

"Yes now, why not," Sherri pushed. You said you were going to take me someplace where we could have some fun. So, now that we're here let's make the most of it."

"But there's not even a dance floor," he reasoned.

"So what; we can make one. We can dance right here to tell you the truth, so no excuses."

"Okay, okay I'll tell you what; the next time they play a song that we can dance some meringue off of then we're on okay."

"Sure that's fine. You can even teach me as we go, Sherri said with a huge smile.

Some ten minutes or so later, it was time for him to show Sherri what he could do on the floor. As it turned out Sherri's attempt at learning something new was mostly amusing to her. They started out at arm's length with hands clasped together. Chulo then placed one hand around her waist and drew her in close until their pelvic areas made contact with each other. With his legs spread apart slightly, he instructed her to place her thigh in between his legs as they swayed their hips to the rhythm of the music. Although a true meringue dance also calls for a series of turns as well as some complete separation from your partner, their version was nothing more than an erotic expression of their emerging lust for each other, as they merely grinded together, twisting and spinning within the confines of a small area. The friction between their bodies felt like it could spark a small fire at any moment. Although a number of eyes were fixated on them, they may as well have been the only ones in the room. At one point they gave up any pretense of doing any real dancing as Sherri simply turned her backside to Chulo, inviting him to grind against it with his clearly aroused manhood. She placed her hands over his which had come to rest on her stomach. Turning her head slightly, she looked over her shoulder into his face.

"Can we go someplace?" she asked without the slightest hesitation.

"Someplace like where?" he questioned back. "Aren't you enjoying yourself here?"

"I am, but I mean like someplace we can be alone," she explained as she turned to face him.

"Well I don't live that far from here."

"Then let's go there. I mean if you want to that is."

"Sure why not; I was just going to have one more drink and then we can get going right after that."

"The last thing Sherri needed at that time was more to drink, but that's exactly what she had when he managed to convince her to drink a shot with him. At least he did order her something more pleasant tasting than one of the shots of scotch he was having would have been. But that's not to say that it was any less potent; especially given that she'd already had 4 cosmopolitans on the night. She didn't know exactly what it was she did receive; only that she downed it with ease. And with that they were out the door.

Neither of them did much talking during the brief drive to his place. Sherri for her part was far enough under the influence that she never noticed that his demeanor which had been so ebullient throughout had begun to morph into one that was almost sullen in comparison. The only real talking he did was while barking out directions on where she was to turn and finally to park as they arrived.

She didn't really know for sure but Sherri believes his apartment was located above a storefront, because she noticed that they walked past one of those steel security gates on the way to the entrance.

"Have a seat on the sofa," he said once they entered. Sherri sat down, placing her purse beside her as Chulo continued on to the bathroom. A few minutes later he emerged and went into his kitchen where he poured and then quickly downed yet another shot of something. He then came and sat next to her before pouncing on her immediately, groping her all over before starting to kiss her; his kisses far more rough than tender. Falling onto his knees before her he started to remove her skirt and then quickly her panties. On cue she allowed her legs to fall open as he placed his head between them. His tongue quickly found her wetness, lashing away eagerly. Certainly she'd had men go down on her more sweetly, but at the time, in her present state, it felt golden as she was bought to an orgasm in a fairly short amount of time.

He then stood and undid his pants revealing a not exactly large, but certainly nice-sized penis to her.

"Come on, suck my dick," he said in a commanding voice. Sherri instantly rushed onto her knees and began to comply. However it became evident to her in a very short time that one thing was for sure; none of that time he'd spent in the bathroom when they had first arrived was on freshening up. It was not as if she was completely shower fresh herself, but she found him to be absolutely rancid. Nevertheless he continued to make his desires clear to her; in an ever increasing tone and with more pointed language at that.

"That's it suck it! Oh you're a fucking nasty little slut aren't you? It was enough to have her wondering how this could be the same person she had met not that much earlier. The one who like a gentleman offered her his jacket to shield her from the chill as they walked to her car once she agreed to spend some time with him. But then he was now fully under the influence of alcohol as well. He grabbed her by the hair and began to forcefully thrust himself deep into her mouth, pulling her hand away each time she attempted to grip his penis in order to control the tempo and the depth of his pumps. She started to gasp for air, not knowing if the feeling that she may vomit was more from the sweaty odor of his genitals, the pushing to near her gagging point or both. Beyond spilling her insides, she thought she might just die right there when he pressed his scrotum against her lips for several seconds before placing himself back in her mouth.

"Ah yeah, check you out; go ahead you filthy bitch. Take this shit whore."

As much as she may have disliked the things he was saying, at that point she couldn't dispute them. For that is just what she was feeling like; a cheap, dirty, little whore. What had started out as an erotic experience of the type she had envisioned and desired when they had come to his place had now turned into more of an act of violation. More than any feeling of pleasure or satisfaction she felt nothing but relief when he pulled out of her mouth in order to shoot his load all over her face. Not that him doing so would have been her choice if asked. While certainly facials are not something she'd generally had a problem with, she didn't know Chulo at all, unlike her other lovers whom she had taken the time to get at least somewhat acquainted with. In one last act of utter disrespect he next used his cell phone to take a photo of her semen-covered face as she sat on the floor trying to gather herself.

"Oh yeah there it is; another piece of trash added to the collection," he spat.

Unable to hold it any longer, it was at that point that she did vomit; right there on the dark-colored carpet. She was about to see the fury she had just unleashed. To find out just how much of a nasty, angry person Chulo had become now that he was drunk.

"What the fuck? You fucking little bitch; what did you just do on my floor," he screamed over Sherri as she sat on the floor coughing and gagging. She could sense another painful convulsion coming so she rose to her feet as quickly as she could. "Look at this shit," he continued to berate her as she rushed towards his bathroom. She made it into the bathroom just in time to let loose once again; this time into the bathroom sink. Following closely behind her, Chulo exploded once again upon seeing that.

"You dumb ass bitch; you couldn't do that shit into the toilet? What the fuck is wrong with you?" he yelled. As she struggled to regain her composure he grabbed her by the hair. "Look at this shit you disgusting whore." Suddenly the back of his hand crashed against her face, spinning her around and sending her reeling to the floor. Sherri suddenly began to fear for her safety as he pounced on her, again taking a fistful of hair in one of his hands.

"No, no, I'm sorry," she pleaded to no avail. He slammed her face to the floor twice in rapid succession. Never releasing his firm grip on her hair he then yanked her to a seated position. As she started to sob loudly he finally relinquished his hold on her, before getting right in her face.

"I know one thing; you'd better clean that shit out of my sink you nasty fucking bitch!!"

She felt an instant, albeit small sense of relief as he left the bathroom, slamming the door closed behind him. She tried to focus her gaze on the mirror, knowing that the burning she felt in her face told her that some bruising was bound to be evident. Indeed she had a nasty purplish bruise on her left cheek as well as an abrasion dotting her forehead. She tried gamely to hold it together as she ran water into the sink in order to run the vomit down the drain. When she finished with the cleanup she used some tap water to try to rinse the foul taste out of her mouth as much as possible. She then turned off the water and started to open the door slowly, hesitant to come face to face with him again. When she entered the living room the first thing that she could see was him down on his knees on the floor. He was working a scrub brush in a vigorous back and forth motion, in an attempt to clean the area where Sherri had thrown up. He turned and looked in her direction once he sensed her presence, an expression of rage still covering his face. Sherri felt her legs start to quiver and she slowed even further, bracing herself for what might come next.

"Just get your shit and get out. I don't even care about fucking you now. Just get the hell out of my place you filthy slut."

Sherri's mind begged to defend herself. After all it was really he that bought about the vomiting. Between his foul stench and the way he seemed intent of forcing his dick completely down her throat as hard as he could, she couldn't hold it back. Although she didn't doubt that the amount of alcohol she had consumed on the evening played a part as well. But instead she tried to apologize, hoping that would lessen his verbal assault. But that wasn't to be.

"I'm very sorry about your carpet. I think I've had too much to drink tonight so that's why I got sick. I apologize."

"Yeah whatever bitch; just get the fuck out okay. Go ahead and take your grungy ass home or wherever you're going. Just get the hell out of here."

Sherri didn't dare say another word. She simply grabbed up her car keys and her purse and was gone; leaving him there on his knees scrubbing away on his soiled carpet. She walked slowly down the stairs before starting to gingerly make her way down the block towards her car. No sooner than she was seated in her vehicle than her insides erupted once again; heaving violently. She was able to somehow throw the car door open and lean her head outside before making a mess of her car at least.

Once she pulled away from the curb and started to drive she came to the instant realization about something. That being that she didn't really know how to get back to where she needed to in order to be headed home. She was lucky in that there were still people milling about in the area. And she hit the jackpot when a couple she pulled alongside of were themselves headed to I-280. They even told her that she could follow them to that point before heading to where she needed to go. On the fairly long drive home Sherri took some time to reflect. On not only what had just happened but on how much worse still it could have been. She realized that she could have gotten herself seriously hurt or even worse. She imagined no longer being there for her children. And all because of a spur of the moment decision she'd made. If there was any chance at all that she could turn back from the road that she was continuing to travel on, then this was the time.

By the time she arrived home she was feeling a bit better but very far from great by any measure. She couldn't wait to just crawl into the bed for about 10 hours of sleep. But first she just had to go remove the nastiness from her mouth with a good amount of mouthwash and then toothpaste. When she went into the bathroom she noticed that while she did feel a wee bit better, she looked pretty bad. Her pupils were glassy and enlarged, while the whites of her eyes were anything but. The bruises on her forehead and cheek were nothing short of ugly looking. She knew with her having to go pick up the kids some time later in the day, and with Clay returning home Sunday evening, that she had to figure how best to disguise that if not explain it. But for a while the only thing she wanted was her cozy bed, her comfortable pillow and some much needed sleep.

∞∞∞∞∞∞∞∞

Sherri slowly rolled onto her back, while opening and rubbing her still weary eyes. She didn't know how many times the phone had already rung by the time she reacted to it. But she was at least semi- coherent once she managed to roll over and pick up the handset.

"Hello," she groaned into the phone in a voice far from its normal pitch.

"Hello Ms. King?"

"Yes this is she."

"Good afternoon Ms. King, my name is Jason and I'm calling from Master Card.

"Hold on a second, did you say good afternoon? What time is it," she asked while still trying to fully get her bearings.

"It's about 12:45," he informed her, prompting a shocked reaction from Sherri.

"Oh my God, I can't believe it's that late," she groaned.

"Yes it is maam; did I call at a bad time?"

"No, no, no that's not it. Besides if you hadn't called I might have still been sleeping at 4:00," she added, drawing a chuckle.

"Well in that case I'm glad I was able to prevent that maam. But the reason I'm calling you today is that we were sent what we call a fraud alert. Now what that means is that there has been an inordinate amount of activity on your account in a relatively short amount of time. So what we do when that happens is we try to contact the customer; in this case that being you, and double check on the legitimacy of the transactions."

"Okay, exactly what transactions are we speaking of here?" Sherri grumbled in a still unusually deep voice.

"Well we have a number of online transactions from just midnight last night until now. We have Target, Dick's Sporting Goods, Best Buy and Amazon.com just to name some. All totaled we have almost two-thousand dollars in purchases charged to your account since just midnight last night."

"What! You've got to be kidding right?" Sherri yelled out while jumping into a seated position. "Either that or there must be a mistake here. I haven't used the card at all in a couple of weeks at least; and certainly not last night or this morning for that matter."

"Okay Ms. King; well with that being said I guess we're to assume that these weren't your transactions or ones that you were even aware of?"

"Yes you would certainly assume correctly."

"All right, well then that takes us to this. Has your card been lost or perhaps stolen Ms. King?

"Well__no, not that I know of; but wait a minute let me check for sure. I mean I used another card to get gas yesterday evening and I know I saw both of my cards in my purse at that time."

"But you haven't seen them since?

"Hmmm no; can't say that I have but that doesn't mean…wait what did you say your name was?"

"My name is Jason maam."

"Well Jason if you'll hold on for a minute I'll go get my purse and check on this right now."

"Sure Ms. King I'll hold on.

Sherri lifted her pocketbook off her lap and placed it next to her on the sofa before burying her head in her hands. She just couldn't believe it; yet another cruel twist of fate had befallen her. Slumping against the back of the sofa, she blew a big gust of air out from between her lips. She managed to lift herself up after several seconds before slowly making her way back into the bedroom. After falling heavily onto the bed she picked up the receiver.

"Hello," she muttered into it.

"Yes Ms. King I'm here."

"I can't believe this, but yes my credit cards are missing; so now what?

Well the first thing we have to do is to place a hold on your account. What that means is simply that whoever has it and has been on this big shopping spree will no longer be able to make use of it."

"Okay, let's do that right away then," Sherri agreed.

"All right I'll take care of that right now for you. Now basically what it also means is that the person who has your card will also be calling attention to them self with whatever in-person transaction he or she may attempt to make from this point on. So let's just hope that they're greedy enough to keep pushing his or her luck. Now the other thing Ms. King is that you need to think back to when it might have come up missing so that we can determine if it's to be filed as a loss or as a theft. Now in the case of theft I can assure you that you wouldn't be responsible for any of those purchases. Now; on the other hand if you say that you just lost it I can't guarantee that you will be reimbursed fully."

"Well I assure you Jason that I'm certain that my cards were stolen rather than lost."

Okay Ms. King; well in that case I must tell you that the process for the reporting of a theft is quite a bit more involved. You have to first file a police report and then get back to us with a copy of that. In fact you can fax that to us as soon as possible to expedite the whole process. Now being that you said that you know the card was stolen does that also mean that you know who the perpetrator might be?"

As she soaked in everything that Jason had told her something began to dawn on Sherri. Reporting her card stolen would involve being interviewed by the police. And require some telling of where she was when it was taken; and with whom. Suddenly the idea of reporting her cards stolen didn't seem like such a great one after all.

"You know what Jason; let me look into it a little more on my end. I mean I may have just lost the cards, I'm not sure. So before I go to the extent of police reports and what have you, I guess I should be certain. I will call back once I have a clearer idea of things."

For his part Jason was immediately nebulous about the sudden switch. After all it did seem more than a bit far-fetched to think that two credit cards would both be lost at the same time; but he wasn't about to push where he had no business, so instead he let it go.

"Well just call us back whenever and let us know how you want to handle this and we'll go from there okay?"

"Yes of course, I'll be in touch soon. Thank you Jason."

"You're welcome Ms. King and try to have a good day in spite of this whole thing. And also thank you for your loyal business; I hope everything works out with the least amount of inconvenience to you."

"Thanks again, I appreciate that. Take care."

"Bye."

Sherri sat there feeling fully exasperated. Not only had Chulo humiliated and assaulted her both verbally and physically, but she now knew that he had stolen from her as well. She figured he must have gone into her purse while she was in his bathroom trying to get herself together. But the worst part about it was that she felt powerless to do anything about it. After all what could she do; go to the police and tell them that the man she allowed to take her home from some dive bar for sex stole her credit cards? No way; she knew she had to chalk this one up as more of the price she needed to pay for her indiscretions. After a few minutes she got up, determined to shake it all off for now. She needed to gather herself so that she could go get the kids. But before that, she needed a shower in the worst way.

After a long, warm shower, Sherri started to feel somewhat decent again. She felt cleansed and refreshed; well at least on the surface if not in her heart and soul. Now that would take some doing and some time. But she was willing to do whatever it took; she knew now that she had to. She had to do it both for the sake of herself and those around her. For her family in particular, for she knew just how close to the edge she had now gone. And it was time for her to back away from it before she stepped over it. Or more to the point was pushed over. She applied a heavy layer of concealer in an attempt to camouflage the bruises on her cheek and forehead. Once she finally got to the point where she felt it was sufficient she was ready to go. She grabbed her purse and her keys and walked out the door to her car. The moment she sat down inside she decided to call Nina and give her a head's up. Let her know that she was on her way to get the kids. But it didn't take long before that now familiar sinking feeling again started to wash over her. She had been digging for a while and had even emptied most of the contents out, but she knew in her mind that it was not in there. Yes her Blackberry had also been taken. That in itself wasn't the worst part, because she carried insurance on the device itself. But what was truly gone were all of her contacts and other small personal effects. And as many times as she had intended to, she had never created a backup for any of them. Numbers, email addresses and photos were all gone just like that. Many of which she had no recollection of; having always relied on just pulling them up on the device. Saddened again, she stepped out of the car to head back inside. She was going to have to use the house phone to make the call.

The next night Sherri was in the bathroom showering when Clay entered; him having returned from his weekend convention a few hours earlier. After exiting the shower, she was doing her hair in front of the mirror when he came back in to place something in the closet adjoining the bathroom. Once he had done so he stepped out of the closet, pausing just to the right of her.

"Is that some sort of abrasion on the side of your face?" he asked her pointedly.

Her pulse quickened and she hesitated noticeably before responding.

"Oh yeah, I went for a little run on the nature trail in Dobbins Park and I stumbled over some branches that were on the ground. They must have fallen during that bad storm we had Wednesday afternoon I suppose. And you know how clumsy I can be sometimes. I never even saw them there on the ground until I tripped over them. If there's an accident waiting to happen it'll probably happen to me."

"Actually I've never really known you to be very clumsy or accident prone Sherri. Anyway, I'm going to get something to eat and then settle down in front of the television for a little bit.

After she watched him leave the room, Sherri turned to her reflection in the mirror. While the bruise on her forehead had all but disappeared, the side of her face still held the signs of what had taken place two nights earlier. Later that night after Clay had fallen asleep in the chair in the family room, Sherri caught him off guard; undoing his pants as she knelt before him. And to her delight he surprised her just as much when he was completely receptive to her as she aggressively went after what she wanted. The blowjob she gave him was immediately followed by a bout of lovemaking right there on the spot; ending with him entering her from behind as she knelt on the plushly carpeted floor. It was the type of spontaneous action she longed for often, but had too often been denied. She didn't quite know what to make of his rare moment of passion but she wasn't about to question it. Only enjoy it, and hope that it might be a sign of things to come. After all she had decided that it was time for it to be just him for her once again. Recent experiences had served as an eye-opener for Sherri, and she was now quite wary of continuing to push her luck.

CHAPTER TWENTY-TWO

It was just before daybreak when Alicia nudged him awake. Gee had never been mistaken for a morning type, while she was quite the opposite. But it wasn't the need for company that prompted her to awaken him from his deep sleep. It was hunger, or more exactly a craving for something.

"Huh, what's the matter baby?" he muttered after he slowly opened his eyes.

"Garrick I'm hungry."

"Okay, you want some breakfast sweetheart, give me a minute okay?"

"Well I do, but not the sort that you might be thinking; I mean like bacon and eggs or potatoes or anything like that."

"Alright that's fine, what do you feel like having boo?"

"You know what I'm in the mood for? Some jelly donuts."

"Some jelly donuts?" Gee repeated in his trademark baritone.

"Yes; do you think you can get me some?"

"Sure baby I can get you whatever you want. Just give me a few minutes to get myself together okay."

True to his word, Gee was up and at em a few minutes later. Or at least was making a real attempt at motivating himself to do so. It was Monday morning and Alicia had spent the entire weekend with him; sort of a mini trial run for what life might be like once they tied the knot sometime in the months ahead. And he had to admit that he was completely comfortable with the feeling of having her there; especially now that she was carrying their child. He felt an increased need to look after her and to take care of her in any and all ways.

He emerged from the bathroom feeling at least a little energized just by having brushed his teeth and wiped the remnants of sleep out of his eyes.

"Okay love I'm about ready to roll. As soon as I throw something on I'm out. The Dunkin Donuts in the Wal-Mart Plaza opens very early for the off to work crowd so I'll just run up in there and take care of you."

"Oh okay, and since you'll be over by Wal-Mart can you stop in there and get me some ginger ale. It seems to help a bit with my morning sickness."

"Of course I will; you know that," he answered as he slipped into a pair of jeans before throwing on a sweatshirt to go along with it.

"Thank you baby, I love you," she whispered to him.

"Oh yeah, well I bet I love you even more," he smiled before he came over and attempted to kiss her on the mouth.

"Oooh no baby, I haven't had a chance to brush my teeth yet remember," she said while turning away from him.

"Oh please you know I'm not concerned about that."

"Okay maybe not, but I am," Alicia told him.

"But I was only going for a little peck. All right well how about a great big hug instead?"

"Sure, now that I can do."

"MMMMMMMMMMMM," Gee groaned as he squeezed her tightly.

"Ooops let me let go of you. I might be squeezing the baby."

"Baby, I don't think it's that serious," Alicia assured him.

"Hey, you never know. Anyway I will be back in a bit. Oh and by the way, one donut or two?"

"Oh I think you'd better make it two if not three."

"Three; wow you are certainly eating for two now."

"Well one is in case I get the same craving sometime later."

"Understood; but okay let me go. Be back in a flash."

"Alright baby, see you when you get back."

From the moment he started up his engine the first thing that Gee noticed was that he had an urgent need for gas. Had to add that to the itinerary. No big deal he figured. The gas station was on the way to the other stops. In the meantime, Alicia had gotten up herself a few minutes after Gee departed and made her way to the bathroom to do her own morning freshening up. It was while in there brushing her teeth that she first heard the sound of loud knocking and then the doorbell coming from downstairs. As she quickly turned off the faucet that she'd left running while brushing her teeth, the sound grew only that much louder. She spit the toothpaste into the sink before wiping around her mouth. What the hell, she was wondering as she hustled out of the bathroom and grabbed her robe before exiting the bedroom and continuing on downstairs.

"Yes who is it," she asked as she stopped just on the inside of the door.

"Police, open the door," came a loud command.

"The police?" she repeated in a shocked tone. "What on Earth for?"

"Just open the door Miss, do it now."

"Wary of just what might happen next if she didn't comply, Alicia unlocked the front door before slowly starting to open it. But before she could open it fully she was overrun by a crush of bodies. It must have been about 5 or 6 in total; all of whom came barreling inside one after the other.

"Garrick Andrews, where is he?" Rollie, the last one to enter demanded to know. He was the only one out of the bunch who didn't rush right past her and up the stairs.

"Why; what do you want with him?"

"Listen I'm asking the damn questions here, and right now I'm asking you again; where is Garrick Andrews?"

"I don't know where he is," she screamed back at him. But what is this all about?"

"Who are you? Just who the fuck are you huh? Some piece of ass he picked up for the night?"

"No. I'm his fiancée," Alicia countered.

"His fiancée; and you're trying to tell me you don't know where the hell he is? Bullshit! Come on get your ass upstairs," Rollie barked before grabbing her by the right arm and practically dragging her up the stairs along with him.

What Alicia saw when they reached the top of the stairs and stepped inside absolutely astounded her. The other four men were rampaging through the place, tossing aside anything in their path. Cabinets which just moments before had been full of DVD's were empty now; the contents strewn all over the place. Cushions from the furniture were in the middle of the floor, the kitchen almost looked like a tornado had swept through it.

"How we doing guys; anything yet?" Rollie yelled out before releasing her with a nudge that was anything but gentle.

"Nope nothing yet," one yelled back to him as he passed by them on their way to starting on tearing apart another room.

"Well keep looking, we know they're here."

"Will do, and don't worry we'll find them," the second man assured him.

"Rollie resumed his grip on Alicia's arm. "The drugs; where are the god damn drugs!!" he screamed into her face.

"What drugs? I don't know what you're talking about; let go of my arm, you're hurting me."

"Listen bitch I assure you that it'll get a lot worse if you don't tell me what I want to know. Now again, where are the drugs hidden?"

By this time Alicia was crying hysterically. "I don't know what you're talking about, I swear I don't."

Rollie then gave her a hard shove, causing her to crumble to the floor in a heap. As she laid there sobbing he took stock of the present situation before turning on her again. Grabbing a fistful of hair he knelt down until he was right in her face.

"Look I'm going to ask you one more time, where's your fucking boyfriend?"

"I'm telling you I don't know where he is; but please I'm pregnant."

"Oh so you are, are you; like I give two shits about your little Black bastard child. You'll be giving birth behind bars if you don't start talking; and I mean now."

At that point one of the other men intervened on her behalf. It was Mike Marciniak, one of the 2 persons, along with Rollie who were central in putting the entire bogus search together.

"Hey man, relax a bit, we know they're here and we'll find them. So you don't need to do this," he said.

Rollie released Alicia with one final shove before standing over her. He then backed away slowly before turning to Mike.

"I'm going downstairs to relax for a minute; you guys keep looking."

Mike slowly nodded in agreement as Rollie turned to leave, but said nothing. He instead placed a hand on Alicia's shoulder.

"You okay? Let me give you a hand."

"I'm fine," she grunted before pulling away from him and slowly standing on her own.

Rollie was standing outside smoking a cigarette, when the door opened behind him. He didn't turn around to see who it was. Not until he heard someone speak.

"I couldn't help but hear all the commotion; something going on?"

"He turned around to see a tall, fairly attractive fortyish year old woman with blonde hair looking back at him.

"Who are you," he asked quietly as he blew out a long stream of smoke.

"I'm Diana Malloy, I live next door."

"Well we're looking for your neighbor; have you seen any sign of him?"

"Well not exactly up close and personal. Don't see very much of him that way. Just hear him coming and going basically."

"And have you seen either of those anytime recently?"

"Yeah; as a matter of fact he just left. About fifteen minutes ago I'd say."

Rollie's eyes enlarged and his ears perked up at the sound of her words.

"And you're sure about that?" he questioned.

"Absolutely sure; nobody comes in and out of here without me taking a peek. It's sort of what I do. I'm like a one person neighborhood watch squad," she chuckled. "So yeah I looked long enough to know that it was him who I heard walking down the steps and then get into his car."

Rollie quickly tossed the cigarette to the ground before crushing it with his right foot. He then rushed past the woman and took off up the stairs.

He rushed over to Mike the moment he stepped back inside Gee's place.

"Where's the girl?" he asked excitedly.

"I don't know, I think she might have gone into the bathroom," Mike answered.

"Before he could get even get all of the words out Rollie had again taken off. He found Alicia In the bathroom dabbing at her eyes with some tissues.

"Where is he? I know he left here about fifteen minute ago, so I'm gonna ask you one more time. Where the fuck is he? And I swear if you don't tell me the truth I'm gonna run your ass in right now!" His voice grew louder and his tone angrier with each word.

Panic and fear set in on Alicia as she saw the venom in his eyes and tears again streamed down her cheeks.

"Okay, okay. He went to the Dunkin Donuts in the Wal-Mart shopping center and he was going to make a stop at the Wal-Mart also, she said in a soft voice in between her sobs.

"The Walmart over on Route 22?" Rollie questioned her.

"Yes," she replied.

"Rollie then ran out of the bathroom and over to Mike. "I know where Andrews is; you and Taggart stay here and keep searching. Everybody else is coming with me. We're headed to the Wal-Mart shopping plaza; call in for some backup Mike."

Rollie and the three other men raced downstairs as quickly as they could. He stopped for a quick word with them outside the front door to the townhouse.

"Okay here's the deal. We know our suspect is thought to be somewhere in the Wal-Mart shopping plaza up there on Route 22. He might be either at Dunkin Donuts or Wal-Mart itself. Now we also know for a fact that he drives a black hummer okay. So here's the plan; there shouldn't be a whole lot of vehicles in the shopping center this time of morning. So what we're hoping for is this. I'm hoping that we might locate his vehicle in a parking space around one of those two stores, and that he's still inside one of the two. And if he is, we'll just wait until he comes back outside and then pounce on him. That way the chances of him fleeing is pretty much eliminated. Now I requested backup but we're not gonna wait on this one. But, having said that, we don't know if this guy is armed or anything like that but we have to assume that he may be, so be careful okay. Let's go."

Gee was waiting patiently in the checkout line at Wal-Mart. That was one thing about Walmart; whether early in the morning or late at night they were bound to have only one or possibly two registers open. So even when picking up but one item as was the case with him, your wait might well be a lengthy one. He would have called home to Alicia to explain the reason for him not being back so quickly, but he recalled that he left his cell phone in the center console of his hummer. For that reason he also hadn't gotten any of the several panicked phone calls that Alicia had tried to sneak to him from inside the walk-in closet attached to his master bath. Mike had forgone any concerns about her whereabouts and he was getting to the point where he was ready to end the charade of the search and just go to where he knew the stuff to be planted; at least according to Jimmy and Roberto who placed it there.

It was a relief for Gee when he was finally able to checkout. He walked briskly towards his vehicle, of course oblivious to the unmarked vehicles laying in wait for him. Alicia had begun to continuously redial his number; thinking, or at least hoping that he would answer on one of those occasions. As soon as he was seated inside he heard the loud buzz as the phone vibrated once again. He grabbed it immediately and looking at the display saw it was her.

"Hey sweetheart what's up?" he answered using the speakerphone feature.

As soon as she heard his voice Alicia began to speak quickly, and with a clear sense of urgency. "Garrick listen to me, the police are here; baby they're looking for you. They've torn the place up calling themselves looking for some drugs. What's going on baby? I'm scared to death," she whispered.

"Wait, wait, wait, slow down Alicia; they're there doing what? That's crazy; I'm on my way back there right now."

"Garrick no, you don't understand; I think some are headed there looking for you too; you've got to…"

"POLICE; STEP OUT OF THE VEHICLE NOW!! DO IT SLOWLY!!"

Gee turned his head to his left and saw four men dressed in plain clothes. Each of them had a weapon trained on him from about 35-40 feet away.

"What the hell," Alicia heard him say and that was it from him. She then heard a loud voice yelling out once again. "I REPEAT, OUT OF THE VEHICLE NOW! WITH YOUR HANDS UP! NICE AND SLOW!"

Gee sat there stunned; unable to react at first. His cell phone then slipped from his hand onto the floor of the vehicle.

"I'M ONLY GOING TO SAY THIS ONE LAST TIME, STEP OUT OF THE VEHICLE; SLOWLY!"

Gee turned slowly to his left and with his hands extended in front of him slid his left leg out of the Hummer. Just as he was about to step over with his right leg he heard what sounded like the frantic voice of Alicia coming from his cell phone.

"GARRICK! GARRICK, WHAT'S GOING ON!" she was screaming into the phone.

He wanted to say something to her. He knew she was very upset so he just wanted to take a moment to reassure her. Tell her that he would call her back as soon as he could; as soon as this mess was straightened out. The last thing he wanted was for her to go into a panic in her condition.

At about the same time, Mike finally went right to where he knew the cocaine was said to be stashed by Jimmy and Roberto. He and the other officer were ransacking their way through the kitchen when Mike rolled out the refrigerator. He then took a look at the bundles of dope before turning to the other man.

"Hey man, check this out," he said, prompting the officer to walk over to where he stood looking down at the floor. As soon as he reached his side Mike spoke out.

"Well, well, well it looks like we found paydirt."

Gee slowly reached down and while bent over slightly started to grab for the phone. When he got a firm grip on it he started to move it up towards his mouth to speak into it. It was at that moment that the absolutely unthinkable happened.

"HE'S GOT A GUN!!!

The words came from one of the others besides Rollie. It wasn't clear who fired the first shot, but what was beyond dispute was this; all four of the men opened fire within moments of each other. There were a total of eighteen shots between them, with most of them hitting their mark. Not that they were necessary. Gee was gone in an instant; mortally wounded by a slug that penetrated his temple, well before the shots that followed; continuing even as he slumped against the steering wheel.

What Alicia heard told her the worst. The series of pops sent chills through her and sent her into a state of shock. She was momentarily rendered speechless before she managed to snap out of it and react.

"OH MY GOD! GARRICK? OH PLEASE GOD, NO. NOOOOOOOO!

Mike rushed towards her, finding her there on the floor of the closet, the phone by her side. "Hello, hello," he yelled into it after picking it up. Seconds later his partner rushed over to him, stopping in his tracks as he surveyed the scene.

"What's going on," he cried out to Mike.

"I don't know; stay with her, I'm going to try to get Rollie on the radio.

About a minute or two later Mike came rushing back into the room.

"I can't reach Rollie; we need to get over there."

"Well what about the girl and the stuff?"

"We'll leave it as it is, lock up the place and bring her with us," said Mike. "You have a key right," he asked Alicia who nodded back affirmatively after a pause.

Mike did appear to at least to have a bit of sympathy for Alicia judging by something he said during the high-speed drive to the shopping center.

"Listen, I'm sorry for what you had to go through back there at the apartment. We were just trying to get the information we needed out of you. It's just that not all of us are going to go about it in the same way. I really hope you're okay and your child as well."

But Alicia still didn't speak one word during the ride. She merely spent the entire trip just staring blankly out of the window. It was like she was trying to escape what her intuition was telling her. But it was to no avail; she had an eerie feeling that only grew worse the closer they drew to the scene. Sheer bedlam had already ensued by the time they arrived. Police cars were everywhere; both marked and unmarked. Officers were there representing the county police and the prosecutor's office as well as a couple of cars from the local police. There was also an ambulance and a large crowd of onlookers, even at that hour on a Monday morning. Mike found a place to pull the car to a halt and he and the other Detective jumped out.

"Stay here," he commanded Alicia before they raced away from the car. But he probably should have known that was a directive that there was no way she would comply with. Mike and the other officer showed their credentials and were then let past the makeshift barricade that had been erected to keep the curious spectators at bay. He felt an instant sense of relief when he spotted Rollie. He was leaning against one of the cars smoking a cigarette. As he surveyed the scene further he then spotted the other officers who had left the house with Rollie on their quest to apprehend Garrick Andrews. They were situated about 10 feet from each other and it appeared that they were each in the process of being questioned individually by a law enforcement official. Already walking as fast as he could Mike broke into a full-fledged trot as he approached Rollie.

"Hey I tried to get you on the radio; what's going on?"

"We had to do it Mike."

"Had to do what? Rollie, what are you talking about? What happened?"

"Andrews, I'm talking about Andrews Mikey; it looked like he had a gun."

"Where is he Rollie? Where's Andrews?"

"Over there at the center of attention. Right inside that Hummer," Rollie said as he gestured in that direction.

Mike walked towards Gee's vehicle; moving slowly and deliberately. What he saw when he got close enough to see astounded him and stopped him dead in his tracks. The bullet-riddled body of Garrick "Gee" Andrews was still in the same position; slumped over the steering wheel, his arms hanging down by his side. Blood was everywhere as were signs of shell impact. As he turned away from the vehicle he almost bumped into the officer who had arrived with him at the scene. He hadn't even realized he was so close by.

"Why hasn't the body been removed yet," he asked Mike.

"Because they're still investigating the circumstances of what happened."

As he looked up, Mike was instantly shaken by what he saw. Slowly walking towards the Hummer was Alicia. He rushed in her direction, trying to head her off before she got too close to turn her away.

"Come on, I thought I asked you to stay in the car," he said with a stoned-faced expression as he reached for her arm.

"Stay in the car my ass. You have no right or even reason to hold me in there. Besides this is my fiancée that they came here looking for. Now I want to see him; have a word with him even."

"Please Miss; no I don't think you want to see him."

"What do you mean? Of course I want to see him."

"Miss, I'm sorry but your fiancée is dead."

"Come on stop messing around with me; let me talk to him, just for a few minutes."

Mike grabbed Alicia by her shoulders and held onto her lightly as she attempted to walk past him. "I'm afraid I'm not kidding; Mr. Andrews has been killed."

"No, stop saying that, I want to see him; I demand to see him right now and you can't stop me," she yelled loud enough to grab the attention of most onlookers. "Noooooo," her screams pierced the mostly quiet surrounding. "He can't be dead; he just can't."

"She sobbed uncontrollably as Mike escorted her back towards his unmarked squad car. "You; you fucking bastard, I bet you killed him," she yelled in the direction of Rollie when she spotted him off to her right.

"That's right sweetheart, I saw the whole thing; they did kill him," a female voice suddenly called out from the crowd. "In cold blood like it was nothing; like he was nothing. Get yourself a good lawyer, that's what my advice to you would be."

"Shhhh, don't say that too loud," warned another person near the woman. "If they know that you saw too much they might come after you next."

"I'm not worried about that. I'm gonna speak my piece. Our lives don't mean a damn thing to these police. But I got to do what's right in my eyes; and the eyes of the lord."

Clay called Rollie on his cell phone about 15 minutes later. "Hey I just got word of what happened; you okay man?" He asked him in a relaxed manner.

"Yeah, yeah I'm fine."

"Okay good; now are you off by yourself someplace so that we can talk for a second?"

"Hold on give me a minute," Rollie answered.

He then started walking until he reached a location where there was no chance of anyone hearing what he might say.

"All right," Clay began. "First of all what's done is done. And besides we know that neither one of us is exactly gonna be crying over the Black motherfucker's body. But what we do have to worry about of course is managing the fallout from this, because let's face it, it could be major."

As Rollie listened intently, Clay continued. "Now the reporters are probably gonna start arriving any time now. And we both know they're gonna swoop in like vultures; so I just want to make sure that the only piece of dead meat they have to pick at belongs to that filthy spook okay. I was also made aware of the statement you gave in regards to what took place. Now, you've got this all worked out pretty good I'd say, so we're not going to deviate from that story at all. You guys went to arrest a known narcotics dealer at his home; he wasn't there but you got word that he was at or near this location so you and the other officers responded and when you moved in to apprehend him, the suspect brandished what appeared to be a gun, leaving you and the others no choice but to defend yourselves. Perfect; I mean it seems pretty cut and dried to me, but of course you know what the outcry from the darkies and even some of the White ACLU types is gonna be like, so we just have to stay steadfast here. And in time this will blow over; just like similar incidents have in the past. We know it always does."

"Clay, I'm one step ahead of you. I'm fine; got it all under control."

"Great; besides, him winding up dead wasn't part of the plan but he brought it on himself right?"

"Exactly; I gave him fair warning. More than once at that, yet he insisted on trying his luck. Well needless to say the unlucky number came up for him today."

"All right, well it sounds like we're good then. Now I'm not showing up but as you know Jimmy Walter is there and he's going to make a statement on behalf of our office."

The two of them then said their goodbyes before Rollie headed back over to the scene of the shooting where he was met by Jimmy. James Walter was considered Clay's top assistant on the prosecutorial side. A former law-school classmate, Clay plucked him from the private sector where he was ironically working as a criminal defense attorney. But he was now on the other side, and considered Clay's top dog in criminal prosecutions. A short time later the first members of the media arrived as expected, and as also expected came loaded for bear. They first converged on Jimmy who announced that after speaking to the lead officer at the scene he was prepared to make a statement.

The sum of the ad-libbed statement he made was that first of all the officers involved would not be made available to the media. He then added that they would be placed on administrative leave pending a review of the facts in the case. Finally he painted a picture of the incident from the perspective of the officers, making it clear that he fully supported the officers and saw no wrong doing involved at that point in time. Needless to say the story was far different once the reporters were approached by those who say they witnessed what happened and were prepared to speak up about it. First up in that regard was the woman who had earlier so vehemently protested what she saw as not just an unnecessary but basically heinous, killing of an unarmed man. And so it went; two stories and two sides, yet one undeniable truth.

CHAPTER TWENTY-THREE

Sherri and Lily were headed outside; having just finished eating lunch together after a late morning workout at the gym. Signing up for a gym membership at LA Fitness was one of the things she'd done to fill the time that had previously been devoted to her lovers. As they were departing Lily came to a halt as she approached the lobby bar area. Something on one of the televisions overhead had captured her attention.

"Hmmm I only caught the tail end of that story but they said something about the police killing someone in Watchung. I'll have to try to make sure to catch the early evening news later on."

"Yeah me too, because it's pretty rare to hear about anything like that in Somerset county," Sherri noted.

Shortly after 5:00, Sherri's phone rang with a call from Lily. She was in the kitchen just finishing up dinner and the kids were off in their rooms occupying themselves since they had all completed their homework.

"Hello," she answered.

"Hey I just wanted to see if you were watching channel 7. They're just starting that story about the police shooting now."

"You know I almost forgot; let me run and turn on the TV now. Thanks for the reminder."

A few minutes later Sherri was seated there on the sofa; numb and seemingly unable to move. Just sitting there with her mouth wide open until her right hand covered it. She was shocked to the extent that it took her being called 2-3 times before she would snap out of it.

"Mom, mommy, MOM," Tyler was calling out to her from across the room.

"Yes Tyler what is it," she finally said glumly.

" Since I finished my homework, can I play with my XBOX until it's time for dinner.

"Sure go ahead," she replied without ever taking her eyes off the screen. She just sat there in stunned disbelief when the news anchor talked about the man who had been shot dead by the police; frozen as they displayed his picture off to the right hand side of the screen as the story continued. She would stay in that same position for a few more minutes; just sitting there staring through empty eyes, a blank expression covering her face. She looked at either the TV, or just as often nothing; long after the story had concluded. She held that pose all the way up until the phone rang with another call from Lily.

"Wow, can you believe that; you were right, stuff like that just doesn't happen around here too often," Lily remarked.

"No I can't believe it; not at all actually," Sherri replied sadly.

"But I guess it just goes to show you that no place is really safe from that element anymore."

"That element; what do you mean?"

"You know thugs, drug dealers, car thieves, stuff like that. Sounds more like something you'd expect in Newark or maybe Plainfield or New Brunswick but not in Somerset County. But at least they got this one."

"Yeah they certainly did," Sherri said wistfully.

"But how dumb do you have to be to test the police when they've got you surrounded like that. He must have had a death wish I guess."

"Well Lily we weren't there so we really can't say what happened. I mean you heard some of the witnesses. They said that what happened was totally unnecessary."

"Oh come on, what do you expect them to say Sherri?"

"You know, I don't know Lily, but I do know that I just hope the truth comes out; whatever it is."

"Oh my God Sherri, you sound almost like the typical liberal apologist right now," Lily said coldly, cutting her even deeper with a chuckle after the words left her mouth.

Sherri was angered to the point where she didn't want the conversation to continue any longer. She instead just sat there holding the phone in uncomfortable silence for several seconds before fortunately enough another call came in; this one from Clay.

"Listen that's Clay, I have to get that. I'll talk to you later."

"Okay go ahead," Lily responded before Sherri clicked over abruptly, without saying another word.

"Hello."

"Hey it's me," Clay said while sounding a bit weary. "Listen I'm gonna be coming home pretty late tonight in all likelihood."

"All right; is everything okay, you sound tired?"

"Sure everything is fine we just had a little something go down today, so I just need to hang around for some briefings and things of that nature. So I definitely won't be home for dinner."

"Okay well I'll just see you whenever you get here."

"Well that's just it; I don't know when that may be right now, so I just wanted to make sure you say good night and all that good stuff to the kids for me."

"Yeah sure I can do that."

"Alright, I'll see you later."

"Okay bye."

As soon as Sherri hung up the receiver she fell back heavily against the back of the sofa; weighted down by the news that had hit her over the head like a ton of bricks. When Clay finally arrived home at about 10:45 that night he found her just lying across the bed, the room dark except for one small lamp. Not even the television was on but there was Sherri, staring off into nowhere in particular. Initially at a loss as to what might have led to this unusual scene, Clay was able to figure it out soon enough. And with that, he didn't hesitate to tweak her just a little bit by taking a very subtle dig.

"Are you okay? You're laying up here like an eight year girl who's had her puppy run away from home. Hopefully he comes back soon," he teased.

"I'm fine, just tired but I'm good. And I know how concerned you are," she said facetiously.

As Clay headed out of the room Sherri turned off that loan solitary lamp before turning over onto her side. It was just as well that she did so because that prevented her from seeing the wicked smile that covered Clay's face as he departed. Sherri set her mind on trying to get some sleep; something which would be a long time in coming. It was just the first of what would be several long, restless nights.

As blue as her mood was, Sherri could only imagine what Alicia must have been feeling. And indeed absolute devastation could only begin to describe the emotions Alicia was experiencing once what happened had started to sink in. She felt completely empty much of the time, but never more than when she had to break the news to Gee's parents. She had pleaded to be allowed to be the one to tell them, even though they as technically the next of kin, would normally be informed by the authorities in such a case. But they relented, with a couple of detectives even dropping her off at their home in Union Township, since although her car was still parked in Gee's driveway, she felt in no condition to drive it.

Gee came from a solid, traditional working-class family background, his parents having been married 36 years and raising 4 children with Gee being the 2nd oldest. Needless to say his parents were completely crushed by the news, with his mother taking it particularly hard. Marlene Andrews was a tall, regal woman of style and class. She worked as a nurse until recently retiring, although at age 59 she could easily pass for 10 or more years younger. In all the times that she had been around her, Alicia could not recall a time when Mrs. Andrews was anything but cheery. But that changed in an instant after she heard the mournful words. She and Alicia shared a tearful embrace for about a minute as his dad sort of paced around in a dazed state. Two years older than his wife, Gee's dad Wilton works as a supervisor at an insurance company after a previous career as a school guidance counselor. He had always been more of the stoic type, but despite his outward demeanor not changing much, Alicia could tell the anguish that he now felt also. Once he returned his 6'4" frame to a seated position next to his wife he spent several moments simply holding his hands to his head; his fingers brushing through his salt and pepper hair. He too took a turn consoling his wife. They spoke softly about how they had never seen Gee as happy as he had been in recent days, something they attributed to Alicia. This was without them even knowing as of yet of her pregnancy. She briefly thought about whether right then would be a good time to tell them before quickly deciding against it.

Once Alicia managed to compose herself enough to tell them about the details surrounding the shooting from the point of view of the officers involved, their emotions quickly swung from sadness, to that of anger and disbelief. They, just as Alicia had, reacted strongly to any suggestion that their son was involved in the trafficking and selling of drugs. They all vowed to put up a strong unified front. To fight back against any attempt to paint him as such in order to in some way justify the actions of the detectives that morning.

Over the next couple of days a hell storm surrounding the death of Gee formed; only intensifying in its strength as word of the incident took flight in both the local and even to a lesser extent, the national media. 3 of the 4 local New York network affiliates covered the story for 2 consecutive days and CNN ran it on their sister station's Headline News broadcasts. A prominent and controversial group of activists held a rally right in front of the complex that housed the Somerset County Prosecutor's office along with that of the county police. Although no one from the latter was involved in the shooting. The mostly peaceful rally did threaten to take a turn towards something far different when the group holding the rally was taunted by a carload of individuals who sided with the detectives who fired the fatal shots. Fortunately the officers from the Somerville police department who were assigned to the site of the rally just in case any potential disturbances arose, stepped in and ordered the people in the car to move on before things could potentially get out of hand.

For his part, Clay made certain to stay out of the office on the day the rally took place, opting instead for a day of golf. But that did not save him from being affected by it, as the next morning a slew or reporters who had been camped out awaiting his arrival moved in on him as he stepped towards the building. The questions were flying fast and furiously, yet he ignored them for the most part with his only response being a terse no comment when he responded at all. But the members of the media were nothing if not determined to draw something out of him with their pointed questions.

"Is the probe into the shooting pretty much completed, or still ongoing?" came one.

"After having a few days to review the incident do you feel that the detectives involved were completely justified in their actions in this case?

"The civil rights leaders that were here yesterday are demanding an independent probe into the shooting. Do you see any chance of that happening?"

None of those questions drew a reaction from Clay but there did come a series of queries that finally did do the trick. That was when someone yelled out, "What do you say about the accusation that you don't care about finding the truth in this case because you're too tied to the officers who fired the shots? Or, that there may be a certain racial element to not only the incident but your reaction to it also?"

Clay stopped in his tracks at that point; turning and facing the assembled reporters.

"Okay I will say something in response to that, but first allow me to throw out a question to all of you. What do you know about the organization behind this little attention-seeking exercise you all witnessed yesterday? Not much I would guess right? Well, let me say this; my job is to serve the interests of the citizens of Somerset County; not a bunch of hustlers, charlatans and rabble-rousers, who by and large don't live in or anywhere near this county, yet came here armed with an agenda. And that was to garner publicity for themselves as much as anything. Now if you'll excuse me I have work to do for the people who are actually counting on me for just that."

And with that he hurried inside, leaving the press members scrambling to get his quotes out as soon as possible.

Although they were approached, neither Alicia nor anyone from Gee's immediate family wanted to take part in the demonstration, feeling that it was counterproductive and if anything threatened to sway public perception in a way that they would prefer not see happen. They decided that is was just as well that they continue to cast their lot with the justice system to do the right thing in determining whether or not the shooting was justified. But the group did manage to reel in one of Gee's cousins, who ironically enough never even shared much of a bond with him. But she was outspoken which was what they were seeking as much as anything. For their part the Andrews family devoted more focus to what they saw as the libelous manner in which Gee was portrayed. So to that end they decided to seek the counsel of an attorney.

Lawrence Montgomery III was known as much for his flamboyant appearance as anything. He was partial to wearing three piece suits in non-conventional colors such as gold, deep purple and fiery red, usually along with a matching fedora. But there was also no one who knew him who did not respect him as a highly competent and skilled lawyer. He was also known for his relaxed, free and easygoing manner when in the spotlight, and his great relationship and thus unfettered access to key members of the press. And it was this which made him most attractive to the Andrews family. They were determined to stem the tide of public opinion that they saw as possibly working against their son.

∞∞∞∞∞∞∞∞

The funeral for Gee was set for Friday and when that day arrived it was fittingly very gray and gloomy. Sherri had been going back and forth in her mind all week as to whether she wanted to be there; ultimately deciding the morning of the services that she simply had to be. That she at least needed that small bit of closure. The service was heavily attended by dozens of co-workers, friends and relatives of Gee from both near and far. Certainly not wanting her arrival to draw any unwanted attention to herself, Sherri made it a clear goal to arrive on time. At least before the door to the sanctuary would be closed; for opening it thereafter would most likely draw some curious eyes toward her in an attempt to see who was entering. By the same token she also did not want to risk entering too soon when many people would be milling about outside and elsewhere inside the building. So instead she stepped inside just a few minutes in advance of the scheduled start time, saying a brief prayer before taking a seat in the very rear of the church. Even on the overcast day her eyes were covered with dark sunglasses, but that in itself was not anything that was unique as many people do this for funerals, and this one was no exception with several other persons wearing them as well.

As would be expected the service was extremely somber with tears filling the church throughout. Several of Gee's relatives and friends took to the podium to give stirring testimonials before what was a moving eulogy by the minister. The service was also awash in music, some songs being pensive but others almost exultant. Just as she sensed things nearing a conclusion Sherri decided it was time to make a hasty exit. As she stood up to leave her overwhelming feelings were that though it was sad, the program was also a terrific tribute to Gee, and a true celebration of his all too brief life. But as good as Sherri felt for having come to pay her respects to her most recent lover, she nonetheless lost it a bit as she arrived back in her car; breaking down in tears before struggling to compose herself before heading home.

The following Thursday, nearly a week to the day after the funeral, word began to leak out that Clay's office had set up a press briefing for the following day. The general assumption was that there would be an announcement as to whether the internal probe into the shooting had uncovered anything that suggested undue force had been used. So calling on all of his media savvy, Lawrence in turn scheduled what he was labeling as an announcement for later in the same day.

Clay stood in front of the assembled members of the local press and glanced at his watch. It was 10:00 am. Time to get things started and quickly over with he was thinking. He wasn't all that comfortable with having to deal with the media; merely seeing it as a requirement that he needed to fulfill on certain occasions that called for it. And although he didn't necessarily see the Andrews case as worthy of the attention it'd been receiving, there he was, about to address it once again. Hopefully for the last time were his thoughts on it.

"Good morning. Thank you all for coming. I know that you all would like to spend as little time as possible standing here staring at me early in the morning, so why don't I just cut to the chase and let you know what this briefing is about," he stated before pausing.

"Almost 2 weeks ago a team of detectives under my command arrived at the Mountain View shopping center in Watchung with the intention of apprehending one Garrick Andrews. Mr. Andrews was sought for suspected narcotics trafficking, and in fact on the very same morning that the detectives moved in to arrest Mr. Andrews, another couple of detectives did in fact locate a sizable amount of cocaine inside of Mr. Andrews' residence. In the course of attempting to detain Mr. Andrews at the shopping center, the detectives noticed that he was brandishing a metal object in his right hand. This left the detectives in a situation where they felt threatened by Mr. Andrews; thinking he might be holding a firearm. Seeing this, my detectives then reacted as they have been trained to do. That is they discharged their weapons in the name of self-defense against what appeared to be an armed suspect. In the aftermath of this incident it was discovered that what Mr. Andrews held was in truth not a weapon but rather a mobile phone. However, with the facts in this case, as just spelled out to you, it is the judgment of this office that the detectives responded with reasonable force given their perspectives during that split second during which they had to make a decision on how to react to this perceived threat. Therefore, it is our view that what took place and led to the untimely passing of Mr. Andrews was nothing more than an unfortunate accident. Hence it is our decision that there will be no further action taken in this matter. Thank you very much."

As Clay stepped back from the podium he was pelted with rapid-fire questions from the assembled reporters. His only response was that he was not taking questions but would defer to his assistant James Walter to provide answers for them. Within minutes of the conclusion of the press briefing Lawrence had received a call from one of the many members of the press that he maintained a good relationship with. He had reached out to provide him with details of what took place. But while he appreciated some of the details of what Clay has said in his statement, all Lawrence really needed to know was the bottom line. And that was simple. The shooting of Gee had been determined to be justified, there would be no further investigation taking place and the detectives involved would be returning to their normal duties immediately. Buoyed by that information, Lawrence prepared himself for a rebuttal; asking his confidante if he could leak the word to a few of his peers who were present. It was about time for Lawrence Montgomery III to hold his own version of meet the press.

A small group of reporters crowded into Lawrence's office at 3:00. As the attorney representing the Andrews family, they were anxious to hear his reaction to the news Clay had delivered earlier in the day. And they would certainly not be disappointed in hoping that he might also provide them with some good headline material.

After the last person to arrive was escorted into his office by his assistant, Lawrence stepped out for a quick word with her before re-entering a few seconds later.

"Good afternoon, I thank you all for coming by on what was relatively short notice. I don't know if anyone else will be coming, but I've instructed my assistant to simply tap on the door if anyone else does arrive. So I apologize in advance for any possible interruptions. Now having said that, please let me begin." As he circled around his desk to take a seat in his chair he surveyed the group in front of him. There were 4 ladies seated in the chairs he had ringing his desk with another group of 4 men and one young female reporter standing against the wall behind them.

"Okay, as you all here certainly know, Clay King, the Somerset County Prosecutor announced this morning that his office's investigation into the shooting death of Garrick Andrews has concluded. And that given the facts as alleged, he sees no basis for any continuing investigation into the incident. Concluding that it was nothing more than to use his words, an unfortunate accident. So speaking on behalf of the family of Mr. Andrews let me say this; it is not this finding that we take particular issue with. In fact given the circumstances, we grudgingly accept that judgment as we know how difficult it must be to be placed in a situation where the wrong decision in a split second could result in the possible loss of life of one or more members of law enforcement.

However, there is one aspect of this entire incident that we not only dispute, but repudiate strongly. And that is the contention that there was just cause for the attempted arrest and apprehension of Mr. Andrews in the first place. And it is that which we will now wage battle against. It has been alleged that Mr. Andrews was involved in narcotics distribution, a charge that has been thoroughly rejected by the surviving members of the deceased's family as well as his fiancée. Also, in the interest of researching this claim, both I and/or members of my staff, have questioned dozens of relatives, friends, neighbors, co-workers etc. of Mr. Andrews. During this process we have not uncovered even a single individual that has seen any evidence of this charge having any basis in fact. Indeed those who knew Mr. Garrick Andrews the best have dismissed such a possibility as anything ranging from unlikely to far-fetched and utterly ridiculous." As most of those present either extended their digital voice recorders or scrambled to take down notes, Lawrence paused briefly before continuing.

"Now given that, and all else that we know about the young man, we have come to a conclusion of our own. And it is that the claim made by the Somerset County Prosecutor's office and its detectives is a bogus one. Therefore, it is our intent to pursue this further by seeking an independent probe into these charges. Also, to this end, I have contacted a member of the Governor's staff to request a sit-down meeting with the Governor to discuss this matter as well. Thank you very much and now I will take a few questions but no more than that please as I have a very busy schedule lined up as you might imagine."

The first question came from one of the ladies seated in a chair opposite his desk.

"Mr. Montgomery is it your assertion that the charge of narcotics trafficking made against Mr. Andrews was a purposely trumped up one?"

"Well we're not prepared to go quite that far just yet but that is one of the possibilities that we'd like to have looked into yes."

Piggybacking on the same question the next one came from someone standing against the wall. "So given what seems to me to be pretty cut and dried, and that is that you see some sort of frame-up here; what motive do you see for such a thing?"

"Again, we're not quite prepared to go out there on a limb before a probe has taken place, so I'll just reserve any comment on that until the picture clears up a bit. Just one more question please."

The final question was delivered from the same aggressive reporter who had asked the first. "Okay if I may take this a step further; knowing that you feel that there was some dishonesty and questionable conduct involved here, who is it that you see as the source of the false accusation against Garrick Andrews, the Prosecutor's office itself or some individual who may have had some sort of beef with Mr. Andrews?"

"Now that is certainly a good question Miss, but unfortunately it's also one that I cannot answer today as it also goes straight to the point of why we are seeking this investigation. Now if you'll excuse me…"

As Lawrence rose to his feet the group started to file out of his office in a quick but orderly fashion. The expressions on their faces told him that they certainly feel as though they were leaving his office with something good to run with in terms of a story.

∞∞∞∞∞∞∞∞∞∞

The next morning Rollie came almost barreling into the Clay's office. With a smile highlighting his face, he rushed over to embrace him.

"Good morning buddy, how you doing? Hope you're as excited as I was when I got word that I was back on full duty. I'm ready to roll; you did it buddy, we did it, we pulled this shit off Clay."

It didn't take long for Rollie to notice that for some reason Clay didn't share the same joyful mood that he was enjoying.

"Hey man, what's up? You don't seem as happy as I would have thought you'd be. Is everything cool? No more bullshit going down with Sherri is there?"

"Have you seen the cover of the Home News Tribune this morning," Clay asked in response.

"No I haven't, but what's wrong?"

"Well here take a look," Clay grumbled before shoving a copy towards him. "Read these headlines."

The biggest headline was in bold and read as follows:

NO CHARGES IN ANDREWS CASE. PROBE FINDS NO WRONGDOING

As his eyes scanned downward Rollie soon came across the other headlines. They were midway down the page and were the reason for Clay's dour mood.

ANDREWS FAMILY ATTORNEY TO SEEK STATE INQUIRY

ASSERT BOGUS DRUG CLAIM LED TO ATTEMPTED APPREHENSION

Rollie was at a loss for words as he looked at Clay with the same sort of expression he had seen worn by his friend from the time he entered his office.

"Well now you see the potential problem we're looking at right," Clay asked strongly.

Rollie still didn't speak but instead just backed up and turned away, walking into a corner as if he needed to let what he had just read sink in. Moments later he pivoted and walked back in the direction of Clay before taking a seat in one of his guest chairs.

"Yes I certainly see now why you had the long face when I walked in. But then like you said it's only a potential problem. Listen Clay, who all knows about any of what really went down?"

"Well it's just me, you and Mike; oh and dumb and dumber of course."

"Exactly; so that means that there's no information that they can get to build a case on right? I mean they can suspect anything they want, and speculate on this and that or whatever, but the truth is that's all they can do because they couldn't possibly tie us to anything. Well that is unless…"

Rollie didn't even need to complete the thought. Clay knew exactly where he was going. He briefly smiled in Rollie's direction before again turning serious.

"Maybe you need to get back in contact with your buddy's Jimmy and Roberto. Perhaps tell them you have another chance for them to make an easy score."

"I'm one step ahead of you my friend. I'll get going on that as soon as I walk out of here."

As the two men parted ways, the frowns they sported earlier were now replaced by cunning smiles. After mulling things over in his mind for about an hour, Rollie then set things in motion.

"Hey Roberto, its Rollie Celini; you have a minute?"

"Yeah sure I've got a minute, what's up?"

"Well nothing much really; just that I have another opportunity for you guys. Your partner wouldn't happen to be there with you by any chance would he?"

"Yeah he's right here man, we're just shooting a little game of pool."

"That's great; then what I'm about to lay on you, you can pass on to him right away."

"Well I don't want to go into details over the phone but like I said I have another little job for you two. It's something that'll probably be a piece of cake; a chance for another easy payday for both of you."

"Sounds good to me, whatcha got?"

"Like I said I'd rather not go into detail over the phone, but I'm hoping we can meet someplace and discuss it."

"Hold on for a minute okay," Roberto said after a pause.

"Sure, no problem; take your time."

"Okay I just wanted to run this by Jimmy before we go any further, but yeah sure it's cool man, where do you wanna meet?"

"Alright listen, do you know where the old North Branch train station out in Branchburg is?"

"Yeah I know where it is."

"How about Sunday evening at 7:00?"

Roberto took a brief glance over at Jimmy before answering.

"Yeah that'll work, we'll be there."

"Sorry if the location seems a bit far out, but for obvious reasons I have to be very careful; you understand right?"

"Yeah don't worry about it; we understand the risk you're taking. But like I said we'll be there."

Later that evening Clay was seated in his family room with Sherri and the kids. Friday was their normal pizza night followed by a movie at home. Usually they would go out but on that night they went with delivery because of how late Clay had arrived home. Even though she could sense that there was a real chasm that was continuing to develop in her and Clay's relationship, Sherri still always made an attempt to maintain the same level of normalcy that the children had become accustomed to; so this time was precious to her. They were all bunched together on the sofa, Clay flanked by Abby and Tyler and then Zach with Sherri to his left. The movie had just started when Clay felt a vibration from his cell phone. He reached into his pocket and retrieved it, before looking at its display.

"Excuse me but I have to take this," he said as he stood and walked around the cocktail table in front of them.

"Can't you just let whoever it is leave a message and call them back after the movie is over," Sherri pleaded.

"No I have to take this one; I'll only be a few minutes. I'll be right back you guys," he added while looking in the direction of the kids.

Clay quickly walked into the master bedroom before answering.

"What's up Roll?"

"Hey listen I just wanted to let you know it's a go. Sunday evening; I'll give you a call afterwards."

"Sounds good man thanks."

"Okay, talk to you soon."

"See that wasn't too long at all was it," Clay said when he returned to his position on the sofa.

∞∞∞∞∞∞∞∞∞

Running just a little late," Rollie pulled his car in front of the abandoned North Branch train station about 7:07 that Sunday evening. The station had been closed three years ago, falling under the ax wielded by the previous Governor in the form of steep cuts to the state budget. Looking around, he didn't see any other cars as he came to a halt before climbing out of his vehicle. It was plenty dark, with the only light being two amber street lamps about 50 feet away that were separated by 20 feet or so in distance. The fact that he didn't see anyone right away threw him for a moment but any concerns he had were quickly alleviated when he saw the shadowy figures of two men moving towards him. As they drew closer he was able to recognize that it was indeed Roberto and Jimmy.

"Gentlemen, always good to see you two," Rollie remarked facetiously. He noticed Roberto pass a 40 ounce bottle of beer to Jimmy who in turn took a deep swig from it.

"Well I was actually thinking the pleasure is all ours to tell you the truth," countered Roberto.

"Hey Detective, you're not going to cite us for an open container and public consumption of alcohol are you?" Jimmy quipped as he lowered the bottle before handing it back over to Roberto.

"No, I think you guys are good with me, in fact I'd almost like to join you, but not quite," Rollie replied lightly. "Anyway, what do you say we get down to the matter at hand shall we?"

"Actually why don't you hold that thought for one minute," asked Roberto. "I have to go take a piss like right now."

"Sure go ahead, Jimmy and I will just engage in a little small talk while you're gone."

Rollie watched as Roberto walked off to the left and completely around the station to the rear of it before he then turned back to Jimmy.

"So what have you been doing with yourself Jim?" Rollie asked as he slowly walked in front of him.

"Oh just whatever it takes to survive, you know how it is," Jimmy answered.

"Well it looks like things must be going pretty well for you. Is that a new leather jacket you have on?" Rollie questioned while moving in towards him.

"Nah this thing is old as dirt," Jimmy said.

"Oh but I like that though, that's real nice, Rollie said while touching his left hand to it.

"Thanks but like I said it's seen its better days."

"Yeah but I sure like it, nice real nice," Rollie kept repeating. As an unsuspecting Jimmy looked on, Rollie slowly reached his right hand into his jacket pocket. Pulling out a magnum revolver he pressed it into Jimmy's side and fired off a shot; a silencer attached to the weapon effectively muffling the sound. Jimmy's eyes rolled around in his head before he started to crumple to the ground slowly with Rollie guiding him downward. Jimmy was still alive as Rollie moved quickly, grabbing his shoulders and starting to drag him further into the station. He didn't want Roberto to see his extended legs when he came back from behind the station. But Jimmy suddenly reacted; trying to put up some resistance with what was the last of his strength. Just as Rollie let him go Jimmy managed to clutch one of his ankles, causing Rollie to pull out the weapon and fire off two more rounds; one more to the torso and a final kill shot right between the eyes.

Holding the gun behind his back Rollie then walked off to the left in search of Roberto. After walking a distance of about 30 feet he heard the sound of rustling feet behind him in the distance. Roberto had surprised him by circling around the other end of the station. Having come up on Jimmy's body he was now making a dash; fleeing for his life. In his haste to get away he had stumbled down the three steps that led to the ground before scrambling to his feet and racing off to the right. Since he had just come from that direction he knew that Rollie must have gone the opposite way gunning for him.

As Roberto took off into the darkness, Rollie ran after him, firing his weapon several times. With Roberto having a pretty good head start and being far swifter afoot than his heavy-legged pursuer on top of it, any realistic hopes Rollie had of catching up to him were quickly dashed. He knew that his only chance was to pick him off with a lucky shot; in the dark of night at that. He lost even more time by stopping to retrieve a flashlight from his car. But he was figuring that in his eagerness to get away there was also a chance that Roberto could have run himself into something like a tree or tripped over something unseen in the darkness. So he wanted to have some vision just in case Roberto might be down on the ground someplace. It was a long shot, but it was really the only one he had at that point. In truth Roberto was long gone however, having run parallel along the tracks to the rear of the station before making his way up a steep embankment. Still breathing heavily and with his veins brimming with adrenalin, he kept moving at a steady pace; occasionally looking back for any sign of his hunter.

He also wanted to avoid any chance of getting himself pinned up against the Neshanic River which ran about 100 or so yards beyond the rail line. He figured his best bet was to remain alongside the tracks until he no longer could. Doing so also provided him with some light on occasion; if only from the small ones lining the tracks. Suddenly a thought came to him. As long as he stayed on line with the tracks he would eventually run into the next active station on the line; that being the Raritan station. From there he'd be safe for sure; he could perhaps even borrow a cell phone from someone to call his girlfriend to come pick him up. Hopefully there would be someone around who would allow him just a minute of time to make the call. He had left home with his own phone but it now sat helplessly in his pocket, having quickly drained its battery life away searching for a signal, in the semi-rural area with it's very sparse coverage areas. He didn't know the distance he had to travel, but just knowing that he now had a clear destination in mind pushed him to move even faster. He wondered why the thought hadn't come to him right away. It was at least a straight shot; certainly easier than trying to navigate his way back to Route 22 from in the midst of nowhere.

Rollie walked and occasionally jogged probably no more than 75 yards before he gave up the chase. Holding the flashlight in front of him for light, he then headed back towards his car. Stamina certainly wasn't his strong suit and his lungs burned with every step. When he arrived at the car he quickly climbed inside, collapsing onto the seat before reaching for his phone and dialing Clay's number.

Clay was in the midst of a discussion with Sherri in the kitchen when the call came through. Just as two days previously, he excused himself; explaining that he had to take the call in a different room.

"What another secret call that you can't take in front of me," Sherri remarked.

"Well I would think you'd be the last one to bring up the subject of things that are secret," he countered before swiftly walking towards the stairs and down to the empty family room, leaving Sherri to ponder what he meant.

"Hey, what's going on?" he asked upon answering the phone.

"I took care of Jimmy Klevens," Rollie answered proudly.

Clay hesitated briefly, looking over his shoulder before responding.

"Okay that's good, but what about his sidekick?"

"Well that's where there might be a slight problem."

"A slight problem; what exactly is it that you mean by a slight problem?" Clay whispered.

"I'm afraid Roberto got away. Something happened and he was able to get a little jump on me and I just couldn't locate him out here in the darkness."

"Well I guess I don't have to tell you about the trouble that could potentially cause do I," Clay commented.

"Well the way I see it, we don't have to worry about him surfacing anytime soon. The little mother fucker is probably scared shitless."

"Oh, the way YOU see it!" Clay said firmly. "Well I guess that should make me feel all comfortable about the situation huh? Anyway, there's no point in harping on it right now; we just have to hope you might perhaps get another shot at him before too long. In the meantime we keep our fingers crossed. That's really all we can do."

"Yeah you're right about that. And don't worry I'll put the squeeze on some people in the area of his known hangouts. See if anyone has a clue of his whereabouts."

"Okay keep me posted, I'll talk to you soon," Clay said calmly before ending the call and heading back upstairs.

It was close to 8:00 on a Sunday night but there were still a handful of people at the Raritan train station when it came into view. Roberto was very disheveled in appearance with muddy streaks all over his clothing and several abrasions dotting his face. In all honesty he looked like he had just been in a fight in which he came out on the wrong end. And in his mind he really had been, except that he felt like he won. Marked for death and yet standing there as a survivor. Now all he needed was a phone.

He had no luck with the first three persons he approached; with the latter two even claiming that they didn't have phones. The first person, who he had seen talking away on a cell phone when he arrived at the station, simply moved very quickly away from him as she saw him approaching; before he could even ask. That left him with a feeling of disappointment, but he couldn't really blame her once he placed himself in her shoes. A grungy looking man who had seemingly come out of nowhere walking up on her in the dark? He could certainly understand why she might feel a bit antsy. He sized up a 4th person who was sitting on a bench looking through a magazine. It was a thirtyish woman with short blond hair. The way that she was dressed made it appear that she might be going out for a little nightlife. Roberto parked himself about 15 feet away from her on the bench. He noticed her looking up and smiling at him as she sensed his presence. As soon as he took a seat he pulled out his phone and started fiddling with it. After throwing in some deep sighs for even more effect he figured he had successfully given the appearance of someone going through the cell phones blues. So he then called out to her.

"Excuse me I'm sorry to bother you, but my phone has a dead battery and I really," he began before she cut him off in mid-sentence.

"Oh you need to make a call? Here you can borrow mine. That's not a problem."

"I really appreciate you offering like this," Roberto said. "I was just about to ask if I might be able to borrow yours briefly."

"Oh sure no big deal, I think we've all gone through that at one time or another so I don't mind. I mean as long as you won't be calling Europe or anything."

Her quick wit led him to smile as he looked into her friendly eyes. The random act of kindness temporarily made him forget about the tension that he had been under just minutes before so he was able to return the quip.

"I promise I won't be calling Europe. They're in the middle of the night right now anyway."

"Well in that case here you go," she said with an even bigger smile as she handed him her phone."

"Thanks, I'll be calling right over to South Bound Brook and I won't be longer than a couple of minutes."

Roberto took the phone, stood, and starting to walk, quickly called home with the phone being answered quickly by his live-in girlfriend Carmen.

"Hello."

"Hey baby, listen to me; I need you to come pick me up someplace, can you do that?

"Roberto? Whose phone are you calling me from; Shauna Olander who's that?"

"Carmen I'll explain all that later but right now can you just come and give me a ride home please? I'll fill you in on everything when you get here."

"Fill me in on everything. What do you mean Roberto? What's going on?"

"Carmen, please baby can you just come and get me? If not I'll have to try to get someone else," he replied as he walked in a small circle.

"Okay, okay sure I'll come and get you."

"Great sweetie, how soon can you get here?"

"Well first you'll have to tell me where here is don't you think?"

"I'm sorry Carm; you're right; I'm at the Raritan train station. No, no, no wait a second Carmen, there's a Quik Check across the street from the train station, pick me up over there. I'll wait for you inside."

"Roberto, you sound so nervous; what's the matter baby?"

"Not now sweetie, I'll explain it to you when you get here I promise. Just hurry please."

"Okay, okay I'm leaving right now."

"Alright I'll see you when you get here," Roberto told her before ending the call. He then walked back over to the young lady and handed her the phone. "Thanks a lot, and again I really appreciate it."

"No problem; but are you okay man?"

"Yeah sure I'm fine; thanks," Roberto replied but the jitters he was experiencing were evident in everything from his voice to his body language. He quickly looked all around him before hustling out of the train station and scurrying across the street to the Quik Chek. After using the men's room, he prepared himself a cup of coffee. "Hey man I'm waiting for a ride; is it okay if I hang out here drinking my coffee until they show up," he asked the young clerk who rang up his coffee.

"Yeah go ahead that's not a problem, I'm sure it must be getting chilly outside by now."

"Thanks, I shouldn't be too long."

Roberto spent the first ten minutes of his wait standing in front of the large plate glass window; peering outside, before going back to some pacing. He headed over to the magazine rack, glancing at the covers before something else caught his attention. That day's copy of the News Tribune had a headline story related to the possible investigation into the drug charges made against Gee. He snatched up one of the papers and started reading with interest. Just as he neared the end of the article his attention was diverted by the glow of bright headlights shining into the store. Just as he slowly walked towards the window he saw Carmen leap out of the car. Changing direction, he rushed over to the register and handed the clerk a couple of dollars for the newspaper before thanking him again and quickly heading for the exit where he was met by Carmen.

"Baby you okay," she said as she threw her arms around him.

"Yeah I'm good, let's go," he said as they hurried out the door. "Let me drive," he said.

"Okay now you can tell me what this is all about right?"

"Yeah," Roberto said before pausing for several seconds. "Jimmy's dead."

"What! Jimmy's dead; how?"

"Here, look at the headline of this paper."

As Roberto pulled back from the parking space, Carmen scanned the headline before also reading the first few sentences of the accompanying article. At that point she had to stop reading as she lost the light from the store's parking lot.

"Is it okay if I turn on the inside light so I can read the rest of the article?"

"No don't do that," Roberto answered quickly. It was clear he was still at least a bit paranoid. "I just needed for you to look at the headline really."

"Okay fine, I did so now what does that have to do with any of this?"

Roberto ran a hand across his forehead and then through his hair before beginning to speak slowly and deliberately.

"Almost a month ago me and Jimmy were approached by these two detectives about doing a special job for them. As strange as it sounds they wanted us to break into some dude's townhouse yet not take anything. What they wanted us to do instead was plant some drugs inside there. And those are the very same drugs that are talked about in that article."

"So you're saying they had you guys do this so they could set somebody up for a fall," Carmen interjected.

"Exactly, and that's just what happened. And so what happens next; the dude winds up dead when they moved in to arrest him and you see what the fallout is now. So anyway, it's obvious that these guys wanted to eliminate the possibility of what we know coming back to haunt them. Well they got Jimmy, but I was lucky and got away."

"Damn baby that's terrible; this is bad real bad," Carmen lamented.

"I know, I know, that's why we have to get away from here Carmen."

"Get away; what do you mean get away; like where Roberto?"

"I don't know, maybe we can head down to Texas, I have a lot of family down there."

"Oh baby; how can I just up and leave? What about my job and stuff?" What about money? Roberto, I don't know."

"Carmen it's not safe here! They're going to be coming after me, and if they can't get to me they'll come after you. We have to go baby; I'm sorry end of story."

"Okay, but how are we gonna survive someplace else without me working. You're not working and we can't live off of play money."

"I don't know, we can take whatever we have in savings; probably stay with some of my people until we can get ourselves on our feet. We just gotta do what we gotta do sweetheart."

"Okay you're right, we'll find a way. Just thank God you're okay; but poor Jimmy"

"I know, and that's what I mean. If you don't want me to be next we have to get the hell out of town, and we have to do it tonight."

CHAPTER TWENTY-FOUR

Though she continued to occasionally grapple with the same lust-filled thoughts that had led her down the path to danger and deceit, Sherri had began to handle it much better. The incident with Chulo coupled with the tragic death of Gee had both served as wake up calls to her. Awakening her to the fact that what she'd been doing could have ultimately led to her demise as well. Either that or the victimization of someone else that might next be caught up in her tangled web. Not that she had any reason to think that his involvement with her had anything to do with what happened to Gee. No reason that is except her belief in karma; a belief that had her wondering if her day of reckoning might soon also come to pass. She'd gotten the mess caused by the theft of her credit cards straightened out, but there still was no mending of her heart, for she was still mourning for Gee; albeit as quietly and discreetly as was needed given the circumstances. And she had every reason to believe that she'd been able to completely and effectively hide the hurt in her heart from Clay. But there were those moments when she lets loose; allowed the tears to flow, and the sadness to envelop her. Sadness as much for Gee's family as for herself. And especially for Alicia and what had befallen her.

It had been 2 weeks that Roberto and Carmen had been in San Antonio and all things considered, they had sort of settled in already. Carmen had already managed to secure a job at a local women's boutique, though she still hoped to secure another position in the customer service field. The one in which she'd worked before the two of them packed up some of their belongings, and with $3000.00 cash in hand, headed southwest to Texas. She first requested a week of leave; claiming a family emergency, before one week later quitting altogether. Roberto on the other hand was dealing with the same issue he had while back in New Jersey; that being the challenge of finding employment with his criminal record.

It was a Friday and the two of them were enjoying a nice evening down at the River Walk. It was their first visit there since being in town. The weather on the early November day had been beautiful with a high of 76 and even at this hour of 9 pm it still felt like it was in the mid 60's.

"You know Roberto I could really get used to this," Carmen said as they sat outside of the restaurant where they had just enjoyed some authentic Mexican fare. "Here we are in November and we don't need to wear more than a light jacket; even in the evenings."

"So what are you saying; that you wouldn't mind staying here and making it our new home?"

"Maybe," she teased. "I mean we'll see; there are some things we'd have to consider first," she said before taking another sip of her pina colada.

"Things like what baby?"

"Well there is the matter of all of our stuff we left behind for one. I mean I know the lease is about to expire, but if we decide we want to vacate the apartment we'd have to get it all out of there before too long. But how could we get it out if we can't even go back there, let alone get it all down here. And then where we would put it?"

"I know, but maybe we could get our own place soon. I mean I know you're not making that much down at the store but I'm gonna keep looking and hope something comes through for me too."

"I'm proud of you for really trying so hard this time Roberto, and I'm sure someone will give you a chance soon."

"I hope you're right because I'm determined to do things the right way with this new start down here. I don't want to go back to what I left behind. I know where that can lead and trust me either in jail or dead is not where I'm trying to wind up right now."

"Speaking of which; Roberto, are you going to do anything about what happened to Jimmy?"

Roberto hesitated, shaking his head and throwing his hands up. "Baby, what can I do?"

"I don't know, but there has to be something Roberto. Jimmy was basically your best friend for as long as I've known you. You can't just let it slide like that. I mean you couldn't even be there to pay him your respects. That's not right; somebody needs to know what happened before those guys do it to somebody else."

"I know Carmen. Trust me I do, but I can't just try to play hero and wind up dead myself. That's not what you want is it?"

"No of course not, but there has to be somebody you can tell who could take care of this."

"Really like who? Tell me who baby? Should I tell the police? I can't trust the police; they'll just look out for one of their own and try to have me silenced too; believe me."

"I know Roberto, I know. All I'm saying is to think about it. There has to be a way out of this or we'll just be living out of these suitcases forever. And I don't want that; I can't live like that."

He placed his right hand to her face; brushing some of her dark hair away from it before looking into her expressive brown eyes. "Okay baby, let me put my mind to it. I'll see what I can come up with."

"Thanks, I love you papi."

"I love you too mamacita," Roberto replied before turning up his bottle of beer one more time to finish it off. "Come on let's go on one of those romantic looking boat rides," he said just after placing the bottle down.

∞∞∞∞∞∞∞∞∞

Sherri had been spending her idle time during the day getting much more involved in her children's education and various other day to day activities. Since she and Lily had their little falling out they'd seen far less of each other. But even with her more fruitful pursuits it's not as if she didn't still have her challenging moments. Just from knowing what was out there to entertain her at the very least, or tempt her anew. Yet she was pretty comfortable in feeling that she would no longer travel back down that path to her own potential destruction. The memories were all so very fresh in her mind; those both good and bad. And just as she reflected on Gee, she did likewise with Scott the very passionate and sweetly unselfish lover, and also on Craig, the caricature with whom she shared her initial indiscretions which only left her starving for more. And how could she forget her youthful neighbor Darren, the man-child who'd proven to her that he was far more man than child. Then there was Derrick, who strung her along before casting her aside like a child does a toy in favor of a newer one. And yes even the outwardly charming yet benevolent Chulo also played a key part in leading her to where she found herself now. They were experiences and lessons she would take with her as she went forward with her life; determined to take a higher road. But there was the one man who was different; the one who only wanted to be her friend, even when she wanted him in a much different way. He was strong when she was at her weakest point, steadfast in his moral convictions as she so casually tossed whatever morals she had aside. And for that she had treated him so poorly. She felt the need to make amends; she wanted to make things right with Miguel if she could.

She called him on a Monday morning once Clay and the kids had departed; keeping her fingers crossed that he would be available.

"Hello."

"Hi, do you know who this is?" she asked somewhat hesitantly after he answered the phone.

"No I'm sorry I don't; should I?"

"Really; you have no clue?"

"Nope sorry, I'm afraid you must have the wrong number."

"Okay, well I'm sorry to have bothered you, bye." Sherri said sadly.

Just as she was about to hang up Sherri heard the sound of loud laughter coming through the phone. "No don't hang up; of course I know who this is. Hello Sherri."

"Uggggh, why did you do that to me?"

"Gotcha; oh I forgot to tell you about my penchant for kidding."

"Oh okay; well you got me with that one."

"Sorry about that, but I think you had it coming," Miguel said before chuckling once again.

"Yeah, well I guess you're right there. Anyway how are you?"

"I'm doing fine, how about you?"

"I'm doing pretty well, thanks."

"That's good, but this is a surprise; to what do I owe the pleasure of this call?"

"Well I remember how cold I was to you the last time we spoke; so I just wanted to apologize for that."

"Oh its okay, you don't have to," Miguel began before Sherri cut him off.

"No please Miguel, let me do this. I was wrong and I had no reason for talking to you that way when you'd been nothing but a good friend to me. But because I was so wrapped up in my own selfish desires I only wanted what I wanted and didn't care much about anything else. And the funny thing is that out of all of the men that I've met of late you have probably the best qualities and highest character out of any of them. And yet you were the one I gave the brush off to. So again; for that I apologize to you."

"Well I do appreciate it. It's big of you to call and do that, so thank you. And I certainly accept your apology."

"Thanks Miguel; oh and there is one more thing."

"What's that?"

"I think I owe you a lunch; a complete one."

Miguel smiled broadly before replying simply. "Sure, that would be cool."

"Well I don't know when you may be anywhere around here again, but whenever you are; lunch is on me okay?"

"Alright, and actually we have a game at Monmouth University coming up soon so I'll be in the area then. It's on a Monday night so I could probably arrange my schedule to stay in the area long enough to have lunch the next day."

"Okay that's great. Why don't you give me a call a few days beforehand to firm things up?"

"That sounds good to me Sherri, I certainly will."

"Cool, I guess we have a date then. Well not a date, but you know what I mean," Sherri laughed.

"Yeah I know what you mean. Anyway, I have to run and start getting ready for practice, so I'll just give you a call soon."

"Alright you take care Miguel."

"You do the same, bye."

"Bye-bye."

Meanwhile, down at the modest bungalow that his cousin Marisol shared with her husband Carlos and their two children, Roberto was just about to drive Carmen to work. Everyone else had already departed; the kids for school and Marisol and Carlos for their respective jobs.

"Baby I've come up with a plan of sorts. Now I don't want to go into any details until I see how it goes, but I'll be sure to keep you posted," he told her as they walked towards the door.

"Okay that's great Roberto. When are you going to try to put it into action?"

"Actually this morning; right after I drop you off and get back to the house in fact."

"Oh wow, well let's go so that you can hurry and get started with whatever you have in mind."

"Have a good day at work sweetheart," he said to her once he pulled up in front of the store. "I might try to give you a ring later to let you know how it goes okay."

"Sounds good baby; please let me know how it goes," she replied before they kissed good-bye and she departed the car.

The moment he arrived back at the house, Roberto immediately walked back into the spare bedroom the two of them had been using and retrieved something. It was the newspaper he had purchased on the evening Jimmy had been killed. He then sat down on the bed and grabbed his cell phone before opening the newspaper. After finding what he was looking for inside he dialed a number on his phone. It didn't take very long for the call to be answered; a mere 2 rings.

"Good morning Home News Tribune, how may I direct your call?"

"Good morning I was wondering if it would be possible to speak to Ryan Drake."

"May I tell him who's calling and what it's in reference to?"

"Actually I prefer not to give my name out, but you can tell him it's about the case he wrote an article about like 2-3 weeks ago."

"I'm sorry, is there any way you can be more specific sir?" the woman asked politely.

"Okay sure, the article was about the guy who got shot by the cops last month in Watchung. You know the dude they said was a dealer."

"Oh you mean the Garrick Andrews incident?"

"Exactly; that's the one," Roberto said with his voice rising in excitement.

"Well actually I'm not sure that Mr. Drake is out of a weekly staff meeting but I can try his line; hold on sir."

"Sure, no problem," Roberto replied.

About 30 seconds later the young lady returned to the line.

"Sir."

"Yes, I'm here."

"Thanks for holding; but yes I'm afraid Mr. Drake isn't available right now. Is there any way he can get back to you?"

"Um yeah sure; I guess so. Would it be this morning?"

"Well I can't answer that for him, but I would think so. I mean it depends I guess. Do you have information pertinent to the case?"

"Yeah you could say that I do."

"Well sir, I will certainly leave him a message telling him that and I would think he'll get back to you in short order, because this story has been his biggest focus ever since it broke."

"Okay, I'll wait for his call," Roberto said after supplying her with his number.

About 30 minutes later Roberto was lying on the bed, staring at the ceiling and anxiously awaiting the call, when it came in.

"Hello," he answered quickly.

"Hello, this is Ryan Drake. I understand that we need to talk."

"Yeah man I think we do," Roberto began. "You're the dude who wrote the article in the paper about 2-3 weeks ago right?"

"If you mean an article regarding the Garrick Andrews story than yes that was me. I've actually written a series of articles concerning that incident and the subsequent investigation into it."

"Alright then cool; well I think I have something that you might be interested in."

"Okay I'm listening, what do you have?"

"Enough to blow the lid right off this case, but first I have to know that I can get something out of going public with this."

"Well what exactly do you want that to be Mister uhhh; I'm sorry I didn't catch your name."

"That's because I didn't give it. I might do that in time but first let me clue you in on what I'm talking about and then we'll see what you can do for me in exchange for what I'm about to lay on you."

"Ryan shifted in his chair and threw his feet up on his desk. "Okay fair enough, talk to me."

Roberto then proceeded to tell him everything; starting with the initial meeting he and Jimmy had with Rollie and Mike, all the way up to the murder of his friend. Roberto wasn't too far into telling his story when Ryan pulled his feet down from off the desk and sat almost on the edge of his seat. He listened intently, occasionally jotting down some notes on a small notepad.

"Wow. You weren't kidding when you said what you have is major," Ryan said once he concluded. "Wow, he repeated. "Okay, so where are you now?"

"I'm out of the state; holed up down in Texas with some relatives. I know they still want nothing more than to take me out too, so there's no way I was gonna stick around."

"Well don't you think the best thing for you might be to just go to somebody with this?"

"Somebody like who man? The cops? Please, I don't trust any of them. The way I see it, if I went to them I might as well be writing my own death sentence. That's why I called you."

"Okay but what can I really do for you?"

"I don't know man, but you have the power of the press behind you. You might be able to expose this whole thing."

"Yeah but as powerful as what you've told me is you're talking about a couple of cops here; allegedly crooked ones sure;

but still cops. You need some strong evidence when you try to take some of them down."

"So what are you saying? That it's no use, and I wasted my time even telling you this. Come on man that's bullshit," Roberto snapped. "This fucking guy is a dirty ass cop and on top of that a murderer dude. He shot my friend down like it was nothing. No wonder he and his buddies were so quick to kill that guy in his car. That probably wasn't any accident either. I doubt that seriously."

"No it wasn't a waste of time for you to call me. That's not what I'm saying; not at all. Listen, if what you've told me is true I want justice to be served above anything else," Ryan assured Roberto. He then took a deep breath and exhaled. "Listen; let me think about what the next move can be alright. Give me about an hour to come up with something and then I'll get back to you. Can I reach you at this same number?"

"Yeah the same number."

"Okay, I'll get back to you soon."

"Alright I'll be here, and listen up man, if there's any nonsense that goes down I'll just deny that I ever talked to you."

"Okay, okay; but don't worry about that I'm not on the side of the police or anyone else, I'm just on the side of the truth. One hour."

With some time to kill, Roberto decided to take a quick shower and then run out for some early lunch. He took a short drive to a diner he had spotted when he and Carmen first arrived in town. It was while he was there enjoying a meal of veal cutlets with mashed potatoes and gravy that his phone rang. When he checked the display he saw that rather than Ryan it was Carmen calling.

"Hey love, what's up," he answered swiftly.

"Nothing much here, just taking a little break so I decided to give you a call and see what's up with you. Been thinking about what you said before I left this morning. You know, about taking some action today. Anything to report?"

"Yeah but let me get back to you Carm, I want to keep my line free because I'm expecting a call back that could come at any time now."

"Okay baby, like I said I was just checking."

"Well I'll call you back a little later and you never know, I might just have something to pass on then. I'm hoping so; but anyway let me go for now."

"Alright sweetie, I should be taking a lunch about 1:00, so call me back sometime between then and 2:00 if you can okay."

"Okay no problem," he replied before hanging up and immediately checking the time. Almost an hour had passed since he'd hung up from Ryan. Shrugging his shoulders, he then quickly polished off the rest of his meal before requesting his check. At just about the moment his waitress placed it down and walked away his phone started dancing on the table. Grabbing it quickly he checked the display. This time it was indeed Ryan.

"Hello."

"Hey it's me, Ryan Drake. Can you talk now?"

"Yeah sure can, just give me a minute okay," Roberto asked. He then reached into his wallet and placed a ten and a five down on the table before quickly making his way towards the exit. "Okay I'm here, let me just make my way to my car. It'll only take me a few seconds. The moment he was seated in the driver's seat he placed the phone back up to his mouth. "All right I'm here; what do you have for me?"

"Well I think we've come up with a pretty good plan for how to handle this."

"We; who the hell is we man? I told this to you only with the intention of keeping it that way."

"Hold on, I was getting to that. Now listen; I know you said that you don't trust any of the cops and so on and so on, but hear me out. I have this friend with the FBI…"

"The FBI; come on man, what is that about?"

"Wait you didn't let me finish. Like I said I have this friend with the FBI. We went to college together and I've known him for over 25 years. And I can tell you that I trust him completely and you can too. Now he's waiting on the other line but I wanted to talk to you first and then see if we can conference him in so he can also talk to you. You know, to let you in on more of what the two of us came up with before I called you back. Is that cool with you?"

"Damn, I don't know man," said Roberto as he nervously lit up a cigarette.

"Hey, listen I understand your hesitation, but you're gonna have to trust me a little bit if we're gonna work together to move this situation forward and get you out of hiding so to speak. Isn't that what you want?"

"Yeah I would, but I don't know man," Roberto responded. "Hold on, let me think on this for a minute myself okay." Roberto placed the phone down on the passenger seat before leaning his head forward onto his hands which rested on the steering wheel. Deep in thought, he held that pose for about 45 seconds before straightening up and reaching for his phone. "Okay Mr. Drake, I'm leaning on faith on this one here, but let's do it, put him on."

"Great, just hold on one second while I bring him into the conversation."

A scant few seconds later Roberto heard Ryan calling out. "Okay Chris we're a go."

"Alright great, thanks Ryan. Sir, can you hear me okay?" a deep voice called out.

"Yep hear you loud and clear," Roberto acknowledged.

" Hello Sir, my name is Christopher Jarvis and as I'm sure Ryan told you, I'm an agent with the FBI working out of the Newark office. Now Sir do you mind telling me your name?"

"My name is Roberto, that's enough for now."

"Okay that's fine Roberto, just that much indicates that we've broken down at least one barrier already. Anyway Roberto, Ryan has already pretty much given me the details of what you two discussed earlier so there's no need for you to go over it again. And suffice it to say I'm in complete agreement with him that the information you've come forward with is very compelling. Now the problem as I see it is this. It's pretty much just hearsay right now. So the task here, as I see it, is simple. We have to come up with a way to get one or more of the detectives to implicate themselves with their own words. Now of course that is sometimes easier said than done. But I think we can make this happen. How? Well let me lay it out for you."

A clear look of disappointment was etched on the face of Lawrence Montgomery as he approached the group of reporters who had been camped outside of his office. Thirty minutes earlier he had left a meeting in his office with the state Attorney General, who had met with Lawrence on behalf of Governor Christian to discuss the Andrews' family's concerns over the drug allegations that had been made against Gee.

"I'm going to be making a brief statement but please no questions okay," Lawrence opened. After a short pause to allow his words to sink in, he began his remarks.

"After meeting with the Attorney General of this state just a short time ago I can now report to you that the Governor has declined to go forward with an investigation into the charges made against Garrick Andrews. As you all know it was these allegations which ultimately led to Mr. Andrews's death during the course of his attempted apprehension. Both I and the Andrews family are deeply disappointed by this decision but remain undeterred. We continue to maintain that these claims had no basis and as such we are fully committed to pursuing this matter further. What that will entail I am not at liberty to disclose at this time because I have to sit down with the family and decide what exactly the next step will be. Thank you very much."

In spite of the fact that he had requested that no questions be asked, Lawrence's experience in such matters let him know that was about to fall on deaf ears. So it was not at all surprising to him when the questions began firing in his direction as he made his way to his car with the band of reporters surrounding him. He ignored most of the inquiries with the exception of a couple.

"Mr. Montgomery is there still a chance that you will seek a federal probe?"

"That is certainly an option that remains on the table and we will discuss that possibility."

" Did the Attorney General give you any specific reason why the state decided not to pursue an inquiry?"

"Well during the course of the meeting today, it was made clear to me that the Governor and his Attorney General have complete faith in the Somerset County prosecutor's office. And they feel like if they saw cause to make an arrest than they are supportive of that decision. Needless to say we don't necessarily agree. Now if you'll all excuse me I am headed to meet with the Andrews family right now. Thank you."

While he may have been somewhat on edge in the days leading up to the decision made by the man who appointed him as Prosecutor, Clay was once again very comfortable in its aftermath. In fact while he seemed to be somewhat humbled and subdued for a while, it appears that he had now returned to the Machiavellian complex that he had displayed so often over the years. Sherri could also sense that there had been an uptick in cockiness and bravado on his part of late. While he didn't discuss work with her often, he seemed anxious to make it appear ludicrous that a call for an investigation had been made in the first place. But while she hardly knew much about the inner machinations of such a process, she figured it couldn't have hurt to have the man who hand-selected you be the one who made the eventual decision not to go forward with any probe. As for their relationship, it continued to be kind of stagnant, with limited substantive dialogue and even less in the way of passion or romance. The odd thing is that the situation was of far less concern to her. This is in spite of the fact that unlike before, there was no other man in her life filling the void. As she saw it, this was the time for her to take stock of her life; to cleanse herself mentally, emotionally and yes physically, of the things that led her to where she'd been until very recently.

A few days later on what was a Thursday morning, Roberto got off the elevator on the 6th floor of the Hyatt hotel in downtown San Antonio and walked slowly to the right. All the way to the end of the corridor where room 620 was located. He was somewhat apprehensive but didn't feel terribly nervous, though he did pause to take a deep breath before knocking. As he waited for someone to answer his knock he turned and looked down the hall and checked his watch one final time. It was 10:00 on the button so he was right on time. When he turned back towards the door a lump formed in his throat as he heard what sounded like whispers. Seconds later a voice sounded through the door. "Yes who is it?"

"This is Roberto."

"Roberto who?"

"Roberto Torres."

"Okay just stand in front of the door so I can make sure you look like the photo that you emailed to me. Yeah it's you alright," the person behind the door confirmed in moments. A short time later the door opened; inside of it stood a goateed, mid 40's African-American male. He stood about 6 feet tall with a sturdy build and a closely-cropped haircut. After Roberto slowly stepped inside the man quickly closed the door. He then proceeded to check Roberto for any weapons. Finding none, he then offered his hand. How you doing Roberto? I'm Chris Jarvis, nice to meet you."

"I'm good and nice to meet you too. I'm really just ready to get this over with to tell you the truth."

Just as the handshake concluded, Roberto looked to his right to see another man approaching him. He immediately recognized the clean-shaven, bespectacled man due to having seen his picture on the newspaper's website. Roberto had still been following his coverage of the Andrews story in numerous articles he'd written. It was definitely Ryan Drake.

"Ryan Drake; nice to finally meet you face to face Roberto," he said with a friendly but still businesslike smile.

"Same here Ryan," Roberto countered before the two of them also shook hands.

"Alright then, now that we have all of the formalities out of the way I guess we can proceed," Chris said matter of factly and without a hint of sarcasm. "I know you said you were ready to get this over with and so are we believe me."

"Yeah let's do it," Roberto concurred.

"Sure thing; now everything is all set up. Just relax and do it exactly the way we discussed okay. I'll be over there listening and recording the conversation from across the room. Just give me a moment to get the headset on and then once you pick up the phone and I can hear the dial tone, I'll give you a little thumbs up signal so that you'll know to proceed with the call. And just remember we had caller id removed from this line so he won't have any idea where you'll be calling from alright man."

"Sounds good, I'm ready to go," Roberto informed Chris.

In the meantime Ryan moved in to give some final words of encouragement himself.

"You're almost there man; this party is just about over and done with so let's rock and roll buddy." Roberto nodded towards him before Ryan moved to another part of the room as well.

Roberto took another deep breath and blew it out slowly before walking over toward the 2 beds. The beds were separated by a large nightstand on which the phone rested. He took a seat on one of the beds before reaching for the telephone. As he lifted the handset he looked towards Chris who gave him the go ahead signal. He dialed the number deliberately before moving the handset to his ear.

"Detective Celini speaking how may I help you?"

"Hey man this is Roberto Torres."

Rollie shifted forward in his desk chair before responding. "Oh you don't say; it sure is you. What a surprise; I thought you might be dead to tell you the truth."

"Thought I might or hoped I might?"

"Oh come on man, we're old business associates, you know I wouldn't wish something like that on you."

"Well you did a little more than wish it on Jimmy didn't you? So forgive me if I find that a little hard to believe."

"Hey you know how it is; sometimes business deals go a little sour. But hey at least you're okay right?"

"Yeah I am but I don't think I would be if you'd had your way the night you took out Jimmy."

"Hey once again; like I said sometimes things take a turn. It was nothing personal, just business. But I found out that you're a slippery little one Roberto. Where are you calling me from by the way?"

"Roberto chuckled into the phone. It was a slightly nervous laugh. "Nice try detective."

"Hey you can't blame a guy for trying right. If at first you don't succeed try, try again."

"Yeah and I'm sure that you're itching to do just that huh? Anyway, I just wanted to make a plea to you; ask you to stand down. You don't have to worry about me I swear."

"Stand down huh," Rollie said in a tone sprinkled with sarcasm.

"Come on man, I'm begging you, I can't live like this. Hiding in the shadows; looking over my shoulder constantly."

"You're begging me; you're begging me? Listen here you little piece of shit Mexican; you can beg all you want. But what you can't do is hide forever and eventually I'll catch up to you. And when I do you know what's going to happen? "You're gonna be put right out of your misery you understand me. Your pitiful life is going to be over just like your buddy's. And I hope I'm the one that gets to take care of you too you fucking wetback bastard."

"I swear man," Roberto shot back, his voice rising with emotion. "I'm telling you I won't say a word; not a damn thing. Why would I? From the time that we first met with you and that other detective Mike, all Jimmy and I did was what you wanted. There was never any reason not to trust us. You didn't even need to take Jimmy out like that."

"Shut up! Shut the fuck up mother fucker. You know how the game is played and you of all people should have known what you were getting yourself into. Just be thankful that you got away the night Jimmy got his okay; but this conversation is over as far as I'm concerned. Just like your life comprende. You like that? I threw in some Espanol just for you; so I hope I'm clear Lupe." CLICK!!!!

Roberto sat there holding the phone for a few seconds after Rollie had slammed it down in his ear. As he slowly lowered the handset back to the base he looked over to Chris who was removing his headphones. Chris then stood and hustled over towards him. "Great job Roberto. Oh yeah, we've got him. And believe me it's going to be a real pleasure to take down this racist bastard. But just one thing, who is this Mike you mentioned?"

At that point Ryan stepped in to answer the question. "Mike Marciniak; he's another detective that works with Detective Celini."

Roberto fell back on the bed, staring at the ceiling. His emotions had been all over the place: apprehension, nervousness, fear, excitement and now finally; a sense of relief.

CHAPTER TWENTY-FIVE

Ryan and Chris weren't due to fly out until 2:00 that same afternoon so they, along with Roberto decided to grab some early lunch down by the river. Once they were all seated, Roberto decided that he wanted to talk on a lighter level rather than to keep things centered on the case. After all he had done his part and the rest was up to the authorities.

"So you too went to college together huh?" he asked neither of them in particular.

"Yeah we were both in the criminal justice program at Rutgers University," Ryan offered. "That's funny right? I mean here Chris is with the FBI which is something that you might expect with that type of background, and me; I'm a reporter."

"Well that is sort of different; how did that come about?"

"Well I always thought I wanted to be a lawyer, but I took some journalism courses and I really started to take a liking to the idea of possibly being a journalist."

"But not just any journalist," Chris interjected. "Rather a blue-blooded pursuer of truth and justice for all," he joked.

"That's right, that's me all the way. Anyway, I decided to pursue my graduate degree in journalism and so here I am; an Investigative Reporter."

"And he's the very best at it too I might add. Certainly helps to keep me on the right side of the law that's for sure," Chris kidded again.

"Yeah you do seem to be very good at what you do. That's why the article that I first read in the newspaper stuck in my mind, and led to me calling you out of anybody I might have."

"Well that's where the criminal justice degree comes in handy. It allows me to think both like a reporter and someone performing criminal investigations," Ryan noted as Roberto nodded in agreement.

By 12:30 Ryan and Chris were ready to take off for the airport so they bid Roberto farewell.

"Okay now, when I get back and run today's events by my superiors I assure you we'll be looking to move fast on this once I get the green light. Should be early next week; hopefully Monday but Tuesday at the latest I'd say," Chris informed Roberto. "And you've got my number in case you need or want anything okay."

"Same here; if you should need to for any reason; don't hesitate, give me a call," Ryan added.

"Okay guys, but either way I'm sure we'll be speaking again soon," said Roberto.

Roberto dialed Carmen's phone the moment he was alone. "Hey sweetheart can you talk for a bit?"

"Umm yeah sure; I can for just a little while, what's up?"

"Okay this won't take long. I just called to tell you that we pulled it off."

"Oh that's great baby, I am so happy."

"Yeah I guess this could be all behind us before too much longer Carmen."

"So what about that other thing; did you get any feedback on that?"

"Yes I did. The dude from the FBI is pretty sure that at their recommendation any jail time for breaking in and planting the drugs could be suspended and I might wind up with nothing more than probation."

"Oh my God Roberto; I almost feel like celebrating."

"Well let's just wait and see what happens first. I mean they still have to be arrested, convicted and sentenced and all, so we ought to hold off on that for now."

"Yeah you're right we can wait for that," Carmen agreed.

"But I promise when this is really all over; we'll have a big celebration okay."

"Okay, but let me get back to work all right."

"Oh of course you go ahead, I'll see you later on."

"All right, I love you Roberto."

"I love you too Carmen; bye."

∞∞∞∞∞∞∞∞

A couple of weeks later, around midday on a Friday, Sherri was busy folding clothes midday Friday when her cell phone rang. "Hello," she answered.

"Hey it's me Miguel; can you talk for a second?"

"Yeah sure, I'm home but no one else is here. What's up?"

"Nothing much just calling to firm things up for lunch like you asked me to. Are we still a go for that?"

"Oh yes of course. Is your game down here coming up?"

"Yeah, the game down at Monmouth is this coming Monday night."

"Great; any type of place in particular you want to go to?" asked Sherri.

"Nope I'm not real picky so why don't you just choose a place."

"All right; well there's a place called the Bedminster Inn off of Route 287 in of all places Bedminster. That sound good to you?"

"That's fine with me."

"Great; twelve-thirty okay?"

"Yep that's fine, see you then."

"Hey I'm looking forward to it Miguel."

"Me too, it'll be good to see you."

"Well have a good weekend and good luck in your game Monday night. I hope you win so you'll be in a good mood on Tuesday."

Miguel laughed before responding. "Thanks for that, we'll probably need all the luck we can get. You have a good weekend too. Bye."

Monday morning arrived, and with it a healthy dose of damp, chilly air beneath a very sullen sky. It was the kind of morning that signaled you that one cup of coffee probably wouldn't be enough on this day. It was 9:30 and much of the staff and both uniformed and non-uniformed officers at the Somerset County Police complex were settling in for another long day ahead. Most were just drudging along, working their assignments quietly, faces buried in pc's and paperwork; with a few already burning up the phone lines.

The stark quiet made it not at all surprising that pretty much everybody within their sight had their attention immediately diverted when the group entered. Four men and a woman who were all similarly dressed; sporting gold colored shirts under black fleece sweaters with black slacks. One man led the way with the others flanking him. The group stepped briskly before stopping at the first set of cubicles they reached.

"Good morning, we're with the FBI, and we're looking for Detectives Roland Celini and Michael Marciniak," Chris, the one who had led the group in, said to no one in particular.

The persons in the cubes stared at each other; looks of surprise evident on all of their faces. Finally one of them spoke up, albeit haltingly.

"Detective Celini's office is this way," he said while pointing to his right. "Do you want me to go get him for you, or is there maybe something one of us can help you with?" he added, drawing out the last word for added emphasis.

"No that won't be necessary; we'll take it from here thank you," Chris assured him.

"Okay, well like I said his office is right that way, down that hallway. You can't miss it; his name is right on the door.

"Thanks again, and how about Detective Marciniak; where can we find him?"

"His is the 2nd cubicle from the front, in the last aisle before you get to the offices."

"I appreciate it," Chris said before turning back to the group of his fellow agents who were under his command. "Okay here we go," he said softly as the group huddled around him. "Jeff and I will go for Celini. The rest of you grab Detective Marciniak."

Ironically, Rollie was on the phone with Clay when he heard the knocking at his door.

"Hold on a second boss, let me see who this is. Come on in," he barked just after placing Clay on hold.

Rollie's mouth fell open and he straightened up in his chair the moment he saw who it was entering his office. They really had no need to identify themselves; he knew what they were. But in keeping with policy, they did so anyway.

"Roland Celini---FBI. We have a warrant for your arrest," said Chris as he approached his desk.

"What, you've gotta be kidding me; what's this all about," Rollie protested in vain.

"You're under arrest and charged with conspiracy, fabrication of evidence and murder."

"Huh, this has to be a joke right," Rollie interrupted once again, but as he did so the other agent with Chris walked around his desk and after producing a pair of handcuffs from his pocket ordered him to his feet before cuffing him behind his back.

At the same time the other 3 agents had converged on the cubicle at which they had been told Mike was located. Once they discovered he wasn't there they quickly turned to the person seated just behind that location.

"We're looking for Detective Marciniak; do you know where he is," the lone female in the group asked the stunned looking man.

"Yeah I just passed him on the way back to my desk a minute ago. He said he was going to grab a cup of coffee, but I know he stepped into the men's room right after he told me that."

"Come on," she said to the two men with her the moment the words had reached her ears.

Mike was checking his tie in the mirror when they rushed in, with Agent Janice Smart Allen leading the charge. It's hard to be certain which shocked him more, turning to see a woman barging into the men's room, or the words that flew from her mouth as soon as she set eyes on him.

"Michael Marciniak?"

"Yes," he responded as he stepped back slightly, his hands falling to his sides.

"FBI; you're under arrest, cuff him guys."

Rollie was being ushered onto the elevator when he turned as he heard the commotion stemming from Mike also being led in that direction.

"Mike! Stay strong Mike! They've got nothing; stay strong you hear me," he implored him sternly before the elevators doors closed completely.

"We've got nothing? You only wish that was the case," Chris teased once the elevator started its descent.

The reactions from those in the office who had seen or heard all of this play out were striking in their contrasts, with some standing in rapt attention while others sought to give the impression that they were somehow oblivious to what was taking place.

After holding on the line for a few minutes, Clay had finally hung up before dialing Rollie's direct line right back. Then, after receiving no answer on either his office or cell phone, he dialed the general number for the office seeking answers. The call was picked up by one of the two young ladies who worked there as administrative assistants.

"Hey this is Clay King, I was just speaking to Detective Celini but I lost him and now can't reach him back. Do you know where he might have ventured off to?"

"Well Sir," she began in a subdued tone, "I don't know quite how to tell you this, but Detectives Celini and Marciniak were just taken into custody by the FBI."

"They were what?" Clay screamed into the phone. When did this happen?"

"It was actually just within the last few minutes sir."

Clay pulled the phone away from his ear and softly placed it on his desk before burying his head in his hands.

"Sir, are you there?" he could hear the young lady saying faintly through the receiver. "Sir," she repeated a few times.

Finally, Clay straightened up and picked the handset up from his desk. "Yes I'm here," he said quietly.

"Are you okay Mr. King?"

"Yeah I'm fine. Thanks and you have a good day," he said softly before gently hanging up the phone.

Clay stood, walked over to one of his windows and stared out into the gray sky for several seconds before trudging back to his desk where he fell heavily into his chair. His mind hadn't stopped racing since he was rocked by the news on Rollie and Mike; with all sorts of scary thoughts flying through his head. But there was no need to go crazy over it, he convinced himself. After all what was done was done and it didn't necessarily mean that he was next to go down. Maybe they hadn't put everything together. That's what he was thinking. He just had to hope it was more than merely wishful thinking.

Rollie and Mike were immediately ushered into separate rooms at the FBI headquarters building up in Newark upon their arrival. Each of them had declined their right to speak to an attorney at that point and time. In the meantime Chris, agent Allen and their supervising agent sat down to work out a strategy for the interrogation of the two of them. The decision was made that they would be questioned at differing times with Rollie up first.

"Detective Celini," Chris called out as he opened the door for he and Janice to enter the room where they'd left Rollie seated at a desk. "Are you comfortable enough? Can we get you anything? I mean maybe a cigarette or something?"

"No thanks; I've been trying to quit and I'm thinking this might be a good time to just go ahead and do it cold turkey."

"Well that's good Detective," Chris countered as he and Janice sat down in the chairs in front of the desk. "It's good that you're so concerned about your future well-being. But of course where you're headed the future doesn't look so promising anyway now does it?"

"Please, like I said before you've got nothing," Rollie spat.

"Yeah I do remember that and like I told you then I'm telling you now; you only wish that was the case."

Rollie looked over at Janice who smiled broadly, while sweeping her shoulder length red hair away from her face.

"Nice smile angel face. You know I kind of believe you're flirting with me," he said as he puckered up his lips before making kissing gestures in her direction.

"Hardly that I assure you," she answered. You see, I don't find too much appealing about a man who figures to spend much of the rest of his life behind bars. But you know there's always a chance for you to see the light of day a little sooner."

"What are you talking about?" Rollie questioned.

"You see we've been talking and we don't see any clear motive as to why Garrick Andrews would be the target of a frame-up. No priors, led what appears to be a clean life; we just don't get it, so why don't you help us out here Detective."

"Frame-up? I don't know what the hell you're talking about honey, but I do enjoy watching those sweet lips of yours move. So feel free to continue, even though it's not gonna get you anywhere. But it is making me have impure thoughts."

"LOOK WE'RE NOT PLAYING GAMES WITH YOU HERE. WHY DID YOU DO IT?" Chris snapped.

"Hey take it easy brother man," Rollie replied sarcastically. "Why are you jumping in like captain save-a-hoe? You're not, I mean, nah not you two. Honey here looks better and smarter than to travel down the dark path to destruction."

"Listen here," Janice began before Chris cut her off.

"No wait a minute agent Allen allow me. "You know Detective I've been doing this for a while now and I've always managed to remain professional about my job and not allow personal feelings to factor into it. But for the record I happen to think you're a piece of shit and I just can't wait until the day you're behind bars."

"Oh you don't say, well guess what, you might think I'm nothing but a piece of shit, but you really are more like shit aren't you? I mean you're the color of it, you look and you even smell like it, because let's face it, at the end of the day you're still nothing but a low down filthy…"

Before he could finish his sentence Chris leapt to his feet, snatching him by the collar.

"Okay you ignorant mother fucker, I've had about enough of you and I'm about two seconds off your sorry ass; you hear me?"

"Chris no; come on man; don't let him get to you. That's what he wants; the guy's not worth it," Janice said in an attempt to calm his fury.

"You know what, you're right. Let's get out of here; we're wasting our time with this guy."

Even as the two of them turned to depart the room, Rollie threw more darts in their direction. "That's right and next time don't even bother me with this shit because you're getting nothing from me. Not a goddamn thing you hear me. So save your breath, and my time."

Janice grabbed Chris' arm to stop him right outside the door. "So what do you think? I mean the guy is a racist prick, that much is clear. But do you think that in itself would drive him to set Garrick Andrews up for a fall? Because that still begs the question of why him in particular?"

"Yea I don't know," Chris admitted. It's still hard to figure when there's no apparent history between them. Not even knowledge of them having ever met or even crossed paths before this."

"I really think we ought to concentrate our efforts on Detective Marciniak right now," Janice stated.

"Yeah I agree with you; let's do that. But first what do you say we grab some coffee? This could be a long day."

Chris and Janice found Mike to be almost affable in comparison to dealing with Rollie. Unfortunately they also found out that he was no more cooperative in telling them what they really wanted to know. They worked him for a couple of hours before deciding to break for lunch, and also to re-think their strategy.

"I don't know, this guy just seems fiercely loyal to somebody. Now whether it's' to Celini or to someone else is the question," Janice said while they waited on line to be served in the cafeteria.

"Yeah but you know what," Chris began, "he might just be loyal to a fault and to his own detriment. And perhaps that loyalty might just be misplaced."

"You're going somewhere with this aren't you? I can almost see the wheels churning inside of your head."

"I sure am Janice, and I'll get into it more once we sit down someplace."

"So, what are you thinking Chris?" Janice questioned the moment they were seated at a table.

"Okay, now we know that Detective Celini is a real asshole and a miserable sonofabitch, so it's kind of hard to see him having a wife, a family or anything like that; but what do we know about Marciniak?"

"Well nothing about his personal life really. But what you're saying is that if he does have a family we might be able to use that to break him."

"Exactly," Chris said before taking another bite of his turkey sandwich. "Except I'm not sure I would really call it using them. But rather seeing if that loyal streak he has also extends to his family. Because we could just offer him a way to lessen the amount of time he'd spend away from them and behind bars, you know what I'm saying."

"Yeah I do, and you know what; I like the idea. I mean when we were at his desk this morning I didn't notice if there were any family pictures or anything but…"

"It wouldn't be hard to find out," Chris finished the thought for her.

"I'll get on it as soon as I finish my salad," said Janice. "Make a call back down to his headquarters to see what I can find out."

"Okay that sounds good, but just one thing Janice."

"What's that?"

"It may sound strange, but let me say this; if it turns out that he does have a family you might want to try to find out if he has any photos of them at his desk; and if so try to get a hold of one and bring it back here."

"Really, you think that would make a difference in some way?"

"Trust me, as someone who's seen it at work; it certainly does. Having to sit there and look at their family, even if it's just in a photo, can have a powerful effect. And of course as a father myself I can understand."

"Oh yeah I see what you're saying; I'll make the call and if need be drive back down there and take care of it myself." Janice promised.

"Okay thanks; I'm going to work on a couple of things also, so what do you say we meet back here around 4:00," Chris suggested.

"Sounds good; see you then," Janice said before taking another forkful of her grilled chicken salad.

A short time before 4:00 Chris re-entered the room where Rollie was being held.

"What the hell do you want now? I hope you're not back here for some more of your bullshit," Rollie said when he saw him.

"Bullshit? No not at all; but I am here to tell you again that things just aren't looking very good for you pal."

"Listen I keep telling you, you've got nothing and we're certainly not any sort of pals Leroy."

"Really; well I guess I didn't bother to tell you about the nice time we had talking to your old friend Roberto Torres."

"Roberto Torres," Rollie repeated before breaking out into a big belly laugh. That's who I'm supposed to be worried about? Roberto Torres is nothing but a two-bit street hustler, and I'm supposed to be concerned that his word is what's going to burn me? Please stop it; although you do amuse me."

"Oh no see that's where you're wrong; maybe you need not worry about Roberto's words sending you to prison. But you do have to worry about your own."

"Oh yeah, what the hell is that supposed to mean?"

"Let's see if this amuses you okay," Chris said with a straight face. He then produced a small tape recorder, held it in his hand and pressed play. He had it cued up right at the point at which he wanted it to play.

"Come on man, I'm begging you, I can't live like this. Hiding in the shadows; looking over my shoulder constantly."

"You're begging me; you're begging me? Listen here you little piece of shit Mexican; you can beg all you want. But what you can't do is hide forever and eventually I'll catch up to you. And when I do you know what's going to happen? "You're gonna be put right out of your misery you understand me. Your pitiful life is going to be over just like your buddy's. And I hope I'm the one that gets to take care of you too. You fucking wetback bastard."

Rollie's jaw dropped as he listened to the recording; hearing his own voice saying the words that would come back to haunt him. His face turned an ashen shade of gray as he looked at Chris whose face had broken into a wicked grin.

"You heard enough? Because there's more there if you wanna hear it," he said proudly after he had stopped the recording.

Rollie placed his hands on his knees and leaned forward. With his head down he held that position quietly for a few seconds before finally speaking; looking up at Chris as he did so.

"I need to speak to my lawyer."

"Yeah I think you do," a still smiling Chris said before departing.

It was actually close to 4:30 by the time Janice returned from Somerville. After briefly talking, she and Chris were ready to take another shot at Mike. They entered the same room where they had grilled him previously, this time clearly hoping for different results.

"Hey, I thought we were done with the questions," he said after Chris and Janice entered.

"Oh no, we're only just beginning. Come on detective; have you been holed up that long today that you've forgotten how this works?" Chris asked him before he and Janice again took seats across from him.

"No I haven't forgotten at all; it's just that it's been such a long day I was hoping as much as anything," Mike admitted.

"Well," interjected Janice, "we can get this over and done with before too much longer; but that all depends on you of course."

"Hey I told you two before; I don't know anything about any pre-conceived plan to set up Garrick Andrews."

"Yeah we know what you told us detective, but let's just say that we're not quite convinced you've been forthcoming with us," Chris told him. "But as you see now we're not ones to give up without a long fight; so let's just say that we're here for round 13 shall we," he added before turning to his right. "Janice," he said as if he was turning the floor over to her.

Janice slowly reached into a bag and pulled something out before pointing it towards Mike. It was a picture of a very attractive raven-haired woman flanked by two adorable girls. The girls appeared to be around the ages 8 and 6 at first glance.

"Hey, where did you get that?" Mike asked sternly.

"We got it from your cubicle at work where else," Janice told him. "You know you really do have a lovely family Detective Marciniak."

"That's private property; you can't just grab someone's personal things whenever you want to."

"Relax, it's a picture detective. Hardly the type of thing that's going to get a case tossed out of court," Chris countered. "Besides that's not the real issue here."

"That's my family there man; it damn sure is a real issue as far as I'm concerned. Why the hell are you trying to bring them into this?"

"Why Detective Marciniak?" Janice answered. "Well, you seem like the real family type to us. That's the main reason. Let me ask you something; how old are your girls about eight and six I'd guess?"

"Yeah the youngest is six but my oldest is seven. She turns eight on Christmas day."

"Oh that is precious and they are just the most beautiful girls. You must be so proud."

"Yes I certainly am," Mike assured her.

"That's great. Well let me ask you something else detective. And please, hear me out before you answer. How much of their lives are you willing to miss out on in order to cover up somebody's mess? I mean let's see here; you're looking at felony conspiracy and probably falsifying charges and evidence tampering on top of that. I mean because let's face it, the drugs that were planted in Garrick Andrews townhouse had to come from someplace right? So once you add it all up, you're facing a double digit sentence easily I'd say. 10-15 years probably. So we're talking no adolescent years, no sweet sixteen parties and no prom or graduation for at least one and possibly both girls. What a shame that would be. So let me ask you again detective, how much of their lives are you willing to miss; just in order to protect somebody else?"

With each word that Janice spoke Mike's agony deepened. By the time she was done, his head was buried down on the desk. When he finally raised it up he looked at them with eyes that were red and moistened with tears. He used his right hand to attempt to cover them before running it down his face to his chin. He found himself unable to look at Chris and Janice any longer. He didn't want them to see his agony. So he stood and turned his back to them before walking until his feet met the wall. With both hands at the side of his head he rested it against the wall.

"You know," Chris began, "I have a daughter myself. She's much older than your two though. She's twenty and a junior in college. She goes to Wellesley up in Massachusetts. And I've got to tell you I don't know where the years went. It seems like just yesterday when I was buying her dolls and teaching her how to ride a bike. And the next thing I know she's asking me advice about boys and I'm shelling out cash for a gown for the prom. And I don't even want to get into the cost of college, but hey, that's just part of the deal. But I must say all of those memories; they're just priceless. I wouldn't trade them for the world," he concluded before a long pause. Come on detective, we know there's a bigger fish here someplace. Talk to us; we can work something out for you."

Mike slowly turned around. "You can work something out huh; something like what?"

"Well in exchange for your cooperation, maybe we could probably get it knocked down to just a simple misdemeanor charge. Something with no more than perhaps 2-3 years max attached to it," Chris promised.

"Well could I get that in writing?"

"You sure can but not today. What you would have today is my word on it and on that you'd just have to trust me. As soon as you obtained an attorney we'd be able to work it out legally."

"Come on detective, think about what were offering you here," Janice added before standing and handing Mike the photo of his family.

Mike looked at it for a short amount of time before placing it on the desk and taking a seat. He passed his glance back and forth between Chris and Janice, a serious expression on his face. "Okay you've got it; let's do this."

As the two agents both produced small writing pads in preparation for possibly jotting down any notes, Mike drew in a deep breath, exhaled and began to tell his story.

∞∞∞∞∞∞∞∞∞∞∞

Clay had somehow gotten through a day on which his thoughts and focus were elsewhere more than they were on the business of running his office. And as much as he didn't want to dwell on it, he couldn't chase away the thoughts of Rollie and Mike and what were the possible ramifications of them now being in FBI custody. But he also realized that even with his fancy law degree and powerful position, for once he was unable to affect the outcome. All he could do was lean on the hope that neither of them would be broken. Not knowing what was happening had started to gnaw away at him; so he sought an escape. He decided that he would head home and spend some time with his children.

"I was approached by Rollie back in late June," Mike started out. He told me he had this lifelong friend with a possible problem on his hands. Asked if I might be able to help him out. Now he wouldn't divulge too much at that point. He said he'd rather the three of us have a little sit down and they would fill me in then if I was willing to assist them. So we did that within the next couple of days. And that's when they told me just what the issue was. I found out that this friend has a wife whom he had some concerns about."

"What sort of concerns," asked Chris once Mike hesitated.

"He umm, had some suspicions that his wife might be seeing someone else. So they told me that was where I came in. That they wanted someone to tail her for a while; just to see if there was anything there. And that someone was me. For the first four or so days that I followed her there was nothing out of the ordinary; but then that all changed in a heartbeat. It was almost like she had been suspicious and had laid low for a while. But she couldn't pull that one off for very long apparently because soon enough I found out that she was indeed going by some guy's place regularly. Like a couple of times a week, and she'd stay there for several hours."

"And you're sure she was seeing a man on these occasions?" Janice asked at that point.

"Oh I'm damn sure. I caught a glimpse of him seeing her out the door one day. I took some pictures on numerous occasions too. It was him; she was seeing Garrick Andrews."

"Okay then; go ahead detective," Janice said.

"So when I took this information to them; meaning Rollie and this friend of his; they were both livid. I mean both of them were as steamed as you can be; especially after I showed them the photographs. I actually think Rollie might have been angrier than his friend was."

"Well I can certainly see that being the case after what I've seen of him just today, Chris jumped in. "Anyway, I'm sorry detective; continue on."

"I mean don't get me wrong, the friend was angry as hell too, but I could also tell that he was just very hurt over the discovery. I mean how could you not be when you find out that your wife is cheating on you. So, that was when the two of them agreed that Andrews had to pay for what he was doing to his wife."

"Now detective, excuse me for one moment," Chris interrupted. "As obvious as it appears to be on the surface, there was no visible proof the wife was getting it on with Andrews right?"

"Aw come on man," Mike said before turning to Janice. "Forgive me for one second he said to her before looking back in Chris' direction. "Well no I never saw him actually fucking her but seriously man; I mean there's no reason to think they might have been playing bridge for 3-4 hours at a time."

"Oh believe me, I agree wholeheartedly, but I'm just thinking about firmly establishing a motive," Chris explained.

"Oh trust me," said Mike. "At that point a motive was very firmly established, because I can assure you that they were both quite incredulous that not only was she cheating, but that it was with a Black guy. There was nothing but vengeance on their minds you can believe that." And that was what led to them putting their heads together to hatch the plan to take Garrick Andrews down on the trumped up drug charge. So I doubt I need to say much more at this point; you two know the rest obviously. If not I don't think either Rollie or I would be here right now."

"Yeah you're right, except one more thing. We're still gonna need a name;" Chris reminded him. "Who was this friend Mike?"

Mike hesitated, looking up at the ceiling and then back in the direction of Chris and Janice.

"Come on detective, you've come this far. Just give us what we need," Janice implored him.

Rather than speaking, Mike stared down at the floor; his head resting in his hands. His anguish was clear to see, so they allowed him some time. After about thirty seconds he closed his eyes tightly; just as he opened his mouth to speak.

"I'm doing this for my family."

"Yes of course; we understand that, and like we said that's a great reason," Chris said.

Mike lifted his head and made eye contact with the two of them. And then with his eyes wide open, spoke the words they'd been waiting to hear. "It's Clay King; the Somerset County Prosecutor."

As soon as he got the words out Mike stood and turned his back to them. Chris and Janice looked at each other before slowly standing themselves and heading for the door. But not before having some parting words for Mike.

"You did the right thing detective," Chris said.

"Yes you certainly did; both for yourself and your family," added Janice.

"So you were right all along," Janice said to Chris once they were outside the room. "There was a much bigger fish out there for us to catch and guess what, we've got him buddy."

"Oh yeah thanks to a big assist from both Roberto and Mike, we've got him hook, line and sinker. Now let's go talk to the boss about getting an arrest warrant for Mr. King."

"Come on kids its eight-thirty, time to start getting ready for bed," Sherri announced.

"But we're having such a good time; can't they stay up just a little while longer," asked Clay.

"No they can't; I'm sorry but it's a school night. Get up everybody, let's go."

"Hey guys, I tried; but we had a blast while it lasted though didn't we?"

"Yeah daddy; can we play again tomorrow," Zach the youngest of the three asked.

"Sure we can buddy, as soon as I get home from work and get settled in a bit we can do it all over again okay."

"I love you daddy," Zach said before throwing his arms around his shoulders.

"I love you too sport. Have a good night and sleep tight. Don't let the bedbugs bite."

Zach giggled before running off, and in his place came Abby and Tyler who also embraced Clay before telling him good night and heading to their respective rooms. Clay looked at Sherri sternly before she turned and followed the children. Once she was gone from his sight he climbed off of the floor and slowly walked into the kitchen, where he poured himself a glass of scotch. Leaning against the counter, he took a small sip before then downing the rest in one quick gulp. He stared at the wall briefly, exhaled deeply and poured himself another.

CHAPTER TWENTY SIX

It was a little after 9:00 by the time Chris and Janice finally headed home but, their time spent working late had hardly been in vain. The plea agreement for Mike had been drawn up for his attorney to review, and everything was in place for the arrest and detainment of Somerset County Prosecutor Clay King. He would be charged with conspiracy, abuse of office and falsifying records, a litany of serious charges that came with the potential for a rather lengthy prison term. This particular FBI branch had a policy that when possible an attempt should be made to avoid taking persons into custody in full view of their families; in particular any young children. That stipulation of course did not apply to individuals to be charged with violent crimes. But with them finding out that the Kings had three small children it most certainly did apply in this case. So as eager as the two of them were to grab him, this big fish would have to be reeled in the following morning.

Chris and Janice were going over their timeline as they headed to the parking garage and their cars.

"Well I'll be here nice and early as usual, but I figure we can head down there about 9:15-9:30," Chris suggested. "How does that work for you Ms. night owl?"

"It sounds good to me, I'll be ready to roll," Janice assured him.

"I guess we'll take Barry Parks along with us. I know he'll be here and chomping at the bit by that time."

"Great, see you in the morning; bright and early. Well at least early," Janice kidded.

"Okay good night," Chris said with a grin.

"Good night Chris."

The next morning was as crisp and chilly as you would expect at that time of the year but the sky was bathed in brilliant sunshine. Sherri was surprised to find Clay still at home when she returned from dropping Zach off at school. He usually left home by 8:45 at the latest and with her having stopped to pick up an item from GNC on the way home it was about 9:15 by the time she pulled back into the driveway.

"You're running a bit behind this morning aren't you," she remarked when she saw him still getting dressed when she came inside.

"Well apparently so," he replied flatly. "I didn't sleep all that well, so I can't really get going this morning."

"Why couldn't you sleep; got a lot on your mind?"

"I guess you could say that. Maybe I'll try a second cup of coffee because that first one didn't help much."

"I've come to swear by my 5 hour energy shots. I drink one before every trip to the gym and it works wonders for me. Maybe you should try it."

"Well good for you but I'll just stick to my black coffee. Anyway I'm outta here."

"What about your second cup? I can pour it for you."

"What about it? I didn't say I would have it here did I? I'll just wait until I get to the office if that's okay with you. I mean I'm already running much later than usual as you pointed out."

"Okay never mind; sorry I asked. Have a good day and I will see you later."

Clay picked up his briefcase and headed downstairs before walking out without saying another word.

"Okay goodbye to you too; have a nice day," Sherri said aloud after he had left. But she wasn't going to let his clearly dour mood spoil her own upbeat spirits. Her itinerary was all set. She was about to snuggle up on the sofa to watch the Rachel Ray show, then off to the gym before returning home to get showered and dressed for lunch with Miguel.

Clay stepped off the elevator about 9:40 stopping first at Jeri's desk to check for any messages.

"Good morning," he said dryly as he neared her desk.

"Good morning Clay," she responded with far more enthusiasm. "All quiet so far; no calls."

"Great, hopefully it stays that way," Clay said seriously before slowly walking towards his nearby office. Stepping inside, he closed the door behind him, placed his briefcase in one of his guest chairs and stepped around his desk before sitting heavily in his chair. After powering on his computer and checking some emails he stood up and headed for his door once again.

"I'll be back, I'm just going to grab a cup of coffee," he told Jeri before turning in the opposite direction and walking towards the closest break room. He had taken only a few steps before she called out his name leading him to stop in his tracks and face her.

"I just wanted to remind you that you have the 10:00 conference call with those four Chiefs of Police."

"Yeah how could I forget? But I'll be back well before then don't worry."

"Okay," Jeri replied simply as Clay continued on to the break room.

Clay spent the next 5 or so minutes in a conversation with one of his assistant prosecutors after they encountered each other in the corridor before he entered the break room. Once the conversation ended he finally made his cup of coffee before heading back to his office, detouring to Jeri's desk before going back inside.

"Hey did I miss anything?"

"Well Judge Ramsay called and I put him through to your voicemail, but other than that not a thing. And you still have almost fifteen minutes before your conference call is scheduled to begin."

"Well in that case I'd better hurry up and get some caffeine into my bloodstream," he said before taking a sip of the steaming hot beverage. "I'll be inside, just buzz me when the call is ready."

"Okay will do."

He entered his office and again closed the door behind him, placed the coffee down on his desk and again started to walk around it to take a seat. But what he saw as he peered outside of the large window behind his desk stopped him dead in his tracks. There was no mistaking it; he had seen enough of those plain dark-colored sedans to recognize it. And there was no doubt about the attire worn by the man and woman who stepped outside the car when it came to a halt. They stood there briefly before another identical car pulled up beside them, with a lone, identically dressed male climbing out of that one. As he watched them standing there, chatting and then gesturing towards the building, Clay's pulse began to race. He could feel beads of perspiration seeping onto his forehead. He knew he had to think quickly because the man and woman from the first car to arrive were now walking towards the building, leaving the other individual standing alongside his car.

Clay watched, frozen for a moment before he was able to react. Suddenly snapping to attention, he quietly retrieved his keys from his top desk drawer and grabbed his briefcase before slowly tiptoeing towards the door. He opened it just enough to step outside before releasing it to let it quietly close behind him. He looked to his left, and seeing no one quickly turned and headed to the right. Luckily for him the corridor was empty so no one saw him as he opened the door to the staircase about 30 feet away. Dashing down to the second floor, he exited there before hurrying down the long hallway leading away from the elevators. Once he reached the stairwell on that far end of the building he hustled inside and ran down to the first floor as quickly as he could. Slowly stepping outside into the 1st floor corridor he peered down the long hallway in the direction of the lobby. With no one in sight he then turned and walked briskly out of the building through the nearby exit.

Moments later Chris and Janice stepped out of the elevator on the third floor and walked in the direction of Jeri's desk. They didn't get her attention right away, but once they got close enough for her to sense their presence, she looked up from her game of solitaire. Chris, who was already flashing his badge, spoke up well before reaching her desk.

"FBI," he barked as Jeri looked at him and then to Janice who was also flashing her identification.

"Good morning, how can I help you," Jeri asked a bit anxiously.

"Clay King; is he here right now?" a straight-faced Chris asked.

Jeri's eyes stretched wide and she shifted in her chair before answering.

"Yes, he's in his office."

"And where's that," Chris inquired.

"Right this way; first door on the right," Jeri answered while pointing in that direction. "But I should call in and announce you before you go in there."

"Sorry but this is not that kind of visit," Janice chimed in. "But don't worry we'll announce ourselves as soon as we get in there."

"Okay, but I just don't want him to think that I didn't do my job that's all."

"Miss, I wouldn't worry about that; besides, you did do your job. Now it's time for us to do ours. Thanks for your help," Chris told her before turning to Janice. "You ready?"

"Very," she answered.

"Alright let's do this," Chris said before stepping away from the desk and towards Clay's office with Janice right behind him.

He knocked sharply on the door to the office before placing his ear to the door to listen for a response. Hearing nothing, he then knocked again, this time even louder; again with no response. He then signaled Janice with a nod of his head before placing his right hand on his service revolver and slowly pushing the door open before the two of them rushed inside.

"Shit, he's not here," Chris called out. He rushed over to the window and looked outside where he saw the 2 cars they had arrived in parked. "He must have seen us coming in from this window and taken off. Come on let's go."

As she followed Chris out of the office, Janice noticed the cup of still steaming coffee on the desk.

Seconds later Chris was standing over Jeri's desk grilling her with questions with Janice just beside him.

"Now Ms. Barnsworth," he began after peering at the nameplate resting on her desk, "I can tell you now that this is official business that bought us here this morning. We came to take your boss into custody, so I don't think I need to tell you of the trouble you could get yourself into by not telling us the truth here. Now again, are you trying to tell us that you didn't see him come past you?"

"No I didn't I swear; I'm telling you he was scheduled for a conference call at 10:00 and he told me he'd be in his office waiting for it. And I haven't seen or heard from him since. That was just a few minutes before you two came in."

In the meantime Janice had stepped back about 20 feet and was making a call.

"Barry, Mr. King seems to have slipped out before we managed to get up here to his office; any signs of him down there?"

"He did what!" Barry replied incredulously.

"It looks like he saw us pull up from a window in his office, so he took off."

"Well I've been right by the door and no one has come past me or gotten off of the elevator."

Meanwhile back at the desk, Chris was still firing questions at Jeri. "Where are the staircases in the building located?"

"There's one about 30 or so feet down the hall past Mr. King's office and another at the very far end of the building in the opposite direction. But I would have seen him if he had headed that way."

Almost as soon as the last word had fallen from her lips Chris took off running to the close by stairwell. He entered and looked around for any signs of something that might help them, before stepping back inside the corridor calling for Janice.

"Listen I've got to go, but keep your eyes and ears peeled, and get back to me if you see or hear anything suspicious at all," she told Barry while hurrying in Clay's direction. "And just in case, stop any male you see down there and make them show some identification." she added.

"Okay will do."

"That was Barry," Janice informed Chris as she moved towards him. "No signs of him in the lobby area."

"Well I think I know how he left, let's head down and see what these stairs lead to."

The two of them exited on the first floor and jogged down the long corridor leading to the South exit of the building, passing the second stairwell on the way.

"He probably came the same way that we just did and slipped out of this door," Chris suggested once they were standing outside.

"Yeah assuming he's left the building it had to have been through this door because Barry's been all over that main entry. But I'll tell you what, whichever way he came it wasn't very long ago. There was a cup of scalding hot coffee on his desk."

"Dammit why didn't we cover this way in and out too," Chris lamented.

"Hey I've got an idea, let's go check something out," said Janice.

Minutes later they had their answer. Security had confirmed that Clay's car had indeed gone through the electronic gate. A mere seven minutes before in fact. A subsequent check of security camera footage also confirmed his exit point out of the building.

"Okay let's get out of here and figure out what our next move is," Chris said wistfully.

"Hey it's not our fault Chris; this was just to be a routine arrest so we didn't feel a need to worry about securing the grounds or anything like that. And we also didn't know all of the ins and outs of the building."

"Yeah I know, but I just hate that he slipped past us just the same. Who knows, the sonofabitch might be somewhere laughing; feeling like he outfoxed us."

"That may be the case right now; but he certainly won't be smiling when we nail him will he? And you know that we will Chris."

The temperature was hovering around 45 degrees, yet Clay was sweating profusely as he raced into the house. For all he knew the FBI might have notified the local police by now and either or both of them could be showing up at any time to take him in. So he scurried about quickly, gathering up some things and tossing them into a duffle bag before rushing back out to his car, taking a moment to look up and down the block before climbing inside and speeding away. He knew he had taken a huge chance in coming there, but he had managed to get away with it. Now he needed some time to think; to ponder what his next move would be. After driving for a while with no specific destination, he decided to check into a hotel someplace. He wanted to take some time to relax his mind a bit if possible. But he soon found out that wasn't possible.

He wondered if it was even safe and secure to be seated in that room at the Holiday Inn express in Morristown. What if the television networks have been running the story and flashing his face all over the screen? He ultimately concluded that this wasn't quite that big for him to be overly worried about that. He also knew from his own experiences from his time in office that the authorities are not likely to feed the media a story such as his, unless there was an actual arrest to report. They were not known to take situations public which might show themselves in a potentially embarrassing light. They would eagerly report on the arrest or indictment of a public figure; but certainly not so on one that had slipped from their grasp. Every attempt would be made to rectify things before that would happen. But the irony of it all was not at all lost on him. He, the top law enforcement official in Somerset County, had gone on the lam and was now considered just another fugitive from justice. He took a big swig from the bottle of scotch he held in his hand. It was one of the things he had taken from the house in the short amount of time he'd been inside. And at this moment it seemed to him like the one thing he needed the most.

Chris had just spent some time arguing with his boss over the need to put out an APB on Clay. He favored it as he considered Clay a flight risk, but Gerald McClane, his supervising agent was opposed, feeling it wasn't necessary. And it was Gerald who of course had the final say. So in the end, though he was disappointed, Chris accepted that it would just take some good old-fashioned police type legwork to capture him. And whatever it might take he was ready to do, because Clay King was their big fish, and he wasn't about to let him slip off the hook.

∞∞∞∞∞∞∞∞∞

Sherri returned from the gym and   pampering herself with a manicure and pedicure by about 11:45. It was time for her to get showered and dressed for lunch. Thirty minutes later she was ready; dressed in a beige sweater and a pair of jeans with her favorite pair of black boots. She took a final look at herself in the floor length mirror in the master bedroom and content with her appearance, put on her jacket, grabbed her keys and purse and walked out of the house. Not two minutes after she had departed, the police pulled up at the house; their second time coming by already that day in hopes of talking to her, just in the event of Clay having reached out to her.

With every bit of scotch he downed, Clay's emotions seemed to swing more and more on the pendulum. While his current plight had been giving him occasional feelings of gloom it was when he thought of Sherri that his mind flew all over the place. While reeling from the love he knew he still had for her, and lamenting the demise of what they once had together, he was gripped with strong feelings of contempt for her as well.

Sherri arrived at the restaurant first, and explained to the hostess that she would be waiting for her lunch companion to arrive. She then took a seat in the waiting area just inside the entrance. Her wait would not be a long one though as Miguel stepped through the door just five minutes later, a big smile spreading across his face once he spotted her sitting there.

"Hey, sorry I'm late, I think the directions to this place confused my GPS," he joked.

"Oh that's okay," Sherri said while rising up from her seat. "It's only been five minutes."

"Wow so you were counting the minutes huh?"

"Sure you know we girls are all about time," she kidded.

"So how are you," he asked Sherri as they embraced, her head barely passing his midsection.

"I'm good thanks," what about you?"

"Oh I can't complain," Miguel answered.

"My God I'd forgotten how tall you are. My head comes up to like your navel."

"Yes I'm still tall, he grinned."

"Come on smarty pants, our table is ready."

The conversation between the two of them flowed freely from the moment they sat down. Sherri was able to openly share some of the most intimate details of the trials she'd gone through recently. She did so easily due to her having no fear of Miguel judging her. He only did as he always had; that is lent a sympathetic ear and words of wisdom.

"You know it's just amazing that you've always been so understanding and supportive of me no matter what. I can't tell you enough how much that means," Sherri assured him.

"Well that's because like I mentioned in the past, I've been through my own struggles. I ruined what was a good relationship with a great lady because I couldn't defeat my own demons, so I know what you're dealing with and I truly sympathize with it."

The conversation continued on unabated through a couple of interruptions, the first being when they paused to order and of course another as their meals arrived. And about forty-five minutes in would come the third.

Sherri retrieved her cell phone from her purse and looked at the display. Oh it's my husband let me grab this okay?"

"Of course go ahead," Miguel replied before she got up and walked towards the exit of the restaurant.

"Hey Clay, what's up?" she said in answering the call.

"I just called the house and didn't get any answer so I was just wondering where you were."

"Okay; well I'm just having lunch with a friend. Why what's going on?"

"Nothing; I didn't really want anything."

"So that's all you really wanted was to know where I was?"

"Well yeah, I mean no; I mean what are you making for dinner?"

"I don't know yet, maybe a meatloaf or something; I'll figure it out when I get home. But are you okay? You sound a little weird."

"Where are you having lunch?"

"Okay Clay, this is not about to turn into a game of twenty questions is it; because my friend is waiting for me at the table."

"No it's not don't worry; that's the last question."

"We're eating at the Bedminster Inn and my lunch is just sitting at the table."

"Alright I'm sorry, but just one more thing."

"Yes what's that?"

"Do you still love me Sherri?"

"Yes Clay I do. But I have to go now okay."

"Yeah go ahead, I'll see you later; bye."

Sherri returned the goodbye before hanging up the phone and heading back to the table.

"I'm sorry Miguel. And the kicker is he didn't want a thing; nothing at all. Just felt like being a pain I guess."

"Maybe it was just his way of checking up on you," said Miguel."

"You know it's funny that you should say that because it did almost seem that way, but whatever. I'm having lunch. You would think he might have something better to do at work. But anyway, you were saying something about your demons," Sherri added before digging back into her Cobb Salad.

"Oh I was just talking about how I myself ruined a good relationship once because I couldn't overcome some inner things. But I'm a believer in learning from your past and making the most of second chances."

"And are you doing that now?"

"Yes I am. In fact I've been seeing someone who might just have the makings if you know what I mean."

"Oh really," Sherri replied excitedly. "You sneak; you didn't say anything. While we were talking about me and all of my drama, you actually have some good news. Come on tell me about it."

"Well I don't wait to go into a long drawn out thing, but okay."

∞∞∞∞∞∞∞∞∞∞∞∞∞

Clay sat staring out of his car window for several moments after the call with Sherri had ended, seemingly in a trance. When he finally snapped out of it he again reached for his phone.

"Hey Nina, it's me Clay; are you busy?"

"Nope not really, what's up?"

"Well I really wanted to just ask you for a favor."

"Sure what's that brother-in-law?"

"I was wondering if you could pick the kids up from school for us today."

"Yeah of course I can, but is everything okay?"

"Oh yeah everything is fine. Sherri's just feeling under the weather, so that's why I called. I figured that she could be at home getting some rest until I get there with the kids."

"Okay well, like I said it's not a problem at all. You want me to just bring them by the house later for you?"

"No that's okay you can just keep them there until I pick them up when I leave the office today."

"All right, I'll just see you later then."

"Okay thanks Nina. Oh one more thing; have you guys talked to mom lately?"

"Yes we talked to her on Sunday she's doing fine."

"Alright that's great," Clay said softly.

"And what about you; are you okay? You sound a little funny. Like you might be preoccupied or down about something."

"Yeah I'm fine; but listen let me go. I love you guys and thanks again."

"We love you too Clay, bye."

Nina stared into the receiver briefly before hanging it up. She could sense there was something bothering Clay. She just couldn't put her finger on what it might have been."

At the same time, back at the restaurant, Miguel was just about to tell Sherri about the new lady in his life.

"That's fine because I wouldn't want you to go into a long, drawn-out thing anyway. After all I have to pick up my son from school before nightfall, "Sherri chuckled. "And cook dinner and help with homework tidy up the kitchen and so on."

"Okay, okay I get the point. Anyway her name is Naveah and..."

"Oh that's a very pretty name," Sherri interjected.

"Yes it is and she's a very pretty lady but, if you keep interrupting me we will be here all night miss I'm in a hurry," a smiling Miguel kidded.

"All right sorry, I'll be quiet, go ahead."

"Well like I said her name is Naveah, and I met her at a high school. Now I know what you're thinking but no she's not in high school," Miguel chuckled. "I was scouting a kid at a high school game in New Haven and she was the cheerleading coach for the same school he played for. Well after the game was over and most people had cleared out of the gym, I was hanging around waiting to talk to the kid we were interested in. So long story short, there was some eye contact, a little flirting it appeared and the next thing I knew she had come over and introduced herself and we were sitting in the bleachers having a conversation. And so it began and so it has continued on from that day forward."

"Awww, what a sweet story Miguel; that's so nice; now what was she doing there that long after the game was over?"

"She said at the time that she was hanging around with a couple of the girls on her cheerleading squad who were waiting for their ride home. But of course I keep telling her that she was just hanging around hoping I would make a move," he joked.

"Well it's a good thing she went ahead and came over and struck up a conversation. What were you waiting for an invitation?"

"I don't know I was kind of tired, so maybe I just felt like I wanted to spend a little time with the kid we were after, go home and relax and what have you."

"Okay, whatever Miguel. Like I said it's a good thing she took the chance. You men today, I don't know," Sherri kidded him.

"Hey I'm not gonna argue with you there; it's a very good thing for me. But you know what's funny; she said it was her cheerleaders who talked her into coming over to say hello."

"That's too funny; the kids were playing little matchmakers for the adults."

"Yes they were, bless their hearts, and they're good girls too."

"Oh so you've gotten to know the girls she coaches?"

"Some of them, well actually most of them by now; of the ones who didn't graduate this past summer that is."

"I'm not surprised that you said Naveah is a very pretty girl. I would think that must be the case to reel in a man like you."

"Why thanks, you do flatter me and yes she is very pretty; just gorgeous in fact if you ask me. But then I guss I'm a bit biased. I remember when I first saw her at the gym that night that I was thinking to myself that this girl looks sort of like a younger Sade, just with a slightly darker complexion. And she's tall; about 5'9" in her bare feet."

"Well that's certainly good for a giant like you," Sherri chuckled. "And for her because she never needs to worry about whether she should wear heels."

"Yeah you're right; and she's also a complete sweetheart, she's smart and funny and get this; she loves basketball. She said she used to play before she decided to focus on cheerleading in high school and college."

"Wow, I'm so happy for you Miguel. Well for her too because you're a great guy. And it sounds like you two make a great couple. What a nice way to end lunch. Let me try to flag down our waitress so I can get the check, but go ahead you can keep talking."

"So anyway, the kid I was there to see play the night we met wound up going to another college, but I got something even better out of my visit that day I'd say."

"You sure did, no doubt about it," Sherri agreed.

Five or so minutes later they were walking out of the restaurant, Miguel empty handed but Sherri carrying a paper bag holding Irish soda bread.

"Where'd you park, I'll walk you to your car," he offered.

"Okay, its right over here," Sherri said before leading the way. "Sorry but I tend to park far away sometimes just so I can get some extra exercise in."

"Hey, there's nothing wrong with that and it's certainly not a problem for me."

"Anyway, I'm so glad we had the chance to do this again."

"Yeah me too, it was so good to see you Sherri."

"And good luck with everything; you know the job, and especially with Naveah. I don't want to jinx anything, but hopefully she might be the ONE."

"Thanks Sherri, I appreciate that and we'll see; so far so good. We took it nice and slow at first just because we recognized the possibilities early on. I mean even when you and I went to lunch the last time I wasn't sure where things were going with her. I just knew that I was hopeful."

"Well here's my car; thanks again for coming way out here and allowing me to make up for the last time, and please keep in touch Miguel."

"No problem; I enjoyed it, and I sure will keep in contact," he promised.

"Great, well let me go; can I have a hug?" Sherri asked before turning to him with her arms outstretched. "Mmmmm, she cooed as they held the embrace for several seconds. "You're a good man and a good friend," she whispered to him. She then suddenly jumped back, her attention diverted by something she saw out of the corner of her eye.

"CLAY! What are you doing here?" she exclaimed as she turned and saw him slowly walking in their direction.

"What am I doing here? That's a good one Sherri. But a better question is what are you doing here?"

"What? I told you on the phone I was here having lunch with a friend."

"Yeah I know what you told me, and now I see for myself. You had to go find another one didn't you? Even after what happened to the last black bastard you wouldn't stop would you!"

At that point Miguel who'd been standing there looking on in bewilderment spoke up.

"Hey listen man; it's not even like that okay. Like Sherri said we're just friends and that's it alright."

"No you listen; just shut the fuck up," Clay said angrily before turning back to Sherri. "You think I didn't know. Huh Sherri! You think I didn't know about Garrick Andrews?"

"I'm sorry Clay I,"

"Save it Sherri!" he interrupted. All of these years; and while I'm working hard to keep you living a nice lifestyle this is what you do to me? You turn into nothing but a low down nigger slut!" he said with his voice rising with each word.

"Now look, I'm not going to………," Miguel objected before Clay also cut him off in mid-sentence.

"No you look mother fucker; I thought I told your black ass to shut the fuck up didn't I?"

"Clay listen to me; there's nothing going on between Miguel and me. I'm telling you the God's honest truth."

"Well how nice of you Sherri; looking out for your latest boyfriend and everything, "Clay said with more than a little sarcasm. Seconds later his facial expression which had been one of a cunning smile instantly turned sinister. "Well let's see how you feel about this," he barked.

It all happened in what seemed like a split second. Clay reached into his jacket pocket, pulled out a handgun, pointed and fired a shot right into Miguel's chest. Miguel instantly crumpled to the ground; his long frame slumped against Sherri's car.

Two ladies who had just exited the restaurant screamed before rushing back inside once they saw what had happened.

"Oh my God Clay, what did you just do?" Sherri shrieked in horror. "What on Earth did you do?"

"How did you like that huh Sherri? See now he's just like your other nigger boyfriend isn't he? Now come on," he growled before pulling her by her arm.

People watching from inside the restaurant could see him pulling her along on foot. They ran beyond the grounds of the parking lot and onto a trail leading to a wooded area. Someone had already called 911 and with police headquarters only a few blocks away their arrival certainly would be imminent.

"No Clay no, why did you do that," Sherri cried out.

"IS THAT ALL YOU CARE ABOUT SHERRI! IS THAT ALL? WHAT ABOUT US AND WHAT YOU'VE DONE TO OUR MARRIAGE. AND OUR FAMILY! RUNNING AROUND CARRYING ON LIKE A FUCKING WHORE, AND YOU'RE ONLY WORRIED ABOUT THAT BLACK MOTHER FUCKER."

"No Clay I care about us too and I'm sorry, I'm so sorry," she broke down.

"Oh please Sherri don't you think I can see it's all just an act now; that you're just trying to save yourself. WELL TELL

ME ONE REASON WHY I SHOULDN'T PUT A BULLET IN YOUR FUCKING HEAD; JUST ONE GODDAMN REASON SHERRI."

"No Clay, please no, I'm sorry please, really I'm so sorry," she said as he held the gun close to her head.

"You can't can you? All you can do is beg for your miserable life. Go ahead bitch; get down on your knees," he said as he forced her to a kneeling position His left hand held her hair as he continued to point the gun at her with his right ."This is what you do best right? It's what you've been doing for your boyfriends right Sherri. YOU FUCKING DIRTY PIG, I HATE YOU, I FUCKIN HATE YOU. THIS IS ALL YOUR FAULT. ALL OF IT!

"I'm sorry. I'm so sorry but we, we can work this out Clay, we can get past this, "she muttered while looking up at him with tear-filled eyes. "We can start over, work on our problems, and work on our marriage. I can change sweetheart, I already have. Please Clay."

"What are you talking about," he responded in a suddenly calm voice. "I'm done Sherri. They're looking for me. They came for me this morning. Don't you get it; the only thing I'm looking at is a lot of years in a jail cell. That's the only future I have to look forward to Sherri," he said before releasing his grip on her.

"No Clay it's not that bad. It's never as bad as it seems."

Suddenly they both grew silent as they heard voices in the distance. They seemed to be growing closer. "This way, they said he took her up this trail over here, let's go," could be heard clearly.

"Don't you see now Sherri. Its over. They're here for me again. He turned and walked away from her; a distance of about fifteen feet before stopping and facing her. His eyes, which had been fillled with rage had turned sad and then sort of vacant. Take good care of the kids Sherri; you're all they have now. And you can thank them for your life."

Sherri scrambled in a desperate attempt to get to her feet.

"CLAY NOOOOOOOO...........................,"

EPILOGUE

It's been about 18 months now, yet not a day goes by where Sherri doesn't think about the lives she had a hand in destroying, either directly or indirectly. She's tried so hard to put it all behind her, but in her heart she knows that will never completely happen for as long as she lives. But she is in a far different place now, both literally and figuratively. She's moved on from her former home; having sold the house in New Jersey and returned to Massachusetts to be closer to her parents. As for the other side, none of Clay's family outside of Beth has as much as spoken to her since the entire story came out in the days leading up to his funeral. But Sherri likes to think she's a far different person after all that happened. She's even gone back to the workforce; working with the legal aid society in Boston. It's far less lucrative than work at a firm would be, but it makes her feel good to assist those in need. And the kids are okay all things considered. They have their good days and bad days; just as she does herself. She saw a therapist for about six months before deciding she didn't want to do that anymore. It's so hard for her to pinpoint when she really lost control or even why. There were no unresolved issues from her childhood, certainly no lack of self-esteem. As best she can tell, her actions had to do with nothing more than pure unadulterated lust which she simply gave in to. She, along with her lovers had not only bitten into, but then completely devoured the forbidden fruit. But she has made great strides in battling her demons. Since returning home she's reconnected with the Catholic faith in which she was raised. And dating? Well that's the furthest thing from her mind. Maybe one day she figures. But right now she's just squarely focused on trying to figure out who she really is. Not that it matters much now, but she occasionally wonders if the response from Clay would have been as extreme had he found out about Craig or Scott rather than Gee. Maybe she might have changed her ways then, and there would have never been the fling with Gee. And he would still be alive. She actually sat down and wrote a letter to Gee's fiancée Alicia one day. In it she just apologized to her and told her how much she wished she could make it so that none of it would have ever happened. But she wasn't surprised that she never received a reply back. She didn't really expect for that to happen. She realizes that any forgiveness for her would have to come from God. Writing the letter was just something she wanted to do.

Little Garrick Andrews Jr. will be turning 1 soon. Alicia can't wait until he's old enough to understand when she talks about his father.

The judgment is expected to come any day now in the wrongful death suit filed by Alicia and the Andrews family against Somerset county and the county Prosecutor's office. On the advice of their attorney Lawrence Montgomery III, they turned down an offer of an out of court settlement and are awaiting word on if they will be awarded the 15 million dollars they're seeking. The general consensus in the legal community is that even if the judgment falls short of that number that they're likely to be awarded at least half that amount or about 7.5 million. Not that it will matter in terms of bringing the man who was to be her husband back.

Mike Marciniak is counting down the days. There are only 30 more days before he will be released from the halfway house at which he is finishing out his 15 month sentence for his role in the conspiracy which led to the bogus charges being bought against Garrick "Gee" Andrews. But he can see the light at the end of the tunnel and he can't wait to get out so that he too can start a new life someplace else. Somewhere far away from the fingers that would surely continue to be pointed in his direction. Fingering him as the cop who dared break the code and go beyond the blue wall of silence. But he has no regrets, because the fact that he will be able to kiss and hug his wife and kids before too much longer made it all worthwhile for him. It's doubtful that the same could be said for former Detective Roland "Rollie" Celini. It's likely that he might have quite a few things he laments as he serves out the 40 year sentence he received, with no parole eligibility before 25 years. His days are as long as they are miserable now, and on each and every one he wonders if this might be the day they come for him. They being the other prisoners. That's simply a recognized hazard for a former cop now in prison; especially when you're recognized as such and called out on your very first day in the general populace.

Not that Roberto Torres is going to be shedding any tears for him down in San Antonio where he and his girlfriend Carmen still reside. They love it there; especially the winters. And they've even managed to buy a home there just months after Roberto Torres started on his job working at a tire shop.

Sherri recalls the day well. It was one of her sort of down days but the moment she opened that envelope her mood did a .360. degree turn. And now she can't wait for the wedding. She's sure she might be crying every bit as much as the bride on that day. Her friend looked so happy in the engagement photo; and she's so very happy that it seems sometimes good things still happen to good people. And in her eyes they don't come much better than Miguel Larios. She recalls that no one seemed to care about her more in the wake of all that happened than he did. While many others, including some family members and others she had considered her closest friends, turned their backs on her, called her names and ignored her calls; he always took the time to reach out to her. She remembers the joy she felt in an otherwise dark period in her life when she found out that he was going to be okay; that the bullet had missed piercing his heart by a fraction. And now here he was just weeks away from marrying the ONE. Naveah Dennis was one lucky lady and for at least a day Sherri knew she would be one happy friend when Naveah and Miguel would be joined as one.

###

About The Author

Ken N. Robinson has parlayed a lifelong love of storytelling and writing into what is now his first full length novel. Born and raised in New Jersey, he now lives outside of Atlanta and has now begun working on his next book Players and Ballers.